INFRACTUS

Sarah L. Johnson

To Josh,
The end begins with
a book!

Coffin Hop Press

COFFIN HOP PRESS LTD / CANADA

Infractus

Sarah L. Johnson — First Edition

Copyright © 2017 Coffin Hop Press Ltd.

Coffin Hop Press Ltd.
200 Rivervalley Crescent SE
Calgary, Alberta Canada T2C 3K8

www.coffinhop.com

info@coffinhop.com

Publisher's Note: This is a work of fiction. Names, characters, places, and incidents are a product of the author's imagination. Locales and public names are sometimes used for atmospheric purposes. Any resemblance to actual people, living or dead, or to businesses, companies, events, institutions, or locales is completely coincidental.

Book design © 2017 Coffin Hop Press

Cover design © 2017 Coffin Hop Press

Cover Art © 2017 Shutterstock/Tithi Luadthong

ISBN: 978-1-988987-02-6

"The more a thing is perfect,
the more it feels pleasure and pain."
-*Dante Alighieri* *"The Divine Comedy"*

FOREWORD

Everyone has a dark side.

You. Me. That old lady feeding pigeons in the park. The chipper young lady working at the local independent bookstore...

You must know the one I'm talking about: Crazy curly hair, a distant gaze, as if she's always thinking of something, somewhere, else. She has that smile, the one that never leaves her face, even when her eye twitches – ever so slightly – as you reach for the latest potboiler thriller, instead of the unknown local author pile she's casually nudging you towards with a subtle crane of the neck. Or maybe she's measuring you for that coffin she keeps propped up in the back room. Yes, everyone has a dark side, some darker than others.

Which brings me to Sarah L. Johnson, and her latest novel. Her debut novel. The one you must be holding in your grubby little paws, fondling the cover and running your fingers down the spine, shivering in anticipation.

It's true, this is her first novel. Which is not to say her first book. That was an amazing collection of equally twisted, brilliant, and subversive fiction called *Suicide Stitch*. If nothing else, that book proved that Sarah is a brilliant writer with a talent for finding the heart of a great story, ripping it out, twisting it, and tossing it into the air, juggling the bloody thing with literal aplomb.

Case in point: *Infractus*. The book you hold in your hot little hands. Sure, at first glance, it may appear to be a dystopian tale about a nameless assassin finding his way in a post-apocalyptic wasteland. If you watch close, and read deep, you can see that she's actually juggling with the heart of...

Hell, I'm not going to spoil it for you.

The interesting thing about dark sides, is that – *if* you shine a light, turn it up bright, and aim it just right – you can catch a glimpse of what lurks beyond the veil, waiting for that day when gin weakens the border between realities. Then, if you get lucky, *real lucky*, a tiny bit of weird from that other place finds a way across into our world. A *tulpa*, or a *golem* – thought and belief made real - a shadow made solid in the shape of a book.

You? You've got all the luck in the world, my friend. Just look at the shadows you're holding in the palms of your hands.

Robert Bose
Editor, Publisher, Author, Friend
Calgary, Alberta
October 2017

To my parents,
for taking me to church...

PROLOGUE

Someone left a doll on the steps of the station. The fireman saw it as he swung into the parking lot. A naked baby doll, plastic, same as what his own little Jelly-Belly dragged around 'til she was dang near ten years old. He squeezed the 4X4 into his reserved stall and cut the ignition—course she was sixteen now—his boots clomped onto the icy pavement—and last time he called her Jelly-Belly she near bit his face off.

The fireman zipped his parka to his chin. Little Bella weren't exactly little no more either. She'd always been a healthy girl, inherited his stocky genes, but she'd put on more than a few pounds recently, hiding it under those baggy hoodies. She ditched school too, stayed out all hours and came home moody as hell, talking to herself. That worried him some.

I hover in the dark, listening to the fireman's thoughts. He's a good father. Observant to a fault. God is in the details, but get too hung up on them and the Devil walks off with the big picture. A common mistake made by good fathers.

INFRACTUS

Near as he could tell, Bella's trouble started with that buddy of hers. Creepish, fiddle-playing weirdo with a wicked scar slashing through his eyebrow into his hair. The fireman first met the kid a year back when he'd used the big scissors to chew open that mangled Dodge. Parents were pronounced at the scene. Bad skull frac and brain bleeds left the kid in a vegetative state, until two weeks later when the vegetable popped up like a spring onion. A miracle.

The fireman noted a layer of black ice varnishing the station parking lot. Soon as he clocked in he'd send the rookies to spread gravel, maybe reward the most eager conscript with that plastic baby doll—the fireman paused mid-thought when the doll moved. A spastic flail of arms and legs.

His mind goes blank with an electric pop. I'm unable to manifest my own body on this plane, a privilege I sacrificed for what I hope will be a worthy cause.

Unfortunately, in astral form I can do little more than observe. Though sometimes a little is enough. I hurl a mental prompt at the fireman with all the force I can muster. MOVE.

The fireman shot across the parking lot as though shoved by the hand of a giant. Skating over slick pavement, he dropped into a crouch by the steps where his medic training kicked up automatic. The baby lay silent but alert and moving enough to dismiss spinal trauma. The fireman stripped off his gloves and scooped the bitty thing into his hands.

INFRACTUS

A boy. Obviously. Clean, pink, with a good head of black hair. Not more than a couple hours old by the look of the umbilicus. Raw blood vessels in a rubbery yellow sheath, neat cut and cinched off with...hair? A sugar-white braid, long and thin as a shoelace.

"Hell's teeth," the fireman muttered and continued his assessment. Smidge of cyanosis in the extremities, good pulse from what he could tell, legs and arms resisting extension. No indrawing, gasping, or other signs of respiratory distress. Decent APGAR.

Normal baby, almost. Could've been a trick of light bleeding through the lace of falling snow, but instead of the murky slate of a newborn, the baby's eyes were a lighter color. Colors. One green and one blue. If that didn't beat all.

I withdraw from the fireman's consciousness when it occurs to me that the baby is awfully quiet. Not that I expect coherent thoughts from an infant, but this isn't right. He's human. Why can't I hear him? Because I've made a mistake. Already.

The fireman tucked the babe between his flannel shirt and down parka. A damn head-scratcher. Cared for immediately after birth. Cleaned up and left in a place he'd be found quick. Why naked though? No blanket, not even a dirty shirt or a plastic bag to shield his skin from the concrete. It was snowing for Chrissakes. The infant squirmed against his chest, and the fireman peered over his shoulder into the snow-flecked darkness.

Someone wanted this baby to survive, and to suffer.

CHAPTER 1

J ohn huddled cross-legged next to the open hatch where enough light entered the crawlspace for him to read his Daredevil comic. Lately he'd been hiding above the music room during recess. It was springtime. That meant burning eyes, itchy palate, and sneezing endless rivers of clear snot. St. Ann's backed onto a weedy field where the pollen was so terrible it made John want to cut his own head off.

The crawlspace smelled like an old bird's nest, and there were spiders too, but John liked the quiet. He turned the page of his comic book and his heart clenched at the dull gleam of the staple. The coolest part of the story always came at the staple, but before he could read a word, a whimper intruded on the silence. He ignored it, focusing on Kingpin as he cornered a blind and beaten Matt Murdock. A wail rang through the air ducts. John slapped the comic book shut.

He lowered himself through the hatch and laddered down shelves full of xylophones and bongos. Carefully. He'd dislocated his shoulder falling off the roof at the group home. Sister Claudia hadn't been too happy. On the floor, he brushed off the dust streaking his clothes and turning his black hair gray—evidence that he'd been climbing around in places he wasn't allowed. He hid his comic behind the piano and crept into the hall.

Shadows stretched up the walls of the dim corridor, like figures in hooded robes. John's sneakers smooched over the linoleum, and he ignored the tingle between his shoulder blades. A weird feeling he got sometimes. Like someone sneaking up behind him, but he knew better than to talk about it. His shrink already had "deep concerns."

The whimpering led John to the stairwell. Through the glass panel in the door, he saw a first grader huddled on the concrete, clutching the sides of her head. An older boy held her by her hair, a shiny red ponytail wrapped around his fat fist. A pair of scissors flashed in his other hand. Teacher scissors. The kind with long silver blades that kids weren't allowed to use because they'd stab their eyes out or whatever.

John slipped into the stairwell, letting the door snap shut behind him. "Leave her alone."

"This look like your business, you queer-eyed shrimp?" The older boy yanked on the girl's ponytail. She yelped, tears spilling down her red cheeks.

John didn't know the girl's name, but seeing her on the floor with the older boy's scissors ready to chop her red hair off made his insides boil, like the volcanoes they learned about in science. Under pressure and full of magma.

"Don't worry," John said to the girl.

The older boy released the girl's ponytail and turned on John. "You say something, shrimp?"

The older boy was a big problem. Every day he prowled the playground with some other sixth graders like a pack of ugly dogs on the hunt. The boy was a lot bigger than John, but who wasn't? John was in third grade and the same size as the girl on the floor. Sister Claudia promised he'd be tall one day. Said he had long bones, whatever that meant. Sister Claudia had a lot of weird ideas.

The girl scurried behind John, and he recoiled at the sweaty pressure of her hands on his arm. He didn't like anyone touching him, and skin on skin was the worst. The older boy gnashed the scissor blades together, a sound that echoed off the concrete walls and stairs.

"Scram, queer-eyes, or I'll be giving you the first haircut."

John cocked his head and pretended to think about it, but he'd decided how this would go when he was in the crawlspace, stuck at the staple of his Daredevil comic. Matt Murdock's adventures taught John an important thing about big problems. If you didn't fix them on the first try, they only came back bigger.

The girl's sticky hands clutched John's arm again. He grit his teeth and pinched her sleeve, tugging her in the direction of the door.

"You'd better go."

She fled through the stairwell door, ponytail swinging behind her. John's heart beat slowly, and a heavy heat surged under his skin, a creature of molten igneous rock. The girl would for sure be on her way to tell a teacher, which didn't leave him a lot of time.

The older boy dropped the scissors and kicked them away.

"I'm gonna pound your fucking face in—"

Crunch. Sharp on John's knuckles and dull in his ears. Blood oozed down the older boy's chin and sprayed from his lips as he roared, swinging a fist the size of a grapefruit. John ducked and rammed his shoulder into the older boy's stomach, knocking him to the floor. This was how you fixed a problem.

❖❖❖

As usual it wasn't a question of being in trouble, but rather how much. John hugged the wall outside the kitchen and peeked around the corner. The social worker slouched at the table tapping her pen on her notepad. He couldn't see Sister Claudia but heard her opening and closing cupboards. He smelled peppermint. That meant tea. Which meant a serious talk. Not good.

"I'm sorry you had to make the trip on short notice," Sister Claudia said.

"You saw his latest psych evals," said the social worker. "Withdrawn, repressed anger, no empathy. And now this."

"I agree; he's troubled."

"He's a sociopath."

John buried his face into the crook of his elbow, smothering a weird urge to laugh. He reminded himself to look up "sociopath" and "empathy" in the dictionary he hid under his bed. One thing he knew for sure without having to look it up. On Sister Claudia's list of Very Bad Things, what he'd done was even worse than profaning the Lord's name, which had to do with swearing.

"Claudia, we have to pull him, find a more suitable home placement."

A spoon clattered on the table. "He's eight years old."

"He beat a kid toothless."

Without thinking, John tightened his fists. Pain bolted up his arms and his gashed knuckles throbbed with every beat of his heart, as if his hands had tiny hearts of their own.

"He tries to be good, but you have to understand that boy is a demon."

The social worker sighed. "I know you meant that metaphorically."

John didn't know what metaphorically was, but he'd been hearing the demon bit his whole life. Sky is blue, water is wet, God is good, and you're a beast from hell; pass the jam.

"You know him," Sister Claudia said. "You named him, for Heaven's sake. Tell me you don't feel it."

"Sister . . ."

"He's never cried, even as a babe. He hardly sleeps, wandering at all hours of the night. And when he does nod off, the doctors say he doesn't dream. What kind of child doesn't dream?"

"So, he's a fifty-pound time bomb. Not exactly news."

"He bears the mark of the damned."

"Bicolored eyes are a genetic anomaly. Claudia, you can't talk like this. Not with your health issues. They're watching you."

"Am I one of your cases now?"

The social worker's chair scraped back. "I'll try to work something out for the little monster. But I don't understand why you want to keep him."

It was a reasonable question. As a rule, Sister Claudia treated him like a catastrophe—he liked that word—in human skin. Why stick up for him now?

INFRACTUS

John slipped into the closet, peeking through the crack in the door to watch the social worker leave. His nose itched. He held his breath. Sometimes that helped. He'd been practicing and could hold it for a whole minute. When the front door closed, Sister Claudia's outline remained centered on the frosted glass. Her hair, pulled into a bun, made her head appear small on her sturdy shoulders.

"John White."

The back of his neck heated at the full name summoning. John White. Good job social worker, way to have the imagination of a turnip. Everything about it felt wrong. Like masking tape covering his whole face. He couldn't breathe under John White. Sure, he responded to it and wrote it down on his homework sheets, but it wasn't right. Not even close. One day he'd figure it out. Someone would call him by his real name. He'd hear it, and he'd know.

Sister Claudia crossed her arms at her chest. "Eavesdropping is a sin."

Busted. It didn't matter how sneaky he was. Sister Claudia had the instincts of a raptor. Sneezing, he stumbled out of the closet. He wiped his runny nose on his sleeve and waited for the inevitable sermon. Sin, Jesus, hell. Blah, blah, blah.

"You're in deep shit," she said.

John's mouth fell open as she swept down the hall and caught the back of his shirt in her talons. He tripped over his own feet as she dragged him into the living room and dropped him on the lumpy sofa. He braced himself to be eaten alive.

She stood over him, tugging at the sides of her cardigan. "You will write a letter of apology to that boy and his family. Contrite, humble, and above all convincing."

John nodded. First the swearing and now Sister Claudia was telling him to lie? He'd never been sorry for anything. What would that even feel like?

"As for punishment, I've a mind to suspend your library privileges."

He hoped she wouldn't, but he didn't care about that right now. "Sister Claudia, are you sick?"

Her eyebrows knit together. "Of course not."

Lies felt a certain way, like a needle zigzagging over the inside of his skull. He'd always been able to tell when someone was lying. And everyone lied, even Sister Claudia. "Will you get better?"

"John." She sank down on the couch beside him, combing her fingers through his hair. "Such a face you have. Did you know all demons were once angels?"

One of those questions you weren't supposed to answer. Rhetorical. John stared at his shredded knuckles. "That kid was a problem."

"Now solved." Sister Claudia smoothed her hand over his hair again and reached into the pocket of her cardigan to retrieve a small, well-thumbed bible. "We'll start with reading together. Every day."

John's heart cannonballed into his stomach. "For how long?"

"One month." She licked her finger and flipped to the first page of Genesis. "One month for every tooth you knocked out of that boy's head."

He nearly dropped his face into his wrecked hands, but Sister Claudia stopped him with a firm knuckle under his chin. "Stop hurting yourself."

Over the next four months, Sister Claudia read the entire goddamn English Revised Version. Twice.

CHAPTER 2

FEBRUARY 2021

John stood in the dark, staring out the second story bedroom window. In one hand he held a thin length of braided hair, white as moonbeams. He dragged the silky plait over his lips, inhaling the scent of cinnamon. He didn't know whose hair it was, possibly his birth mother's, but it was the only thing he owned that truly belonged to him. Usually he kept it in an Altoids tin under his mattress, but lately he brought it out more often. Because of what he held in his other hand.

He held his breath and made a fist around the rosary he'd found under his pillow. Again. Almost a whole year since he kicked that numbskull's teeth down his throat. John had stayed out of trouble—or at least made sure not to get caught—so what was with the Jesus choker?

What was the big deal in the first place? The older boy didn't pick on the littles anymore, and he kept his distance from John. They all did. Even the girl he'd saved. She was smart enough to understand that what he'd done had nothing to do with her. She was only a catalyst. John liked that word.

INFRACTUS

He rolled the chipped wooden beads between his fingers and glanced at the glowing hands of the wall clock. He'd been holding his breath for almost two minutes. The rosary was just a thing, a stupid thing, but Sister Claudia stuffing it under his pillow night after night and never saying anything about it made his stomach feel like a paper bag full of spiders.

Sister Claudia still ruled the home, but the other sisters carried out most of her orders now. They told the kids Sister Claudia was fine. Lies. Between his sinful eavesdropping and Internet research at the library, John figured it out. Sister Claudia had a lump of meat in her head that didn't belong. A big problem, and getting bigger.

The clock ticked. At two minutes and four seconds, John reached what books on free diving called the break point. Used air whooshed out of his lungs. He drew a long clean breath, opened the window, and chucked the rosary into the frozen flowerbed. He paused for a moment, leaning out the window and rubbing the braid between his fingers. Snowflakes melted on the back of his neck as he searched the darkness. He had that feeling again. The one he got sometimes, drifting along the edge of sleep, or sneaking down an empty hallway at school. A feeling of being watched. He cranked the window shut and locked it.

Sleep wasn't happening, and the middle of the night was the best time to do homework. He had a lot of homework now, because the school put him in a special class for smart kids. At first it seemed like a weird punishment for the crime of using his brain, but at least school wasn't so boring anymore. He had a current events report due in a week, and he'd picked the recently ratified Global Nuclear Disarmament Treaty as his topic. The treaty said that all nuclear weapons in the entire world would be disassembled by the year 2030, and he'd found a library book about the Manhattan Project that was actually pretty cool. Extra research meant a better grade, and good grades went a long way toward keeping "deeply concerned" grown-ups off his back.

John sneaked past the other boys snoring in their bunks. He slipped into the hallway, and meant to head downstairs to grab his book, but saw light shining under Sister Claudia's door. He tiptoed over the worn carpet, avoiding the squeaky spots, and when he got closer, he found her door open a crack. Sister Claudia never left her door open. When he was little, he'd thought she passed through keyholes like a vampire.

He peeked through the crack, expecting to see the inside of a church with a giant bleeding Jesus on the wall. But her room was just a room. A small cross above a regular bed like they all had. Made hard and neat, the same way she forced everyone to do it. John didn't mind. He liked order.

Sister Claudia sat fully dressed on the edge of the bed with her open bible in her lap. Her hair fell down to cover her face and her shoulders trembled under her cardigan.

John nudged the door open. "Sister Claudia?"

"I can't read it." She blinked at the pages pinched between her fingers. "I can't...I can't see."

Without asking, John crawled onto her bed to kneel behind her. He gathered her hair in his hands, brown waves smelling of soap and peppermint tea. Softer than it looked. He swept it over her right shoulder so he could see over the left. The gospel of Zechariah marched down the pages in tiny type. One of the better books in John's opinion, because it was short and had apocalyptic stuff in it. He liked that word: "apocalyptic."

John read out loud. "And the Lord said unto Satan, *The Lord rebuke thee...*"

Sister Claudia's tears dripped onto the pages as he read. John wondered what crying felt like. He continued sounding out words he didn't understand. Words like "iniquity" that sounded bad, and "asunder," which he'd look up later because he liked the shape of it in his mouth. He read until her shoulders stopped shaking. He read right into the New Testament through the fourteen generations of begats from Abraham to David. He read until his throat went scratchy and she sent him back to bed.

The next night, John found her rosary under his pillow again, along with her well-thumbed bible. The rosary went out the window. Her bible, he kept.

CHAPTER 3

AUGUST 2022

Sweat pooled in John's ears as he listened to the fan slop hot air around in the darkness. While the other boys snored into the crooks of their arms, John mapped constellations in the stickers Sister Claudia allowed him to put on the ceiling in the hopes that it might keep him in bed at night. Like what reality was she living in?

He sucked at sleeping. Insomnia it was called. He had a book about it hidden under his mattress next to the cinnamon Altoids tin. A shaft of light from a streetlamp fell across the plastic Jesus on the wall beside John's bed. He didn't believe in God, but it must be rough for plastic Jesus, melting on His cross. Hot as hell. John mashed his face into the pillow and laughed.

Hot as hell, and maybe even hotter. He'd long since kicked away the covers, and his pajama pants clung to his legs like wet towels. Even in the dark he could see the dinosaur pattern. Too freaking babyish to believe. He was ten years old, but a stringy runt, and in the home, you got stuck with what fit out of the hand-me-down heap. Beggars can't be choosy, Sister Claudia proclaimed. Easy to say when you were mostly blind. He flipped his pillow and dropped his sweaty head on the temporarily cool surface. The fan growled.

Sleep? Yeah, right.

He rolled out of bed, ditched the dino pants, and pulled on a T-shirt, cut-off jeans, and his sneakers. An extra blanket under the covers would pass an open-door bed check. Halfway out the window, however, John heard the squeak of mattress springs.

The new kid's paper-plate face hovered in the darkness. "Where you goin'?"

"Go back to sleep."

"I'm gonna tell."

John grit his teeth. This new kid had so far demonstrated himself to be an incorrigible snitch. But John had ways of dealing with snitches. "Tell anyone and I'll cut your goddamn tongue out."

The new kid's paper-plate head vanished under his blanket. John dropped onto the lower pitch of the roof. The lattice creaked as he climbed down to the flowerbed. He was careful not to squish Sister Claudia's hollyhocks. When you were up to very bad things it was smart not to leave evidence. He pinched off a withered blossom and brushed soil over his footprints. Then he ran.

Frame houses gave way to dented trailers and empty lots full of ragweed. He held his breath as he sprinted past those. Stupid allergies. At least he'd been spared freckles and red hair.

At the edge of town, he flew onto a path curling through a grove of aspens. His sneakers thumped over the dirt in a steady rhythm. He slowed to a panting trot at the end of the path where the trees opened onto the shoreline of a lake.

INFRACTUS

The "beach" was nothing more than rocks and sour mud squishy enough to slurp the shoes off your feet. He hopped stone to stone until he reached the dock where he wiped the sweat from his eyes and caught his breath. The curved blade of the moon glowed in the sky and stars glinted like knifepoints on the surface of still black water.

John stripped down to his underwear, raced across the warped planks of the dock, and dove in. The water was warm and tasted like bagged grass clippings after a week in the sun. When he surfaced, he took a dozen deep, rapid breaths like the pearl divers he'd read about. If you scrubbed the carbon dioxide out of your blood, you could hold your breath a lot longer.

He filled his lungs one last time, packing the air in until it pushed his stomach out and stretched his ribs apart. The stars above disappeared as he flipped himself head down and kicked.

He counted in his head. One hundred eighty was the magic number. The closest he'd ever come was one hundred sixty-four. On the bottom of the lake, he pulled himself along in the dark by grabbing handfuls of slimy weeds. Pulling and counting, pulling and counting. At eighty-three seconds, he reached a cluster of man-sized rocks.

Glacial erratics—that's what they were called. Chunks of mountains chipped off and carried away by traveling glaciers during the ice age. When the ice melted, it dropped them wherever. Alone in a place they didn't belong. Odd rocks. Misfits.

One hundred twenty. Two minutes.

Bubbles flew from his mouth as his lungs partially deflated. Like a freshwater starfish, he latched onto one of the rocks. Edges, slick with algae, bit into his arms and legs. Mud squelched between his toes as they wedged in at the base.

One hundred sixty.

His heart banged against his ribs and the numbers sloshed in his head. One hundred seventy. He pressed his forehead hard into the rock. One hundred seventy-five. Dirty air raced up his throat. One hundred seventy-eight...nine...one hundred eighty.

Three minutes.

He braced his feet and pushed off. The rock shifted slightly, its massive weight pressing against his ankle. Not enough to crush, but enough to pin. His lungs screamed as he tugged at his leg and shoved at the rock. Cold fire swept his oxygen-starved brain.

Air hunger, serious air hunger, was the weirdest thing. Time transformed into a melted marshmallow stretching out forever on a single sticky thread. Until he reached the break point.

His body gasped for air his brain knew wasn't there. Water boiled into his lungs. He coughed, dragging in another scalding wave. Then, like a drawstring pulled tight, his windpipe closed. He fought against his own body, strangling even as he continued gulping water into his stomach.

His struggle ended the way most things did with him. Getting bored and wandering away. His legs went limp and his head fell back. He stared up at the surface. Too dark. Too far. His arms flopped like they could swim away and save themselves. But it was too late for them. Too late for everything.

The Internet described drowning as a peaceful experience. And it was, a bit. His thoughts grew still and clear. He knew he was dying, only it didn't seem important. His throat remained sealed, but the feeling was merely information, neither good nor bad. Laryngospasm. He'd read about that on the Internet too. He knew it wouldn't let go until he lost consciousness, or went into cardiac arrest.

But he didn't blackout, and his heart didn't crash either. Not exactly. Instead, he felt the link between his mind and its meat pod snap. Then he felt nothing at all.

Interesting.

Death was like the bottom of the lake. Dark and floaty. Except he didn't have to hold his breath because he had no need to breathe. If there was a white light, he had no eyes to see it, and no legs to run toward or away. As he floundered, it occurred to him that his last words were: "I'll cut your goddamn tongue out." It was only meant to terrorize that bratty little snitch, but what if there was a God? He probably wouldn't appreciate the profaning of His name.

Sister Claudia made hell sound like a spider-infested garden, with each descending circle weedier than the last. But what if Heaven was a giant church, with a giant plastic Jesus hanging from the wall? What if you had to sit on those hard benches and read the Bible forever? He'd rather spend an eternity sneezing in the weeds.

And what about reincarnation? If that was the deal, his Karma could be a problem. Claws and teeth were the tools of survival in his world and he was a survivor, or he had been, before he died. He figured the best he could hope for would be an intelligent animal. Something that couldn't drown would be cool. His argument for manta ray was coming together when a voice punctured the silence.

INFRACTUS

A voice he knew, but couldn't remember how. The voice pulled him. Not forward or back, but through and out. Beyond. The melted marshmallow stretched and folded back on itself. Seconds, years, hours, days. Impossible to know.

Beyond was a dark place, but not totally. Almost warm but cold too. Quiet but not silent. Every sense deprived, but not completely. The edge of everything.

Liminal, the voice said.

The word wasn't a part of the boy's vocabulary. He'd need to look it up. Were there dictionaries in hell? The voice whispered his name. Not John White, but his real name. A name he knew, but couldn't hold in his memory. Could he be dreaming?

The dead don't dream.

"I'm dead?"

You should be, reckless thing. You're lucky I've had my eye on you.

That prickly sense of being watched, or the memory of it, poured through John's consciousness. The presence. This was its voice.

"Uh . . ." John said. "Are you God?"

Not yet. The voice chuckled, a soft tremolo full of secrets. One day He will send Her, and on that day, you will begin to understand. My plans are already in motion, and make no mistake, this world will be mine. But if you choose correctly, it can be ours.

"You know my name." John had never begged for anything in his life, but he'd never wanted anything this much. Only a thin white braid connected him to where he'd come from. "Please, you're the only one who can tell me."

INFRACTUS

Do you think I wanted it this way? I offered you everything... The voice sounded hoarse, as if each word were a wadded-up piece of sandpaper. One day I hope you'll forgive me, but until then stop trying to kill yourself. Now, wake up.

The command shivered in the center of John's awareness. Pain, if that was the right word, ripped through every unraveled bit of himself. Strands twisted together, smaller and tighter, into a thin white braid pulled through the liminal space.

Water spewed from his mouth and nose as he coughed his ribs to bits. When it passed he found himself on the ground twenty yards from where water licked the muddy shore. He whipped his head back and forth. Trees, mud, water, mud, trees. Nothing. No one.

Foam bubbled from his lungs into his mouth. Words skipped across the surface of his mind like flat rocks. He couldn't remember. He tried to stand. Couldn't do that either. Instead, he slumped to the soggy ground and puked.

Eventually he hauled himself to his feet and started his way down the path through the trees. A few blocks from the house, he sagged against a chain-link fence, panting. His raw, leaky lungs struggled for every breath. Then he realized his face was six inches from a tangle of weeds and enough pollen to make his head explode.

Aw, hell.

But his nose didn't so much as itch.

When he reached the house, he stood on the front lawn, staring up at the second story bedroom window. Not happening. He shambled around back, to the kitchen door that never latched properly. He jiggled the knob until it swung open. Darkness greeted him with the muffled growl of fans. Situation normal. He tiptoed into the kitchen.

"John White."

His body locked. The light snapped on. Sister Claudia. Only Sister Claudia. At the kitchen table. Wearing a robe? He assumed she'd been born wearing slacks and a cardigan. In front of her she had a Braille edition of Hardy Boys: The Twisted Claw. He'd checked it out of the library. What was she doing with it?

His wet chest rattled. "How'd you know?"

"Not exactly a three-pipe deduction." Sister Claudia shuffled over to him and rubbed hard circles on his back as he coughed and coughed. "Who else sneaks in at the devil's hour smelling like a wet dog? John, are you all right?"

His teeth chattered, and he didn't speak for fear of biting his tongue off. His bones rattled. He couldn't breathe. He was alive when he should be dead. He was a very bad thing. Starving for air and full of dirty water.

A noise he didn't know he could make clawed out of his chest and up his throat. Hot water dripped out of his eyes and he buckled to the floor. Sister Claudia gathered him in her arms, and for the first time in his life he didn't fight her.

"John, tell me what happened."

"Something's...coming . . ." That was it. He had no words for the voice in his head promising terrible things he couldn't remember. So, he sagged in her arms, pressed his face into the fleece of her robe, and cried.

CHAPTER 4

JUNE 2025

Afternoon sun pelted John's head as he dawdled down the street, mindful not to step on the dandelions growing up through the cracks in the concrete. Dandelions didn't belong anywhere, and everybody hated them. They were pernicious. John liked that word, and he liked dandelions. He also liked walking to and from school alone. Finally. At thirteen years old, he was the only kid left at the foster home. His social worker had given up, content to hope that he'd age out quietly and not axe murder anyone on her watch.

Anyway, it wasn't like he needed a babysitter. Sister Claudia needed taking care of now. The homecare nurse was on the porch when he unlatched the gate to the front yard.

"Welcome home." She hooked his arm and hustled him through the front door. "She's having another episode. Oxygen sats are dropping. I'm going to have to dose her—"

"Not yet." He shrugged her hand off his arm, toed off his shoes, and headed down the hall to the den that now served as a hospital room. The nurse didn't have to tell him. He'd heard the shouting halfway down the block. Sometimes Sister Claudia wasn't herself.

"Show your face...fucking traitor. I see you!" Sister Claudia gasped, collarbones jutting, temples and cheeks hollow enough to hold water. A few months ago, she'd stopped eating because she choked every time she tried. Something about the swallow reflex not working. So, the doctors installed a tube for feeding in her stomach, put one under her nose for oxygen and one in her arm for medicine, though they only gave her fentanyl and morphine now.

"I said...I see you...I see . . ."

The room smelled like rubbing alcohol and the cream the nurse used to prevent pressure ulcers. "Sister Claudia."

Blind eyes locked onto his. "John White. Where've you been? Sneaking out again?"

"School." He squeezed her outstretched hand. This touch was allowed only because it calmed her down.

"And what did you learn today?"

"Russia disarmed their last nuclear warhead. That leaves China and the US."

"World peace in your lifetime, imagine that."

Was the absence of nuclear threat the same thing as world peace? John wasn't sure, and he didn't like the way she referred only to his lifetime. He settled in his usual chair by her bed and reached to crank the window open. "Your hollyhocks are blooming. I staked them up yesterday."

She slid back down to her pillow. "I dreamed of rain. Is there a storm coming?"

He tipped his chair back toward the window and saw clear sky with a solid mass of thunderheads moving in from the west like a giant steamroller ready to flatten the world. "Tell me about your dream."

She eased onto her side, brushing a hank of brown hair behind her ear. "I was in the desert. Not the sandy kind with dunes, but the scrubby sort, with cacti and Joshua trees. It started to rain, and I found shelter in a tunnel that opened into a cavern. Though it could have been a ballroom, lit with torches. So many different colors of stone. Pink, orange, and blue, with veins of blood red and black pearl."

"You were talking to someone in your sleep."

She pressed her mottled eyelids shut. "A man. I couldn't see his face, but in his left hand he held a sword. A silver blade with an inscription. I didn't recognize the language, but somehow, I could read it. The Archangel Michael, who is like unto God and stands against the Dragon."

"Michael sounds like a badass."

"Language."

"Sorry," he mumbled, not sorry at all. "So, you saw the Archangel Michael?"

"I saw the sword." Claudia's pinpoint pupils fixed on him. "But that man was not Michael."

"Maybe it was the Dragon?"

A laugh rattled her skeletal body. "Oh, you evil thing."

The nurse popped in, checked the monitors, and gave John a thumbs-up as she departed. Claudia groped the top of her bedside table until her hand landed on a coil-bound book. Ever since learning Braille on The Twisted Claw, she couldn't get enough Hardy Boys, and what was not to like? They had pirates, bank robbers, forged paintings, buried treasure, secret passageways, and crooked cops. They were awesome.

Sister Claudia nudged the book toward him. "Would you read to me?

In the Daredevil comics, when Matt Murdock went blind, Stick trained him on his other senses until he could see through sound, taste, touch, and smell. Matt Murdock hadn't been prepared to lose his sight. Neither had Sister Claudia. In the event of sudden blindness, John would be prepared.

He closed his eyes and stepped off the moonlit porch. Grass crushed like damp velvet under his bare feet as he explored the backyard. A screech in the trees formed an owl in his mind. The neighbor's sprinkler system came on, throwing enough mist into the breeze to raise goose bumps on his arms. He reached out, gripping the pole of the swing set, abandoned in the yard like a skeleton stripped of flesh. Flaking metal stuck to his hand and he saw rust behind his closed eyelids.

The prickle of grass on the soles of his feet gave way to a hard, pebbled surface. He'd reached the pavers leading to the back gate. Twenty paces to the shed and ten in the opposite direction to the garden that used to smell sweet and spicy, but now stank of bitter green weeds. At least he wasn't allergic anymore.

He stood utterly still, listening, feeling. The wind picked up. He smelled rain.

INFRACTUS

I watch him skulk about in the dark, eyes closed, arms outstretched like a ghoul. A strange and beautiful boy. John, they call him. One night I read over his shoulder as he flipped through an entire book of baby names. Perhaps hoping for one to strike a chord? He'll be waiting awhile yet.

Now he pauses. As usual I'm dying to know his mind, and as usual I'm met with impenetrable silence. My first mistake, though he is otherwise flawlessly human. I veer off to listen to the ones I can hear.

The nurse. Awake in her bed and flitting between concern for a child at risk and her desire to be done with this wretched contract. Claudia sleeps, dreaming of death in color and light. The boy she calls John occupies those places in her heart both tender and fearful, as if she herself had cradled his womb-damp body to her breast and willed into him the air of this earth. A mother's love. The only religion worth believing in.

He slips back into the house. I'm tempted to follow. To spread myself over his slight adolescent body and let his warmth bleed into my nothingness. But there's work to be done.

Weapons of mass destruction nearly disposed of. World peace is at hand. But while their collective human gaze is fixed on that pie in the sky, weapons of strategic destruction are shifting into position right under their noses. Classic misdirection, and after decades of painstaking work, it's almost time.

In the morning John shambled into the kitchen. The nurse dunked a tea bag into her mug. John sniffed the air. Not peppermint. Raspberry.

"Did you sleep at all?" she asked.

He shook his head and dropped into a chair. She poured him a bowl of Cheerios, plunking it and the milk jug on the table in front of him. Weird, because she'd never done it before. She was a palliative care nurse, not a nose-wiping nanny.

"I was up half the night myself," she said. "She's taken a turn. You'll want to stay with her today."

John stared at his bowl of Cheerios, the only kind of boxed cereal Sister Claudia would buy. "I have a math test."

"Blow it off. I'll write you a note."

Just as well; he'd tank the advanced placement exam trying to take it when he was this tired. He closed his eyes, hooking his finger over the top of the bowl. He tipped the jug and heard milk swirl into the spaces between the Cheerios, lifting them until the cold wet surface touched his fingertip. A trick he'd learned while practicing things blind. Except this time, he didn't stop pouring. Milk spilled over the rim of the bowl and pattered onto the floor. A part of him, the John White part, strained at the only thing tethering him to existence—the weakening thread of Sister Claudia's life.

The nurse set her mug down on the counter. "Go. I'll take care of this."

Rain sheeted down Sister Claudia's window but John cranked it open anyway. "I rode my bike by the river yesterday. It's really high. Saw some trees floating in it. Lots of garbage too."

"Don't tell me about garbage," Sister Claudia grumbled, more lucid now that the nurse lightened her morphine. If the pain bothered her, the alternative of dying in a stupor bothered her more. "I suppose you climbed down that cliff of a bank to get a closer look?"

"I've done it a hundred times."

"Only takes one fall to be washed away."

"Another piece of trash," John said, watching the blinking lights on the monitors. The nurse had already silenced the alarms. That was what happened when you died slow. You lingered until only the machines cared, and then they were shut off too.

Sister Claudia slipped in and out of sleep. A priest arrived, administered last rights, and departed without a word to the sullen kid in the chair by the window. By noon, it was raining harder than ever. The hollow of Sister Claudia's throat sucked in with every breath, and she was too weak to do much more than blink. John reached through the side rail of her bed. She wrapped her fingers around his. It didn't seem right to him that someone still alive could feel so much like a bundle of dead twigs.

"Are you ready?" she asked.

A noise like rushing water filled his head, and a milky haze clouded his sight. He realized that being prepared wasn't the same as being ready.

Nothing left to say, and nothing more to be done. John picked up their latest Hardy Boys, closed his eyes, and began to read aloud, running his fingers over the raised bumps that formed words in his mind. Sister Claudia fell asleep, but he kept reading.

Frank and Joe had turned the antiquity thief over to the fuzz when Sister Claudia slipped away. John expected a death rattle, or the sound of a balloon slowly losing its air, but Sister Claudia's final breath sounded the same as any breath before it. The only difference was that nothing came after. Nothing but the rain.

CHAPTER 5

Without Sister Claudia to anchor him, he drifted. For days, or so it seemed.

In reality, weeks slipped away as he traveled by bus, by foot, and the odd truck bed. He couldn't recall exactly how he'd spent that time. All he knew was that he'd gone west until there was nowhere to go but into the water.

Wind whipped through his hair and his shoes sank into coarse sand as he gazed out at the waves. He'd never seen the ocean before. It smelled like old washcloths and roared like a nightmare. A deep, dark forever.

At his back the weight of the city bore down on him. Spears of glass, steel, and concrete thrust up into a flinty sky. He spotted a shaggy blond surfer in a dry suit running down the deserted beach with a yellow board tucked under his arm.

"Never seen swell this big make it into English Bay," the surfer said as he raced past the boy and charged into the water with a hooting battle cry. Raindrops pattered against the boy's jacket as he watched the surfer paddle out into the angry ocean.

INFRACTUS

"Storm's coming."

Startled, the boy turned to find another man standing right beside him. Ragged black coat, violin case strapped to his back, hair lashing around his head in the high wind. The man inched closer and brought with him the faint smell of forest fire. "You on your own?"

The boy backed up. "No."

The boy didn't think the man was much older than the surfer. His face wasn't wrinkled, and his hair and eyebrows were dark as scorched wood, the left split by a scar that ran all the way up his forehead. His eyes were the warm brown of Sister Claudia's leather-bound bible, currently stashed in the boy's backpack with a white braid pressed between its pages.

"What do you want?" the boy asked.

The man flashed a toothpaste commercial smile that didn't fit with his grubby clothes. "Got a place to stay?"

The boy turtled into his jacket and shoved his hands in his pockets. For weeks he'd been numb. Now all sorts of feelings were creeping in. Cold was the least of it.

"This is a rough town for a little mouse." The man stuck out a clean hand with trimmed nails. "I'm Zee. You got a name?"

The boy shrugged. What was he supposed to say? I had a name, but it was the wrong one? I have a name, I just don't know what it is? Surf crashed onto the beach. In the distance a monstrous wave roared up, and he glimpsed the surfer gliding along on his yellow board. Zee watched too.

"Some people don't know when to pack it in," Zee said.

INFRACTUS

The boy watched the tip of the surfboard gouge into the wave and flip end over end. The surfer flew through the air and dropped into brown water that swallowed him like he'd never existed in the first place.

John White was dead. Sister Claudia was dead. Zee's hand landed on the boy's shoulder, a heavy weight he almost shoved off, but at the moment it was the only thing holding him in place. The only thing keeping him from running into the ocean.

"C'mon, little mouse," Zee said over the shrill wind. "Storm's apt to get a lot worse before it gets better."

CHAPTER 6

Mouse huddled on the curb at the edge of Pigeon Park at two in the morning. Under a streetlight, with one sneaker planted in the gutter of Carrall Street, he turned the wavy pages of 1984, by George Orwell. He'd found the slim volume abandoned in the rain on a bus stop bench. People did that sometimes—finished a novel and left it behind. Back at his roach-ridden eastside studio, Mouse set the soggy book by the window to dry. Normally he hid his assortment of chewed over paperbacks from Zee to avoid an interrogation. However, his mentor had vanished on one of his walkabouts a few weeks ago, taking only his fiddle.

Mouse finished the chapter and gazed up into the warm September sky. No rain. No clouds. In Orwell's book, Pigeon Park would be the Prole district. But most lowlifes were smart enough to figure a kid reading by streetlight in one of Vancouver's roughest neighborhoods was perhaps best left alone. And if they didn't, they deserved what they got.

Orwell's version of 1984 never came true. Not exactly. There were no thought police or mandatory morning exercises, and people were still allowed to write with pens and paper, but there were other things. Worse things. Mouse hadn't gone to school for the last year, but he kept up with the news. He knew about rampage shootings, Sharia law, and the economic shitstorm of tanking commodities. He knew the American government had reneged on the nuclear treaty, refusing to dismantle the few remaining silos dotting the interior of their country. The rest of the world had their junk in a tolerable twist over that one.

But there were also people who left their books on benches, so it wasn't all bad.

A shadow sliced between the light and his open book. Mouse scowled up at a figure in a long coat haloed by the street lamp. "You're back."

Zee slung his arm around Mouse's neck and dragged him into something halfway between a hug and a sleeper hold. "Don't ever count me out, kid. I always come back."

Mouse shoved him away. "Where the hell were you?"

"Investing in our future. Bella says with trade embargoes on the States, they'll be starved for everything, including chemical distraction. Demand for Canadian glass is gonna be huge."

Mouse peered at Zee over his book. "I don't want any part of your dope business. I told you that already."

Zee chuckled. "Aw, that's my little straight-edger."

Mouse dog-eared the page and set the book down. "Boosting cars and fencing whatever happens to fall off a truck is one thing, but why sling meth like a loser, when you're smart enough to be a suit with a legit job, loads of money, and an overpriced condo in Yaletown?"

Zee dropped beside him on the curb, rested his elbows on his knees and tented his inscrutably clean fingers. "Say you were in the system right now, where you ought to be. Say you've got a family with their own Yaletown digs. They feed you a hot breakfast every morning, help you with your science fair project, and remind you to brush and floss before lights out. Sounds perfect. But every morning, you wake up wondering if today is the day they change their minds and send you back? Odds are the next time you'll end up a statistic. Living someplace where Mom drinks herself to sleep and Dad crawls into bed with you."

Mouse shielded his eyes from the headlights of a passing car. Newer BMW. Judging from the speed, the driver wasn't cruising to buy drugs or sex, but rather lost and terrified to find himself in the ghetto at night.

"What does my hypothetical foster perv have to do with you?"

"People with a lot to lose live in fear, Mouse."

Mouse contemplated this. After Sister Claudia died, he split because he wasn't interested in having decisions made for him. In the book, Big Brother controlled people through fear. Mouse chose a life where he could be the one in control.

"Better to be free on the streets than afraid in your ivory tower," Mouse said.

His ear struck the sidewalk before he registered the backhanded blow to his face. He stifled a cry of shock, though he shouldn't have been surprised. School was in session, and Zee had a unique instructional style.

"Ivory tower? I think baby Jesus just crapped the manger," Zee said, grabbing Mouse by the throat and hauling him up against the light pole. "You read too much, kid. Open your eyes. Analyze the details. I'm free. I'm fearless. I'm also an unscrupulous criminal. Maybe a little less freedom and a little more fear is what this world needs."

Mouse fought against the choking grip. He clutched Zee's shoulders and brought his knee up. Zee anticipated the shot to the groin, but not the hook to his chin.

"Hells bells." Zee staggered backward. "This time last year you never woulda landed that punch. Nice work."

"Good teacher," Mouse said, wiping the blood off his mouth.

With a cryptic gleam in his eyes, Zee scooped the book up and handed it to Mouse. "I ain't the Devil, kid. I'm just his advocate."

Mouse held the book against his chest. "You've been gone a long time. Fat Bella's pissed."

"I'll see her tomorrow," Zee said, rubbing his jaw. "Bring her some fresh gossip. She can't stay mad at me forever."

True, but she could definitely stay mad long enough to rearrange Zee's facial geography. Mouse was about to suggest extreme caution when a tremendous bang punched through his ears and ripped the air out of his lungs. His vision blurred and he found himself horizontal on the concrete again, his book sprawled open next to him. When he could focus again, he saw Zee's mouth moving but heard only the ringing in his head. Above them a reddish glow bloomed across the sky. Zee grabbed his shoulders, pulling him up. Dragging him back.

"Come on...outta here...before—"

Mouse caught only the blunt edge of Zee's words. Another shockwave slammed into him and they tumbled to the shaking ground.

INFRACTUS

Over and over, the explosions shook the earth and drummed through his bones. Over, and over, and over.

When things got weird, the first thing to go was Mouse's sense of time. He could have sworn only minutes had passed since that first explosion rocked the city. Minutes. Sliding by more quickly than he could track them.

Smoky thunderheads had piled into the air, smothering a previously clear sky. The ground crunched under his shoes. Mouse looked down at a carpet of glittering, glowing red and orange. Like Christmas lights or hot coals. He didn't understand. Not at first. Then a row of windows in a burning high-rise shattered, raining broken glass over a world on fire.

Zee. Mouse shouted but couldn't hear his own voice. He whipped his head around. People teemed through the streets, eyes wide and white like terror-blind rabbits. Little kids in pajamas clung to their parents. A barefoot couple ran down the street holding hands while an old man shuffled along cradling a cat in his arms. Everyone on their phones. No one getting through.

"Zee!" he shouted again, mute air racing through his vocal cords. A rumble traveled up through his shoes into his legs. The burning high-rise began to collapse. Floor upon floor, ejecting a spray of dust and ash. It had to have been burning for hours. How long had it been? Why couldn't he hear? A hand clamped onto his wrist.

"I'm here. I've got you," Zee said. The words were mushy in Mouse's ears, but he heard them.

INFRACTUS

Zee towed Mouse through the mob and threw him on the back of a motorcycle. Mouse banded his arms around Zee's waist as the bike rumbled to life beneath them.

They zigged and zagged their way down East Hastings, away from downtown, which seemed to be ground zero. At the corner of Cordova, a refrigerator-sized chunk of concrete fell onto a car trying to nose its way through the hysterical throng clogging the road. Zee steered the bike up onto the sidewalk to get around the wreck. Up close, the reek of spilled gasoline engulfed them, and Mouse recognized the car as the shiny BMW that passed by earlier. The buckled driver's side door hung open and Mouse glimpsed a man's hand. Gold wedding ring, white shirt cuff, and blood streaking through a fine layer of airbag dust. Mouse's teeth clacked together as the bike lurched off the curb and dropped onto the asphalt. Zee gunned the engine.

The ringing in his ears faded, but the screaming was worse. Even the noisy motorcycle and the sirens shrieking in all directions couldn't smother the sound of human terror. Dozens of people on the ground, trampled, or pasted by falling debris. Smoke belching out of broken windows carried the oily stink of burnt meat. They zipped past a woman sprawled in the gutter in front of a smashed-up pharmacy. Shards of glass gleamed in her bloody hair and a toddler sat in the street beside her, wailing.

"Zee, stop."

Zee glanced over his shoulder. "Forget it, Mouse. Kid's already dead."

"Stop!"

INFRACTUS

When Mouse started to jump off, Zee skidded to a halt.

"Goddamnit, you got a death wish?"

Mouse raced to the end of the block where the kid was begging to get run over or flattened by another falling chunk of skyscraper. Mouse checked the mother's neck for a pulse he knew he wouldn't find. A white paper bag lay torn open beside her, a bottle of liquid penicillin inside. Her skirt was torn and her blue underwear hung off one of her ankles. The baby's footy pajamas were soaked in blood from her crushed skull.

"Mama," the kid bawled, tears drawing pink veins down his dirty cheeks.

Half a dozen men waving machetes and bats piled out of a burning pawnshop across the street. Mouse scooped the kid up and ducked into the glass-strewn doorway of the pharmacy. The looters marched on, but not before Mouse saw the blood spattering their faces and dripping off their weapons. Mouse analyzed the details. The woman went to the drug store to pick up medicine for her baby when the explosions started. She was probably still hiding there when those assholes barged in to sack the place. They raped her, kicked her head in, and left her kid for dead. A police cruiser zoomed by in a flash of red and blue and howling sirens. Too late. Always too late.

The baby continued to cry, burying his wet face in Mouse's chest. Mouse ran his hand over blond curls and hefted the soft fuzzy weight higher in his arms. Fresh blood soaked into Mouse's shirt. It couldn't all be the dead mother's. He located a tear in the sleeper by the kid's shoulder and found a deep cut underneath.

Zee roared up on the bike. "Christ, Mouse. You picked a hell of a time to go Mother fucking Theresa."

"He's hurt," Mouse said, swinging his leg over the seat and winding one arm around Zee while hanging onto the kid with the other. "We need to get him to a hospital."

With a squeal of tires, they sped off, sliding through the human carnage, and dodging the gangs of looters. Near Burnaby they were able to pick up some speed. Smoke whipped through Mouse's hair and burned his eyes. He pulled his jacket around the kid who'd settled with his thumb plugged into his mouth and Mouse's shirt bunched in his fist. Every minute or so a fire truck or ambulance screamed by in the opposite direction, headed toward the flaming carnage of downtown.

"Should we flag one of them down?" Mouse shouted.

Zee yelled back over his shoulder. "You should've tucked that whelp under his dead mama's arm and walked away." Mouse tightened his hold on the sleeping toddler, and Zee shook his head. "When the world's on fire, Mouse, all you can do is let it burn."

They found the same apocalyptic mayhem in Burnaby. Flames, rubble, melted plastic, and blood in the streets. Could Zee be right? Could the whole world be on fire? Mouse pictured his book, unfinished on the sidewalk, curling into ash. He thought of the red light filling the entire sky.

By the time they crossed the Fraser River into Surrey, the baby was dead.

CHAPTER 7

Mouse ran through the charred remains of Stanley Park, the acrid air cool on his feverish skin. If he slowed now, he might stop. If he stopped, he might fall. What he carried on his back was worth killing for, and he was fifteen, about the worst age there was for a street kid. Old enough to be useful. Young enough to be used. He'd been running for months and wondered if he'd ever be able to stop.

By now Zee would be in the alley off West Georgia Street, kicked back with Fat Bella and a jug of something undrinkable. Zee wouldn't care that Mouse was late. Zee wasn't the one running out of time.

Above the black bones of cedars, he could still see the smoke. An hour ago, he'd been in a boat, crossing the harbor under the smoldering congestion on the Lionsgate Bridge. Apparently, a fuel tanker rolled over and the whole thing went up in a massive inferno. His throat burned from the fumes and his nerves were shot from the water crossing. A whole lot of goddamn trouble to do something he swore he never would.

INFRACTUS

He ran past a cluster of whores loitering around a fallen hemlock at the edge of the park. The girls called after him in shrill voices. Teenagers, strung out on glass, with hard red mouths, bruised skin, and dead eyes. Junkies. Losers. Trading the only thing they had on the cheap. Since that stormy morning on the beach, Mouse had lived by two rules. He wouldn't sling dope or flip tricks. Nothing in the world could make him that desperate.

Then the world changed.

Adventus. That's what people called it. The night bombs, missiles, and gas line explosions wiped out pretty much all supply chain and communication infrastructures. Television, cellular phone service, and Internet didn't exist anymore. The dire lack of information seriously fanned the flames of public hysteria. With no electricity or running water, and dwindling reserves of food and fuel, the streets erupted in riots so violent people were literally torn apart.

It took months for radio to come online, and it did so in the form of continuous news broadcast called the Stream. Unfortunately, the Stream confirmed what Zee already suspected. A-Day happened everywhere. All over the world. With nuclear disarmament nearly complete, this was the last thing anyone saw coming. Especially since it didn't appear to be an attack on one nation by another. In most places, the damage from bombs and missiles could be traced back to their own military stockpiles. Like a suicide pact between every country on earth. Not surprisingly, countries that'd held onto their nukes suffered the worst damage.

Running on the street would attract attention, so Mouse put his head down, walked fast, and struggled to quiet his breathing. He swerved around a woman who'd staggered from a doorway long since relieved of its door. His stomach lurched at the sour stink of cholera. Her sunken eyes pleaded and her fingers grazed his arm, but he kept going, telling himself not to look back, knowing he would anyway.

The meat wagons hadn't made their daily pickup, and Mouse saw the woman seeing the others. Corpses, like wads of spent chewing gum lumped in the gutter or collapsed in other doorless doorways. Mouse nearly tripped over one as he watched the woman shamble, aimless and resigned. She'd be on tomorrow's wagon.

A cramp twisted his guts into a hard ball and he stumbled again as his vision swirled. If he kept walking he'd fall. If he fell, he might not get up. So, he ran. He sprinted down the rubble-choked ruin of West Georgia. A grinding hum in the near distance accelerated into a roar. He ducked into the narrow alley as a convoy of tanks rolled around the corner.

Zee lounged on an upended crate with his fiddle across his lap. He picked up the bow and dragged it across a cake of rosin. "Look what the cat coughed up."

Mouse dragged his feet to the opposite wall and slid his backpack off his shoulders. Too heavy, like everything else these days. The pack thumped to the ground, raising a puff of yellow-gray ash. He gulped air and commanded his knees to stay in their upright and locked positions. Fat Bella sat next to Zee in her typical uniform of leggings and an oversized hoodie. Both watched Mouse intently as though they were in a velvet-draped theatre box rather than sitting on milk crates against a brick wall in a filthy alley. They'd been there awhile, judging by the half-empty plastic jug between them. Mouse recoiled at the odor of rotten cherries and yeast. He wondered if he looked as rough as they did.

The details. Fat Bella wasn't so much fat as she was huge and capable of punching a horse to the ground. Mouse figured she was thirty, but the rind of dirt and ash made people look different. Kids appeared younger, and adults older. Soot beaten into the lines of Zee's face aged him into his forties. Only the scar splitting his eyebrow remained pale and clean.

Fat Bella said Zee got in a bad car wreck when they were kids. She said he was in a coma for weeks, that all his hair fell out. Bella also swore the King of England offered her a handful of diamonds to pee on him. She believed both stories to be true. Turbo crazies like Fat Bella posed a technical difficulty for Mouse's lie-detecting talent.

Zee swigged from the jug and winked at Mouse. That could be good or bad. His mentor was never an easy read, and the worst thing you could do was ask.

"What's with the flag?" Zee pointed to the banner hanging off a barrel-snouted tank as it trundled down the street. Mouse rubbed his grainy eyes and peered at the strange flag he'd seen popping up more and more. A black circle on a gray background. Like a bloodless version of the Japanese rising sun.

"Emblem of the new world," said Fat Bella. "Belongs to an outfit called Panopticon."

Zee took another drink. "What's a Panopticon?"

Bella swiped the jug out of his hand. "Like I got the time? Learn a book, dumbass."

Zee's ignorance sent the lie detector needle skittering over the inside of Mouse's skull. Then again, Zee made a point of speaking in half-truths, so it was hard to say exactly how much he knew. Mouse shivered even as beads of sweat threaded down his spine. He wanted to close the deal and scram, but this was information worth having.

"Why is the Army suddenly wearing this Panopticon's patch?" Mouse asked.

Bella sipped and shuddered. "When FEMA, NATO, and Red Cross went tits up, the UN tapped these Panopticon guys to shovel through the mess and get people to act right again. Word has it they used to be in the private security biz."

Zee inspected his bow. "Like mall cops?"

"Like Blackwater, dipstick. Like private armies in every corner of the goddamn planet."

"Right." Zee scratched his head through the knit cap he wore. "The Blackwater."

The Fool. Zee's favorite role, though he would play any part to get what he was after. Never be yourself if you can help it, Mouse. Because yourself usually sucks, and it isn't what other people wanna deal with. Mouse would bet anything Zee knew more about this Panopticon thing than he was letting on.

"Where'd you hear about it?" Mouse asked Bella.

"Flag speaks for itself dontcha figure? And I'll tell you something else. My contacts are saying there ain't no government anymore, not nowhere. Even the 'muricans are rudderless. Whitehouse down and dusted."

"Shame, that." Zee dropped the rosin into the open fiddle case at his feet.

"The Stream hasn't mentioned anything," Mouse said.

Bella's broad body shook with laughter. "Forget the Stream. You want the straight dope on the state of affairs in Denmark you come see Fat Bella. Mark my words boys, these Panopticon guys are shady motherfuckers and them black-eyed flags are the thin edge of the wedge."

Mouse drew a triangle in the ash with the toe of his boot. Streamcasts were tolerably useless, but radio was low tech, reliable, and the only media outlet. Too bad the news tended to be local stuff. Go here. Do this. Bread lines, water depots...outbreak reports. World events were sparsely detailed. Between the Stream, the rumor wheel, and Fat Bella, everyone knew something. No one knew enough.

"It's been eight months," Mouse said. "They're still not saying how it happened. How every country in the world managed to blow itself up on the same day."

Bella belched, covering her mouth with her slab of a hand. "That Islamic State thing. Terrorist cells working in every major city."

Mouse risked leaning against the wall. Casual, as though he were taking a moment to think. Leaky A-Day theories abounded. Muslims, Christians, Canadian radicals, Vegans. Mouse didn't offer an opinion. He didn't know enough about the world and didn't have the energy to chase down the words. Not with the fever poaching his brain.

"ISIS? Get real," said Zee, tightening the pegs on his fiddle. "We heard it from you first, Jelly-Belly. A-Day happened everywhere. Hundreds of thousands of bombs, a few nukes. Roads, rails, pipelines.

Airports and seaports. Global supply chain blasted to hell. Cue looting and riots. Now every ash-dusted cranny of the world looks like the friggin' East End. Know what kinda time and planning and resources that would take? Personally, I'm thinkin' aliens."

Bella cuffed Zee's ear. "Call me Jelly-Belly again, I'll knock you into last Thursday."

Zee rubbed his reddening ear and waved Mouse over with a clean hand. "Let's get down to business. You got something for me?"

Mouse unzipped his backpack and pulled out a grocery sack. He breathed through his mouth to mitigate—that was the word—the flowery perfume. "North Van is a dead zone. Had a hard time finding anything that hadn't been set on fire at least once."

"Them kinda places is all over now," said Bella. "South of the border, it's like someone drew a giant black X from Nevada to Michigan, Idaho to Missouri. Nuked by their own warheads. Ain't nothing left but blighted wasteland."

Zee passed the jug her way. "How would anyone here know shit about friggin' Nevada?"

"Specialized frequency. All my contacts are on it." She offered the jug to Mouse. "Wanna drink, kiddo? Little yeasty, but not so thick as the last batch."

Mouse shook his head. A mere sniff of Zee's prison brew made his esophagus shrivel up. As for the so-called contacts, Fat Bella was fully whackadoo, but also super smart, and rarely wrong about this stuff.

"Anyway, I got what you asked for." Mouse tossed the grocery sack across the alley. Zee snagged it and pulled out one of the hotel-sized bars, still wrapped.

"What folks'll do for a bit of soap these days. Little bricks of gold."

"The vultures chasing me with machetes seemed to think so. Your turn, Zee."

Zee tucked the fiddle under his chin, picked up the bow and dragged a low hum from the strings. The bang of an explosion ripped through the smog. A common enough occurrence that Mouse hardly flinched. Moments later, a helicopter whipped across the yellow sky and military sirens squealed.

"Ooh, they're playing my song." Bella hefted herself to her feet. "Gonna check the scene. Get my information right from zero ground."

"It's ground zero," Zee said with a jaunty reel. "Say hey to that fireman o' yours. Something going on there I should know about?"

"Ain't like that. He knew my Daddy is all, way back."

"Your old man still up North?"

Bella laughed. "Thinking of a visit?"

Mouse pressed himself into the brick wall, trying his best to become invisible. Zee never talked about his life before and when Bella rambled too far into the past, he was quick to shove her back to the present. This was definitely information worth having.

"Your daddy never liked me much," Zee said.

"If he knew what kinda trouble you'd got me in, he prolly woulda killed you."

"Hey, it worked out in the end."

Bella clenched her fists. "For you."

Mouse held his breath in the conversational pause. What kind of trouble? One of Zee's fledgling scams? Something worse? Zee's eyes flicked toward him. "Curiosity killed the cat, Mouse."

Mouse lowered his gaze to Bella's big toes poking through matching holes in her slippers. Zee cared a lot about Bella, but he'd still screw her over in an eighth note if it meant getting what he wanted. Mouse hated him for that. Hated that it only reinforced what he already knew. Affection was a parasite. It bound two people together and sucked the life out of them both.

"Enough with the jig down memory road," Bella said. "I gotta split. Get my ear to the dirt. Catch the signal." She reached over and ruffled Mouse's filthy hair. "Get some vitamins, kiddo. You're white as bird shit."

Zee played a bouncy tune until Fat Bella lumbered around the corner, then a wolfish white smile stretched across his face. Zee took excellent care of his teeth, and taught Mouse to do the same. It's the appearance of quality. You can charge more for shit that looks better. No one's gonna empty their wallet for a guy with dirty hands and a mouthful of rotten chompers. Not unless they're being mugged, and that's not how we roll. We're businessmen.

Mouse didn't smile back. "Whatever game you're on, I'm not interested."

"You're slumming, Mouse. Was a time you wouldn't touch a bag of glass with lead lined gloves."

"It's not for me."

"Who do you think you're fooling? I know what's putting you to the bricks like a boiled string bean. I know what you need. And I know how bad you need it."

Mouse needed a hospital admission chit. Without ID, the only official way to get a chit was to apply for ID, which took weeks.

INFRACTUS

Tolerably pointless when the cholera would kill you in a matter of days. The unofficial way was to bribe the admitting officer with high-grade glass only Zee could get his hands on.

"We had a deal."

Zee set his bow down. "Two years ago, I tucked you under my wing. Made sure you got a proper education."

"And you got your cut. I don't owe you anything."

Zee taught Mouse how to crack locks and boost cars, how to negotiate and fence, how to sniff out desperation and ruthlessly exploit it. It was from Zee that he'd learned to build a big picture out of small details, how every interaction and observation offered something of value, maybe not on its own, and maybe not right away, but all information is worth having, Mouse. More intel equals more leverage. Mouse learned fast, yet his mentor remained superior at the art of being a double-crossing sonofabitch.

"What do you want?" Mouse asked.

Zee's eyes drank him in, shoes to shag. "Ever had a woman?"

His hands went clammy. An honest no could be dangerous as a fabricated yes.

"Or maybe you like boys." Zee grazed the fiddle strings, making them sigh. "Two years and I don't even know what lifts your luggage."

Mouse wasn't sure himself. It was hard to think about sex when you were busy enough trying to avoid rape. And riots. And starvation.

"First love, Mouse," said Zee. "That's the one that wrecks you."

"For fuck's sake what do you want?"

"One hour." Zee's eyes roved over his body again. "I get one hour, and the dope is yours."

INFRACTUS

Mouse jerked his head back, smacking it on the bricks. He'd run up against his share of complicated perverts and Zee's gender indifferent kink for jailbait was hardly a secret. He should have seen this coming. And he would have, but he'd been stupid enough to assume a degree of something, respect maybe, between them.

"No deal."

Zee pointed at Mouse with his bow. "I'm offering the staff discount here, and that's me looking out for you–"

"Like hell it is." Mouse grabbed the bag of soap and stuffed it in his pack. "I'm not one of your junkie crank divers."

As he stalked toward the mouth of the alley, the fiddle began singing again. Sad, like a funeral.

"Things'll get better," Zee called out over his dirge. "It'd be a shame to let the fever take you now."

Mouse's stomach rolled. The hollow-eyed woman, whose papery hand grazed his arm, was merely one of the dozens he saw every day, puking and shitting themselves inside out, their guts turned to milk. Blue corpses stinking up the streets. Fat Bella told him the cholera pandemic would cull the human herds by a third before public sanitation was a thing again.

From the velvet lining of his fiddle case, Mouse watched Zee pull a slip of paper embossed with a red cross. He tugged off his cap and ran a hand through the cyclone of hair brindled with ash. "Not gonna let you die, Mouse. You know I won't."

Mouse thought of the baby he'd tried to save on A-Day as he trudged back into the alley, stopping with the toes of his boots an inch from Zee's. "What about all your rules? What happened to watching the world burn?"

Zee tipped his face to the strip of sky between brick walls. "Never met a rule I didn't break eventually."

Mouse tried to understand. Zee had over two years to make his move, why now? And what about the fever? He didn't seem the least bit concerned about getting sick. None of it made sense. Lies and truth. Trust and treachery. And those were just the things Mouse had words for. He missed words. He missed dictionaries and libraries and stories and information. That was an old life. With rules that didn't work anymore. Since the day they'd met, Zee taught Mouse how to survive. Maybe Zee was still teaching. New lesson for a new world.

"This won't make you less lonely," Mouse said.

Zee stood up and tucked the chit into Mouse's pocket. "I know."

The gloved grip of an indeterminate number of hands lifted Mouse onto a cot covered in a white sheet. When was the last time he'd seen something so clean? All around he heard the rush of people: displacing the air, talking, whispering, crying. Under the bite of bleach, he smelled bile and death. He rubbed his cheek against the cool linens.

How long had he been here? His memory blurred backward. Too far. All the way to naked skin and the taste of wood smoke. Zee's mouth on his. Zee on top of him. Inside him. It hurt, but he still got hard. He didn't want to, but he spunked all over the place, which was so beyond embarrassing. Beyond any word for any feeling. Like a silent blast rupturing every molecule of his being. He'd trembled in Zee's arms, his mouth pressed shut, holding back the terrible nothing inside. Zee held him and whispered over and over the same empty words: I'm here...I've got you . . .

Mouse gagged. Someone rolled him to his side and shoved a metal basin under his chin, but he didn't puke. He wouldn't. Not yet. Where was he? Coal Harbor. Field hospital. He remembered the sign. Zee kept his promise? Where was that evil bastard anyway?

"Hey, kid," Zee said, hooking a chair leg with his foot and dragging it over to the cot.

"Go away," Mouse croaked.

"I'm sorry, Mouse. I'm so damn sorry."

Mouse heard Zee's voice and smelled his smoky smell, but it couldn't be Zee because Zee never apologized. To anyone. For anything.

"Not gonna defend myself. I wanted to be your first. Guess I didn't know any better way to say goodbye."

"Wait." Mouse flung his arm out and clawed at Zee's sleeve. "Don't go."

"It's time, Mouse. I'll be seeing you."

He felt Zee's lips against his forehead, heard the scrape of a chair, and the zing of a curtain pulled along its track. The words rolled through his fevered mind, snowballing bigger and bigger until he saw only white.

CHAPTER 8

It rained the day Mouse turned seventeen.

He huddled on the ledge of the broken window of his Yaletown flat, watching the downpour hammer Pacific Boulevard. Winter wind sprayed him in the face and he withdrew deeper in his hoodie. Rain like this reminded him of Sister Claudia. She hadn't believed in birthday gifts or parties, but she always baked cakes for the kids. Confetti, lemon, or carrot. For John White it was always Devil's food. The woman had a sense of humor. He was glad she died before A-Day. For a lot of reasons.

Watery shadows played along the mildewed walls and flaking ceiling of Mouse's dumpster-sized room. Yaletown real estate had seen better days. The building had neither heat nor electricity, and when it rained hard, the whole neighborhood smelled like sewer. Still, it didn't have bedbugs, the rats weren't too bad, and a steady roof over his head was a tolerable change.

There were no rules when it came to survival. Zee hammered that lesson home before he left, and by the time Mouse left the hospital, Fat Bella had vanished too. Mouse forged ahead alone, doing everything he said he never would in order to survive. Zee was right though, things got better. Now he scuffed by acquiring contraband for anyone who had the creds. Life under Panopticon's black eye was still hard, but no longer desperate.

On the street below, Mouse heard the sliding rumble of a van door and the wet struggle of someone being stuffed inside. Happened every day. Panopticon had eyes all over, and if they didn't like your face, they sent their patrol around to erase you from existence. Their motives were ideological, but also practical. Panopticon purchased the unquestioning love of their citizens with food, water, housing, and harsh treatment of undesirables. The latter conveniently provided a limitless supply of able-bodied "criminals" to work in Panopticon's mines, refineries, factories, and farms.

Hunger gnawed in Mouse's gut. Earlier that day he'd managed to procure a few gallons of sterno for one of his clients—not easy with strict fuel rationing—and now he had money in his pocket, enough to buy something that didn't come out of a can. Bread, cheese, or even apples. His mouth flooded at the idea of tearing through red skin into tart white flesh. A nearly carnivorous craving, though he couldn't remember the last time he'd eaten meat.

In the midst of his food fantasy, he heard a knock at the door.

"Hullo," said a muffled voice. "Anyone home? It's Jenny."

The details. Jenny was a trader he'd met while waiting for his sterno client near the Stroll. When she approached he'd expected her to hustle him. Instead she pointed out a spot on a brick wall where someone had painted an electric blue fish. He liked that she noticed such a small thing. He liked the tattoo that circled her wrist, finely inked script she allowed him to read by slowly rotating her hand.

take care that no one hates you justly

He also liked that she used her real name instead of some dumb hooker handle like Rapunzel or Sapphire. Jenny was a regular name for a regular girl. A good fit for an experiment he'd been considering.

He left the window ledge and crossed the room to open the door.

"Sorry I'm late." Jenny's knees quivered below her vinyl raincoat. "Had to stay out of sight until that patrol went on its way. D'you know the water runs right into your building if the front door gets left open?"

She twisted a bit of soggy yellow hair around her fingers. That afternoon her nails had been orange. Now they were metallic purple. Mouse wondered where she got her nail polish. Her smile flickered. Probably wondering if he was planning to murder her. He opened the door and waved her in. The experiment had begun.

Jenny shucked her wet coat while Mouse dug the agreed upon sum out of his pocket. She tucked the creds into her giraffe print bag and got down to business, pulling her dress over her head and letting it drop to the floor because he didn't have so much as a chair for her to put it on. Next, she unhooked her pink bra and skimmed off her panties.

For several seconds Mouse studied her. He'd never seen a totally naked girl before, not a live one anyway. Her chest was nearly flat as his and she had no hair at all between her legs—most pro traders removed it to keep from catching lice. He scanned himself for some sign of attraction to her female body.

She hauled him out of his hoodie and his T-shirt and his other T-shirt, laughing when she got tangled up in all his sleeves.

"Gosh, you smell nice," she said, prompting him to lie back on the sleeping bag.

Earlier he'd bought some soap and paid for the luxury of a tepid shower. Seemed the considerate thing to do. Her weight settled against him and somehow his face ended up mashed into her bald armpit. She smelled like cotton candy—or his vague memory of it. He adjusted his position under her and went sliding onto the floor. He flinched as his shoulder blade skated over the icy tiles. They bumped heads as he wriggled back.

"Ow."

"Sorry."

Her legs swished over the nylon sleeping bag as she straddled him, unzipped his pants and pulled a foil packet from her bag. "Want me to put it on? I don't work without so don't even ask."

"I can do it." He peeled the condom open and wondered who hooked her up. In books, there was always a Big War, brown leggings, and kids gutted each other for reasons that were vague, yet super important. That was fiction. The reality of a post-apocalyptic society? Everyone had the clap.

Christ, he missed books.

Mouse gazed up at Jenny's unfocused pupils. She was high, but he didn't see any track marks on her arms or legs so she probably didn't inject. Between that and the rubber, hopefully he wouldn't catch hepatitis.

"Need a hand?" she asked.

"No."

"You sure?"

"Yes."

"Let me try."

Mouse squeezed his eyes shut. Every part of him but the part that mattered went rigid at the slide of Jenny's skin on his, the tickle of her damp hair, and her stroking fingers. She was supposed to touch him. He was paying her to touch him. It wasn't the same as those other times, when he'd been desperate. When he sold himself to men who'd used him every which way. This was supposed to be different.

He pushed Jenny's hands away. "Stop."

"Sure?"

"Yeah." Experiment over.

"S'okay, kid. It happens." Jenny shimmied back into her underwear as though his catastrophic failure to get it up were about as remarkable as a dented soup can. "Blight it, I'm starved. Got a few more creds? We could do something. Stroll's gonna be dead tonight on account of the rain."

Dazed, Mouse twisted until he could reach into his pocket for the rumpled polymer bills he'd earmarked for apples. He tossed the money on the floor near Jenny's giraffe bag.

"I know a place where we can get animal crackers and listen to records," she said, her head popping through the top of her dress. "It's a mosque, which feels kinda disrespectful, but since Panopticon says people ain't allowed to do church no more . . ."

Mouse rolled over, burying his face in his sleeping bag. The experiment not only failed, it burned down the entire lab. He wanted something normal. That was why he picked Jenny. A young pretty girl. The exact opposite of those men, those lonesome losers and kinky weirdos. This was regular. This was what he wanted. So, what the hell?

"Some other time, then," she said. "I'll see my own self out."

Through the down of his sleeping bag, he listened to the plastic flap of her coat, and her high-heeled shoes ticking across cracked tiles. A draft as the door opened and a draft as it closed. Rain blew in through the broken window. Happy fucking birthday.

Fire truck lights flashed red and white against the smoggy night sky. Patrollers brandished their black batons and viper stun guns, shouting at the surge of onlookers to get back. Mouse stood behind the barricade of sawhorses and fluttering yellow tape. The hospital was still burning. The fire started that morning and spread like dragon's breath. The smell of braised flesh hung in the air like a meaty fog. Mouse pulled his shirt over his nose.

Fingers of flame crawled from broken windows on the lower floors and disappeared into fat plumes of steam. Enough heat radiated from the blaze to sting the raw scrape on Mouse's cheek. The client who'd tried to short him on a box of batteries crawled away with a broken nose, and only that because Mouse happened to be in a hurry. Now he was actually late. He hated being late. He shoved his way through the crowd, past the hospital, and zipped down the smoky street.

Distorted old-world industrial techno led Mouse down into the basement of the West Side mosque. Fat Bella had been right when she said Panopticon's black-eyed flags were barely the beginning. Since then they'd insidiously dug their hooks into this and that until they controlled the entire world with their cameras, curfews, patrols, and work camps. Now they'd banned religion. Not a tragedy in his view, but even if the practice was outlawed, houses of worship were still places to gather.

The basement was hot and reeked of marijuana, unwashed bodies, and the cloying bloom of poppy resin. A few dozen people lounged in the hazy candlelight, alone or huddled in small groups. Mouse waded through them until he found Jenny settled in the corner on a pile of mildewed prayer rugs.

For whatever reason, Jenny seemed to think their abortion of a date all those months ago cemented between them the bonds of eternal friendship. An early display of what he'd come to think of as Jenny Logic. So, when she'd pestered him to come here, going on about how riot cool it was, he should've expected a grungy opium den full of strung out losers.

Mouse flopped down next to her half-shouting over the music. "We're gonna get bombed just breathing in here."

Her fingertips grazed the tender side of his face. "You've been fighting again."

"A bit."

Jenny worried a lot, but Mouse knew what he was doing.

Violence is a commitment, Mouse. No room for half measures. If you're gonna throw down, you throw down hard.

Jenny offered him the open bag of animal crackers, but she did it without a smile or a joke or any of the usual Jenny conversation starters.

"What's wrong?" he asked.

Jenny hugged her knees. "Did you see the hospital fire?"

"Still burning." Mouse peered into the bag. "These smell like furnace dust."

"On the Stream they're saying Ori Mane did it."

Ori Mane. A name Mouse heard more and more these days. On the street, and on the Stream. No one knew exactly who Ori Mane was, only that he and his crew claimed to be freedom fighters and called themselves Jackals. Panopticon called them terrorists. A matter of perspective, considering the way they ran up and down the east coast of the Pan American Division, PAD, disrupting surveillance, raiding government storage depots, ambushing supply convoys, and now supposedly blowing up hospitals.

"Doesn't make sense," Jenny said. "Ori Mane fights for the people. He's the good guy."

"No such animal," Mouse said, sorting a handful of crackers into lions, giraffes, elephants, and monkeys.

"But the Stream said—"

"And who controls the Stream?" Mouse snapped. Jenny Logic confused him at the best of times, but now it threatened to tear his head inside out. "For all we know Panopticon torched the place themselves. Why do you even care?"

Jenny shrank into the corner like a kicked puppy. "There were kids in there, Mouse. Babies."

"Mmm hmm. Hey, why do you think the monkeys wear pants?"

Timid to ferocious in the time it took to jump to her feet, she stood over him, glaring. "You are such an asshole!"

INFRACTUS

Mouse watched, bewildered, as she slung her giraffe bag over her shoulder and stalked off through the smoky miasma.

◈◈◈

The blackened wreckage of the hospital made for tolerably easy, if unstable, climbing. Mouse hoisted himself onto twisted steel beams and scrambled up demolished bits of staircase. Falling was always a risk, but he'd been climbing since he could crawl and was more worried about the patrol. They'd waste no time throwing him over the razor wire into a work camp.

By the time he reached the ninth floor, his head ached from chemical fumes and he was covered in soot. He splashed through puddles of dark sludge under a blackened PICU sign and kicked over a partially melted acrylic tub. It was empty. He stuck his hand through one of the warped portholes and grazed the scorched mattress. He didn't especially want to see a burnt-up little skeleton, but there had to be something here. A clue that would help him understand.

Kids died all the time. The baby Mouse grabbed off the street on A-Day died. Were the runts who died in the fire more important? He didn't get it. Empathy wasn't his strong suit, which usually suited him fine. Filtering someone else's emotions through the messy trap of his own often left him confused. Until a fat drop of water splatted on his head like a Newtonian apple, and the mystery broke open.

Jenny Logic. She wasn't angry because he didn't care about the kids. It wasn't about the kids at all. She thought he didn't care about her. It was a friend thing. Caring about each other's cares, even if you didn't understand.

Another drop hit the crown of his head. "I am an asshole."

INFRACTUS

Jenny backed away from the warped ladder rising five stories to the roof of the condemned East End tenement. "Are you fever drunk? I'm not climbing that."

For all his planning, Mouse hadn't considered that Jenny might be afraid of heights. "The wall brackets are rusted. But it's safe if we go one at a time."

She tucked her hands into her armpits and peered up and down the deserted street. "Coming on full dark."

"They only do ground patrol here. Hurry, we're going to miss it."

"Miss what? What am I risking labor camp, the lockjaw, and a broken neck for?"

He pointed at her yellow stilettos. "You'll want to take those off."

She sulked out of the shoes, exposing glittery toenails—probably a gift from one of her regulars. Mouse slouched against the bricks, hands diving into his pockets. Acid chewed at his too-long-empty stomach. Jenny was clearly still miffed at him, and he'd convinced her to miss a night's work for this. What if she didn't like it? Her painted mouth curled as she jammed her shoes into her giraffe. He hoped she wouldn't notice the dead rat inches from her bare feet.

A klaxon shouted through the fading light. They covered their ears as the alarm collided with crumbling concrete and rattled the bones of stripped cars. The final blare left in its wake something deeper than silence. A vacuum. Empty buildings yawned into their shadows. Mouse nudged the rat carcass into the gutter with the toe of his boot.

"Well, that's curfew," Jenny said, and climbed onto the ladder. From the fourth rung she scrutinized him. "Whatcha waiting for?"

"It won't take the weight. You have to go up first . . ." He trailed off hearing the sound of an engine. Chunky tires over rubble, around the corner. Two blocks away? Maybe only one. This not a minute after curfew. Patrollers, with their stupid orange pageant sashes and viper stun guns. Keen to pick some low hanging fruit.

"Blighted hell." Mouse dashed down to peek around the corner. He saw headlights.

"C'mon!" Jenny said.

"It might not hold."

"You'd rather get pinched?"

Mouse weighed the details, formed two divergent scenarios in his mind. Die quick from a crushed skull, or slow in one of Panopticon's camps. He gripped the first rung of the ladder as the light sharpened and the engine growled louder.

"Mouse!" Jenny reached down grabbing his hand.

He clambered up, gripping the ladder above her head, and placing his boots on either side of her bare feet. The ladder groaned. Rust rained on their heads. Jenny's bleached hair scratched his face. The patrol jeep slowed, preparing to take the corner.

"Don't let me fall," she said.

They climbed together, not looking down. On the roof, they peeked over the edge, watching the patrol rumble by, its tail dimming to a pair of red eyes in the raised dust.

Mouse pulled a blanket from his backpack and spread it out on the concrete.

Jenny stamped her bare foot. "You little shit. Better not've pulled me up here just to get me on my back."

"Actually, I did."

Jenny crossed her thin arms over her chest.

"C'mon," he said, rubbing his clammy hands on his jeans.

Lying side by side, they watched the atmosphere glow opaque red as the universe above faded to black. Megatons of ash and chemicals thrown into the air on A-Day had dirtied the sky into nothing but a blighted blue memory.

Jenny drummed her fingers on her stomach. "So?"

"Watch."

Drop by drop, sunlight bled out of the haze. Jenny wriggled her shoulders. "What am I watching . . .?" Her breath left her in a soft rush. A moment later, black mascara tears rolled over her temples into her hair. "Oh."

Mouse pointed out the brightest twinkle in the red-tinged darkness. "You can only see them if you're high up in a Blackout Zone."

"I forgot what they looked like," she whispered.

"Jenny. I'm sorry...about the hospital fire thing."

He hadn't planned to apologize. It just came out. And for the first time in his life he meant it. Jenny rolled and her lips molded to his like warm wax. He didn't move. He didn't know what to do. Was kissing part of being friends?

Jenny pulled back with a shy smile. "Y'know, I never been on a proper date."

"You think this is a date?"

"Naw." She used her sleeve to rub her lipstick off his mouth. "It's only that I never fucked a guy without getting paid for it somehow. Not even the first time."

To his way of thinking, that was simply good business. Not the point. This was another friend thing. Sharing secrets. "Me either," he admitted. "I figured it might be different with you."

Jenny snorted. "Because I got a kitty? Or because you were the trick and not the treat."

"Both."

"You should've told me."

"I didn't know you."

"Yahtzee." She clucked her tongue. "I coulda been a hole in the dirt for all the difference it woulda made. You're the type needs something going on up here first," she tapped his forehead, "like a brain connection."

Maybe she was right. Not that it changed anything. Who was he supposed to connect with?

People are tools, Mouse.

Use 'em, and chuck 'em back in the shed.

Mouse disliked how often he thought of Zee. Disliked the way he thought of him even more. Not fondly, but not unfondly either. A connection.

As though sensing his distance, Jenny rolled away to root in her giraffe. Mouse pressed his heels down into the concrete. He didn't expect Jenny to stop using because of him, but did she have to do it now? He sat up, scowling at the view across the intersection of Carrall and East Hastings, into the void of Pigeon Park, and the bleary halo of Gastown beyond. The stars were only part of it. Up here you could forget you were staring at a post-apocalyptic hellscape. You could pretend Vancouver was as it had been before A-Day. Dirty lights in a broken city full of crackheads. And for some reason he'd decided to share his rooftop with one of them.

"Made you a present," Jenny said, pressing something heavy into his hand. He held up a golf ball-sized mass of copper wire. Cut, coiled, and crimped into the shape of a dragon. Jenny pointed to the glass shards she'd affixed for eyes. "They're blue and green, like you."

The lump of repurposed scrap wasn't useful. Nothing he could fence for a few creds or a future obligation—he collected markers like Jenny collected garbage for her junky knickknacks. The dragon was worthless. But it felt good in his hands as he traced the gleaming arc of its outstretched wing.

"Why a dragon?"

Jenny shrugged. "Why not?"

The copper warmed as he handled it. "They're monsters."

"So are you. So am I. We do what we gotta. Doesn't mean we're bad."

"Speak for yourself."

"Yeah?" Her grin revealed a missing bicuspid. "Ever kill anyone?"

He leaned in until their noses almost touched. "What do you think?"

She shifted her gaze back to the stars. "I think you're dangerous."

The girl is more right than she knows. I unfurl over them like a magic carpet, listening to the drift of her thoughts. She wonders what he's thinking, and that makes two of us. She likes the feeling of their arms pressed together from their shoulders all the way down to their fingers, not linked, but still touching. She rubs her bare foot against the rough tread of his boot. It's no easy thing being his friend. He'll never tell her exactly what he feels. But lying next to him, on a rooftop with patrols prowling the streets below, she feels safe, and happier than she's been in a long time.

CHAPTER 9

Mouse unzipped his jacket, letting salty summer air ripple through his T-shirt as he followed the sea wall. Waves crashed against the concrete barrier below and the seagulls screeched above. He wondered where in the blighted blue hell he could find Kentucky bourbon in Vancouver. At nineteen, he'd built a solid reputation on his ability to acquire contraband. Ironically, Panopticon's patrol officers were among his best clients.

Behind him he heard the click of approaching heels. Seconds later, Jenny's arm slid through his. For over two years they'd maintained their unusual friendship. No one was more surprised by this than Mouse.

"It's been weeks," Jenny said, resting her head on his shoulder. "Where've you been?"

"Around."

"Round and around and around." Jenny skipped about to face him, reaching into his open jacket and threading her arms into the sleeves alongside his.

He wriggled away. "Stop touching."

"I'm cold."

Jenny wasn't cold. Jenny was in withdrawal. Could be her latest attempt to spin dry. More likely she'd run short on creds. Mouse shrugged out of his jacket. "Here."

She wrapped the jacket around her shoulders. "Last time we hung out you were all over me, and now I can't touch your arm?"

His face heated as their artless encounter at the mosque came rushing back to him. Most of it hazy. His only clear memory was Jenny shotgunning a stream of smoke in his mouth. She let him think it was just weed. By the time he tasted syrupy sweetness mingled with the herbal edge of marijuana, it was too late.

"I wasn't myself," he said.

"I know. You were laughing. Having actual fun."

Never be yourself, because yourself usually sucks. Zee's wisdom stood the test of time.

Jenny's tongue poked through the space left by her missing tooth. "We need to talk."

"No, we don't. Unless you're knocked up or something."

"Got my rag last week." She pulled his jacket tight around her shoulders. "I heard on the Stream that lots of people's innards are toast from radiation and what not. Probably couldn't get pregnant if I wanted to."

His annoyance boiled over. "And what do you want, Jenny?"

"Bite my head off much? I only wanted to see if you were okay...with what happened."

For weeks Mouse felt only dire embarrassment over the incident, but now he realized how angry he was. She had no way of knowing about Zee because that name had not crossed his lips since the bastard lit out of town. Still, she knew enough to know better.

He wheeled on her, and her flinch only fed his temper. "You blew opium in my face until I was high enough to fuck on a grimy basement floor in front of all your junkie friends. You want to know if I'm okay with that? How stupid are you?"

She clutched his arm with chilly fingers. "Mouse, I'm sorry."

He toyed with the idea of slapping that pathetic apology right off her face. But then he'd be just like her stepfather, her brothers, the boyfriend who pimped her out at age thirteen. Even now Mouse saw resignation in her eyes. He would hit her and she would take it. Wouldn't even hold it against him, because to her that was what guys did. Angry as he was, vicious as he could be, Mouse was not that guy. Probably.

He pushed her away about half as hard as he wanted to. "Don't touch me."

"Hey, cool it," a voice said and meaty hands grabbed his shoulders from behind. Mouse whirled around, swinging, but Jenny yanked him back before his fist could connect with the bespectacled face of a middle-aged man wearing sandals with socks.

"Who the hell are you?" Mouse snarled.

"Lemme handle it," Jenny said, and approached the man, each click of her heels like a gunshot. "Problem, mister?"

A flush ran upward from the man's neck to the skin visible through the thready comb-over on his scalp. "I was out for a constitutional and I saw this kid harassing you."

INFRACTUS

"You're gonna want to keep walking," Mouse said and stumbled when Jenny shoved him back again. He didn't know if he was angry with the man for getting the wrong idea, or possibly having the right one.

The man eyed Mouse, clearly unimpressed. His mistake. Mouse knew he didn't look like much—lanky would be a generous description—but he was strong, fast, and his pulse had dropped deathly low, the way it always did before very bad things happened. Jenny scowled over her shoulder as if she knew exactly what he was thinking.

"I appreciate the consideration," Jenny said. "Too many folks jog the other way when they see someone in trouble. But I'm fine and dandy."

"At least let me see you home." The man cupped Jenny's elbow. "These days patrollers will toss you in a camp just for keeping the wrong kind of company."

Jenny gently lifted her arm away. "That's real sweet, and if you wanna take a stroll with me during business hours, you know where to find me, but my personal life is none a yours. Understand?"

The man nodded, mortified. "You take care, then. And you," he pointed to Mouse, "have some respect. That's no way to treat a lady."

Mouse watched Jenny's delusional customer plod away. Like a carpet salesman. A sad sack of crushed dreams. A loser. Without agreeing to, they resumed walking. She tucked her chin into the collar of his jacket and her hands into the pockets. A leaden weight settled in his stomach. The carpet salesman drew reasonable conclusions. An angry kid about to give his girlfriend a black eye. The worst part was that Mouse knew how close he'd come to doing just that.

INFRACTUS

He reached out and tugged on Jenny's sleeve. "You okay?"

Jenny stopped and handed him her giraffe bag. She slipped out of his jacket, flipped off her shoes, and in broad daylight sprinted down Sunset beach, kicking up sand and leaving a trail of clothes. Mouse glanced around at the few people milling about, paying no attention to the naked girl running into the surf. He followed her trail, gathering up her stuff as he went.

His throat constricted and his heart battered his ribs. He tugged off his boots, stripped off his clothes, and stashed everything under a rock. Seaweed tickled his ankles as he waded into the gray water. When he was chest deep, Jenny was already halfway out to the buoy. A wave crashed over his head, flooding his mouth and nose with salt and dirt. As a kid he'd been a strong swimmer. Now his limbs flailed and his lungs stiffened, his phobia gripping him like a riptide. So, he swam across, rather than against. He focused on slow even breathing, until muscle memory kicked in and he stretched out into a rhythmic crawl.

Jenny clung to the buoy, her lips blue with cold and her pale hair plastered to her head.

"Are you out of your goddamn mind?" He grabbed onto the buoy and wiped the scummy water from his eyes. "The Eye has cameras everywhere. We're going to get arrested. Naked arrested."

Jenny groaned. "Buzz kill."

They bobbed up and down, and Mouse groped for the right words. As a rule he didn't tell people how to live, but in this case: "Jenny, watch it around that carpet salesman, okay?"

"He's harmless. Lonely is all." She stared into the sky and back at him. "Why do you hate the water?"

"Because it's cold and gross."

"And that's different from the rest of our lives how?"

A shudder ran down his legs. "I drowned once."

"Shush, for real?"

"I was just a kid and I should've died. I think I did, for a few minutes."

She frowned and her chin dipped into the water. "Mouse. I promise I was only trying to help you relax, but it shouldn't have happened that way, not between us. It was stupid. I'm stupid."

"Don't," he said, knowing she believed it to be true. "You teach me stuff all the time, and I don't want you to be scared of me."

"Only a dummy wouldn't be at least a little scared of you." Her smile quivered. "Still friends?"

"Sure, whatever."

She threw her arms around his shoulders and kissed him hard.

"You're pushing it," he mumbled against her lips.

Jenny tucked her face into his neck. "Did you see anything when you drowned? A white light? Angels?"

"No. But I was allergic to pollen before, and after I wasn't. In retrospect, drowning was totally worth it."

She pushed off against his chest and yelled into the sky as she backstroked toward shore. "Probably brain damage."

In his nineteen years, Mouse couldn't remember a night as hot as this one. Safe to say the nuclear winter was at its end. It was Jenny's twenty-second birthday and to celebrate they'd climbed up to their rooftop. Heat radiated out of the concrete beneath them and through the unzipped sleeping bag they'd spread out. It was almost unbearable, but the roof was quiet and dark, and safe enough for him to mostly relax.

Jenny swept her hand across the reddish sky. The tattoo circling her wrist contrasted sharply with her pale skin. "I'm going to paint the wind."

"You can't see the wind—hold still."

He clutched her ankle in his lap and repaired a smudge in the lacquer he was applying to her toes. He'd given her the nail polish as a birthday present. The bottle called it "Confessions." Looked pink to him.

The wind she wanted to paint did little to cool the sweat on his naked skin. Sweat from the hottest sex he could imagine. Literally. Like screwing on a stovetop. They'd nearly cooked themselves. Still, it was better than that first time at the mosque, when he'd been so fucked up the whole thing felt like an out of body experience. This time he was present. Awkward at first, but Jenny wasn't shy about showing him what to do and that helped a lot. They took their time. He made her come. Now he was giving her a pedicure and listening to yet another one of her tolerably ridiculous ideas.

"Always gotta marsh my mellow." She rolled over to fish in her bag. Aside from a fresh coat of nail polish she wore nothing at all, and with every movement her spine tried to chew through her skin like a stretched out set of teeth. He knew she was using hard again, blowing all her money on glass and forgetting to eat. "Anyways, it's not about seeing. I wanna paint how it makes me feel. Get it?" She pulled out a pack of matches and lit a neatly rolled joint. "What I'd give for real paints. Blight it, I gotta go to work soon."

He stretched out beside her. "D'you ever think about doing something different?"

"Like what?" She clamped the joint between her teeth, pulled her knees up and admired her pink toenails. "Slave in a shop all day and make half the creds I get in three hours a night? It's not bad work. Leaves plenty of time for my art, I make people feel good, and my regulars are sweetie pies."

"Like the carpet salesman? He still coming around?"

"Let it go, Mouser. Working girls are weirdo bait. Comes with the job. You want a toke? Hundred percent pure ganja, I promise."

Mouse pinched the joint from her lips. "Don't go. I can pay."

"Fuck off," she croaked, exhaling a ribbon of sweet smoke into his face. "Pretties are one thing, but I don't want your goddamn money. It's not like that with us."

"I just—"

"Shut up." She shoved him onto his back and laid her head on his shoulder. "I don't need a pimp, or a daddy, or a boyfriend. I make my own way, and I don't need you to tell me how to do it."

He inhaled deeply and held the smoke in his lungs. She'd misread his intention. He didn't think of her as his property, his responsibility, or anything. He liked that she could handle herself. He liked that she didn't lie. Not ever. He suspected she didn't know how.

The pressure in his lungs intensified as the seconds added up. He rarely smoked, but when he did he enjoyed the drift of ideas across his consciousness, coalescing and dissipating before he could understand the shape of them. Ephemeral, that was the word. Stars glimmered above. Each time he and Jenny came up here, more of them poked through the thinning haze. Soon there'd be whole constellations. He couldn't remember their names, but he'd learn them again as soon as he could see more of those tiny suns, far away, burning up, flaming out. Stars. Stars. Starzzzzz. What kind of word was that anyway?

Tolerable grass.

He wanted to ask which of her sweetie pies hooked her up. Could be a useful connection. But Jenny wasn't hustling him. He probably shouldn't hustle her.

"Strange boy," she said, tracing one of his ribs with a pink fingernail, and then tickling him.

"Gagh..." He coughed the smoke out of his lungs, rolled onto her, and pinned her hands above her head. It confused him, how the slick glide of his stomach over hers could skeeze him out and make him hard at the same time. "Strange?"

"Different is all. Not sweet. Not even very nice." She giggled and wrapped her legs around him. "I like you anyways."

He dropped his head between her breasts and laughed into her cotton candy skin. Jenny Logic. It could be damn funny.

Mouse hurried down Carrall Street. A possible source for Kentucky bourbon had agreed to meet him at the train yard five minutes ago. For a person like Mouse, punctual by nature, lateness induced a singular anxiety that used to drive Zee bananas. Goddamnit, stop freaking out. Ever hear of lowlife standard time? See these guys wearing watches? Fucking hell, Mouse.

INFRACTUS

He crossed West Cordova and headed into the network of alleyways snaking through Gastown. Hopefully the bourbon guy was serious enough about doing business to wait. The deeper into the labyrinth he went, the narrower and darker the alleyways got. When he rounded the last corner into the corridor that would empty onto Water Street, a smell stopped him in his tracks. Not so pungent as it was distinctive. Light trickled into the narrow pass through the garbage piled high on both sides of the alley. Mouse inched his way along and crouched to examine three whitish lumps scattered over a dark stain on the asphalt. Teeth. Closer to the ground, the smell intensified. Overripe and sweet, like opium. He scanned the heaps of trash around him. Against the bricks, under a pile of broken pallets, he spotted a bare foot.

His heart thumped slow and heavy as he cleared away wooden planks and wet cardboard. The smell grew stronger, more metallic, confirming that there was no reason to rush. Nevertheless, he worked quickly. Fire roiled under his skin as bit by bit he uncovered the body. Hair, black with dried blood. Almost nothing left of her face. He held her cold hand, pushed back the sleeve of her jacket, and rubbed his thumb over pale skin and black ink: Take care that no one hates you justly.

Grief eluded him, but a restless irritation crept under his skin. Like spiders. A constant itch reminding him of what wasn't there anymore. He climbed up to the rooftop and stared into the muddy red sky only to realize he'd never cared about a bunch of stupid stars half as much as

Jenny had. Now she was dead, and nothing was good anymore. Nothing was anything.

The carpet salesman was a big problem. Fixing him would take patience.

For two weeks, Mouse waited, watched, and planned. He allowed his quarry time to relax. Day by day the scrapes on the salesman's knuckles healed into scars Mouse knew like the back of his own hands. Though he'd never used his fists to beat a ninety-pound girl to death.

Mouse arrived on Water Street at dusk and found Misty waiting for him. The sorority of pro traders normally coiled up and rattled their tails at anyone prying into their business. Not this time. Jenny had lived by the words inked into her skin and her sisters loved her. Mouse had taken his request directly to the top. An old world stripper, ruthless hustler, and de facto empress of the Stroll, Misty was not to be fucked with. You didn't pull anything on her turf without first securing her permission. But Mouse needed more than that. He needed her help.

Mouse followed Misty into the shadowed doorway of a boarded up storefront. "It's the carpet salesman."

"Carpet salesman?" Misty reached into the canyon between her augmented breasts, and produced a flat aluminum case from which she pulled a hand rolled cigarette. She placed it between her velvet-red lips and Mouse dug an old zippo out of his pocket and lit it for her.

"Comb-over, glasses, sandals with socks. He's been skulking around the Stroll the last few nights. Leaves without buying, but he's working up to it. I need you to give him a push."

Misty studied him through the rising curl of cigarette smoke. "Sure you wanna do this?"

"Will you help me or not?"

"For triple."

"Double."

"Triple. Danger pay, kiddo." She cocked her head so as not to exhale cigarette smoke in his face. "Since I'll be servicing a known murd'rer."

"Take him into that alley and make sure he's facing away from the street."

Misty examined the red paint she'd transferred from her mouth to her cigarette. "This is personal for you, Mouse. Personal can go sideways real fast."

"It won't."

Venom glittered in her black eyes. "I'm indulging you, kid. Against my better judgment. If you get squeamish, or otherwise cock this up, I'll have your pretty head on a plate. Understand?"

He handed over the last of his bourbon money.

Two hours later, Misty delivered what he'd paid for. The carpet salesman had his back to the street and all his attention on the trader kneeling at his feet. Mouse hid in the shadows not ten feet away, waiting. He recalled all the times and all the alleys where he'd been on his knees. Desperate. Like Jenny had been desperate. Flat broke and jonesing. Rather than ask her friend for help, she made a decision that got her killed. Stupid junkie.

When the carpet salesman started grunting and making the other sorts of noises guys did when they were getting close, Mouse emerged and tapped him on the shoulder.

The carpet salesman's head snapped around, eyes bleary. "Buh-what?"

Mouse extended a hand to Misty and helped her to her feet. She wiped her red mouth and stuffed her plastic tits back into her shirt. Her expression reiterated her warning as she stalked past him out of the alley. While not part of their formal negotiation, Mouse knew she'd ensure they weren't disturbed.

"What do you want?" The salesman staggered back, hitching up his pants. "I have money...take it...whatever you want."

"Remember me?" Mouse advanced, driving the salesman farther into the alley. "That day on Sunset, you were following Jenny, weren't you?"

"Who?"

"Blonde, pink toenails, few more teeth than what you left her with."

"Think you got the wrong fella."

Mouse shuddered at the drag of the needle in his head. "You're not a very good liar."

The salesman's lips went white and tears pooled in the dark wells under his eyes. "Honest, I don't know what happened. I snapped...I don't remember."

"You remember enough to know why I'm here."

"Because you love her. I loved her too."

Mouse shrugged. "Are you ready?"

"Are you?" the salesman asked, feebly attempting to engage his backbone. "You're just a kid. Takes a man to kill in cold blood."

Mouse pulled a box cutter from his pocket and thumbed the wheel. His blood wasn't merely cold it was glacial. If you're gonna throw down, throw down hard. He tightened his grip on the knife. This was how you fixed a problem.

After he solved the carpet salesman equation, Mouse plodded back to Yaletown where he climbed the ten flights to his little room with the broken window. Without washing up or even stripping off his bloody clothes, he huddled into his sleeping bag and passed out.

A few hours later he woke up. Numb. He stared at the water-stained ceiling Listened to the night patrol growl down Pacific Boulevard. Slept some more. Woke up. Blaring curfew alarms. Drenched in sweat and chilled to his marrow, he slid deeper into the sleeping bag and dreamless oblivion. He didn't even try to keep track of time as the cycle of lucidity repeated itself over and over.

Through the walls he heard the crash and bellow of domestic rumbles. His hands throbbed. Had he punched the carpet salesman? He couldn't remember. Anger, rage, fury. He searched for remnants of feeling but found none. Words and nothing more. The ceiling dissolved and he hovered in a red haze. Counting stars.

Claudia, Zee, Bella, and Jenny. Anchors. Holding him in a place that otherwise held nothing.

Attachments are a bitch, Mouse. Make it hard to keep your eye on the long game. Hell, I would've marched on ages ago if it weren't for you...you don't even know.

Mouse pulled the sleeping bag over his head and set himself adrift in the musty darkness.

INFRACTUS

I lost him. After A-Day, I got busy, didn't check in as often as I should have, and I lost him. Finding someone who doesn't want to be found is difficult, especially when you can't hear his inner voice. I didn't have time to comb through the mental musings of thousands of humans, hoping to pick up some trace. So, I delegated. I outsourced.

Now I'm hanging from the rust-stained ceiling over his sleeping form. He's alive, but not well, and covered in blood under that sleeping bag. None of it his.

They do have a way of dying, the ones that attract his attention.

Perhaps it was rash, but imagine my surprise to find him still carrying on with that yellow-haired whore. The so-called carpet salesman helped me sever that attachment. One shallow scrape peeled back the man and unleashed a horror. Do I feel bad? Yeah, a little. And perhaps I'm a monster, but like all of us, He made me in His image too.

I call his name. Drive it down like a nail into the mantle of sleep where his dreams would live if I allowed him such an escape, which I don't. Too risky. Again, I call to him. Not John White, not Mouse, but his real name. It hurts me, the way he huddles deeper into himself at the sound of my voice.

He needs to suffer. I know this. I planned for it, but it's changing him. So much rage. His first kill, a massacre that shocked even me. I thought I'd be able to control, or at least contain, him like a Mouse in a maze. So naïve. Every big project is bound to run into a few snags. Plans evolve. The lost boy is now a man. I call to him and he curls up tighter. He knows, but he will not remember.

He isn't ready. And I suppose neither am I.

❖❖❖

INFRACTUS

Mouse came fully awake the second morning after his first kill, certain that someone was in the room with him. If that hadn't roused him, his nuclear need to piss would have. He poked his head out, wincing at the early light slicing through his window. The door was barred from the inside. He was alone. He went to rub his eyes and found something wrapped around his torn knuckles. A white braid, now marred with rusty red stains. He didn't remember digging it out of his pack. Must've done it in his sleep, dragging it into the sleeping bag and curling around it like a goddamn security blanket.

"Fucking hell," he grumbled, struggling to peel off the sleeping bag fused to his clothes with dried blood. He crawled across the tiles and shoved the braid into his pack next to Claudia's bible, Zee's rosin, and Jenny's dragon. Four objects. All he had to show for his entire miserable life. Hatred licked through his insides like a furry black tongue and his stomach gurgled. When had he last eaten? Two days ago? Three? He needed food. But he'd surrendered the last of his cash to that greedy bitch, Misty. There was a woman who knew how to negotiate. Christ, he had to piss.

Every muscle ached as he hobbled down the hall to the communal water closet and pissed for an eternity. He rested his pounding head on the wall, waiting for his bladder to empty. His mouth was so desiccated he could hardly swallow against the acid surging up his esophagus, and he smelled utterly rank. Marinating in a dead man's blood and his own sweat for thirty-six hours in August might have had something to do with that.

Still wearing his bloody pants and hoodie, Mouse shambled outside and into the sunny morning. He threw up a hand to cut the glare. To his left, two figures in suits stood in a wide stance taking up the full breadth of the sidewalk.

"Excuse us," said Suit One, lips snapping into a tight smile. "Might we have a moment of your time?"

Mouse's hands wound into fists and he shifted his weight onto the balls of his feet. After six years in a barn full of owls, it didn't take much to kindle his fight or flight instinct. The trick was making the right choice. "Who's we?"

Suit Two wore sunglasses, and her smile had some teeth. "Word is you performed a bit of community service the other day."

Neither Suit offered up papers, badges, or ident of any kind, which couldn't be good. Mouse missed the old world, where even Mormons wore nametags.

"Here to jam me up?"

"No," said the Suits in unison.

"Then fuck off."

Language. Sister Claudia's rebuke rang in his memory, but he was fresh out of care. When he tried to sidestep, Suit Two blocked him with a palm against his chest. "Hear us out, kid."

He sensed steel beneath her low voice and light touch. Like animal control moving in on a cornered cat. Soft gloves to handle a monster. He shifted back on his heels. She lowered her hand.

Suit One cleared his throat, and the sun glinted off his slicked back helmet of hair. "We have a proposition for you."

Mouse jerked his thumb in the direction of the Stroll. "Gastown. Ask for Wally, he'll do you both at once."

Suit Two stifled a snort.

INFRACTUS

A blush reddened the tips of Suit One's ears. "We represent the interests of a program that would put your talents toward the rebuilding of human civilization."

Suit One's speech was more than weirdly formal or even crisp. He had a way of sharpening every word into a barb meant to stick. Mouse tugged a hand through the filthy tangle of his hair. "You're talking government. Panopticon?"

Suit Two flashed her teeth again. "Your words, not ours."

All information is worth having, Mouse. Zee's words echoed in his head and he drew his hood up to block the sun. "What kind of program?"

"Neutralizing targets deemed threats to human security," said Suit One. "In lay terms—"

"You want me to kill people?"

"Already popped your cherry," Suit Two said, yawning. "Nice work, by the way. Very thorough."

He shoved his blood-smeared hands in his pockets. "You've been watching me?"

"The Eye watches us all," said Suit One. "We would see your potential realized, rather than wasted. We want to give you a better life."

Mouse appreciated that the Suits didn't soft-pedal their intentions, but Panopticon gave nothing without wanting at least as much in return. So far, their version of a better life included curfews, cameras, DNA linked idents, censorship, and outrageous propaganda. Mouse knew Big Brother when he saw it. 2032 was looking a lot like 1984. Christ, he really missed books.

"Consider your future here." Suit One clasped his hands in front of his buttoned jacket. "Marginalized citizens often end up in the camps. I hear they're quite unpleasant. Not to mention the promising developments in neural remapping as a means of rehabilitation for criminals and subversives."

"Neural what?"

Suit Two put a finger thumb gun to her temple. "Electrochemical lobotomy, kid."

Mouse shook his head. In what world did a conversation like this happen? They were in the middle of the street at eight in the morning. Witnesses everywhere. Electric vans whirring about making deliveries. Kids throwing rocks at the seagulls. Traders coming home to roost, while others hurried off to their day jobs. Even a few tweakers were up and skittering about, red-eyed and junk-sick, on the hunt for anything to keep their clocks from winding all the way down. His world.

Suit Two removed her shades. Eyes like winter rain inventoried the ghetto of Pacific Boulevard. "You're better than this. Telling me you wouldn't kill for a chance to get out?"

"You'll come to our Facility," said Suit One. "There you'll be educated and trained. Not to mention properly fed and clothed."

That got his attention. "Educated?"

"We have a core program of required studies. Beyond that your academic pursuits are limited only by your desire to pursue them."

"And you'll be paid." Suit Two threw her shades back on. "A lot."

"To be a hitman?"

"A professional." Suit One handed him a card. "This address. Tomorrow. 0500."

INFRACTUS

He held the card, impossibly white in his grimy hand.

A big opportunity is like a poison apple, Mouse. Could end you, or it could lead to your happy ever after. Point is, you only get one bite.

"Don't be late," Suit Two said. "And for Christ's sake clean yourself up. You look like a maniac."

"To say nothing of the smell," Suit One added, setting his teeth into his lower lip, incisors and canines oddly small and widely spaced.

Mouse considered his foul self in contrast to the shiny shoes and creased slacks of the Suits. They had lots of school. They lived in clean rooms with electricity and hot water. They probably had windows with glass in them, soft new socks, and refrigerators full of eggs and cheese. Sure, they were killers, but they probably never went to bed bloody.

People were born to die. Good people like Claudia and Jenny, bad people like the carpet salesman. Dead was dead, and this was his one bite. Had he come this far to live as a sheep, or as a dragon?

"Hey, kid," Suit Two said. "What's your real name?"

Mouse saw red through his closed eyelids. "I don't remember."

CHAPTER 10

YEAR 4 POST ADVENTUS
THE FACILITY, KILLEEN, TEXAS

The case lay open in front of him on the counter of the firing range. Black felt hugged the outline of a SIG Sauer P226 DAK.

Long name for something so small. All around him he heard the clacks and clicks of his fellow recruits getting to know their weapons. Most seemed well acquainted already. It wasn't like he hadn't seen one before, but he'd never so much as touched a pistol, let alone fired one.

Funny thing about guns, Mouse. Pull a piece and people tend to get ventilated. Besides, they're tacky as hell. Any thug can pull a trigger.

But he wasn't a mouse anymore. He didn't know who he was. Four days ago, he'd been subjected to a thorough delousing and medical exam. When the processing team ascertained—amazing how quick the words came back—that he had neither fleas, nor heart defects, nor syphilis, he'd been given clothes. Khaki pants and a blue short-sleeved button down, so new and clean they drove him to distraction with their odorless sterility. Then he boarded an airplane for the first time in his life. A jet with only six seats. None of the processing team said a word to him on the flight. He mostly stared out the window and toyed with the pearly plastic buttons on his shirt. Flying was an awful lot like riding the bus, but noisier, and less bumpy.

Five hours later he landed on a runway in Texas where the heat rising off the tarmac threatened to vaporize him. A uniformed soldier in an electric jeep drove him to a small campus of beige buildings where the black sun flag was conspicuously absent. The soldier told him it used to be part of Fort Hood, an old-world military base. The soldier also mentioned that everyone else had arrived hours ago by ground transport. He didn't know who everyone else was until he was escorted into a classroom that smelled of artificial pine and fresh paint. Of the ten desks, nine were occupied. Six boys and three girls, around his age, with a raw, recently scrubbed look about them, all dressed in the same khakis and blue shirt. They twisted in their seats to assess the latecomer.

Suit One stood at the front of the classroom, broad shoulders perfectly square. Suit Two lounged off to the side in the shadow between windows. He hadn't seen them since they'd handed him that card. Suit Two's wide set eyes locked onto him. "Clean up nice, kid."

An obvious lie he didn't acknowledge as he slid into the empty desk. During processing he'd been locked in a room with a mirror. An honest to god, shiny, unbroken, full-length mirror. His reflection shocked him. Without a layer of dirt and scruff over his hunger-sharpened facial bones, he was dismayed to see how completely undangerous he looked, how small and childish.

"Welcome to the Facility," said Suit One. "From this moment forward you are no longer ladies and gentlemen. You are recruits. You may address myself, my colleague, and your other instructors as 'Sir,' and while you are permitted the use of your verified surnames on an informal basis, your official identification will be a number."

He imagined serial numbers being long with dashes and letters, so he was surprised when Suit One began listing them off.

"Radcliffe, one. Ito, two. Lusczak, three..."

On it went, and since he had no name, verified or otherwise, he was simply Nine.

"Each of you were selected based on your potential to graduate from this program as an agent with a highly specialized skill set. I say potential, because half of you will wash out in the first two years."

The Asian girl, Ito, snorted. "Wash out? That code for bullet to the head?"

Suit One's lips thinned. "Whenever possible, we prefer not to waste the enormous amount of resources we invest in our recruits. If a recruit does not qualify for field status, and proves amenable, we arrange transfer into a suitable position within the organization. Analytics, most likely."

Nine couldn't help noticing that the word Panopticon hadn't been uttered even once.

"And if I'm not amenable to your desk job?" Ito asked.

"Early retirement," said Suit Two from the shadows. Nine detected a slight drawl in her voice and wondered if Texas was her home state.

Suit One cleared his throat and shot the pristine cuffs of his white shirt. "Your daily schedule will consist of a fourteen-hour block of lectures, labs, physical conditioning, and tactical drills."

"And if you survive year one," Suit Two added. "It only gets worse, so buckle up."

Ito's hand shot up. "Tactical? That's weapons, right?"

"Wrong," said Suit One. "It's strategy and technique, as applied to a variety of catalogues including ballistics, blades, and hand-to-hand combat."

"How much of that fourteen hours is school stuff?" asked the one called Lusczak.

"More than enough to challenge you."

Radcliffe, a blond moose about twice Nine's size, plucked at his blue shirtsleeve. "And how dang long do we gotta wear these faggy rags? Thought we'd be uniformed up in camo."

"This is not the military," said Suit One. "You are not soldiers. You are not a unit or a team. You are not here to make friends, and all you need know about the chain of command is that you are on the bottom. You will learn, perform, and adhere to a basic code of orderly conduct. Failure to do so will result in logical consequences. As for uniforms, your current ensemble is your uniform until you wash out, or earn your suit. Any other questions?"

Only about a million. Like Radcliffe, Nine expected the Facility to be a lot more regimented. From what he could tell, the recruits were a pack of hooligans, and he didn't exclude himself from that assessment. Nine figured that explained the presence of armed guards that outnumbered the recruits at least three to one.

"We will reconvene tomorrow at 0700 in this classroom. Now you may follow my colleague to the supply depot where you'll be issued your kit and room assignments."

Suit Two snapped her fingers. "Chop chop, little lambs."

Chairs grated across the linoleum and Nine found himself in a single file line following Suit Two down a wide beige hallway.

"Fun fact." Suit Two spoke loudly enough for her voice to echo off the painted bricks. "Right now, y'all are trudging in the boot prints of not one but two old world rampage killers. In 2009 an army shrink went bugfuck and shot up the place. Happened again in 2014. We're going to teach you maggots everything those poor bastards never learned. Finesse."

Finesse was about the last word that came to mind when Nine thought of Suit Two. Their line rounded the corner to an office with a woman behind a desk and a rolling trolley loaded with bulging duffel bags.

"This is your kit," Suit Two said, hoisting up one of the bags. "Everything you need to get by on the day to day around here. Clothes, bedding, toothbrush, pit stick, plugs for the bleeders, and a computer tablet loaded with your study modules. Gonna hit the books hard in a couple days, so you illiterate dumbasses better relearn your ABCs real quick."

Five years of squalor and a whittled down definition of basic necessities had prepared Nine for a lot, but not this, not clothes, beds, and books to be just...handed to him. Ten pairs of new boots squeaked on the floor and some of the recruits mumbled to one another, but one voice rose above the others. Radcliffe, the moose.

"Hey, you. Yeah you, pretty whore with the freak eyes. Scrawny faggot. I'm talking at you...Jeez, can't you speak? Or does that mouth only open to suck?"

INFRACTUS

Nine let the taunts bead up and roll off, until a spit wet finger dug into his ear. He let his fist fly. An action that split open his recently gashed knuckles and resulted in his first trip to solitary confinement.

Two guards marched him three stories underground where Suit One waited outside the door of a windowless cell, his mouth compressed into a colorless line. "Your psychological profile indicated a high probability of disruptive behavior. So far you're performing exactly as predicted."

Nine shrugged. "Someone thinks I'm worth the trouble. Not you, I'm guessing."

"Indeed not." Suit One ran a manicured hand over his hair. "I think you're trash, with perhaps a glimmer of potential. Time will tell. Meanwhile, if you choose to behave like an animal, we'll happily throw you in a cage."

The guards tossed him into the cell. The door clanged shut, the light went out, and the pat of shiny leather shoes faded down the corridor. Suit One might be able to scare oafs like Radcliffe into behaving, but Nine wasn't afraid of the dark or of being alone. He was different.

Nine explored his accommodation, running his hands over four walls, a bucket, and a cot with a thin mattress smelling of bleach. He made a few circuits to see if he'd missed anything. Then he lay down on the cot and counted the spots his brain projected into the darkness in front of his face. He reflected on what he'd left behind and wondered if he'd made a mistake. He didn't miss Vancouver. He didn't miss the filth, the cold, and the hunger. And the Facility was orderly, which he liked. He missed Jenny, but no matter where he went, she'd be gone. So that was that.

Already the Facility was better in almost every way. Except one. Out there he'd been vulnerable but free. In here he was a prisoner and there were rules. Life at the Facility could be tolerable, or difficult. Nine wondered what he would choose, and he was still wondering when he fell asleep.

❖❖❖

Solitary on the first day. Well done.

"Shut up."

So, you're speaking to me again.

"I don't even know your name."

But I know yours.

"Yeah, the shiny toy you've been holding over my head my whole life."

I've given you more than you'll ever know.

"And now you're using me. To rub out people who put ugly marks on your perfect world."

If it matters to you, most of those people deserve what's coming to them.

"Most?"

There's nuance to this work, more than you might think. Ito and Lusczak, they'd dismember a baby without hesitation. Others, like Radcliffe, have a stubborn sense of fair play. You're a bit of both. Life's not fair, but you've still got a rule or two, and as long as an order doesn't cross your line, you won't hesitate.

"And what if I draw the line at killing anyone?"

Is there anything else you're good for?

"Go to hell."

Been there. And I've missed our talks, by the way.

A clang startled him awake. Sudden light scalded his irises and made him sneeze.

"Solitary sucks, right?" Suit Two's shark face came into focus. "I was a recruit not too long ago, and I practically lived down here."

Nine swung his legs over the side of the cot. "What do you want?"

"Time to join the rest of the class. You're already way behind."

"How long?"

"Only two days." Her teeth sawed into her lower lip. "Feels longer doesn't it?"

A liquid chill filled his lungs. Two days gone in the space of what felt like two hours. He wasn't hungry or thirsty. He didn't even need to piss. Those two days were more than gone. They'd been stolen.

Suit Two gave his cheek a friendly slap. "Chin up. Radcliffe has one hell of a shiner, and the Facility has a lot to offer. Five years to learn all the ways you can hurt a person. You'll like that."

"You think I'm a psychopath."

"Nope," she said. "But I am. My personnel file is seriously scary. You're different, kid. Better maybe, but you've got a mean streak, and you were hard to find, even for me, and that's saying something. Believe me, they want you here."

They. The Program. The Facility. One of Panopticon's slimier tentacles, strategically hidden from their citizens. The Suits hadn't stumbled upon him. They'd been sent. Suit One had little choice but to acquiesce—another remembered word—to Panopticon's whim to scoop a mouse out of a Vancouver gutter. Nine wondered how long they'd been watching him.

"Study hard," Suit Two added. "But don't let them learn more from you than you learn from them."

Nine couldn't argue with her logic. For now, he'd follow the rules. He'd pay attention, and eventually he'd draw his line.

Suit Two led him up to the showers where he found his kit waiting on a bench. Unlimited hot water, soap, and toothpaste. Alien pleasures he didn't have time to linger over. When he came out wet haired and swimming in a fresh blue shirt and khaki pants, she raised an eyebrow. "Goddamn, you're a bag of bones. We need to fatten you up."

"Planning to eat me?"

Suit Two's brow pinched into a frown. "Well...you never know."

Oblivious to his unnerved silence, she handed him a computer tablet, and Nine followed her as he flipped through the first few chapters of the module on ballistics, boggled by the feel of technology in his hands. They walked outside and down a narrow street to a hangar converted into a firing range complete with bulging rhomboid panels affixed to the walls and ceiling. She left him at his assigned station with a gun he had no idea what to do with.

"Is there a problem with your weapon, recruit?" asked Suit One, all resonance flattened out of his voice by the acoustic baffling.

"Nossir," said Radcliffe, nudging into Nine's space. "He's helping me out. I never used a SIG before."

"Indeed?"

"Lemme go at it one more time." Radcliffe, his eye still purple, clawed the pistol out of the case, pulled back the slide and pulled the trigger once. "First reset." Pulled again. "Second reset."

Suit One pointed the toe of his polished shoe toward Nine. "Since you've caught up so quickly, perhaps you can refresh us on the purpose of the DAK's dual reset."

Nine stared hard at the gun, running the pages of schematics and notes through his head. "Eight pounds of pull on the first reduces the risk of accidental discharge. Six on the second allows you to fire successive rounds quickly."

"Are you quite certain?"

"Yes, sir."

Suit One's nostrils flared. "We move onto live fire in five minutes," he said, and abandoned them to instruct the class on proper grip and stance.

"Bullets here," Radcliffe said, smacking the magazine into the grip. "Give it a try."

Nine dropped the magazine out, pulled back the slide, dry fired twice, noted the difference in force required to pull the trigger. "You know he didn't buy that."

"Still saved face," said Radcliffe as Suit One droned on behind them. "Quick study, that'll come in dang handy, I bet. Most of these dum-dums barely know how to read, but I can tell you got smarts. Do you really not have a name?"

Nine reloaded the magazine and pulled the slide back. "I have one. Just don't know what it is."

A barrage of live fire broke out, making conversation impossible even with the acoustic dampening. Radcliffe returned to his own station. They donned their ear and eye protection. Nine watched Radcliffe grip the gun with one hand, support from below with the other, and blow three neat holes in the paper target's center of mass.

Nine mimicked Radcliffe's grip and stance, tried to concentrate through the muffled blat of gunfire, and pulled the trigger. The hole never appeared. He'd completely missed the target. He fired again and hit the shoulder, fired again and hit the white space beside the head.

He cradled the SIG in both hands. No wonder Zee hated guns. Small, heavy, and heartless. Immeasurably worse in inexperienced hands. Delivering horrible damage to things you weren't even trying to hit. The SIG didn't deserve to be that powerful.

They emptied magazine after magazine into the paper targets, and while Nine improved, he failed to produce the neat cluster Radcliffe did. A few hours later, Suit Two returned, circulating through the funk of hot metal and sweat permeating the hangar. Away and back, head swiveling side to side like a hammerhead. When she swished by Nine, he glimpsed a splash of red on white under her jacket.

An air horn sounded. That meant weapons down, immediately, no exceptions.

"Chow time," Suit Two shouted. "Stuff your face, compare groupings, rub one out, whatever you gotta do, but be back here at 1300."

Suit One leaned in to speak to her. She knocked his hand off her shoulder and swam off. As she passed by, Nine saw the blood on her white shirt again, bigger, redder, right over her heart.

INFRACTUS

In the mess hall, Radcliffe gestured to the seat next to him, but Nine carried his tray to an empty table, and stared at his food in a barely gagged panic. A sandwich. He poked the soft brown bread and pulled the slices apart, exposing a layer of peanut butter and jam. There was an apple, whole and not even a little rotten, some sliced up sausage that he banished to the far edge of the tray and covered with his napkin to keep the smell down. He wrapped his hands around the glass of milk, hardly believing how cold it was. A surreptitious glance at other recruits shoveling sandwiches into their faces. None of them losing their shit over their lunch tray. Although they'd been taking regular meals up here while he'd been stuck in solitary.

Two days. Well attuned to the nuances of hunger, Nine knew that his stomach ought to ache but he felt only vaguely hollow.

He peeled the lid off a cup of rice pudding topped with flecks of what looked like dirt or mold. He sniffed and a memory billowed in his head. Sister Claudia stirring a cauldron of oatmeal for breakfast. Mostly she served it plain, but in her better moods, she'd sprinkle in some cinnamon and sugar. Nine's heart collided with his ribcage. He set the pudding down with icy hands.

So much. Too much.

After choking down half his lunch, and reading through the next few modules on his tablet, Nine returned to the hangar with the other recruits. The targets were now set up fifty yards away. Suit Two was nowhere to be seen.

Suit One retrieved a black rifle from his counter. "This afternoon's session will be introduction to assembly and operation of your rifle. Even those with experience would do well to pay close attention. We are not training you as marksmen. We are training you as snipers, and if you think those things are the same or even similar, I'll refer you to my AWOL colleague, who will happily illustrate the difference in a way you will never forget. When she sees fit to return, that is."

It was the closest thing to an emotion Nine had seen from Suit One. He'd probably tried to track down Suit Two over the lunch break. Tried and failed. Anyone that good at finding people would know a thing or two about hiding.

Each recruit was assigned a gas-powered, magazine fed rifle based on the old world M16 platform. Suit One walked them through basic stripping. Ejecting the magazine, pushing pins to separate the upper and lower portions, disassembling the stock and removing the buffer and recoil spring, pulling out the charging handle, removing the firing pin and bolt from the carrier assembly, and putting it all back together again. Suit One explained the function of the front and rear sights, telescopic stock, and firing modes.

"You'll notice," said Suit One. "That your rifles have only single-shot and three-shot burst capability."

"No full auto?" asked Lusczak.

Ito thrust out her chin. "Why the hell not?"

"So, goons like you can't panic and empty a whole magazine in two seconds," said Nine.

Ito sneered. "Eat me, you skinny freak."

Radcliffe guffawed the way only a corn-fed moose could.

"Nine is correct," said Suit One. "One shot, one kill. Fully automatic weapons are for disposable infantry and blunt instruments, not high-value assets. Your value, Ito, has yet to be determined."

Ito glared needles at Nine, but kept her mouth shut. Suit One went on to explain the sensors, computer, and other telemetry equipment they would be learning to use once they mastered the fundamentals.

After a couple of hours spent stripping their rifles, Nine edged over to Radcliffe. "I think Ito wants to kill me."

"Ito's an angry b-i-t-c-h. Smart too. But heck, I dig it. She's kinda hot."

"If you say so."

"Don't you like girls?"

"Equal opportunity hater." Nine said, and before Radcliffe could ask another nosy question, he asked one of his own. "Why'd you help me before?"

Radcliffe gave him a sheepish look. "Fair's fair. You got thrown in solitary over something I started. Gee whiz, I only wanted to see if the rumors were true."

"Rumors?"

"Before you got here, we heard some guards talking about a street kid coming in from Canada, a real scrapper. Guess I had to see for myself."

Nine shivered at the faintest scratch of deception. "I know what you're doing."

"Yeah?"

"Ito's smart, but a hothead. Lusczak is vicious but not so bright. The rest are probably going to wash out. You figure it'll be us leading the pack."

"They don't want us making friends." Radcliffe rolled his bulky shoulders. "Doesn't mean we gotta be enemies. And that stuff I said, about you being a whore...I was just trying to get a rise. I can tell you're no pro trader."

Nine loaded his bolt back into the receiver. "What difference does it make?"

"It's a cruddy world, okay? We've all done things. Gosh, none of us would be here if we had anything close to a better choice. So whaddya say, we cool?"

Nine was sorting out a response when Suit Two strolled up in a fresh shirt with the smell of Facility soap clinging to her damp hair.

"Ma'am—I mean, sir," said Radcliffe, dropping his gaze to the floor.

"He-Man and Skeletor, friends at last."

Nine shook his head in confusion.

"Old world cartoon," said Radcliffe. "He-Man wears these furry panties. Total fag."

Nine gave him a look. "What is it with you?"

"Huh?"

"Toxic masculinity lecture isn't slated for another few months, kids." Suit Two rubbed her hands together in an unpleasant rasp. "Ready for live fire?"

"Yessir." Radcliffe said, only too eager to retreat to his station.

Every recruit seemed similarly wary of Suit Two. Over lunch Nine heard them say she'd be teaching them hand to hand combat, and even Ito sounded nervous under her macho posturing.

"Pick up your rifle, recruit," said Suit Two.

Nine donned his ear protection, and nearly slithered out of his skin when her body pressed up against his back and her wiry arms came around him.

"Hands here, and here," she said, placing his left hand on the pistol grip and the right on the hand guard. "Noticed you're a southpaw. I assigned you a left eject, so the casing won't burn your arm."

His muscles shriveled at her touch as her voice filtered through his earmuffs.

"The SIG is an effective tool, but a tool all the same. A rifle is a part of you. If I wanted to touch your nose, I wouldn't think about aiming, I'd simply reach out and do it. Your rifle is your arm. The bullet is your fingertip. You need to reach out, and just know it'll happen."

Nine snugged the buttplate to his shoulder, the way Suit One told them to. He lined up the target through front and rear sights, and slowly squeezed with the ball of his finger. The rifle kicked against his shoulder, and a hole opened in the middle of the target's head. He barely heard the bang.

Suit Two's arms tightened around him. "Again."

He fired twice more. All three shots formed a tight grouping on the target, and it felt right. Like swimming. Like muscle memory. Like something he'd done before.

CHAPTER 11

S himmering thermoclines flowed over the baked earth and scrubby vegetation. Sweat pooled in the small of Nine's back and tickled down his ribs. His mouth felt like sand. Three years at the Facility, and he didn't think he'd ever get used to the furious heat of a Texas summer. Roasting under the camouflage of his ghillie blanket, he lay motionless in the dry grass, sighting down the barrel of his rifle.

The basketball-sized drone hovered and shifted at a range of 600 yards. Designed to simulate the movements of a human target, the drone was also equipped with long-range sensors. If the sniper shifted too suddenly, or even allowed the sun to reflect off the sweat on his forehead, the drone would report and the recruit's score would drop accordingly.

Nine manually dialed in on the drone, which pissed off the computer. Details. The rifle had sensors feeding into a module that performed the ancillary tasks a spotter would usually handle, like measuring temperature, wind speed, distance, and target proportions. The computer squawked its sighting calculations in his earpiece. Nine wished he could switch off all that fire-by-wire shit. Of course, the rifle's tech was synced with the Facility's mainframe, and any meddling with their hardware would be reported.

Everything he did got reported, from the number of rounds he used in a drill, to the grams of protein he consumed at breakfast. Panopticon's gaze, though unofficial, was as strong at the Facility as it was anywhere else. Maybe even stronger.

A deep breath scorched his nose and his eyes poached in their sockets. The other recruits were spread out on either side of him. Only five of the original ten.

During a three-night survival exercise, Burns bugged out and got himself shot. Dalek, too cocky for her own good, challenged Suit Two to a sparring match, and after Suit Two scrubbed the floor with her, Dalek climbed into the whirlpool therapy bath and sliced her wrists. An inspired mess, according to Suit Two. Jiminez, Kowalski, and Cote washed out and were remanded to some government crypt for failed investments where they worked as analysts.

That left Radcliffe, Ito, Lusczak, and Parr. Each one boiling away under their own grass blanket, barely able to focus through the haze, desperately attempting to complete their ten-drone objective so they could get out of the sun before it killed them, which was a thing Nine hadn't known could happen before he came to Texas.

Since Suit One loaded them onto the truck and out to this desert furnace, the other recruits had managed four or five drones each, whereas Nine was currently sighting down number ten.

The electronic voice quacked in his ear. "Recruit Nine. Acknowledge recommended sight adjustments. Recruit Nine. Acknowl—" Nine ripped out the earpiece and peered down the scope, realigning his shot. He pressed the ball of his finger on the trigger. The drone flew apart.

The crack of the gas propelled round was still dissipating when a leather shoe scuffed across the dirt in front of him, spraying dust into his face. He threw off the blanket. "Dangerous, sneaking up on someone during a live fire."

"We alerted you to my approach." Sunlight gleamed off Suit One's cured hair helmet and mirrored sunglasses. "You removed your earpiece. Again."

Nine stood up, brushing the dirt from his pants. "I'm done here."

"You rely too heavily on the computer."

A cold needle scraped the inside of Nine's overheated skull. "I don't use the computer at all, and you know it."

"You can't be performing the math in your head that fast."

Actually, he could, and sometimes did. Mostly it wasn't necessary. But he wasn't in the habit of defending himself. Suit One breathed hard out his nose and signaled one of the guards. The guard sounded an air horn and all fire came to a standstill.

"Recruits," Suit One shouted with a smile that showed his tiny teeth. "Nine has completed the drill in record time, thus raising the bar for the rest of you. You will remain in position until you've neutralized an additional five targets on top of the required ten."

Four ghillie blankets flipped back and five sweaty faces scowled in Nine's direction.

"What are you doing?" Nine whispered.

INFRACTUS

Suit One patted his flawless forehead with a white handkerchief. "Outstanding performance deserves recognition. Congratulations Nine, you're dismissed."

Parr appeared ready to cry, Lusczak mouthed an obscenity, Ito's rage all but bled from her eyes, and even Radcliffe wore an expression of loathing that did not suit his face at all. Nine frowned at Suit One. "You're going to get me killed."

"I suggest you make the most of your air-conditioned afternoon."

Nine packed his gear and plodded to the waiting Jeep. The driver reached into his satchel and retrieved a can of cola. Of all the bits of old world to bring back. First, Cheerios. Now, Dr. Pepper. With muttered thanks, Nine accepted the warm can, fiddled with the tab until he figured out how to pop it open and gulped the hot fizz as the driver sped down the dusty road back to the Facility. The cola left him thirstier than ever and coated his mouth and tongue with a thick sticky film. Before A-Day, people drank this stuff all the time, though Nine rarely had. Sister Claudia viewed soft drinks as liquid sin and would have crucified herself before allowing it in her home. And Zee was dead set against anything that might ruin his perfect teeth.

Nine drank the last drops out of the can and wondered what he should do with his last few hours of life.

While he'd been ready for anything, the last thing Nine expected was nothing. The week passed without incident. On Friday night, Nine turned in early with a pile of textbooks. His room contained a steel bed, locker, and desk, all the same shade of Facility Beige. Basic, but private. Single rooms were not intended as a luxury. Intense physical conditioning, fierce competition, and an alone-in-your-cell-at-2200 curfew went a long way toward discouraging the formation of social bonds among the recruits. Not that this was a problem for Nine.

Since the moving target drill, Ito and Lusczak exchanged only the required words with him between dirty looks, and even Radcliffe made it clear that they were no longer the friends Radcliffe had imagined them to be. Parr spent two days in the infirmary with heat stroke, after which he was discharged by way of washout lane.

But the social exile was a holding action and there was no worse feeling in the world than waiting for the other shoe to drop.

Nine settled on his bed and dove into his study materials. He had papers due in organic chemistry and North American history, and an upcoming practical exam in applied psychology, aka Interrogation & Torture. In the beginning, the recruits practiced on each other, but now they extracted real intelligence from real criminals and terrorists before they were sent off for remap or to a labor camp.

Applied psych was a popular class. Ito and Lusczak liked it because they were violent creeps. Radcliffe appreciated it as a means to an end, but occasionally threw up after conducting his interviews. Nine's affinity for the art of persuasion was more complex. The details: thanks to years running grifts with Zee, Nine had a knack for establishing trust and bonding with the subject—so much that he rarely had to inflict physical pain at all. And his built-in lie detector ensured his intelligence was of the highest quality. The other recruits wrote him off as squeamish, but for all the clean sophistication of his technique, Nine suspected he was the cruelest of them all.

INFRACTUS

The chem text tumbled out of his hands as he lay back on his pillow and stared at the pocked tile ceiling. Memories of emerging constellations rinsed away any desire to study. He missed those nights on his rooftop, answering to no one, gazing into a red sky. He'd learned a lot at the Facility, but already "Nine" was a layer of scales ready to be shed.

Hours later, Nine stirred awake to darkness, the chirp of crickets, and Suit Two, sitting on him like a djinn out of an Arabian horror story.

"3:00 a.m.," she said. "Devil's hour."

Nine blinked the sleep away. She'd been gone for weeks, following up on a lead regarding the whereabouts of Ori Mane.

"My books?"

"Threw 'em over there." She cocked her head toward his desk and the tumbledown pile of texts. "That's some hardcore academia. History? Philosophy? Why?"

"The Panopticon," Nine said. "Designed by Jeremy Bentham in the 18th century. A prison with cells lining the inside circumference of a tower and a guard blind in the center. Prisoners assume they're under constant surveillance and conduct themselves accordingly. By leaving the watching to the watched, one concealed guard can anonymously control an entire population."

"Huh?" she said.

Suit Two couldn't care less about how few people had access to that knowledge or how Panopticon was redacting and revising old world history. She didn't care because her intelligence wasn't the kind fed by libraries and lectures. Her education was embedded in her DNA. Instinct and adaptation honed over thousands of years, all of it pounding through her blood every second of every day. At the Facility she taught them blade work and hand-to-hand. Gory tales of her field exploits abounded. The recruits were scared shitless of her, and now she was in his room, right on top of him.

Nine tried to squirm away but her thighs tightened around his hips with the threat of planet crushing force. "Get off me."

"Figures you'd be an egghead."

"I'm serious." Her body heat stirred up a froth of acid in his stomach. "I'll get busted for breaking curfew."

"Golly, we wouldn't want to get in trouble."

Admittedly it sounded riot lame, but a legit concern regardless. Facility life had done nothing to tame his savage insomnia and he frequently broke curfew. There wasn't a single wall or building on the base he hadn't scrambled up and over while avoiding cameras and motion detectors. In three years, he'd only been caught a couple times. But a third strike meant another stretch in the hole where time slid around like oil on ice, unpredictably pooling, shrinking, and freezing. Even then, solitary wouldn't be so bad if he could shake the feeling that he wasn't actually alone.

"What about Ori Mane?" he asked, drawing on his training to start an adjacent conversation. Get the subject to talk, about anything at all. The modules called it priming. "Did you catch him?"

"Animal like that doesn't get caught, he surrenders. And he's not ready." She stared into space as though recalling a scent, one she knew she'd come across again. "Though I did have a blast neutralizing a Jackal cell."

Nine didn't doubt it. Forget remapping or labor camps. If Suit Two was involved, there wouldn't be enough left to reassemble, let alone rehabilitate.

"Got back yesterday. You-know-who suggested I keep to myself until I felt more regulated, but I heard you aced the moving target drill and wanted to offer congratulations."

She reached behind her body and Nine braced himself for a congratulatory crushed sternum or a felicitous knife to the spleen. What she produced, however, was not a blade or cudgel. Nine's breath caught as he followed the elegant lines. Black steel barrel, wooden stock and hand guard, swept back bolt, modified telescopic sight. "Springfield. M1903."

"Belonged to an old-world sniper once." Suit Two presented the rifle like a ceremonial sword.

"You're giving this to me?"

"Kid, you've already got the gift. Believe me, this beauty wants you as much as you want her."

Nine watched Suit Two's eyes devour the rifle in a way that made his skin flush even as his stomach heaved. She laid the Springfield in his hands, and he savored the weight before reluctantly setting it aside. "Thanks, but you didn't break into my room to congratulate me."

"Clever." She pressed her fists into the pillow on either side of his head. "You're thinking of lighting out."

"Maybe."

"The Eye believes in return on investment, kid. They'll burn you."

"They won't find me."

"But I will. Don't think I could stop myself."

Sitting back, she shrugged out of her jacket. Nine recognized the expression on her face. She was about to do something weird, like the time she suggested he and Suit One could work out their differences by taking a bath together. She unfastened the buttons of her shirt and slipped that off too, exposing a lacework of scar tissue over her arms, her chest, and the muscles of her stomach. Fine lines swept across her skin like calligraphy. Most old and silver. Some raw.

On many occasions, Nine had noticed the scars peeking out of her cuffs, or spied a speck of blood here and there on her white shirts. He'd drawn reasonable conclusions, but Suit Two wasn't a cutter. She was an artist.

Her fingers dug painfully into his chest. Between that, the rifle, and her strange mutilated beauty, she'd pressed buttons he didn't know he had, and he cursed his responding body in every silent, hateful way he knew. Three tolerably grand sex-free years. Even on furlough when the other recruits went into Killeen, blew their whole stipend on mescaline and traders, and razzed him relentlessly for abstaining. Jesus, if they found out about this. Well, they probably wouldn't believe it—thank hell.

"My colleague wanted to teach you a lesson," she said, "but I got him to call off the dogs. Told him I'd handle it."

He heaved himself to the side rolling her beneath him on the narrow bed, "And if I don't want to be handled?"

"But you do. You always have." She turned her face into his pillow and inhaled, her eyes rolling back. "I'm an animal, a monster, poison with a pulse. I disgust you and you're dying for a taste. I don't need to punish you. You're going to do it for me."

Nine clutched her arms, wanting her to disappear, holding her in place. His fingertips automatically read her scars. A story written in a mad language for the blind.

Stop hurting yourself.

Sister Claudia's voice echoed from his past and only now did he hear the despair in her words.

CHAPTER 12

It seemed drug money could buy anything but a decent sofa. Carrall Hastings tried to contort around the spring poking his back, but couldn't with his arm pinned beneath the snoring woman. Her purple dreadlocks made his skin itch something awful. Typically, he couldn't tolerate extended touching. In this case it lent authenticity to the construct. A couple of junkies sleeping it off on the infested cushions.

Carrall waited, watching pedestrian traffic outside flicker through the steel mesh covering the basement window. Inside, glass dust swirled in the light of a low winter sun. Soon now. He closed his eyes, both blue thanks to a contact lens, and inhaled the bouquet of marijuana, fungal feet, and his own overspray of woodsy cologne. He tapped his fingers to the beat of pre-millennial grunge pouring from the stereo. Typical crack shack. Riot sound system and a sofa requiring up-to-date vaccinations.

The exterior door to the corner of 34th and Steinway slammed. Carrall counted the trip trap of size thirteens down ten, eleven, twelve stairs. A stumble on the last. The metallic fumble of keys. A jiggling door knob. More key fumbling. Someone was anxious. Good. He kept his eyes closed and let his head drop back, gelled hair crunching against the shredded upholstery. His arm had gone to sleep under the purple dreadlocks.

The door hinges squealed, and Carrall recognized Wyatt's breathless voice traveling across the room. "Hey. Hey, buddy." The music cut out and Wyatt slapped Carrall upside the head.

"Fuck Daisy Duck," Carrall groaned.

"Wakey wakey," Wyatt said, jostling his shoulder. "You straight?"

"Uh?"

"Come on, man. You cranked up or what?"

"No. Not mostly." Carrall injected a hint of slur into his voice. Not that it was all an act. Merely breathing the air in this place gave him a buzz. He examined the woman passed out in the crook of his elbow. "Whoa, ugly alert. Should I chew my arm off?"

Wyatt grabbed a fistful of purple dreadlocks, dragging the woman off the couch and dumping her on the floor. Based on her snoring, it didn't disturb her nap. Carrall winced at the bite of pins and needles under the phony tattoos covering his arm. Wyatt cleared aside the razor blades, pipes, and burner phones littering the coffee table and perched on the edge. "Bad news. My brother never picked up the money."

Carrall rubbed the feeling back into his arm. "Money?"

"He's due to meet the cook in an hour." Wyatt tugged his hair into wiry spikes. "He's not answering his phone. You seen him?"

"Little bro? Probably partying somewhere." Carrall thought of the last time he'd seen Wyatt's poor dumb brother, laid out under some bushes in Astoria Park with his poor dumb neck broken. "Can't you do it? Cook just wants to get paid for his product, yeah?"

Wyatt shook his head. "He's riot paranoid about the Eye nosing in on his business. Thinks every car coming down the street is a black van. He's completely off tech. No computers or phones. Barely trusts my brother, and he won't deal with me at all, on account of some history I got with his ol' lady."

"Ain't paranoia if they're really after you." Carrall stretched his arms above his head. "Those black vans pull up to a house in the middle of the night. Bag up whole families. Kids, dogs, pet turtles, and shit. Remap all of 'em."

"Relax, Panopticon's got bigger fish to fry. It's not like we're Ori Mane and his Jackals. Torching hospitals and raping orphans. I got an understanding in place with the local patrol."

Carrall nodded. Wyatt wasn't stupid so much as he was short sighted. Panopticon didn't believe in catch and release. They would happily fry any size fish. In fact, it was the unusual spending activity of those bribed patrollers that drew Panopticon's eye to Wyatt's sidewalk empire in the first place. In other news, Panopticon could tone down the Jackal propaganda. No one knew exactly who Ori Mane was, not even Suit Two, and Panopticon was trying so hard to paint him as the boogieman that Carrall was beginning to wonder if the guy even existed.

Wyatt yanked his tufted hair again. "Goddamnit, I don't care if he's the only family I got, I'm going to kill that kid."

Carrall Hastings chuckled.

Some details. The cook was an off-gridder supplying a rapidly growing portion of New York with high-grade amphetamine. To draw him out, Carrall spent the last few months getting friendly with the two brothers heading up the cook's distribution network. Wyatt organized the business at street level, but his brother had been the bagman and sole contact where the cook was concerned. With little brother conveniently AWOL, Wyatt had little choice but to ask his new best friend to cover the drop.

"I need you buddy." Wyatt clapped both hands on Carrall's shoulders. "You come through for me on this, you're my new brother."

Carrall tensed under Wyatt's touch. "C'mon, man. This ain't my scene. I'm an artist, and money is so dirty, y'know?"

Wyatt squeezed. "Exactly, you fucking hippy. I know you won't screw me over."

This was Carrall's first assignment out of the Facility, but it wasn't his first grift, not by a long shot.

Scumbags won't trust anyone they see as competition. Take yourself outta their game. Make a big ornery deal of your principles. If they want to rule the world, all you want is a little island to call home.

The confidence game. Zee played it like no other, and he'd taught his Mouse well. The Facility provided him with an extensive formal education, but those street skills were the reason Panopticon tapped him for this job.

"Tell him my brother's got gallstones." Wyatt paused, turning his head and sneezing over his shoulder. "You smell like a two cred trader."

Carrall's liberal application of body spray served two purposes. One, it kept him in character. Two, it kept people out of touching range. Usually.

"What's the word, brother?" Wyatt rubbed his hands briskly up and down Carrall's tattooed arms. "You in?"

Carrall closed his hand around Wyatt's wrist while discreetly reaching between the crusty cushions for his knife. "Where do I meet this cook?"

Minimal light penetrated the scaffolding under the partially rebuilt Hellgate Bridge, but the wind carried through just fine. Carrall popped his collar against the stinging sleet. Two down, one to go. He'd left purple dreadlocks alive, sleeping next to Wyatt, dead with a blade between his ribs.

He shivered, from the cold and the amphetamines coursing through his system. Goddamnit, would this cook guy hurry it up? He turned his back to the wind and reached in his pocket, closing his hand around the icy grip of the SIG. Pistols never warmed to his touch. Or he never warmed to theirs. The curse of a trained sniper. He had a relationship with his Springfield that he couldn't imagine forming with a soulless lump of handheld polymer like the SIG. The Springfield, however, was rather unsuitable for concealed carry.

A shadow appeared at the top of the embankment, a man slowly making his way down the slushy slope. Carrall gave a shivering wave. The shadow man ducked under a bar of scaffolding, straightened and came no closer. "You're not my contact."

"You the cook?"

"What's the password?"

"The passw—are you fucking with me?" Carrall hefted the duffel bag slung across his shoulders. "I don't know how many creds are in this bag, but it's heavy, okay? It's contaminating me. I'm supposed to give this to the cook and no one else, so that's why I'm asking."

The shadow man stepped into a shaft of light. A regular guy, on the stocky side, bad skin, thick eyebrows under a fringe of sleet-wet hair. "I do represent him, but I'm not the cook."

The burr of a lie rolled between Carrall's brain and skull. As the cook reached for the bag, Carrall retrieved the SIG from his pocket. The cook's breath escaped in a fog. "Whoa—"

Carrall squeezed eight pounds out of the trigger. To discharge the SIG, you had to mean it. The cook crumpled to the ground before the sonic crack could ricochet off the iron trellis of the bridge.

"Nothing personal," Carrall said, crouching next to the body to pick up the brass.

He could have done it faster—fast enough that the mark never would have seen the gun—and point blank was a touch dramatic. But Wyatt and his brother had been chores. The cook was the reward. Carrall wanted to see his eyes. Terror. Anticipation. He'd earned it. His first assignment in the field. Three marks. He'd hit them all with nary a hiccup.

"Mr. Hastings." A voice lanced through the shadows like a javelin.

Carrall watched two figures make their way through the maze of scaffolding.

"What are you doing here?" Carrall asked.

INFRACTUS

Suit One surveyed the scene, snowflakes settling on his shoulders and melting on his glassy hair. "Think of us as Plan B."

Suit Two crouched next to the cook's body. She tugged off her gloves and held the cook's dead hand between hers as she pressed her face into his neck, sniffing. Carrall wasn't surprised. Suit Two was a barely domesticated animal. A minimally restrained psychopath. She glanced up with her shark smile. "Did you have fun?"

Carrall shivered. "Not as much as you're having."

Suit One grasped Carrall's jaw with hard leather fingers, moving in until they were almost nose-to-nose. "Mr. Hastings, I do believe you are intoxicated."

"This the part where you date rape me?"

Suit One retreated to arm's length. "I suppose there's little point to lecturing you on the law of diminishing returns as it pertains to embedded assets. You could've compromised the entire operation while under the influence of psychoactive chemicals."

Suit Two joined them, naked hands tucked in the pockets of her long coat. She nudged Suit One's arm. "Seriously? You're gonna narc on the kid?"

Suit One grimaced. "Congratulations, Mr. Hastings, on the technical success of your first assignment. I'm going back to the hotel to submit my report. I suggest you find a place to hole up and dry out. You'll be hearing from us soon." With a nod to Suit Two, he made his way out of the scaffolding and back up the embankment.

As soon as he was out of sight, Suit Two sidled up closer. "Not many operatives can handle embedded work without getting emotional or fucking up."

Carrall kicked at the slushy gravel. "I handled it fine, so what's his problem?"

Suit Two rolled her eyes, not unlike a feeding shark. "Drawing an undercover gig for your first assignment is like getting called up to the show out of little league. He didn't want to put you up to bat, and now he's pissed because you knocked it out of the park."

"He's babysitting the rookie, I get it. But I've always wondered how you got stuck with Agent Dad." The contact high from glass dust made him reckless, allowing words to fall like drops of blood that could easily send her into a frenzy.

"The truth?"

He mirrored her razor-sharp smile. "I'll know if you're lying."

"He's not your handler. He's mine. On file I'm your direct superior, but anytime I'm deployed to a populated area he sticks to me like shit to a shoe. You can bet he's up there watching us right now. Apparently, I'm unpredictable."

This only confirmed what Carrall had long suspected. Cunning and feral, Suit Two was the best bloodhound Panopticon had. They'd chosen her to bring him in because they knew she could find him. Connect with him. Suit One's job was to make sure she didn't kill him.

"Dogs like you and me are hard to leash, kid. They'd put us down if we weren't irreplaceable." She inched even closer, inhaling. "Jesus, you smell like a whore."

Carrall seized the lapels of her coat. Underneath he saw the top two buttons on her shirt were open, exposing filaments of scar tissue spidering up to the hollow of her throat. "And how did you find me tonight? Followed your nose?"

Her fingertips crept up his arm and jammed her thumb against the inside of his bicep above his elbow. "You ought to find a doctor. I think you've caught a bug."

Stunned, Carrall searched her face, finding only the carnivorous glee she saw in everything reflected back at him. "A chip?"

"Didn't hear it from me, but I know a guy in California," she said. "Barclay's not a surgeon, but he's connected. He'll hook you up."

"How? When?"

"When do you think?"

Carrall scowled. "You drugged me."

"After, not before," she said. "And don't look at me like I'm some kind of Delilah. You were a flight risk, and they get one into everybody, one way or another. At least my way was fucking awesome—and ironic, since I don't need a bug to find you."

"Awesome" was one adjective. "Terrifying" was another. But it was clever. The morning in question, he'd woken up so battered and gouged, he wouldn't have noticed a tiny incision not made by her nails or teeth. Not that Suit Two required ulterior motives to play rough.

"Don't be grouchy. That was years ago. We've had some good clean fun since." Suit Two pointed at the duffel bag next to the cook's body. "And now you're skipping away from your first job with a fat bonus."

Carrall wouldn't admit it to her, but he'd never had money before. At the Facility he'd needed only petty amounts, and on the streets he'd risked his neck daily just to keep from starving to death. As of this moment, that duffel bag contained more money than he'd ever seen in his twenty-five years of life.

"Made your bones tonight, kid." She slipped a plastic key card into his hand. "Come see me when you're done. No drugs, no bugs. Promise."

She slipped away into the shadows, but Carrall didn't twitch a muscle until he was sure she was gone. With cold fingertips, he pinched the blue contact lens out of his green eye. He snatched up the duffel bag and weaved his way out of the scaffolding.

Take what you've earned and pay what you owe, Mouse. Nothing more. Nothing less. We're criminals, but we're not crooks.

Carrall threw the money, the brass bullet casing, and the contact lens into the treacherous currents of the East River. Zee was a hypocrite. Carrall was a professional.

He'd made his bones. This was his life. No turning back. He flipped Suit Two's key card over and over in his hand, picturing the web of scar tissue covering her hard, muscled body. She'd left, but he still felt like someone was watching him.

He flings the card into the river. I cast myself out, listen for the slap of plastic on the water's surface, and reel myself back in. Though not present in any physical sense, I keep my distance all the same.

He stares across the water, the lean slash of his body shivering as silver snowlight trickles over the cold angles of his face. Expressionless. I never could tell what he was thinking. He chucked the card though, which means he's matured. Frankly I'm relieved. That woman is claws-out psychotic and human bodies are so fragile.

The temptation to reveal myself is strong, but my regular vessel is far from here and I'm not fond of possessing strangers. Just as well. It's not time. One day She'll come for him and I'll be held to account for what I've done. We all will.

CHAPTER 13

The assassin waited on the curb outside a high-rise piercing the Austin sky like a blade of light. All Panopticon buildings were designed like this. An exterior of solar plates stitched together with polymer beams. Clean and efficient. Blinding under the sun, but those inside could see everything.

At midafternoon, the sidewalk nearly melted his boots. He adjusted the strap of the long canvas tube he carried across his back, the kind meant for rolled up plans, electronic display mats, or concealing a M1903 Springfield rifle. Christ, he hated Texas. The lingering vestiges of the old-world military industrial complex, the reptilian stink of the Facility, the crickets, and the hideous heat. He hadn't been back since graduation.

Traffic whooshed by in both directions on the busy street. Electric motors all but noiseless, leaving only the sound of tires grinding over asphalt and the odd tap of a horn. The assassin glanced at his watch. Finally, a motorized sedative of a sedan slid up to the curb. The assassin loaded the rifle and his pack into the back before settling in the front to stare into his own mismatched eyes, reflected in mirrored sunglasses.

"You're late," the assassin said.

Suit One shoulder checked and slipped smoothly into traffic. "I was not aware we were operating on your timetable, Mr....What are we calling you today?"

"Nice car," the assassin said, sinking into his seat.

"Sneer if you must, but the Citizen-A is equipped with solar microcell paint, comprehensive safety features, multiple GPS tracking beacons, and the most efficient electrics ever rolled off the assembly line. Soon, everyone will be driving them. It's good to see you, agent."

The lie gouged a trench in the assassin's brain. He and Suit One detested each other. It was their thing. Only Suit One had a fetish for pretending otherwise, and their conversations left the assassin with operatic headaches. He put on his own non-mirrored shades, wishing he could blot out the sun altogether.

Suit One handled the wheel with both hands. His cuffs reached precisely an inch from his jacket and as always, his hair adhered obediently to the curvature of his skull. The assassin guessed Suit One to be in his mid-forties by now, but other than a bit of salt at his temples, and a sharpening of frown lines, he hadn't changed since they'd met eleven years ago.

"How have you been?" asked Suit One as the car buzzed along the divisional highway heading north out of Austin. "Talkative as ever. Surely you must have something to say. We haven't seen you in nearly six years."

"So great, right? Thanks for spoiling it."

"We've kept you busy with solo assignments, and you've performed adequately."

The assassin grunted. The agent formerly known as Recruit Nine was their sharpest shooter; his embedded work in New York was now taught as part of Facility curriculum, and if he needed additional proof that he was at the top of their game, it was this: if they had someone, anyone, better, he'd be dead.

Suit One continued, "We thought you'd enjoy some teamwork to cleanse the palate."

Teamwork. A word he did not like. "What I'm hearing is that you need my trigger. And now that you have it, can we not talk?"

When they reached Killeen and the Facility, sickening nostalgia swamped him. Same sand colored institutional buildings and smartly paved roads. They passed the firing range, the gymnasium, and the modular classroom with narrow windows where he'd written hundreds of exams and attended thousands of lectures. Since then he'd killed a lot of people. Terrorists, gunrunners, drug dealers, and other assorted dirtbags. No kids though. Basic, but that was his line, and as long as an order didn't cross it, he'd do the job. No hesitation.

They whizzed by the supply depot that also housed the solitary confinement unit. The assassin wondered if there might be a recruit underground right now, reflecting on whatever very bad thing he'd done.

Suit One drove his criminally uncool car all the way to the end of the campus, into a hangar where techs in flight suits were fueling a small turbo prop and giving a woman in a suit a wide berth.

"My colleague has come to see us off," said Suit One, sounding as thrilled as the assassin felt.

Every couple of years Suit Two would drop into his life like a grenade, do some damage and leave him shell-shocked. Suit One might have the personality of a parking lot, but at least he kept his hands to himself.

Now Suit Two crossed her arms over her chest. Though her eyes were hidden behind mirrored glasses, the assassin recognized the pissed off clench of her jaw as he and Suit One got out of the sedan.

"Sneaking off to Nevada without telling me?" she demanded.

"Nevada?" the assassin said. "Why the hell did you summon me to Texas?"

"With your whereabouts unknown, Texas seemed a logical muster point," Suit One said, and turned a gentler tone on Suit Two. "Intelligence places the target at the verified coordinates. Your skills are not required on this assignment."

"Who's the target?" the assassin asked.

"Intelligence?" She ripped off her glasses. "That's my recon! Two weeks crawling around the Waste, with my nose in the dirt and sand between my teeth. Now you're trying to take credit for the collar!"

Even the techs flinched as her voice ricocheted of the steel walls of the hangar like wild arrows.

"Calm down," the assassin said.

Her knuckles clapped across his face. "Why don't you go ahead and jump up my ass."

Been there...but he held the words back, knowing she might actually laugh. Funny Suit Two was even scarier than Ragey Suit Two.

And besides, she had every right to be angry. He rubbed the sting out of his cheek. "Hey, I know how you feel. He rode my rep all the way up the ladder to assistant director of our nonexistent program."

Suit One's face went from annoyance, to exasperation, to resignation in a series of nearly invisible shifts in facial tension. Buttoned up as ever. Suit Two allowed him to lead her to the other end of the hangar for a private conversation that did not appear to be going his way.

"Nameless," a voice boomed and the assassin was surprised to see a moose in a flight suit loping toward him.

"Radcliffe."

"Gee whiz, it's been a hound's age."

"You're a pilot now?"

"Useful skill for a hitter, you ought to take it up."

"I like to drive."

Radcliffe sniffed at the dopey Citizen-A. "You know you're a dang legend around here? Recruits find out we came up together and they wanna know your origin story."

"What do you tell them?"

"With the amount of time you spent in the hole, I'm surprised you even graduated. Who knew you'd turn out to be such hot stuff."

The assassin got his rifle and bag from the car. "I've got a few miles on me, and the road rash to prove it."

Radcliffe cocked his head toward Suit Two. "Like I said, legendary. And here I always thought you were a fag."

INFRACTUS

Nothing could have stopped Recruit Nine from punching this berk in the face. But at the age of thirty, the assassin had developed some restraint. In a way, he supposed he missed Texas.

Their flight finally got off the ground the next morning. The Suits sat side by side in their khaki jackets and pants tucked marine-style into their boots. The assassin wondered if they intentionally wore matching desert adventurer costumes or if they were so in sync that they chose it independently.

By the window, Suit One dove into his tablet, attending to whatever administrative tasks were required of an assistant director. Suit Two fidgeted, slouching, sitting up, drawing her knees to her chest, or flinging her legs into the aisle.

The assassin knew only that they were headed to the Waste. A deserted territory consisting of old world flyover states. Wyoming, South Dakota, Iowa, Nebraska, Utah, Nevada, and most of Colorado. The last remaining Weapon of Mass Destruction stronghold on earth, and almost all those warheads detonated in situ, producing a huge area of nuclear devastation. A-Day happened everywhere, but in the Waste, it salted the earth.

"What's the mission?" the assassin half-shouted, because Radcliffe's plane was noisy as hell. "Don't tell me we're going to the Waste to clear out a kite nest."

Suit Two leaned into the aisle with a grin. "Kites don't exist."

A bitter joke. Panopticon dismissed them as a myth, but kites were real as rusty nails. Named for unclean birds of prey, they nested in the ghost towns dotting the Waste. They took to the highways, rumbling with rival clans and ambushing travelers. Kite attack survivors were few, and in most cases, they would've been better off dead.

"Who's the mark?" he asked.

She nudged his knee with her boot. "Remember years ago, when I told you Ori Mane wasn't ready?"

"Ori Mane?"

"You were more fun back then."

He rubbed her dusty boot print from his pant leg. So, Ori Mane did exist, and perhaps now he was ready to surrender.

"Orders are to take him alive," she said, tracing the scars on the inside of her wrist. "I don't like that."

The assassin understood why Suit One wanted to leave her behind. Suit Two had tolerable difficulty parsing nuances like "look, but don't touch" and "catch, but don't kill." Panopticon wouldn't risk elevating a man into a martyr.

He reclined in his seat and contemplated his priorities. Working for a government he hated to destroy something a deeply decayed part of him might actually believe in. But he had no grounds for refusal. Unless Ori Mane began his freedom fighting reign as an infant, he had to be well into adulthood, and they weren't even going to kill him. He glanced over at Suit Two, picking her nails, and wondered where she drew her line, if she had one at all.

They landed at a small airfield on the California side of Lake Tahoe, less than five miles from the Nevada border and the official demarcation between civilization and the Waste. They disembarked into the cool morning. The assassin inhaled Northern California air that he associated with grapes, sunshine that didn't hurt, and getting

INFRACTUS

Panopticon's blighted tracking chip dug out of his arm. It reminded him of Suit Two's friend Barclay, a man as solid as she was crackers, and perhaps the one person in the world the assassin trusted.

Radcliffe hung out the door of the aircraft. "Safe travels."

"You're not coming?" the assassin asked.

"I don't work in the Waste," said Radcliffe, all humor draining from his expression. "Nothing in that dusty hell is worth it."

The assassin noted the sting of a partial-lie buried in that statement. He'd always suspected Radcliffe was from one of the Waste states. Iowa, or some such.

Suit One snapped his fingers and pointed to the other side of the airstrip.

"Butter my biscuit," said Suit Two, lowering her shades.

The assassin followed her gaze to the edge of the runway and a sleek Mercedes sedan with low profile tires and tinted windows. The kind of environment-hating, driver-loving work of automotive art that still ran on a mix of petrol and electrics. The assassin's feet itched for her pedals and his hands ached to wrap around her wheel. "I'm driving."

"Shotgun," Suit Two added.

"Bulletproof body panels and glass. Reinforced tires," said Suit One. "Coordinates should be programmed into the GPS."

The assassin took his rifle out of its canvas tube and loaded the five-round clip. He opened the door of the sedan and the creamy smell of hide wafted out as he tucked the Springfield behind the leather seat. Next, he jammed a magazine into the SIG, his ugly but useful foster child of a gun, which fit nicely in the center console cup holder. He ran his hand over the spotless dash, embossed with the letters AMG.

GPS reported their destination about 250 miles away in Nevada, where a town called Goldfield used to be. The map software suggested it would take four hours to get there. The assassin imagined he and his new life partner, Mercedes, could cut that time down considerably.

"Road trip, y'all." Suit Two dived in the driver's side door and clambered over the console into the passenger seat. "Let's hit it."

They merged onto the divisional highway heading east toward Carson City and within minutes they crossed the border into the Waste.

"I've quite a lot of work to do," said Suit One. "So, if you don't mind, I'm going to commandeer the back seat as my office. Pretend I'm not here."

"Way ahead of you," said the assassin.

Suit Two scowled. "Make an effort, will you? It's not that hard."

"We're never going to take a bath together."

"Why not? I've climbed into the tub with him lots and—"

"And I have repeatedly asked you not to," Suit One interrupted, a hint of color flushing his cheeks. "I don't know how you keep breaking in."

Suit Two twisted in her seat toward Suit One. "I get that you don't like it. But it's the only time you're not distracted by something else. And once you stop yelling at me, you have to admit, we've had some good talks."

Her explanation actually made sense. When Suit Two needed to be heard, she'd find a way to make you listen.

"Still messed up," said the assassin.

"It's not like we had relations. Don't be gross."

"So, I disgust you?" Suit One said. "But not enough to keep you out of my bathtub."

Suit Two tossed a shark grin over her shoulder. "You couldn't handle me, old man. I'm merely explaining to our protégé here that not everything is about sex."

The assassin sighed. "I wish nothing was."

"Bullshit." She jabbed him in the ribs. "Remember Nepal?"

"I remember telling you my arm doesn't bend that way, and trekking all the way down from Annapurna Base Camp with a dislocated elbow."

She laughed. "That's what Himalayan hash is for."

"Do we need to have another conversation about drugs, agent?"

The assassin shook his head. "I'd love it if we never had another conversation at all, ever."

They drove. The assassin kept a heavy foot on Mercedes' accelerator, and an eye out for kites. That and Suit Two's tragic attempts at car games were enough to break up the monotony. Three hours into the drive, Suit Two pressed her face to the passenger window, squinting into the tall weeds on the right side of the road. The assassin hadn't experienced an allergic reaction to pollen in twenty years, but his sinuses tingled with the memory.

"Stop," said Suit Two.

"What is it?" Suit One asked.

The assassin consulted the GPS. "We're thirty miles out from the coordinates you gave."

"Fuck the blighted coordinates." She unbuckled her seatbelt and reached for the door handle.

"Jesus." The assassin screeched to a halt in the middle of the highway, grinding off a good portion of Mercedes' tread. "What in the blue hell are you doing?"

She cracked her door open and leaned out, peering into the gently swaying weeds. Suddenly the side view mirror exploded into shards, housing and all.

"Get down," Suit One shouted over the wavering echo of the gunshot.

The assassin grabbed Suit Two's arm, yanking her back into the car. Another bullet smashed into the passenger window exactly where her head had been a heartbeat ago. He glimpsed a flash of red retreating through the tangle of weeds.

Suit Two leapt out of the car and charged into the brush. An instant later Suit One was racing after her. The assassin grabbed his rifle and followed.

Suit Two didn't hesitate, clearing the weeds and continuing her sprint across a fallow field cut down to stubble. On the other side of the field, about three hundred yards ahead, the assassin saw a dilapidated house and a tilting collection of outbuildings. Suit One called after her. A puff of dirt shot up at his feet, followed by a bang. The assassin hauled Suit One back into the tall weeds.

"Cover her," Suit One commanded.

The assassin pulled back the bolt on his Springfield and dialed in on the scragglebeard on the porch aiming his rifle at Suit Two. The assassin fired, and before scraggles fell down the front steps, he'd chambered another round for the gunman in the front window. The assassin was not often involved in firefights, and it was riot fun, except Suit Two was going to get her batty little head blown off.

A bullet thwacked into the dirt twelve feet away. The assassin returned fire and sent the shooter winging off the roof into a cluster of tumbleweeds caught between the house and the garage. Four down. Silence descended on the valley.

Suit One had his binoculars out. "I don't see any more. These are kites, not terrorists. What on earth is she doing?"

An answering roar erupted as a vehicle, a hybrid of bus and tank, tore out of the rotted shed, chunky tires chewing up the earth. The war wagon trundled its way onto a gravel road, swung around a hill and out of sight.

Finally Suit Two turned and waved them down. Suit One swiftly texted into his phone as they ran through the field, meeting Suit Two outside the wind-torn fence surrounding a yard dotted with spiky patches of yellow grass and a rusted-out Buick sunk up to its wheel wells in the earth.

"Mane knew we were coming," she said to Suit One. "Probably saw one of your dumb drones sweep in for a low pass. That's why he evacuated his crew."

"I've never heard of Jackals and kites working together," said Suit One.

Suit Two leaned against a splintered fence post. "If anyone could make it happen . . ."

"You're sure it was Mane?" asked the assassin. "Did you see his face?"

"Didn't have to." She closed her eyes and dragged a long breath through her nose. "Smell that?" The assassin didn't smell anything but diesel exhaust. She inhaled again. "It's him."

"How do you know?"

"Because all I see is fire."

The assassin understood. He'd seen that particular vision before, eyes wide open. A world in flames.

With his white handkerchief, Suit One dusted off his sunglasses. "I've got drones tracking the vehicle. A military convoy is en route to intercept."

"Army?" The assassin slung his rifle across his shoulders. "You trust those meatheads not to shell our target?"

"Derision and paranoia. You really haven't changed."

"We should catch up."

"Indeed," Suit One said. "We're done here."

But Suit Two was not done. She was busy. Deep, long breaths transformed her sinewy body into a bellows. Even her temples hollowed with each inhale. Then she snapped her head toward the yard so fast her hair flew out in a dark fan.

A smile sliced across her face. She skipped over a broken post trailing barbed wire like rattlesnakes half-hidden in the dead grass. Her voice swept low to the ground, musical and coaxing. "Come out, come out, I know you're here."

A boy emerged from behind the rusty Buick. Bronze face and dark eyebrows powdered with dust. No more than fourteen, he wore the clothes of a larger man, cinched by a leather belt with a sheathed knife attached. The boy gripped a revolver with both hands, an old Smith & Wesson. "Stop. I'll shoot you. I will."

"One of Ori Mane's baby soldiers. I hear he likes them young." Suit Two made a show of tallying the dead men sprawled in the yard. "He didn't share you with those dirty kites, did he?"

"Shut up. He takes care of people. You don't know him."

"I know he left you here, alone."

Suit One texted busily, waiting for Suit Two's game to play out. The assassin didn't like this. Ori Mane had no business dragging a kid into the Waste to begin with, but to abandon him? There were plenty more kites circling the territory.

"Just go," the kid said, voice cracking.

"Did he tell you not to worry?" Suit Two asked. "That he needed a little more time, and that we wouldn't hurt you, because you're a kid?"

"C'mon, leave him alone," the assassin said.

She didn't appear to hear him and neither did the boy. She'd wrapped them both in her spell, creating their own pocket outside of space and time. There was a word for that, a perfect word, but the assassin couldn't quite reach it.

"We take care of people too." Slowly she peeled off her jacket, hung it on the Buick's hood ornament, and held up her hands. "See? Unarmed."

A trickle of sweat cut through the dust on the boy's cheek. "Stop it. Please, stop."

"Brave boy." Suit Two advanced until the barrel of the revolver pressed into the center of her chest. She clasped the boy's elbows and slid her hands down to where he gripped the pistol, his knuckles ready to slice through his skin. "Shh, you don't need this."

The boy's fingers relaxed under Suit Two's touch and the gun thumped to the ground. The assassin darted forward. "Don't—"

But she'd already pulled the boy's knife from his belt and slipped the blade neatly under his sternum. He gasped, a sound of surprise, and relief.

"Nighty night," Suit Two murmured, cradling him as his knees gave out. The boy expired without complaint. Suit Two kissed the tip of his nose. Then she got up and grabbed her jacket, flapping out the rust flakes. "Time's a wasting, fellas. Let's go bag us some terrorists."

They piled back into the car, the assassin behind the wheel. Suit One continued texting whomever it was he received orders from or issued them to. He didn't care about the boy. To Suit One that kid was just another tumbleweed, thrashing itself to bits on its way across the desert.

"That way," Suit Two said, pointing east.

The assassin stomped on the gas. "You...are the worst."

"Says the guy who once murdered an old woman in her bed."

"Unless that kid was also the head of a child trafficking ring, this is completely different."

"He would've been remapped. I did him a favor. Don't be such a priss."

If he weren't driving, he would have punched her. No kids. His one line, and she put him in a position to cross it. He didn't kill the boy, but he didn't stop it either, and in this case one basically amounted to the other.

So why didn't he try? Some details. The boy was good as dead the moment Suit Two sniffed him out. To stop her, the assassin would have had to kill her. A big problem. Sure, the boy was brave, but bravery, like stupidity, wasn't rare or special. People like Suit Two brought something unique into the world. Something they took with them when they left. Much as he loathed her, the assassin couldn't face the idea of an existence that much more homogenized. So, he made a choice. Sacrifice a sheep to save a dragon.

The assassin propelled Mercedes closer and closer to her red zone, as they accelerated deeper into the desert. They followed Suit One's directions down a single lane road with a blanket of dirt blown over it and a fresh pair of tracks running down the middle. In the distance he spotted part of a chain link fence and a sign. As they drew closer he was able to make out the words:

RESTRICTED AREA

51

"Area 51?" the assassin asked.

Suit Two clapped her hands. "Aliens and UFOs!"

"Doubtful, the base was obliterated on A-Day," said Suit One. "There's a small corner of the administrative section left standing at the edge of the Groom Lake salt flat. We suspect Jackals have been using it as a bivouac for years. We've got aerial surveillance, but if they reach the base, we'll be hard pressed to root them out."

A dust wake came into view. The assassin maintained their speed, estimating the war wagon to be a couple miles ahead. "What's the play?"

"Convoy is in position," said Suit One.

Suit Two frowned. "You're not going to let the Army collar him, are you?"

"They have orders to disable and secure the vehicle. They are not to engage. Keep following, I'll tell you when to stop."

Suit One's explanation bothered the assassin. For one thing, he was lying. About what, he didn't know, but something was going down. Was Suit One planning to kill Ori Mane after all? It would be easy to arrange an accident, a miscommunication with an overzealous military detachment. Suit One wasn't the mutinous type, but the assassin had an all too fresh reminder that given the right application of force, anyone could be knocked across their line.

The assassin made eye contact with Suit Two, who bared her teeth in response.

"What are you doing?" said Suit One, jostling against his seatbelt as the assassin hooked the wheel right, wrenching them onto a dirt road leading up a low rise. "You are not authorized to change course, agent. Turn around."

"I think we'll have a better view from up here," the assassin said. "And anyway, it doesn't matter, does it? They've got their orders. Once the scene is secure we'll head back down."

Suit Two braced her hand on the roof of the car as they jounced along the rutted lane. "Unless there's something you're not telling us?

You've been awful chatty with whoever's on the other side of your phone."

"Stop the car." Suit One repeated.

The assassin brought Mercedes to a gentle halt on the crest of the hill. Suit One was outside with his gun calmly aimed at the assassin before he and Suit Two could unbuckle their seatbelts.

"This is insubordination," said Suit One. "I'd be within my rights to shoot you both."

The assassin climbed out of the car. "You're not going to shoot both of us."

Suit One fired. The assassin's left shoulder went numb, then hot. He fell to his knees and Suit One stood over him. "Not both. Just you."

He gritted his teeth against the flare of pain and assessed the blood soaking into his shirt. "Are you insane?"

"Consider that a shot across your bow," Suit One said, holstering his weapon.

Suit Two knelt in front of the assassin and tore his sleeve down, exposing a profusely bleeding furrow along the side of his shoulder. "Flesh wound." She used his sleeve as a bandage, tying it around his arm. Then she patted his head and hauled him to his feet. "You were right about the view. Check this out."

The assassin followed Suit Two to the edge of the ridge where Suit One stood overlooking what remained of the Area 51 Air Force base, a small cluster of buildings surrounded by rubble on the edge of a salt flat that stretched beyond the horizon.

"Where's the Army?" Suit Two asked, noting the complete absence of vehicles and personnel.

"They'll be along directly."

The tank-bus came into view, roaring down the road, drawing closer to the base, when suddenly it shuddered and fishtailed, nearly rolling as it came to a stop. Someone had buried a spike strip. Someone knew, well ahead of time, that Ori Mane would be heading this way.

"I want you to understand," Suit One said. "You've made not a bit of difference by defying orders. You've only ensured damage to a common interest."

The assassin couldn't help himself. "For the look on your face? Worth it."

On the road below, Jackals piled out like clowns from an old-world Volkswagen. All of them wore desert nomad scarves wrapped around their heads and faces.

"That's him," Suit Two said, pointing at a figure directing the others out of the tank and toward the base where they began running.

The assassin didn't bother asking how she could identify a faceless speck from five hundred yards away. If Suit Two said it was Mane, it was Mane. When the last Jackal was out of the tank, Mane himself began running. Something about his gait struck the assassin as familiar, the turnover of his boots and the extension of the legs. No one outside Mane's inner circle knew his face. It was possible he and the assassin had met before, but no face emerged in his memory to match the long-legged stride.

Mane fell into the dust a moment before the crack of a rifle filled the pale sky. Another Jackal, large and broad, hoisted Mane up and dragged him along. Mane still ran under his own power, but he was definitely hit.

"What happened?" Suit One asked. "Who fired that shot?"

The assassin retrieved his rifle from the car and lay on his stomach at the edge of the ridge, observing through his scope. Another shot rang out, missing Mane and his partner by about a foot. Even expert snipers had trouble with running targets. And a target running perpendicular to your hide site was the worst. Rather than aim for the mark, you had to aim ahead, calculate, extrapolate, and hope your mark intercepted your bullet's trajectory. The sniper was good, but not good enough.

The assassin shifted his sights and dialed up the magnification. He spotted the gunman, a thousand yards away, splayed out on a slab of rock jutting from the hardpan. Completely exposed in his flight suit, the scope on his government-issue rifle catching the sun. Goddamnit.

He should have known when Radcliffe so adamantly insisted nothing could drag him into the Waste. Not a lie exactly, but not the truth either. Indecision. After dropping them off, he must have taken the plane and flown to Goldfield, hoping to head them off at the pass. But he didn't have Suit Two's nose. He didn't know Mane and his Jackals had fled those coordinates.

"What are you waiting for," Suit One demanded.

"You didn't set this up?"

Another shot. This one drilled a Jackal in the back and his chest cavity erupted in a spatter of blood and tissue. The big guy dragged Mane around their fallen comrade and carried on.

"Agent, it is imperative that Mane reach the base alive. Take that gunman out, immediately."

"It's Radcliffe."

Suit One managed a human expression for a microsecond before realigning his features into robotic indifference. "You have your orders."

The assassin squinted through the scope again. Radcliffe laid down his rifle and looked directly at him, shrugging as if to say, 'Fair's fair'. Like Suit Two, Radcliffe believed Mane worthy of an honorable death. The assassin understood. But you could believe something with all your might and still be wrong. Ori Mane left a kid alone to die in the Waste. He didn't deserve a clean end. Radcliffe on the other hand . . .

The assassin let his breath out and slowly increased pressure on the trigger. A pink mist sprayed from the back of Radcliffe's head as the shot rippled across the desert. The assassin dropped his forehead onto the dirt. "Fuck."

"He was done, kid." Suit Two's hand rested on the back of his neck. "You did right by him"

"Don't touch me." He rolled away and onto his feet. He wondered if it came down to a moment like this for everyone in their line of work. A moment where you were simply done. Full stop.

The last few Jackals made it inside the base, probably thinking it was only a matter of time before Panopticon sent drones to bomb them out of existence. Suit One briefly texted into his phone and led Suit Two down the ridge to crouch behind Mercedes.

Too late the assassin realized why. A blast clobbered his eardrums and shook the earth. He lost his balance and something bit into his skull before he sank into the thick soup of unconsciousness.

❖❖❖

INFRACTUS

In darkness, he splashed around until he glimpsed flickers of light and heard the burble of running water. Coral, rust, turquoise, and onyx streaked across the stone sky in a gory sunset. He couldn't feel his legs or arms. He couldn't see or think clearly, but he knew this place. He knew this cave.

I wasn't expecting you.

The voice came from everywhere and nowhere, from without and within, neither male nor female, old nor young, but familiar all the same.

Seems you've managed to hit your head again.

"Sister Claudia...her dream. This is her dream."

Ah, yes. Before I learned that those close to crossing the veil are more sensitive. I often wonder how many visions I've unwittingly transmitted.

His own vision blurred until he could no longer see the striated dome overhead. "Is this a real cave?"

After a fashion. It's a lacuna.

"Right...that's the word I was looking for earlier. But it's a real place, isn't it?"

You place such stock in reality. As if it were immutable—

"I like that word. Immutable."

Yes well, you have a concussion to tend to.

"Sword," he said, unable to feel the sound in his mouth. "That's a weird word."

You'd better not have damaged that brain I worked so hard to create for you.

"You created me?"

Decreated, more like.

"Huh?"

You are becoming, again, and for the very first time. Each day a little more. Each day a little different.

"Ah. I don't get it."

You rarely do, though someday I hope. But duty calls, for both of us.

"Wait."

I'll see you soon.

The assassin squinted into the light of a red sun, dimmed by an enormous plume of dust. He found himself sprawled on his back, ears buzzing, head resting on what felt like a pillow of broken pottery. Hours had passed, maybe, though he couldn't recall how he'd spent them, finding only black gouges like empty eye sockets. He often wondered if his insomnia and dreamlessness were the cause, or an effect, of waking to find holes punched in his life where time and memory ought to be.

Fresh blood slicked his fingers when he palpated the back of his skull. Not hours, a minute, maybe. Another grossly distorted chunk of time. He'd taken more than a few hits to the head in his life. Perhaps he'd sustained mild brain damage.

Staggering to the edge of the ridge, he expected a heap of rubble where Area 51 used to be. Instead, he saw a deep trench, perhaps thirty feet across, circling the perimeter, effectively turning the base into an island.

Suit Two lurched out from behind the car, eyes unfocused, she tripped over her own feet several times before she reached him. The assassin knew Suit Two to be a lot of things but clumsy was not one of them. She hadn't seen this coming any more than he had. Suit One emerged next, removing plugs from his ears. "Well, that was bracing."

"What the hell did we just do?" the assassin said, barely able to hear his own voice.

"This is the Colony," said Suit One, "Last prison on earth. We'll have guards on the ground, drones in the sky, and supplies will be airdropped. No one gets in. No one gets out. Ori Mane and his Jackals want a free and lawless society? Now they can have it, within their own borders. Rather fitting don't you think?"

"We were never going to take him in."

Suit One's smug mouth opened in a toothy smile. "Do you think I'd be out here to serve as a member of a common bag team? We've made new world history, agent. In a few hours this will be all over the Stream."

"Too bad you won't get credit, not publicly."

"Unlike you, agent, I understand the role we play. We are the hidden machinery that keeps our civilization from falling into another dark age."

Every word rang with truth, or the truth as Suit One saw it. He was a believer, keeping the shadows of anarchy at bay. Though the assassin could argue that too much light was just another kind of blindness. "You've got a situation."

Suit Two sat in the dirt cross-legged. She'd rolled up her sleeve and scored a circle into her arm with a sharp rock and was going around again carving deeper, blood running down to pool in the bend of her elbow.

"Our common interest," said Suit One, whipping out the handkerchief that for years the assassin dismissed as an affectation. "Now do you understand?"

Suit One dropped to one knee, reached for her bloody hand, and jerked back as Suit Two lunged at him, bearing her teeth and falling into a predator's crouch balanced on her knuckles and the balls of her feet. Her bloodied shirt was nearly transparent with sweat and her chest heaved like a greyhound.

"I stopped the boy's heart," she growled. "You'd put him in a cage, so he can see outside and never forget he's trapped. Dead is better. I don't put things in cages."

The assassin caught her around the throat and the waist as she lunged again and sliced at Suit One's face with the rock. Blood beaded along a shallow rent in his cheek.

Suit Two flailed in the assassin's arms, flinging drops of blood and sweat into the dusty air. Her leg hooked behind his knee, dropping him to the ground on his back. Cymbals crashed in his ears and his vision shattered. He expected her to drop a rock on his head but instead she scuttled back to Suit One, all but crawling into his lap. She buried her face in his neck, her whole body shuddering, her arm painted red like a demonic transplant.

"There now," Suit One said, holding her and pressing the hankie to her wound. "It's over."

The assassin had to give Suit One credit. Engineering a ruse like this wasn't easy. They'd hit a few snags. Soon the brass would arrive to find a trail of casualties consisting of kites that weren't supposed to exist, a child about twice as old as the number of bullets in his revolver, a Jackal they weren't supposed to kill, and a Facility-trained agent. They'd all crossed lines in order to meet their objective.

A gust of wind sent dust particles swirling in strange directions and for a moment the assassin saw the outline of a vaguely human form. Maybe he was paranoid. Time to implement his exit strategy. He snatched up his rifle and started back toward Mercedes. Somewhere, an ocean was calling his name.

Weary of my vessel's frailty, I hover on the rise in astral form. Moments ago, he found me in the dark. Now I join him in the light. The Suits perplex him. Even I don't fully grasp the nature of their bond because they themselves cannot define it. Humans are limited in that way, as are all creatures above and below. And these two in particular are a rare coupling of weird.

He and I haven't talked much lately. This last decade I've watched him emerge, more patient and controlled, the anger of his youth dormant. But pressure will build over time. I'm counting on it.

Meanwhile it's not enough to seize control of this world. I'm more ambitious than that. I'm conditioning the human race to do what has never before been accomplished: to bow before a single faceless authority. For all my minor slip-ups, I must say it's ticking along rather well.

CHAPTER 14

Noel Bland's feet squished into the mat at the bottom of the climbing wall as he gathered up chalk bags and harnesses. A mess left behind by the group of secondary Ed. students. Animals. Even at thirty-seven years old, Noel remembered well enough what it was like to be a teenager. While his life had been far different from that of these privileged brats, he'd had as little regard for adult expectations. He unhooked the carabiners from the harnesses and dropped them in their proper compartments in the storage bench. The clack of steel on steel bounced off the concrete floor and exposed ductwork on the ceiling thirty feet above.

"Noel?" Grayson Hillaby called from the utility closet that served as his office. "You're not cleaning up after those kids, are you?"

"Bunch of them ditched harness near the end to do some bouldering, and I didn't leave enough time."

"Don't cover for them." Grayson appeared in the doorway of his office, an alpine god with dark tousled curls, sun-toasted cheekbones, and clear green eyes. Noel had a green eye too, but he kept that secret under a blue lens. He dropped the chalk bags into the basket and clapped the dust from his hands.

"Thanks again for subbing," Grayson said. "Saved my life."

"Aw, shush," Noel said with a bashful shrug.

Grayson wandered up to the deserted storefront, grabbing a tablet off the desk. He frowned at the screen. "Have to fill in these blighted forms for the Eye's safety audit. Next they'll want me to suit everyone in bubble wrap before they step on my wall."

The needle zigzagged along the inside of Noel's skull, but he nodded in sympathy. Panopticon did expend a staggering amount of energy attempting to rescue people from their own stupid. But if Grayson hadn't been working on the safety audit, what was he working on, and why lie about it?

"We still on for the Chimney tomorrow?" Grayson asked.

Noel eyed the discarded snarl of ropes on the floor. "Think I'm ready?"

"Hell yeah, you need a real challenge."

"I guess." Noel fidgeted, shifting from foot to foot. Truthfully, he'd been climbing his whole life, free soloing structures considerably less stable than a mountain. He could easily scramble up Alexander's Chimney without a rope, but playing the talented novice invited Grayson to take a special interest, which played right into Noel's scheme.

"Let's do it then." Noel set to untangling the ropes. "First mountain, gee whiz."

Grayson chuckled. "I'll be gentle, promise."

INFRACTUS

Some details. Contrary to Panopticon's propaganda, the Jackals weren't an organized network of bloodthirsty terrorists. Since Ori Mane's incarceration seven years ago, an operation Noel personally participated in, the Jackal movement had receded into scattered pockets of resistance with widely varying agendas and jealously guarded secrets. It took finesse and patience to feel these guys out. Noel joined Grayson's climbing club nearly two months ago and only now was the work yielding potential fruit.

"Sure I can't pay you?" Grayson said. "The amount of time you put in around here, getting coffee, hauling gear, and covering classes. Feel like I'm taking advantage."

Noel waved him off. "Happy to help, and the kids were super fun."

The kids were not fun. The kids were obnoxious pukes. But Noel Bland was too nice to let that bother him, so he let it go, pulling and gathering, pulling and gathering, until he'd wrapped the rope in a neat butterfly coil. He hung the coil on a hook and glanced up at the tinkling of the bell above the storefront door. A woman in a peasant skirt strolled in, accompanied by an eight-year-old boy capped with a dark bramble of curls.

"Family." Grayson rounded the desk, arms out to enfold the new arrivals. "My beautiful wife and the Infernal Fernster."

Noel waved. "Hey, Tara."

"Hey, yourself." Tara flipped her blonde braid over her freckled shoulder as Fern disentangled himself from the parental group hug. "I was going to call you. My cousin can't stop talking about you since the barbecue. He says you're sweet as cherry pie."

Noel offered up a bashful smile. "He said that?"

"Can I give him your digits?"

Tara's smile and voice were cheerful as ever, but Noel noticed she was pale under her freckles. He hung the last rope on its hook and made his way up to the front. "I appreciate it, Tare-bear. But I basically fled Los Angeles for Granolatown to get away from relationship drama."

Tara leaned back against her husband. "So, have some fun. Call it a rebound."

Noel frowned. "Do you not like your cousin?"

Grayson slid his arms around her waist. "Babe, sometimes a guy needs to be a lone wolf."

"Yeah, Mom. You're being embarrassing," Fern added.

Tara threw her hands up in weary surrender. Fern held out his fist and Noel bumped it with his own. "Ditching summer camp, mister?"

"Dentist. And I got no cavities. Not even one. Wanna see?" Fern opened his mouth wide.

Noel chucked the boy under the chin. "You'll want to keep that up. No one trusts a fella with a mouthful of rotten chompers."

"Who told you that?"

Noel turned his hands into pretend claws. "A monster...with perfect teeth." Fern giggled, but covered his mouth immediately as if remembering that giggles were for girls or babies or something.

Grayson held Tara's face between his craggy hands. "Whassup, pretty lady?"

"Give us a lift home? We hoofed it into town, but it's hot already, and I've got this headache. Came on suddenly."

"Aw, babe," Grayson kissed the top of her head. "Sure, just lemme—shit, I've got another class in five minutes."

Slinging his backpack over one shoulder, Noel seized the opportunity. "I'm headed out. Want a ride?"

Tara smiled weakly. "You're a lifesaver."

"Cherry."

"Smartass," she said and then laid her hand on Grayson's scruffy cheek. He turned his head, pressing his lips into her palm. Noel found the intimacy between the two of them repellant and riveting. Fern stared at the ceiling, supremely bored.

"Take care of your mom, Fernster," said Grayson as they filed out the door. The bell tinkled above as Noel absconded with Grayson's wife and child.

Once inside Noel's appropriately dull electric sedan, Tara fell into silence, staring out the window. Noel checked his rearview mirror. In the backseat Fern's curls bounced over his forehead as he bopped along to music piped into his earphones. "Want to take him to his day camp?"

"He's staying with me," Tara said.

"Okey doke." Noel drove down an avenue lined with elm trees. "Tara, I didn't mean to be rude about your cousin, I'm just not ready to—"

"I'm pregnant."

"What?" Noel stopped at a red light.

Tara peeked over her shoulder at Fern, still bopping away. "Grayson has so much going on, I didn't want to drop it on him in the middle of his day." Her pale cheeks flushed. "Is it weird that I'm telling you?"

"A bit," Noel said, and laughed at her dismayed expression. "C'mon, Tara. You say whatever you need to. Stays right here."

Noel wasn't surprised that Tara would confide in him. Noel was an expertly designed trap, after all. Built on the affable moose platform, everything about Noel invited confidence. He was kind and capable, the solid buddy, the gay best friend—a bit of spite that would send Radcliffe into fits were he not already dead. The point was, people trusted Noel.

"Did the test while Fern was in the dentist's chair. Not a minute later, I got a phone call."

"Yeah?"

She crossed her arms over her stomach. "Some chirpy hag from Citizen Wellness. Seems the tests are bugged now."

"Dang."

"She blabbers on about their schedule of required doctor's visits, blood work, and ultrasounds. Gave me the hard sell on signing my family up for that horrible Guardian program. Implanted microchips. Can you believe it? They want to tag us like animals."

Noel's hand strayed from the wheel to rub the nearly invisible scar on his inner arm. "So, don't do it. Guardian is voluntary."

"There's a moment, y'know? You're on the toilet, staring at the stick you peed on. Suddenly you've got a little secret inside you, and you're the only one who knows." Her hand splayed over her abdomen. "They knew before I did."

Noel steeled himself against cringing when she clamped her freckled hand over his. Her wedding ring dug into his knuckle.

"This world, Noel. It's terrible to say when so many people can't have babies at all, but it might be best if this one didn't take."

Noel agreed. Years of poisoned air and water left a good portion of the already decimated population with limping sperm and rotten eggs. The human race was in danger of extinction, which Panopticon used to justify their lurid intrusion into people's reproductive business, especially when it came to successful breeders like Tara Hillaby. Noel didn't understand the drive to procreate. Fern was a tolerable kid and all, but why would anyone deliberately add another sheep to Panopticon's dull-witted flock? What was the point?

Noel parked in the shade of a pear tree. Fern was already unbuckling his seatbelt.

"Later, crocodile," Noel said.

"In a while, alligator," Fern replied.

Noel watched Fern sprint across the lawn to the Hillaby's ramshackle bungalow. A place where Noel had been invited to share their meals, their laughter, their life. He pulled his hand out from under Tara's. The tug of her skin against his made his stomach crawl up inside itself.

"Thanks for the lift," she said.

Noel gave her a sympathetic smile. "Talk to Grayson, okay? Tonight. Sooner the better. Get things sorted."

Tara swallowed hard. "Okay."

Fern called to her from the porch. She ducked out of the car and Noel drove off, hoping she'd take his advice.

CHAPTER 15

LONGS PEAK, COLORADO,
PAN AMERICAN DIVISION

Noel jumped off the Broadway Ledge into thin air. Nylon rope zinged over his gloved palms as he rappelled down the lichen-stippled rock of Alexander's Chimney in the Colorado Rockies.

"Noel," Grayson called from above, following him into the shade of the Chimney. "Where's the fire? Control the descent."

Noel slowed the play of rope through his hands. "Sorry. Gee whiz, it's easy to get carried away. This is riot."

"Yeah, it's riot." Grayson slapped his chalky hand against the rock face. "But that's a three-hundred-foot drop. You go splat, so does my business, true?"

"Right," Noel said. "Splatness equals flatness equals very bad things."

Grayson sent down a grinning thumbs-up, and they continued to rappel in silence but for the muted tap and scrape of their shoes on limestone. "I got a confession, buddy. Didn't invite you out here just to climb a mountain."

"Oh yeah?"

"How'd you like to go out with me tonight?"

"I don't fool with married men."

"Not asking for a date, handsome." Grayson smoothly descended until they were side by side.

"Okay," Noel said, clutching his rope with both hands. "What's going on?"

Grayson pointed to the sky. "Remember the rush up there? Top of the rock, no one but God watching?"

Noel gave him the side eye. "God?"

"I'm talking about freedom, buddy. We go through life, tracked, monitored, and profiled. They know everything about us, and what do we know about them? Nothing. Panopticon is a shadow regime with total control and zero accountability. They claim they saved the world, but all they did was turn it into a prison. And it's not just the cameras. We got GPS tracking in our cars and phones. They log everything we read, watch, and listen to. They censor the media. Redact our emails. Now there's this fucking Guardian chip."

Noel winced because hard words hurt him in all his soft feelings. "This rant have a pointy end?"

Anchoring his feet, Grayson played out his rope and laid back until he hung almost perpendicular to the rock, facing up into the true blue sky. "There's a meeting tonight. With people who remember how things used to be. I want you to come."

Noel gauged their distance from the ground. "Didn't realize you were so political."

"There are no politics in a police state. The tech they use to spy on us out there is bad enough. With Guardian, they're inside you. And if you shine on the chip, they figure you're a subversive. That's when the baggers come."

Noel's shoe brushed over the rock, sending a crumble of dust downward. "Grayson, you're playing with super-serious fire. You've got a wife and a kid. You need to have a care."

"That's why I need good men I can trust." Grayson gripped Noel's shoulder. "You'd give a stranger the last cred in your pocket and the skin off your back if they were jammed up bad enough. You'll turn the other cheek, but you won't look the other way. You tell me I'm wrong about that."

Wrong, Grayson. Way wrong.

"Jeez, okay." Noel shrugged Grayson's hand off his shoulder. "I'll go to this meeting, but no promises."

"Meet me at the clubhouse at eight. We'll go together."

"Yeah. I'd rather get there on my own."

Grayson pushed his sunglasses back on his head. "You don't trust me?"

"Man, you basically told me you're a flippin' Jackal. A terrorist."

Grayson pulled a face. "I'm no terrorist."

"We could get remapped just for talking about this stuff. For all I know you're gonna drive me out to the Waste and leave me for the kites."

Grayson's mouth opened. A pause in breath. Eyelids twitching. Noel knew this look. A man on the verge of acting against his instincts. Grayson drummed his fingers on the rock. "Sorry buddy, but rules are rules. First meet, I gotta bring you in under a blindfold."

INFRACTUS

Damn. Noel hoped it wouldn't come to this, but they were only two hundred feet to the base of the Chimney. Panopticon wanted information and an accident. If he waited much longer, the fall wouldn't kill the most unterrifying terrorist in the blighted blue world. Noel had served his purpose and was no longer useful. His smile vanished as he dropped one hand from the rope and let his shoulders fall back, loose and relaxed. He tilted his head side to side, stretching his neck. The novice tension and mildly dumb sweetness dissolved, revealing someone quite different.

Grayson braced his feet and leaned away. "Noel?"

"Not really." The assassin tilted his head back, pinched the blue contact lens out of his green eye, and blinked rapidly before refocusing on his target. "Much better."

Grayson shook his head. "Who are you?"

"No one you want to know."

Grayson scrambled. Not far. It was called a chimney for a reason. The assassin locked his belay tube, retrieved a utility knife from his waist pouch, and took hold of Grayson's rope. "Sharing time, Grayson. You're going to tell me where that meeting is and what you and your Jackal buddies are up to."

Grayson jammed his hand into a small gap in the rock. "Really think I'll rat out my crew?"

"You know how this ends. The question is what happens next. Did you know Tara's pregnant?"

Grayson blanched. "What?"

"She told me yesterday, when I had her and your son, alone, in my car."

"Stay away from my family, you bastard."

"For what it's worth, I don't do kids."

"Tara doesn't know anything."

"Don't be so sure."

"I swear she doesn't."

"Swear all you like. I said I wouldn't hurt Fern, but I will kill his mother in front of him if you don't start talking. Now."

Grayson's clear eyes clouded. "Mile west of town. Brown trailer off the 119."

"And what are you working on? The truth please, I'll know if you're lying."

"We're going to bust Ori Mane out of the colony."

"Jesus, Grayson." The assassin shook his head. "If I had an old-world dime for every Jackal scheming to—and how exactly were you and your oatmeal eating militia going to accomplish this?"

"Exactly?" Grayson said. "We haven't figured that part out yet."

The assassin withdrew the knife and hung from his rope, honestly disappointed. Why did every Jackal seem to think they could waltz into the Colony, aka Area 51, aka the most heavily fortified military installation on the planet, and waltz out with Ori Mane on their shoulders? Few had seen the Colony in person. Even if Grayson got past the ground patrol, there were aerial assault drones to contend with, not to mention traversing the canyon circling the colony itself.

A shame. Grayson Hillaby was a good man. If Panopticon had known about this crackpot plan ahead of time, they might have simply had him remapped. Although given the choice between an electrochemical lobotomy and a bullet, the assassin knew what he'd pick.

"Are you ready?" the assassin asked.

"You must hate this part," Grayson said. "After throwing yourself into it, sharing our lives. Must hurt to let go."

Conflict rose up in the assassin like a flash flood. "You don't know a thing about me."

Grayson released his fingerstack hold in the rock. "I know you can be better."

The assassin acted fast, grabbing Grayson's hair, yanking his head back, and smashing his face into the rock. Bone crunched. The impact screamed up the assassin's arm and into his shoulder.

Unconscious, the mark dangled in his harness, chin to chest, blood dripping from his forehead. Perhaps a fatal injury, not that it needed to be. The assassin positioned the knife precisely where he'd made the first shallow cut, and sliced clean through.

Cratering from a height of two hundred feet, a body didn't break, it burst.

"Nothing personal," the assassin muttered to the mess at the bottom of the chimney. Preventable accidents were the best kind.

I'm an invisible mist in the pines, far enough away that he won't get the hinky feeling of being watched. I'm cautious about that now. Can't risk rocking the boat so close to the end of the voyage. From here he's particularly small against the mountain. A tiny pebble, yet so much depends on which way he rolls. I watch him zip down the chimney at a speed that makes me nervous. I saw him fall once. You could say it left an impression.

❖❖❖

Outside the Hillaby's house in Boulder, the assassin peered through the kitchen window. He saw Fern on the living room floor, crawling around a partially assembled jigsaw puzzle, studying it from all angles while Tara curled on the couch, braid trailing over her shoulder. She read from the tablet on her lap and sucked on an orange Popsicle.

Panopticon hadn't marked Tara, nor would they. Breeders were valuable, and babies were breadbox godlets. The assassin knew precisely two things about infants. They made noise and excreted different sorts of slime. He'd been a baby once. Clearly hadn't impressed his mother overmuch. If he were to tell Tara he'd been dumped on the steps of a fire station hours after being whelped, what would she make of it?

She smiled around her Popsicle and laughed. A few hours of light remained. Soon, she wouldn't be smiling. For an instant he wanted to knock on the door. She'd invite Noel in, offer him a Popsicle. He'd help Fern with his puzzle and maybe ask Tara what she'd been reading. He wondered if she always read on tablet, or if she preferred old world paper like he did. You could learn a lot about a person based on the condition of their books. Dog-eared pages and cracked spines, or crisp and smooth from gentle handling? He wondered if Tara kept a journal.

You must hate this part.

Shut up, Grayson.

From his backpack the assassin retrieved a plastic bag and set it on the porch. Twenty-five thousand creds. Half his pay for murdering her husband. Grayson staked his life on Tara's ignorance, but in the assassin's experience, women had a way of knowing things. Things they couldn't. Things they shouldn't. Tara was too smart not to put her husband's accident and Noel's disappearance together. Panopticon didn't like people who were too smart. Hopefully she was smart enough to keep quiet, for Fern's sake, and that of her baby—if she managed a live one. And the money would come in handy for her.

Compensation. Nothing more. Take what you've earned and pay what you owe. Good advice from a bad man. The assassin made these anonymous drops all the time, but Tara would know who left this one because Grayson was no ordinary mark. He was a good man.

The assassin checked his watch. Time to go. Panopticon would be tracking him soon, if they weren't already.

CHAPTER 16

THE WASTE,
PAN AMERICAN DIVISION

anopticon is pleased to announce streamlined Guardian registration. Simply fill in an online request and within twenty-four hours a technician will arrive for the in-home consult and implantation. The procedure is comfortable, convenient, and provided at no end user cost. Citizens registered with Guardian enjoy improved outcomes from injury and illness, and early studies suggest an increase in rate of conception and live births. With continuous location and vital sign monitoring, Citizens and their children will never be without access to emergency assistance and medical care. Panopticon protects families. Register yours today.

The assassin snapped off the Streamcast as the car's electric motor hummed up to speed on the divisional highway. Noel Bland had done his job. It was a relief to go back to being no one.

A feeble whine slithered from the Citizen-A's motor when the assassin put the accelerator to the floor. Christ, it would be nice to have a real car. Something old world, like that gorgeous Mercedes he'd relinquished years ago. But Suit One's prediction had come true. C-As were the most common mode of private transport in the Pan American Division, and common was the first step toward being invisible.

Thanks to some clever tampering, the GPS upload would report Noel Bland's car traveling south. But in fact, the assassin was headed northeast through the Waste.

He squinted through his sunglasses as he drove down the crumbling state highway. Around 8:00 p.m. he passed a Welcome To Iowa sign collapsed over a newer model C-A with the doors ripped off and two empty baby seats still strapped in the back. The assassin never traveled unarmed, but when he drove through the Waste, he packed extra heavy.

At dusk he pulled off the highway, onto a narrow lane running through a cornfield. Twisted stalks battered the sides of the car. Warped remnants of old world agriculture gone wild, re-seeding themselves year after year. The assassin stopped the car and retrieved his tablet from his bag. Time for some housekeeping.

Panopticon kept tabs on everyone, especially its operatives. The assassin disliked being tracked, and false GPS data was just the beginning of his elaborate misdirection. Using a cloned ID, he logged into the public transportation network. A few keystrokes placed Deacon Priest on a jet leaving Houston, bound for Italy.

Like Noel, Deacon Priest was a known entity. Panopticon would follow Deacon's digital trail across the Atlantic as he checked into an expensive hotel in Venice, and ordered up cheap champagne and two top-shelf traders. Women, because unlike Noel, the Deacon persona was aggressively hetero. Prostitutes, because Panopticon would expect some mild misbehavior from Deacon. Panopticon was all about math. If traceable movements fell within predictive parameters, they'd believe he was in Venice getting laid, when in fact he was alone in the middle of the Waste.

The assassin got out of the car and stretched his stiff arms and legs. He popped the trunk and retrieved a jar of peanut butter, a loaf of bread, and a bottle of water. With his SIG at his side, he ate sandwiches and watched fireflies emerge to light up the encroaching darkness.

The job was done, but his stubborn worry about Tara remained. Grief made people unpredictable. If she made a fuss she'd get remapped and Fern would get shunted into the system. The assassin knew first-hand how that story ended. He threw his half-eaten sandwich into the field for the rabbits.

Embedded work. Most operatives couldn't handle it without getting emotional or fucking up. A few years ago, it was Lusczak. Dumb, brutal, notoriously obedient Lusczak. He'd infiltrated a medium threat Jackal cell and bought himself a dozen bullets when one of them got suspicious. Suit One claimed Lusczak perished in the line of duty. But Suit Two let the truth slip. They didn't make him. He blew his own cover. What can I say, kid? He was done.

But the assassin wasn't even close to done. He was fine. Tired, maybe. Working round the clock for the last two months. Noel Bland was the best guy ever. He wore a natural fiber wardrobe, employed lexical throwbacks like "gee whiz," and smiled all the goddamn time. Noel Bland was exhausting.

Maybe he should have boarded a plane to Venice. He imagined sprawling on a soft bed in a dark room, pigeons warbling in the morning and the spiraling songs of the gondoliers at night. A vacation would be a tolerable change. Booze and sex. Except he had the alcohol tolerance of a nine-year-old, and the mere suggestion of being naked and interlocking with a stranger left him limp as a dead earthworm. He'd far rather be in the middle of an irradiated cornfield where the fireflies outnumbered the stars. His eyelids grew heavy.

A moment later he jolted awake to full dark and a deep chill settling into his muscles, stiff from a day of climbing. "Fuck," he muttered, glancing at his watch to find three hours ripped from his life in the space of a long blink and a sense that he'd gone somewhere, said something, or seen someone. And he couldn't remember. He could never remember.

Not only that, but for those three hours he'd been prime kite bait. So, he packed it in and vowed to keep his eyes wide open until he'd cleared the Waste.

He drove another full day, catching a few hours of sleep outside the post-nuclear ruins of Chicago. Then more driving. Over darkened roads and sudden bridges. He drove and drove until he ran out of dry land.

At one in the morning, the assassin stood on a beach outside Bar Harbor, Maine. Rolling waves whispered in the deep coastal darkness. Grayson Hillaby was a good man.

You must hate this part.

Sweat beaded on the back of his neck, cold as gunmetal against the warm night. He trudged away from the surf, away from the whispering water. A word. A name. Something he knew, but couldn't remember. A very bad thing.

INFRACTUS

Some jobs were tough, and he'd been doing this long enough to recognize his own pattern. The kill, the getaway, and the brooding. He hiked up to the boardwalk and from there headed toward the glimmering lights of town. He had a safe house in the nearby Acadia wilderness preserve, but he'd go there later. Right now, he needed a diversion.

The Beluga. A riot-leveled dive on the docks, with sticky booths, and a long bar covered in about a hundred flaking coats of varnish. A few traders scoped him out, but not one of the dozen or so patrons lifted their heads when he crossed the floor and climbed onto a stool. The bartender shoveled ice into a glass, poured an imprecise measure of clear spirit, and slid it across the bar.

The assassin picked up the glass and sniffed. "Blueberries?"

"Lowbush," the bartender said. "House special."

Panopticon's onerous restrictions on liquor drove most pubs to source their own moonshine. And it was special all right. Though not as vile as some of Zee's homebrewed experiments back in the day. He knocked it back and signaled for another.

As he lingered over his fourth draught of ichor, a beautiful trader perched on the next stool. "Don't see too many fellas from away in he-yuh. You like Bar Hah-bah so fah?"

Not his type. Too young. Too harmless. A conversation though? Why the hell not? Sometimes he liked conversation. With people. Talking good.

Bar Harbor was very fine so far, thank you. The trader smiled prettily, and before an intoxicated diversion morphed into a rare craving for human contact, the assassin pressed two hundred creds into the beautiful boy's hands. "Go away."

A few solitary ounces later, the assassin wondered what was worse, lowbush, or a bullet to the brainpan. He scraped a nail along the bubbled lacquer on the edge of the bar. The crash of waves against the pilings below tumbled through his brain like heavy fog.

The front door swung open, banging against the wall. The assassin nearly fell off his stool. Two men lumbered in, one after the other, their tiny heads squeezed between massive shoulders. They stomped up to the bar, dragging with them the stench of lobster boat.

"Couple o' glasses," one of the two grunted at the bartender. "An' don't think none about wahterin' her down."

The bartender nodded, eyes on the pour. Satisfied, the lobstermen turned their broad backs to the bar and made a show of casing the room the way mean drunks do when they're fixing to start a fire. Their attention settled on the beautiful trader, now sitting alone in a booth with his phone, texting away the minutes until closing. The lobstermen gestured and joked loudly between them. The boy's lovely features pinched when the oafs began clomping across the floor in his direction. Someone needed to throw a blanket over this. The assassin felt a craving for human contact coming on.

Getting their attention was not difficult. A slurred taunt about dogs and cats, or mothers and sisters, he couldn't remember. Nor could he remember who hurled the first fist. The first of many.

Seriously? How many times do I have to keep you from drowning yourself?

INFRACTUS

The trader's body is smaller and weaker than the one I'm used to occupying and I can feel the soul in here with me, freaking out. Once I vacate he'll lose memory of the experience, but it's still uncomfortable. I miss being able to physically manifest like I used to. In my own skin, not some borrowed shell. I'm restless. Eager to spread my wings, so to speak.

I stumble and fall back on my unfamiliar ass. His waterlogged weight presses me down into the sand, and he doesn't stir as I wriggle out from beneath him. He goaded those goons into beating him unconscious, but now he's fallen into the deep sleep of the dead drunk. This is a moment I don't intend to waste. I sink my fingers into his wet hair. Black as purgatory. I press my smooth young cheek to his and kiss his cold mouth, tasting blood. He groans softly. An unconscious utterance. An old name he breathes into me before I can pull away.

"Michael."

The assassin woke expecting fire. Instead his senses were swamped with crashing surf, wet sand between his fingers, and a briny stink in his nose. He squinted into an overcast sky. Smoke, he could have sworn he smelled it. He propped himself up, triggering a cascade of sharp and dull aches through every muscle. His face itched under a wash of dried blood, the taste of rotten blueberries filled his mouth, and his clothes were covered in what appeared to be a crust of vomit and low-tide detritus.

He fell back into the sand with a painful thud. "This is why we can't have nice things."

INFRACTUS

A breeze drooled over him and something vibrated at the small of his back. His phone. Deacon's phone. They were calling him? He contorted like a rusty robot until he could reach his jacket pocket. According to the phone, it was seven in the morning in Bar Harbor, but their intel would place him in Venice where it was eight, or six hours, whatever. Deacon had a busy night. He'd be sleeping it off. The phone rang and rang.

He ignored the screech of his ribs and filled his lungs with salty air, exchanging the crisp chill of the Atlantic for the dank heat of the Adriatic, cementing himself into character. Deacon Priest. The taste of bad choices and stiff, aching everything provided solid framework for the fiction. Never be yourself if you can help it, Mouse.

Just before the call rolled, Deacon picked up. "What."

"Mr. Priest. What a pleasure." Suit One enunciated in his distinctive way that made even vowels sound pointy.

Deacon yawned, envisioning the hotel room. Heavy wood, white walls, drawn curtains. In the shadows he could make out empty bottles and half-eaten plates of Venetian room service. Champagne flutes marked with lipstick. Two shades. Stagnant air thick with alcohol, perfume, and expensive sex.

"Is this a bad time?" Suit One inquired.

The assassin imagined long hair trailing across rumpled sheets. The slope of a female shoulder, her arm draped over the other sleeping trader. Hopefully the squawking gulls passed for warbling pigeons over the airwaves. A headache stomped his eyes shut.

"You'd better have a good reason for calling me."

"How is Venice?"

"What do you want?"

"We have an assignment. Time sensitive. Though we deeply regret troubling you, Mr. Priest."

"Don't call me that."

"What would you prefer I call you? Noel Bland, Carrall Hastings...Mouse? Surely you've outgrown that silly moniker."

"I'd prefer you not call me anything, or ever." He winced as a needle of pain stabbed his eye. Suit One didn't get it. Every alias represented a shard of his personality. He'd yet to come across a single name able to fuse them all, and so he lived as a collection of splinters. "Why are you calling me? Where's Suit Two?"

"Indisposed and behaving herself, I hope. Is a little cooperation too much to ask, Mr. Priest? We're on the same side."

The hell we are. He bridled at Suit One's passive probing, doublespeak: "we this" and "we that." At least Suit Two had no interest in toeing the Panopticon line. She simply liked to hunt people down and kill them. So much easier to talk to. Unbidden, an image unfolded in his mind of her dark hair and smirking shark face on the hotel pillow next to his.

"How time sensitive?"

"Seven days. Shall we arrange transport?"

He plucked a rope of seaweed off his legs and hurled it back in the water. "I'll take care of it."

"Very good. And while we've got you—"

"Got me?"

"An expression, Mr. Priest. You've taken great pains to ensure that we have no means of directly tracking you." Keys clacked in the background. "Not to worry, we understand and even appreciate your...eccentricities."

With the drag of the needle over his brain, the assassin understood and appreciated that Suit One was a liar who regarded the assassin as an enormous chore and as soon as he ceased to be of use to them, he'd be worm food.

"Your last assignment," said Suit One. "Did you extract the location of Grayson Hillaby's cell and the nature of his activities?"

The assassin felt a bout of eccentricity coming on. "No."

"He wouldn't talk?"

"No."

"You couldn't persuade him?"

"No."

"I'm surprised. You're a man of considerable skill in this area."

The assassin rubbed his forehead with the heel of his hand. "You know how these true believers are. They can name, rank, and serial number their way through a live flaying."

"A logical argument."

"More logical than sending a hitter for information."

"Reductive, don't you think, Mr. Priest? Regarding this new assignment, if you feel we've overestimated your ability to meet multiple objectives . . .?"

"Said I'd take care of it, didn't I?"

"Then we won't keep you from your guests a moment longer. We imagine you have yet a few more hours to make the most of...Venice."

An electronic snap terminated the call. The assassin threw the phone onto the sand, grinding a filthy word between his molars. It was a ticklish relationship he maintained with Panopticon. He didn't trust them. They didn't trust anyone. He should have seen this coming. They wanted Grayson dead, but they didn't need any information because they already knew.

Always a game with them. Always their game.

The innuendo about torture. The implication that the assassin enjoyed cruelty for cruelty's sake. As if he were that simple. Physical pain could be useful and interesting, but the anticipation of pain? That peak of psychological sensitivity? That was something else. Spinning on that sharp point was a unique kind of torment, and it fed something in him, made him the worst kind of sadist and the only operative capable of breaking Grayson Hillaby in a manner both brutal and bloodless. A few strategic threats against Tara, and Grayson disintegrated like a paper soldier in a wet trench. He'd died a traitor to the men who'd trusted him and betrayed by a man he trusted. A friend.

The assassin hauled himself off the beach, located his car by the decommissioned ferry terminal, and found a nearby charging station where he locked himself in the restroom to wash up and inventory the damage.

Under the filth and blood his face wasn't bad. The rest was a different story. His arms and legs were a mass of bruises and livid boot prints decorated his ribs, which struck him as funny, until he laughed and immediately doubled over, gasping.

Certainly, it wasn't the first time he'd picked a fight he knew he couldn't win. He thought of Zee, smart enough to rule the world, yet he'd chosen the gritty life of a street person. And Suit Two, shrouded in scars. Were all creatures with few natural predators compelled to destroy themselves?

Dressed in clean clothes from his bag, the assassin plugged his car into the pillar. Like the other customers waiting for their batteries to charge, he reclined in the front seat of his car, rolled down the windows, and switched on his tablet. He'd considered stalling another twelve hours, just to be belligerent, but that might elicit another detestable phone call. Is a little cooperation too much to ask? Yes, it sure as hell was. The aversion ran deep, all the way down to his misanthropic nucleotides. He did not play well with others.

The file decrypted.

Name: Liza Ayomori

CIN: 3784-26097

Location: Kaylee, California, Pan American Division

*August 15th; terrorist attack; public; blade preferred.

From his bag, he retrieved a pencil and notebook. Relics. Most people wrote on devices, and restricted drive space forced the use of cloud storage. The assassin had a contraband three-terabyte drive, but in strategy mode he still preferred the physical continuity of pencil to paper.

He called up the public record database. These days everything was public. Only the Eye didn't have someone looking over its shoulder. Not that anyone would know where to look. Panopticon had their mirrored buildings, their departments and directors, and a parade of official mouthpieces on the Stream. Marionettes. Whoever tugged the strings kept hidden behind the stage.

Liza's citizen ident came up first. Headshot on the left. Vital stats on the right. Born in East Asia Division. Redesignated to Pan American Division at age three. Black hair, brown eyes, five feet, one hundred pounds. A little thing. And young. In seven days, Liza would be eighteen years old.

No kids. It paid to be flexible in life, but this was a hard line he'd drawn. His only rule, and his reasoning was simple: what kind of psycho kills kids? Not that Panopticon had any reason to murder children. They were a resource with no sense of old world entitlement to things like privacy or inalienable human rights. And children were a threatened species.

He thought back to the incident in the Waste with Suit Two and that baby Jackal, but this was different. In one week Liza would be an adult, however nascent. With that in mind he approached the job like he would any other.

Delving further into the public record, he began to construct a profile. Liza lived with her parents and attended the university in Kaylee. First year pre-med. Before that, secondary Ed was a deluge of activity. Mathlete—so that still existed—environmental club, yearbook committee, first chair flute, debate team, swim team, golf team, chess team, knitting circle...Jesus Christ, no wonder they wanted her dead.

Typically, his targets were legitimate garbage. Liza wasn't the kind of trash he usually wheeled out to the curb. Next, he hacked into the Eye's surveillance cloud. Proper stalking—with a dark green van, binoculars, and legwork—yielded more reliable information. But at the moment, the digital ether was all he had. Surely, he would find evidence of something horrific. He jotted down notes, savoring the scratch of graphite on paper.

Evil Robot

Cannibal

Slam Poet

He rapped his pencil on the paper. Electronic metadata only painted a more vibrant portrait of perfection. The details on Liza. She swam on weekday mornings before classes, called her grandmother on Wednesday nights, tutored with her father every Monday, and visited one Ayham Geremia in his dorm two or three evenings a week. More tutoring? Unlikely, since she rarely left before midnight. Liza had a lover. Seemed frivolous in contrast to the rest of her life, but nevertheless Liza and Ayham were in contact multiple times a day by phone and text and they went to old world movie screenings most weekends. These things pointed to a comprehensive relationship, which meant boyfriend. Perhaps former, as all contact had come to a halt three days ago.

A green light blinked on the dash, indicating a fully charged battery. The assassin shoved the tablet back in his bag. Off-grid mischief was possible, but when? Almost all her time was electronically accounted for. Doubtful she had phony avatars bumbling about the mainframe like he did. To his knowledge only Barclay could hack that deep, and his services weren't advertised in the directory.

Occam's razor held that if it walks like a duck and talks like a duck, it's probably not a zebra. This wasn't about anything Liza did. It was about headlines. An innocent butchered by a Jackal on her eighteenth birthday. The Streamcast practically wrote itself.

The road through the Acadia wilderness preserve wound up and around Mount Desert Island. Granite boulders and ocean on one side. Dense forest on the other. The assassin left his car in the Cadillac Mountain turnout and continued on foot down an old carriage road. The booming ocean faded as he hiked deeper into the woods, hemmed in by stands of cedar, larch, and spruce.

When he came to a stone bridge, he climbed down the shallow ravine. Under the bridge, in a crack in the abutment, he found the iron latch. He dug his heels into the spongy carpet of larch needles and tugged. The door was on hydraulic hinges, but still a solid slab of granite, and his ribs protested as he wrenched it open just wide enough to squeeze through.

Earthy air wafted out of the tomb. He ducked inside and switched on the light. The eight by ten space contained two fuel cells, a small heater, a cot, and a storage unit that ran the entire length of the far wall.

He had other safe houses across the PAD. Regular apartments, held in the names of aliases unknown to Panopticon. But the Acadia installation was the most secure, in spite of having no security at all aside from a hidden latch on a goddamn heavy door. During prohibition the place had been a cache for booze smuggled over from Yarmouth, Nova Scotia. He only found it because he'd been a weird kid who went through an obsession with the diaries of maritime rumrunners. Old world history books were rare these days. The assassin doubted there were many people alive who would think to search for an ancient smuggler's hole on a sparsely populated island.

Acadia was his vault. A place to keep things he didn't want to lose.

Firearms occupied most of the storage unit. A variety of pistols, his treasured Springfield rifle, ammunition, and components for explosive devices. But he didn't need a gun for this assignment. He opened the bottom drawer of the unit and pulled a small strongbox from under a folded army blanket.

He sat on the cot with the box in his lap and lifted the steel lid. The box contained only four items. A white braid, a tattered bible, a cake of gold-flecked rosin still bearing the score marks of a bow, and a copper dragon, glass eyes glinting in the low light. One green, one blue. Handling these objects used to make him angry. Angry because he still didn't know who he was, because Jenny and Sister Claudia were dead and he missed them, because Zee was probably alive and he missed that bastard even more. But the years banked his anger. Now he felt nothing. He closed the box and slid it back into the drawer.

Absently rubbing the boot prints on his ribs, he opened another cabinet and took out a med kit containing painkillers and bandages. He'd need both for the next few days. Finally, he opened one of the long drawers and evaluated his assortment of blades neatly arranged in their proper slots. Decisions, decisions.

CHAPTER 17

KAYLEE, CALIFORNIA,
PAN AMERICAN DIVISION

Deacon Priest waited in his car across the street from Liza Ayomori's house on a chilly northern California morning. He dragged his windbreaker out of a backpack covered with HALO decals in varying stages of peel and flake. For all his oversexed alpha swagger, Deacon Priest was an enormous geek. He couldn't get enough of old world video games. He'd found the backpack years ago in an abandoned kite nest and had to keep it. Nostalgia, perhaps. At the Facility, he hadn't gotten along great with the other recruits, but grudges were holstered for the sake of the occasional HALO night.

Deacon fed his arms into the sleeves of his windbreaker and studied his reflection in the rearview mirror. Five days post-brawl, a bit of yellow discoloration remained around one eye, and he had a small cut on his forehead. Nothing that would attract attention.

Early light flooded the street but the curtains remained drawn across the picture window of the Ayomori's split-level. The houses on either side differed minimally. Swept porches, tidy flowerbeds, and lawns sparkling with dew. What would it be like to grow up here? On a street where people wrapped their roses in burlap on frosty nights, and even the gutters were spotless.

In the space of a generation, Panopticon had taken the world from wreckage to utopia, at least it seemed that way here in the suburbs. But Deacon's mere presence on this street proved that things were not always as they appeared.

At 6:47 a.m., the front door opened. Liza Ayomori was different in person. Not radically. Just rounder. Slightly plumper than he'd expected. This was why he did his own surveillance. Digital couldn't tell you everything.

Rounder-in-real-life Liza had dressed for the chill in a bulky sweater with her jacket zipped halfway. A backpack hung off her shoulders and a tote bag swung from her hand. She tucked her hair behind her ears, closed her eyes and stood on the porch, facing the sun. Taking a moment. Deacon liked her already.

When he'd first arrived in Kaylee, Deacon drove up and down every street within a mile radius of the Ayomori residence. Next, he'd studied a map of the city's pathways. Familiarizing himself with the mark's environment. He applied the routine to every job, even the milk runs. Procedures were important.

Some details. Liza lived less than a mile from the university and had neither a driver's license nor a bicycle permit. Based on that, Deacon figured she walked to school. Likely alone. Ayham Geremia lived on campus and none of her other friends were enrolled in the summer session. Once Liza's blue-soled sneakers rounded the corner, Deacon got out of his car, shouldered his own backpack, and followed.

INFRACTUS

Liza took the route he'd plotted as being most likely, leaving the residential area, and turning onto a busy street running along the river. A footbridge ferried them across the water, and it was another bustling half-block to the campus. Liza walked quickly but her head hung down and she fiddled with the straps of the backpack as if she were uncomfortable.

Deacon waited on a bench under an oak tree when Liza passed through the glass doors into the athletic center. He wanted to follow. He wanted to watch her hair flow like an ink spill behind her as she cut fearlessly through the water. Too bad creeps who watched young ladies swim were conspicuous. Anyway, he wasn't going to drown her. Not little Liza. The Eye wanted splatter. They wanted Deacon to cut her heart out in the village square. To the casual observer, drowning wasn't that dramatic.

Cutting her heart out wasn't an option either. That would take too long. Which wasn't to say he didn't plan to make a mess, only that he wouldn't dawdle over it. He'd selected an Emerson Commander for the job. A paring knife would get it done, but for Deacon Priest, life was a giant video game and theatrics were critical. Forged in the old world, the Commander's four-inch blade sported a vicious recurve that flashed in the sun and would look deadly on camera.

Liza emerged from the building an hour later, hair damp but neatly combed. Deacon hefted his HALO backpack onto one shoulder and shuffled into the medical sciences building, following Liza to her first class, organic chemistry.

In the lecture theatre, Liza kept her jacket on and sat up straight, not in the front row, but in the seat closest to the exit. Interesting.

INFRACTUS

Deacon slouched into a chair in the back, doing his best to appear not thirty-seven. Luckily, he had an age-ambiguous face. The rest was attitude. A little naïve. A lot sleepy, perhaps from playing first-person shooters all night. Zoned out.

The instructor read from the notes displayed on the view panel. She recited formulas and properties and atomic numbers, gave out the reading for next class, and opened the floor. Deacon expected smartypants Liza to ask a question—probably one she knew the answer to—but she didn't. Instead she typed constant notes, her gaze rising and falling, absently finger combing her hair as the last of the pool water evaporated. Deacon imagined the smell of chlorine on the nape of her neck. That was one area where games failed and real life won every time. Smell made things real.

A young man two rows behind Liza asked about the pharmacological application of a compound they'd studied.

The instructor glanced at her tablet. "That is beyond the scope of this curriculum."

There were no more questions.

Pan U was a place to expand your mind, or rather extend it, on a narrow trajectory that discouraged any detour into critical thought. Deacon was fortunate. The Suits recruited him when he was nineteen, and the world a mere step ahead of ruin. They sold him on the promise of a legit unsanitized old-world education. Overnight he went from being an ignorant gutter mouse to living at the Facility where he spent the next six years feasting at the tree of knowledge like a perspicacious fruit bat.

But the Facility was more prison than school. While the recruits did occasionally discuss Foucault's theories on social control and Nietzschean moral genealogy, their interests ran mainly toward blades, ballistics, and bare hands. They were also big on field trips.

Liza's university offered a civilized landscape of higher learning, though few of the students had ever heard of Foucault. Knowledge was power, and Panopticon was stingy with it.

At lunch, Deacon hid in an alcove in the commons while Liza shared a concrete picnic table with her biology lab partner who chattered at lightspeed while Liza nudged her fruit salad with her fork. Afterward she plodded to her next class, more listless than ever.

That evening, Deacon waited outside Liza's house. Based on her Internet activity log, she spent Tuesday nights studying. At exactly ten o'clock, her window went dark.

Liza was not what he'd expected. She hadn't flung her smarts at the dullard masses. Hadn't made a single comment in class. Why so withdrawn? She'd gone from ravenous joiner to non-playable character. It had to be the boyfriend. She hadn't made contact with Ayham. Probably thought she had all the time in the world to patch things up.

Deacon imagined getting out of the car and knocking on her window. She'd throw back the curtain and lean out in her cupcake pajamas and they'd dialogue. He'd tell her that the game had changed, and she didn't need to worry about Ayham or anything else ever again. All she needed to do now was bleed.

A psychotic storyline, but everyone had dreams. Deacon just had his while he was awake. The electric motor whirred as he drove away down the clean street. "See you tomorrow, Liza."

Deacon rose from the uneven terrain of the hotel mattress after a few broken hours of sleep. In the dark, he crossed the matted carpet and retrieved the knife from his bag. The recurved blade gleamed orange in the light from the parking lot.

She was only a girl. The wet paint in Panopticon's scheme to smear the Jackals with a broad red brush. Rounder-in-real-life Liza was marked, and if he didn't do it, they'd send someone else. Someone bloodthirsty like Ito. At least Deacon could make it fast and near painless, while still putting on a show. He was a professional.

He straightened the bed, squared corners, not a wrinkle in sight. Then he ate a bowl of Cheerios in front of the window. Not his favorite food, but definitely a dietary staple. You could get them anywhere and they tasted exactly the same as they had before A-Day. Beyond the parking lot, traffic lights blinked yellow over the intersection of two empty streets. Liza's city slept hard at night.

Hot water gushed through the scale-stippled showerhead. Standing under the spray, Deacon reviewed the storyline. A wannabe Jackal on a quest to make a name for himself. After the shower, he selected an ancient Borderlands T-shirt for old world street cred. He passed on a shave because the black stubble made him feel like a grizzled marine in Call of Duty.

By the time the sun squinted over the horizon, Deacon was parked across the street from Liza's house. By the time she stepped onto the porch, he just wanted to get it over with.

Again, Liza closed her eyes and smiled into the sun. The same backpack hung from her shoulders and the same tote swung jauntily in her hand as she skipped down the stairs and trotted along the sidewalk. Liza was happy.

Deacon locked onto her as though analyzing her on-screen stats. For a homicidal Jackal's purposes, the girl was perfect. Small enough for easy handling, with a soft plasticity to her, like a doll. He followed her along the street, weaving through the flock making their way to work or school, most of them bleating into their phones. There was no risk of losing her. Liza stood out, her hair bouncing and shiny in the morning sun.

Panopticon wanted gore-streaked witnesses to a random act of brutality. The Streamcasts would be sensational. Loud words, scary bad guys, lock your doors, get a dog, hide your kids, and so on. In a matter of minutes, Deacon Priest would deliver the goods.

Happy birthday, Liza. I'm going to make you famous.

She got on the bridge spanning the sluggish green river. Deacon followed, feeling the wooden deck vibrate with hundreds of footfalls. He began closing the gap between him and his intended.

Then Liza stopped. Deacon lurched to a halt, nearly colliding with her. The tote fell from her hand, plopping onto the deck. She knew. The way women know things. In a slow pivot she faced him, her skin washing out from gold to gray. "Why are you following me?"

INFRACTUS

Time went cross-eyed. Liza was no longer Liza. In her place he saw bleached yellow hair and smudged lipstick. A tattoo circling her wrist. Take care that no one hates you justly. His fingers wrapped around the contoured grip of his knife. Solid. Familiar. Sunlight glared off the recurved blade, momentarily blinding him. He blinked. Time snapped back into focus.

Liza. Not Jenny. Liza Ayomori. The mark. Breathing in quiet hitches, her eyes locked on his knife.

"Please," she whispered.

"It's not personal."

Her hands moved to cradle the small bump stretching the blue linen over her stomach. Rounder-in-real-life Liza. Easy to miss if you weren't looking for it. But now it eclipsed everything. It complicated things. Another pregnant woman? What were the odds? And why would Panopticon mark a breeder? Unless they didn't know. Like hell. They knew, and they wiped that information from her profile because they didn't want him to know. No kids. Did this count? Liza's splayed hands shielded it, as if her soft flesh and bird bones constituted any sort of protection from his blade.

"You don't have to," she pleaded. "You don't."

Droves of pedestrians swept by in both directions. No one paying attention. Not yet. Nothing had changed. She was still the mark. But he was no longer Deacon, the silly video game obsessed persona he'd chosen for this dog of an assignment.

Riot-blighted hell.

The assassin whipped his hand around the back of her neck and drew her close, as if hugging her. Liza's cry jammed in her throat when the knife cut through her shirt to graze the skin of her stomach.

"Quiet, or this thing will be born in pieces."

A whimper pulsed behind her lips.

"I can help you, Liza. But only if you follow my instructions. Understand?"

Her vertebrae slid under his palm as she nodded, and her breath misted through his Borderlands shirt. He smelled her toothpaste and the faint familiar scent of cotton candy. He slipped the pack off her shoulders, letting it fall on top of her tote.

"You swim every day," he said. "Would you say you're a strong swimmer?"

Another nod.

"Good. Now scream, and make it loud."

"But you said—"

"Do it," he snarled, spinning her around to face the foot-traffic, and dragging her back with him until the bridge rail pressed against his spine. He slung his knife arm across her chest, resting the flat of the blade on her shoulder.

Liza's shriek sliced through the commotion like a guillotine.

The shivering deck stilled. Over two hundred people on the bridge, and every one in tableau. The assassin tightened his grip. On the knife. On the girl. On himself.

"You're all sheep!" he shouted in Deacon's commanding voice. "Can't think for yourselves. Food for the machine. Take a good look, people. This is what happens to sheep."

INFRACTUS

The crowd stared, wide-eyed and immobilized.

The assassin whispered in Liza's ear, "Wait for me around the bend, under the train bridge."

"What?"

"Liza, you're going to have to trust me."

He knotted his fingers in her hair, cranked her head back, and cut her throat.

CHAPTER 18

Liza's blood poured hot over the assassin's arm. Not the arterial spray he'd originally planned, but enough to impress.

Enough that she'd die if she didn't get seen to. Enough that she might die anyway.

He waited long enough for any cameras pointed their way to grab a bloody lensful before he scooped Liza up and tossed her over the side of the bridge. The splash was a thunderclap against the cloud of silence. Liza surfaced face down, the current dragging her downstream.

Time to go.

No one screamed. No one tried to stop him. No one moved.

Sheep.

He cleared the crowd in seconds and ran like hell. Every instinct tugged at him to sprint in the other direction, toward the train bridge. But he couldn't be seen headed that way, and Liza Ayomori couldn't be spotted alive. Not now. Not ever again.

Near the car he caught wisps of babble mingled with Security Patrol sirens. Focused behavior was an irresistible lure. One of the flock breaks formation and the rest follow suit. Blighted sheep. Not that it mattered. Not that anything did. His existence narrowed to a single purpose. Save Liza.

INFRACTUS

Critical details. Assuming she didn't drown—she won't; she's young, she's strong—he had maybe ten minutes. Fortunately, he'd poached that med kit from his safe house, but it constituted a stop-loss measure, not a lifesaving one. She'd need stitches, intravenous fluids, and a huge hit of broad spec antibiotic for river amoebas. She needed all of that. Never mind how the thing—the pregnancy—might complicate her situation. But pregnant women had extra blood or something, so that was good...maybe?

This was a terrible plan. It wasn't a plan at all. You couldn't fake a person's death, not in this age of surveillance. But there was no stopping now. As a teenager, he'd been suicidally fond of running across rain-slick Vancouver rooftops at night. The trick was in allowing absolutely no room for caution. Any attempt to slow down would translate into a skid off the edge and a plunge to the pavement.

When he reached Liza's street, he threw himself into the car and sped off down the side roads he'd committed to memory the previous morning. When he swung onto the river boulevard downstream from the bridge, he checked his rearview mirror and saw the crowd swelling the way crowds do at rumors of exceptional events. Deacon Priest gave Panopticon everything they wanted. Almost.

The tires bumped over the curb onto the grassy bank. Beneath the framework of iron and rivets, he spied a sodden heap of discarded clothes swaddling a discarded girl. Gravel dug into his knees as he knelt and rolled her onto her back.

"Liza." He cracked the med kit and ripped open a gauze pack. "Wake up. You have to stay awake."

Her closed eyelids tightened when he pried her clammy fingers from her neck. She coughed, forcing a gout of blood from the six-inch slice across her throat.

"No," she croaked, batting him away. "No, no, no."

"Stop." He caught both her wrists in one of his hands. "Liza, I'm going to help you, but you have to let me."

She didn't fight when he pressed the gauze to her neck. Blood soaked through, so he added another layer, taped it, and brought her left hand back to the bandage. "Keep pressure on it. Like that. Good."

Next, he unfolded his bloody knife, gripped her right wrist and jabbed the tip of the blade into the top of her hand. Liza squirmed, but he held her down, probing around until the blade scraped the edge of something plastic. From there it was a quick if painful matter of prying out the ladybug sized Guardian chip. At least these bugs weren't grafted to a major artery like his was. He considered smashing the chip with the heel of his boot but instead threw it in the river where it would be carried far and away. Tears flowed down Liza's face and she sobbed silently, cradling her hand to her chest.

"I'm sorry, Liza. I had to do it, otherwise they'd find you." He wrapped another length of gauze around her hand, unnerved at how little the wound bled. "We have to go now."

The river had sucked her shoes away and he noticed her painted toenails. Ten pink half-moons. Her feet dangled like dead minnows as he hoisted her into his arms, grunting at the strain on his bruised ribs. Liza was small, but between the bridges she'd acquired the density of a dying sun. Dying, but not dead. Not yet. Liza was an overachiever. A winner. No way would this take her down.

He gently wrestled her into the back seat and draped his windbreaker over her.

"Thank you," she mumbled, pulling the bloody windbreaker up to her chin.

What was he supposed to say to a kid thanking him for brutalizing her? He shut the car door. Liza needed help. There was only one place he could go.

The C-A's pathetic motor whirred away down the divisional highway. He trained the rearview mirror on the back seat, on Liza. It wasn't Jenny he'd seen on the bridge. He knew that, and it still freaked him the hell out. He hadn't thought of Jenny in a long time, but now he felt her cold hand in his, and smelled the clotted blood in her hair. The road swerved in and out of focus.

Jenny was the only friend he'd ever had. He'd known she was in trouble. He could have done more. He gripped the steering wheel tightly and glanced over his shoulder at Liza. Decision made. He would not let her down.

CHAPTER 19

NAPA, CALIFORNIA,
PAN AMERICAN DIVISION

Panopticon's Department of Citizen Wellness is pleased to implement MediGuard, an application designed to function in concert with Guardian to optimize medication regimens through improved patient compliance. Dosages can be precisely titrated, side effects immediately identified, and if medication is taken incorrectly or not at all, care providers are notified. Fertility treatment efficacy is particularly improved with MediGuard. For convenience, this new application will automatically integrate with your Guardian profile unless opt-out protocol is observed. Panopticon supports every citizen's right to wellness. Register your family with Guardian today.

The assassin slammed the accelerator to the floor, for all the good it did in this toy car. An eternity of divisional highway finally led him to a road winding through the green hills of the Napa Valley. He didn't like the waxy pallor of Liza's face, or the amount of blood soaking into the upholstery. He knew his way around a knife but he wasn't a surgeon. It was a blind cut and he'd hit the jugular.

"Hang on, Liza. Almost there."

INFRACTUS

At the north end of the valley, he drove by a collapsed brick and timber platform for a train that once carried tourists through wine country. Massive corporate vineyards, long since abandoned, left vines weaving wild through the encroaching brush. The unkempt slopes blurred past until the assassin turned onto a dirt road leading between two small hills and through a wrought iron gate with the words Laughing Corpse arching overhead.

A quarter mile past the gate, the road forked. Procedure dictated he go right, drive up to the white house, and wait for an escort. This time he veered left, navigating the dusty ruts at a barely reasonable speed until a big red barn came into view. The beating heart of this little vineyard.

Sentries hidden in the trellises would have him in their sights. On the road he'd considered alerting Barclay to his imminent arrival, but in certain cases it was better to beg forgiveness than ask permission.

The assassin crept up to the barn and killed the motor. He exited the car, keeping his movements simple and deliberate. He had his SIG in the cargo pocket of his pants, but he wasn't about to wave a gun around. Not when any sudden action could be interpreted as a threat. Liza tumbled heavily against him as he dragged her out of the car.

The barn's double doors hung ajar in reluctant invitation. Inside the smell of oak and earth saturated the cool air. The assassin listened but heard only his own steps echoing off the concrete floor and Liza's shallow breath against his chest. On either side of him steel racks rose to the rafters, loaded with hundreds of casks containing thousands of liters of wine.

Laughing Corpse not only aged but also fermented their product in oak barrels. The artisanal method required strict temperature control provided by a closed circuit of pipes filled with coolant that turned each rack into a heat sink. The assassin acquired the coolant and helped install the system in exchange for a one-time discount on Barclay's exorbitant fees.

"Hold it." A voice boomed through the cavernous space. "You are trespassing on private property. State your business, stranger."

The assassin cleared his throat. "I'm a client of Barclay's and I'm going to keep walking, so you can either shoot or let me in."

Silence. Hidden in the racks, the sentry would be conferring with his superior, or with Barclay himself. Voice only. Cameras were against the Jackal code. If you wanted to watch someone, you did it with your own eyes and risked being watched yourself.

"All right, stranger. Go on through," said the sentry.

A silver-haired woman met them behind the racks at the back of the barn. With a rough hand she brushed the hair off Liza's face and stood back, fingers pressed to her chin. Several seconds passed. The assassin's arms ached, and his ribs were ready to snap.

"I guess you'd better follow me," the woman said, and led the way through a door and down a short ramp to an underground corridor where institutional lighting tinted her hair metallic green. "Infirmary is just ahead."

"Is there a doctor?"

"You're talking to her. I'm Pearl. And I excised a piece of government hardware from your arm many moons ago."

Barclay fiercely protected the identity of his assets, and while the assassin had visited the vineyard many times over the years, it was always by appointment. Pearl had obviously been working with Barclay for ages, yet the assassin hadn't so much as caught a glimpse of her before today. "Nice work. Hardly a scar."

"For what you paid, I should hope not," Pearl said as they entered a bright clean room. "Dean? We have incoming. Hypovolemia, if I'm not mistaken."

A young man with a stethoscope around his neck wheeled a crash cart up to a gurney. "What do we got? What's her name? How old is she?"

"Neck wound." The assassin deposited his burden on the gurney, her skin blue against the white sheet. "Liza. Eighteen, as of today."

"Conscious?"

"In and out. Mostly out."

Dean snapped on a pair of purple nitrile gloves. "Airway patent? She breathing okay?"

"I guess."

"How many weeks?" Dean pointed to the swell of Liza's stomach.

"I don't know her."

Dean glanced at Pearl and back to the assassin. "But you know her name and birthday?"

"I don't know her," the assassin repeated.

"Liza?" Dean said, his face close to hers. "Can you hear me? Open your eyes if you can hear me, Liza." No response. He pried her eyelids open, shining a penlight and flicking it away. "Pupils equal and reactive." He pinched and released the tip of her index finger. "Delayed cap refill."

Pearl snatched the stethoscope from around Dean's neck, plugged it into her ears, and pumped up the cuff around Liza's arm. The valve released with a hiss. "She's guttering. Hopefully we can place a line without resorting to a nasty cutdown."

Dean held Liza's hands in his. "Squeeze, Liza. Let me know you're in there. Come on now." No response. Dean ground his gloved knuckles into Liza's sternum. She gasped and her eyelids fluttered.

"Be careful with her," said the assassin.

Dean shot him a fierce scowl. "Sorry, Liza. Had to wake you up a little. Stay with us, okay?"

The assassin stood back and kept his mouth shut while Pearl placed an intravenous needle and hung a bag of saline. Next, she filled a syringe from a vial and injected it into the line. Epinephrine, the assassin figured. It would tighten up the circulatory system and make the most of her reduced blood volume. Liza's hands clenched and a cracked whisper floated from her lips.

"Say that again, Liza?" asked Dean, and when she uttered the same words he turned to Pearl, shaking his head.

"It's Japanese," the assassin said. "She's asking for her mother, I think."

Dean's professional detachment wavered as he squeezed Liza's arm. "You're gonna be okay, darlin'. I promise." After getting the nod from Pearl, he pinched the edge of the gauze at her neck and peeled it back. Liza's throat smiled up at him in a wide red grin. The gauze fell from Dean's fingers. "Jesus F. Christ."

Pearl leaned in to examine the wound. "At least one point of visible jugular perforation. No apparent arterial damage. Single cut. The implement must have been extremely sharp. Someone did this deliberately."

With their attention on Liza, and the situation approaching majestic levels of awkward, the assassin slipped out of the infirmary. He hustled down the hall, rounded the corner, and nearly ran right into the barrel of a rifle.

Colin Barclay towered over the assassin. Hell, at six and a half feet, Barclay was a tower. A hard-faced black man of sixty-eight years, the proprietor of Laughing Corpse Vineyard, and a tolerable fortress of authority. Currently attached to the trigger end of gorgeous lever-action Winchester.

The assassin put his empty hands up. "How've you been, Father?"

"Fair to middlin'," Barclay said in his deep rasp. "Think it's time you told me just who in the hell you are."

"No one you want to know."

"Twelve years too late for that." Barclay glared down the barrel. "Intercepted the video feed from the bridge in Kaylee, you son of a bitch. I ain't even gonna speculate as to why you'd slice open a little girl in front of the world and then bring her here."

"It's complicated."

"You'd think I could smell an operative by now. How many have they paid you to kill?"

"More than you could count with your socks off."

"I trusted you."

The needle dragged along the inner curve of his skill. "No one throwing around that kind of cash makes a living doing God's work, but you took my money anyway."

"Accusin' me of situational ethics?"

"Is there any other kind?"

"It's all over the Stream. They're blaming Jackals as usual, but I s'pose you already know that."

"Planning to shoot me, Father?"

"You know damn well, I ain't." Barclay lowered the rifle. "I'd appreciate the same consideration."

"I only kill Jackals when I'm getting paid."

Barclay grunted and led the way down the corridor, up the ramp, into the barn and out the side door. Midday sun stung the assassin's eyes and torched the vine-quilted slopes.

"Well don't just stand there with your teeth in your mouth," Barclay said. "Get marching, Deacon."

The assassin glanced down at his Borderlands shirt. Of course, Barclay knew Deacon Priest. Barclay gave birth to him, figuratively speaking. The assassin rubbed his bloody palms on his pants and followed. Undoubtedly more sentries were watching their boss hike into the vines alongside a stranger with red-washed hands. A stranger who first visited Laughing Corpse twelve years ago in need of a surgeon to snip out the tracking chip grafted to his brachial artery.

"How could you not suspect?" the assassin asked. "Considering our common acquaintance."

Barclay made a face like he'd bit into something bad. "That viper. Shoulda known anything she brought my way would be poison."

INFRACTUS

The assassin couldn't argue. He hadn't seen Suit Two in over three years, and if his luck held out he'd never suffer her presence again. "You two go way back, I guess."

"Her mama and daddy were members of my parish in Texas. I baptized that girl."

"Suit Two is Catholic?"

"Proof enough that a sprinkle of water on a kid's head don't mean shit."

"Was she always . . .?" The assassin twirled his index finger at his temple.

"Misfortunately a computer science degree and an MDiv don't make me a head shrinker."

The assassin had known Suit Two half his life. They'd been physically intimate as two people could be. Yet he'd rarely thought of her as a person with any kind of history.

"I don't even know her name," he admitted.

"She know yours?"

The gruff finality in Barclay's voice indicated the question was rhetorical and the discussion over. If nothing else, priests were good at keeping secrets. Which explained why almost no one knew that the humble vintner with the folksy dialect was also a genuine pre-millennial hacker. Put Barclay in front of a computer and those gnarled hands transformed into weapons of mass digital destruction. Far from being a white hat, Barclay commanded a mercenary fortune to program and upload the assassin's avatars into Panopticon's mainframe. Some, like Deacon, Noel, and Carrall, the assassin used for work. Others enabled him to live anonymously in a fishbowl world, and you couldn't put too high a price on that—though Barclay did his best.

The assassin scampered along in order to keep up with the old man's long-legged stride. On either side the vines grew up and over wire trellises forming a green cavern weighted with blue-black clusters. Cabernet, if he remembered correctly.

"Early bud break this year?" the assassin asked.

"Yessiree. Had smudge pots burning off frost three nights out of seven. In a month's time we're going to have the biggest crush in an age—not that my harvest is of any particular int'rest to a government hitman."

The assassin stopped in the middle of the path. "I never said I was good."

"And I never did ask, did I?"

They resumed their stroll at a slower pace. Each step a tacit question met with silence.

"Why does this feel like confession?"

Barclay flicked a wriggling caterpillar off a leaf. "You're the one what still calls me Father."

"Ever think it was for the best?" the assassin asked. "By the time the Eye squashed religion under their boot, it wasn't like you were doing anything particularly priestly."

"If caring for the cholera stricken ain't God's work, I don't know what is."

"Probably done more good as a Jackal than you did as a priest."

"Can't say I planned it that way," Barclay said. "Church shut down and I had nowhere else to go, so I tramped back to the place I spent every one of my childhood summers. Grandpa's vines were in a sorry state. Figured I might try nursing 'em back to health."

"How do you go from saving Grandpa's vineyard to thieving medical supplies from the government?"

"Couldn't ignore what all was going on outside these hundred acres. Folks facing government treatment worse than their affliction. Docs with the will and the skill to help but no supplies or equipment to do it. I had connections from my days runnin' the field hospital. And we ain't thieves. We're diverters."

"Your larcenous fees have diverted a substantial enough portion of my income."

"Yuh," Barclay said with a raspy laugh. "And thanks to your gen'rous patronage, the Eye is all but directly funding terrorism. Reckon' there's some poetry in that."

Barclay made it sound civilized, but the assassin knew better. Stealing from the Eye was not a gentleman's game. Barclay remained a man of faith, but he was a dead shot with his Winchester, and he surrounded himself with individuals similarly sure.

"Tell me about that girl bloodyin' up my infirmary. I'm thinking this ain't a typical day at the office for you."

The assassin pictured a gray-faced Liza on the gurney. "I don't do kids. Just a rule I have."

"Good rule."

The assassin kicked a dirt clod off the path. "When she was crying for her mother, I felt...I don't even know what to call it."

"That'd be guilt."

"Guilt." He tested the word on his tongue. "You think?"

"Trust me, son. I'm an expert," Barclay said, producing a hand-rolled cigarette from the pocket of his work shirt.

The assassin held out his bloody palm to catch a cabernet leaf fluttering down from the trellis. Five overlapping lobes and a ridged network of pale green veins on the underside that he traced with his fingertips. A tactile language. Like Braille. Braille he could read, but he didn't know the language of the vines. Not like Barclay.

Barclay scraped his thumb over the head of a match. The assassin caught a whiff of burning sulfur followed by the mellow aroma of hothouse tobacco. He let the leaf fall to the ground. "The Eye thinks she's dead."

Barclay exhaled smoke through his nostrils. "You ain't in an enviable position to be asking favors."

"Where else was I supposed to take her?" Along with guilt, it also hadn't occurred to the assassin that Barclay might refuse. "I know you never trusted me, Father. But I trust you."

"S'pose I agree to this. If she pulls through—"

"She will."

"It's gonna cost."

"Always does."

If Barclay thought his excessive monetary demands constituted some kind of deterrent, the assassin was tempted to set him straight. After years of grinding poverty, he'd assumed money would change his life. And it did. A bit. He never had to worry about where his next peanut butter sandwich or bowl of Cheerios was coming from, which was no small thing. But beyond necessities, money meant almost nothing to him. Whatever price Barclay named was merely a number to fill in on the transfer.

"Another thing," Barclay said. "Sanctuary extends no further than the girl and her babe. We're quits, you and me."

"Look after her, Father, and I'll never darken your gate again. But if anything happens to her, or the kid."

"Don't you threaten me, boy." Barclay jabbed a gnarled finger into the assassin's chest. "We'll keep her safe all right, but I sure as hell ain't doing it because I'm scared a you."

The assassin bowed his head. "*Mea Culpa*, Father."

"You're a right mouthy bastard." Barclay pinched out his cigarette and dropped the butt into his shirt pocket. "Not all folks got to be leaned on to do the right thing."

They ambled on. The assassin glanced around, seeing only vines and the occasional intersection of paths. The sun burned directly above like a yellow bowl on a blue platter. He had no idea where they were.

Barclay slowed. "Think I hauled you out here to shoot you?"

"Starting to wonder."

"Ye of little faith." Barclay reached between the leaves and twisted a cluster of cabernet in his square-nailed hand. "My grandpa planted these vines almost a hundred years ago."

"I didn't know that."

"Cock-eyed venture. His own kin laughed and said he'd starve. Was a time in this country when no white man'd serve negro plonk at his table."

The assassin found it hard to fathom, being that he was only fourteen years old when A-Day did the world an ironic favor, eradicating most racial prejudice by painting everyone the same sallow shade of ash.

"Five years," Barclay said. "That's how long newly planted vines take to produce anything useful. If they ever do. Long wait when you've invested your life in bald land. Couple hard winters, a few droughts. Those vines might-could ruin you." He released the grapes and they drooped on the vine. "Just got to believe they won't."

"Vines can't survive on faith alone."

"I ain't finished." Barclay inspected the grub holes on a discolored leaf. "Faith's no substitute for good sense. So, pray for sun, but light those smudge pots. Never know when you'll get a late frost or an early bud break."

The assassin realized that right here, right now, he was seeing all of Barclay. Not a shard. Not a splinter. This was the whole. A man working the soil, smoking homegrown tobacco, and imparting scraps of knowledge about vines and life.

"Stay on this here path." Barclay pointed to the dirt at their feet. "It'll get you where you need to go."

"Thank you, Father. For Liza."

Barclay dropped his granite palm on the assassin's shoulder. "Go with God, son. And don't come back."

CHAPTER 20

BALI, INDONESIA,
INDIAN SUBCONTINENTAL DIVISION

Panopticon's Department of Media Standards released its quarterly discussion and analysis, detailing Internet content, television, films, and books flagged for removal from public domain. Between the tireless work of Media Standards and ongoing efforts of citizens to observe and report, all forms of media will continue to be an enriching source of education and entertainment. Panopticon supports every citizen's right to protection from abusive media content . . .

Noel Bland tuned out the blathering Streamcast and stared out the window at the glittering carpet of ocean below. Advancements in aviation meant that an eighteen-hour flight in an old world 747 now took only ten. A good thing, because his next-seat neighbor had a neck tattoo and a habit of vigorously clearing his throat every few minutes. Noel chewed on his homicidal irritation when neck tattoo nudged his arm and pointed to the screen above. "You seen this?"

Noel shifted his arm out of nudging range and saw that the Stream had moved on to replay footage of Liza Ayomori's memorial. Mourners who'd never known her clogged the streets. They followed the hearse and left in their wake a carpet of flower petals so thick you'd swear the sky had opened up and rained carnations. The last image was that of a white casket being unloaded and carried into the government cremation facility. A modern-day Madonna slaughtered by a bloodthirsty Jackal.

"Gosh." Noel placed his hand over his heart. "That poor little duck."

Neck tattoo cleared his larynx again. "Still haven't found the freak who did it. They're calling him the Baby Butcher."

"Really?" Noel concealed his mild delight. "You know, I heard her parents put her backpack in the casket."

Nearly a month had passed since Noel, aka Deacon, dragged that same backpack off Liza's shoulders. He'd expected something to come unhinged, but so far Barclay's lecture had been the worst of it. He'd received yet another loathsome phone call from Suit One, who reluctantly admitted that the upper echelon viewed the lack of a corpse as a stroke of good fortune. Nothing for Liza's weeping parents to say goodbye to but her sad little backpack.

Yet another thing to feel guilty for. Goddamn Barclay. Since that day in the vines, the only communication between them had been a terse email. One sentence acknowledging receipt of funds and below that a single word. CARMEN. The seatbelt sign lit up and the plane banked.

"So, what brings you to beautiful Bali?" neck tattoo asked.

Noel buckled up. "Business."

Liza was an aberration. A change of scene and a new assignment were exactly what he needed, and he'd complete this one flawlessly. He was a professional.

INFRACTUS

❖❖❖

The terminal doors at Ngurah Rai slid open and the tropical air enveloped Noel like a warm wet womb. He breathed deep, letting the humidity bathe his throat and lungs, parched from the mechanically chilled airplane. Afternoon sun warmed his face and he smelled the dishrag odor of the ocean in the distance. He slung his long canvas tube over his shoulder and wheeled his suitcase behind him, rumbling over cracked concrete past the clots of new arrivals conversing in English, Indonesian, and Balinese while loading their luggage into C-A Taxis or platform scooters.

On the edge of a dirt lot that served as long-term parking, Noel approached a man in a lawn chair holding a black rooster on his lap. Noel held out several folded polymer bills. The man stroked the rooster's glossy feathers and reached into his satchel, emerging with a key. No ident, signature, or digital trace marked the transaction.

The car wasn't a Citizen model, but an ancient biodiesel Honda. Not an unfamiliar ride. Before A-Day, he'd boosted dozens of them with Zee. Of all his criminal pastimes, auto theft held the fondest memories.

Noel opened the hatch and slid the suitcase and the canvas tube inside. To get his rifle on a public aircraft he used his government clearance to bypass security. The clearance meant he could bring absolutely anything on board without inspection, but it also alerted Panopticon to his location. Since they were expecting him to surface in Bali anyway, it was a tolerable trade off. This was his comeback, and he needed his Springfield.

❖❖❖

Fear is in the mind.

INFRACTUS

Noel braced himself as a roaring wall of water flipped his surfboard and tossed him into the air. Salt water blasted up his nose and down his throat. The underwater portion of the wave held him down, spinning him like a sock in a washing machine. His head pounded with the building pressure in his sinuses until finally the massive kinetic force shoved him to the surface. He gulped air into his irrigated lungs and followed the leash from his ankle back to the board.

Blighted hell.

These were the famed Uluwatu waves. Modest height. Crushing momentum. Every day, for the last five days, he paddled out and endured the same terrifying roll. Every day he faced his fear. Neither his phobia nor his surfing saw improvement. And this was the kinder, reefless, white sand portion of Uluwatu.

While Noel collected his bearings, a surfer with tightly braided hair sneered at him and slid ahead to pinch the next wave. She was welcome to it. Seawater sloshed in his stomach as another swell heaved him upward and he glimpsed a man with shaggy gold hair waving at him from a point past the inside break.

Finally.

Noel paddled over, preparing for first contact with the mark.

"Yo." The mark jerked his thumb in the direction of the woman setting herself up on Noel's wave. "Gonna let that pula kahula drop in on your ride? You teach people how to treat you, bro. You get snaked, you gotta snake 'em back."

"Gee whiz," Noel said. "I'm getting killed out here. Drop-in's are the last thing I'm worried about." He straddled his board and stuck out his hand. "Noel."

INFRACTUS

"Scooter." He threw his hand into Noel's with a wet clap. "And your biggest prob is tension. Loosen up, bro. You, me, the ocean. S'all the same thing."

"What's that?"

"Water."

The choking anxiety loosened around Noel's neck as he rubbed the sting from the handshake out of his palm. Up close he saw veins of reflected light flicker in Scooter's sea-green eyes. Lean strips of muscle corded his arms and torso and despite considerable time in the sun he appeared a decade younger than his thirty years. Scooter was a serious athlete and the Big Kahuna around these parts. Except he wasn't big, he was little, five-foot-three in shoes, which he almost never wore.

Some details. Scott "Scooter" Isaak had no credit accounts, formal employment, or fixed address. Flagged for possession of contraband media a few months ago. No charges, which implied the offending article was some tattered bit of old world, like a pornographic magazine or a recording of subversive ukulele music.

For the last five days, Noel lurked in Scooter's long shadow. Like most people, Scooter had a routine. In the mornings, he ran an informal surf school, teaching fundamentals in exchange for peanuts, sometimes literally. When not shredding big waves or trading lessons for legumes, he socialized. Scooter had all the friends. Old and young, wealthy and poor, locals and foreigners—bules. His entourage followed him everywhere as he walked and talked like a tiny white Jesus.

So why not remap him, Noel wondered? Hook him up. Hollow him out. Since when were surfing vagabonds a clear and present danger to Panopticon's shiny blue world?

"I heard stories," Noel gestured toward another insidious wave making its way inland, "but these are the hardest breaks I've ever surfed."

Scooter grinned. "Think this is harsh, try getting reefed at the temple cave."

"You go there a lot?"

"Every day." Scooter swiped beads of water from the waxed deck of his board, and squinted at Noel. "Man, have we met before? Cause I swear I've seen you somewhere about. It's the eyes."

Noel averted his bi-colored gaze. Surfing and contact lenses didn't mix. "Think you got the wrong fella."

"Maybe." Scooter frowned briefly. "Hey, I'm headed in for some grindage. Wanna tag? I know a dude, and his wife makes these banana fritters. They. Are. Awesome."

"Sounds super," Noel said. Bait and hook. Sometimes it was too easy.

They paddled on their stomachs until they caught a long wave and proned out all the way to the beach. Noel had never been so grateful to set his bare feet on scorching sand. Scooter dropped his board near a pile of others on the beach. "Stash your stick here. Joint isn't far. We'll take the heel-toe express."

Equatorial sun bombed Noel's shoulders through his rapidly drying rash guard as he followed Scooter's bronzed back a short distance to an open front warung. The sandwich board outside boasted a menu written in English with chalk letters crowding together and eventually spilling down the right-hand margin.

"Selamat siang, Wayan," Scooter called out as they ducked under the shade of the clay tile roof and into a fragrant cloud of coconut, peppers, and frying dough.

A man slicing tomatoes behind the scarred counter sized them up. "Ah, there he is. Where you have been so long?"

Scooter trotted his fingers along the counter. "Here and there."

"Collecting friends like rotten jackfruit collects flies." Wayan wagged his cleaver at Scooter. "I know what is good for you today. Nengah!" Wayan called over his shoulder.

A round female face peeked out from the kitchen. Scooter zipped around the counter to hug the woman off her feet, right out of her orange flip flops, which clapped to the floor one after the other. Nengah squealed and planted a kiss on Scooter's temple before she shooed him away and wriggled her toes back into her sandals. Scooter came up behind Wayan and squeezed his shoulders. "You lucky bastard."

Wayan slid his knife into another ripe tomato. "Your meal is much expensive if you are to be kissing my wife."

Scooter gave a theatrical bow. "Take it all. My gold, my castle, my conquered lands."

"Easy promise for a vagrant."

"Ouch, dude." Scooter pulled a lumpy hemp wallet out of his pocket. "So happens, some well-heeled bules paid me in actual cash creditos."

Wayan pointed the silver tip of his knife at Scooter and spoke to Noel. "My friend, you know this guy? He's trouble."

"That's what I hear," Noel said

"Sit, vagrant." Wayan resumed dicing tomatoes. "Wayan and Nengah introduce your skinny bule friend to the best food on the island."

Noel and Scooter claimed a table with mismatched chairs that wobbled on the uneven floor. Scooter curled up cross-legged in one chair. Noel sat like a regular human in the other. Nengah arrived with two bottles of beer and a plate loaded with golden fritters. The aroma of hot oil and powdered sugar stimulated pleasure centers in Noel's brain he didn't know he had. Nengah clapped her offerings down on the table and departed with a light hip check to Scooter's shoulder.

"She's sweet on you," said Noel.

"Sweeter on him." Scooter watched Nengah, as she trailed her fingers over the back of her husband's neck on her way to the kitchen. Wayan shivered, but never missed a beat dicing his tomatoes. Scooter sighed. "I met her first, buncha years back. Gnarly chick. Then, like an epic merv, I introduced her to Wayan."

"Stole your girl?"

"Naw. Me'n her were friend-zoned, solid. Can't fight the soul mate thing."

Noel rolled the icy beer bottle between his hands. "You don't believe in that, do you?"

"Soul mates?" Scooter ripped a sugar dusted fritter in half with his teeth and mumbled. "Man, I wish I didn't."

Noel suspected Scooter wasn't talking about Wayan and Nengah anymore, but more pressing appetites eclipsed his desire for details. The pastries were hot and crispy on the outside and silky-sweet in the middle, with chunks of melted banana. Noel decided he'd found his soul mate in Nengah's fritters.

Unable to go more than a few seconds without talking, Scooter launched into a recount of the time he lived in Mexico with an iguana named Larry. "Chill roommate, but she had this jones for scaring people."

Noel washed down another bite with a few swallows of beer, concealing his distaste for it. "You named her Larry?"

"No," Scooter answered polygraph-style. "So, she'd hide under the bed, in the laundry hamper, on top of the fridge, wait for me to come along and jump out. First time I about shit myself."

The stories continued. Odd events in exotic locales, making it sound like he'd spent a lifetime in each far-flung corner of the world. Hardly plausible for a man of only thirty years. But so far, not a zig nor a zag of the lie detecting needle in Noel's head.

By the time the Scooter Show paused for breath, they'd hit the bottom of a second round and Nengah replaced the demolished plate of fritters with bowls of meatball soup. Noel balked. His native diet consisted of four things, none of them meat. Quite the opposite of the Balinese, who would eat anything with wings but a plane and anything with legs but a table. He didn't want to insult Nengah and Wayan by asking for peanut butter and bread, or Cheerios.

"Soup's safe, dude," Scooter said. "Grade-A beaks and flippers."

Noel spooned through the broth, contemplating the meatballs. "Gosh, I'm sorry Scooter. I can't eat anything with a face."

"Veg-head, eh? I can dig it. Long as you don't mind if I chow while you tell your story. Feels like I've been doing all the chin-flapping."

"You talk too much." Noel's words came out thick and blunt. This after two whole beers. A sturdy toddler could drink him under the table. Now he'd have to be vigilant. "No story, really. My life got derailed. Came here to get back on track."

Scooter worked his fingernail under the label of his beer bottle. Noel had observed that in a bar setting, people could be separated into two groups: those who peeled labels, and those who didn't. Scooter was a label peeler. Unexpected. It spoke to a certain social discomfort, a restlessness. Not a vibe Noel otherwise got from Scooter.

"Derailed?" Scooter smoothed the edge of the label back onto the glass. "Mind if I ask what kind of train wreck chased you to the other side of the world?"

Noel pushed his bowl away, harder than he meant to. Broth spilled over the rim. "A friend died. Only knew him a couple months, but he and his wife practically adopted me into their family. Maybe it's dumb, but I've been a mess ever since. The more I try to fix it, the worse it gets. What do you think about that?"

Scooter studied Noel through half-hooded eyes. "Two things. First, it doesn't matter how long you know a person. That's family. And nothing hurts worse. Believe me, I know."

"And second?"

"Sounds like you're used to paddling hard to get where you want to go, mate. Could be life's way of saying you need to take a beat. Sit still. Let the sets come to you for a change."

Damn. Between Grayson and Scooter, Panopticon had zero love for green-eyed charmers. Blight of a deal. Under different circumstances.

Wait, was this more guilt? Yeah...definitely guilt. Barclay. A pox on him. Noel glanced down, surprised to find he'd undressed his own beer bottle down to naked glass. This job was a basic hit and run. Noel didn't need to get within a hundred feet of Scooter to meet that objective. Yet here he was, breaking bread with him. Why? Another unwelcome rhetorical question.

Scooter drew his knees up again and stared at Noel. "Not to kick a beached whale or anything, but I never forget a face, and I've seen yours before."

"Don't know what to tell you."

Scooter gnawed on his thumbnail. "It'll come to me."

Probably just inebriated paranoia talking, but Noel thought he detected a hint of warning in that statement. Before his suspicions could drag him further afield, Scooter reached out, resting his hand on Noel's wrist.

"Come to the temple cave tomorrow. Bunch of us meet there at sunrise to hang out and talk."

Sounded Grayson-ish. Noel assumed the kill order had something to do with Scooter's contraband media rip, but maybe it was something more sinister.

"Talk about what?" asked Noel.

Scooter spread his arms out like wings. "Anything. Everything. Good people chillin'. Usually cap it off with a few waves. Energy's sweet that time of day. We can introduce you to Uluwatu properly—without the snakes."

Noel considered the shreds of label around his bottle. "D'you ever think you shouldn't try so hard to help people?"

"Nope." Scooter shifted to dangle one bare foot off the side of an empty chair. "So how about it? Temple tomorrow?"

Noel stood on legs wobbly as the table and chairs. "Why the heck not? Maybe I'll find what I'm hunting for."

CHAPTER 21

Pura Luhur Uluwatu stands against the darkened horizon, its multi-tiered pagoda reaching for the heavens. While the old-world Balinese didn't build their houses of worship on sand, they had no problem digging the foundations into the edge of a cliff dropping two hundred feet to the Indian Ocean. The farther back you go, the more balls human beings had when it came to erecting monuments.

Bali has nine of these directional temples. Pura Luhur's perch on the tip of the Bukit peninsula supposedly protects the island against evil spirits from the southwest. From the northeast, I spot him loping down a heaving stone path, a long canvas bag slung across his back. He stops outside the temple gate, guarded on either side by stone renderings of Ganesha. They regard him with silent disapproval.

I'd be lying if I said I wasn't nervous. Thirty-five of the Thirty-six are dead. After Grayson whassisname, I thought She would come running. No dice. That left only Scooter, but I didn't have the guts. Truly, I never expected I'd have to take it this far. So, I stalled and sent him after an innocent lamb, a young woman with child for crying out loud. Talk about your desperate bids for attention. And still nothing.

INFRACTUS

Now I'm nearly out of time. I need Her here, and this is my Hail Mary pass. It's going to work. It has to.

At 4:45 a.m. the temple grounds were deserted, though far from silent. The assassin wondered if the atonal symphony of croaking frogs ever paused for an intermission. They were even worse than the crickets in Texas. He followed a dirt path through a maze of darkened warungs and surf shops, until he came to a staircase pouring down into the limestone bowels of the peninsula. He switched on his flashlight, training the blue beam on the badly crumbled steps until his feet landed on the floor of the cave.

Wet sand slushed under his boots. Awakening air currents stretched and yawned, ruffling his hair and stirring up the smell of low tide rot. With one hand on the damp gritty wall, he groped his way to the mouth of the cave, where sand and stone framed a window to the legendary Uluwatu temple surf. Big waves, shallow water, and a reef hungry for human flesh.

He checked his watch; Scooter and his surfies were due to assemble at six. That gave the assassin over an hour to set up. He jogged along the narrow strip of beach between the ocean and the cliffs towering overhead. About a hundred yards from the cave, he spotted a ledge protruding from the cliff side. Sharp stone cut into his hands as he climbed the fifteen or so feet and heaved himself onto the ledge. The shelf provided more than enough room to work, and was partially concealed by overhanging vegetation. He couldn't have ordered a better hide-site.

He unzipped the canvas bag and lifted out his rifle. Over a century old, and heavy at eight and a half pounds, the Springfield had none of the flashy tech of a modern rifle. Computerized sighting modules, complex railing systems, multistage recoil absorption, and sound suppressors. The Springfield wasn't even collapsible. Most gearheads would look down their nose at the Springfield for the very reasons the assassin loved it.

The basic mechanism of firearms was simple: pin hits primer, igniting gunpowder, and the expanding gas propels the bullet down the barrel. Why complicate it? From both a practical and aesthetic standpoint, less was more. The Springfield was admirably simple, with elegant bolt action, perfect rifling, and a wooden stock that welded warmly to the assassin's cheek, its secret heart beating with his. A gift from Suit Two. Though to her mind, she'd merely handed over what already belonged with him.

Before entering the Facility, he'd never fired a gun in his life. Extensive training honed his talent, but in the end, it came down to nothing more than a feeling. A moment where the world evaporated, leaving only his rifle, his target, and a sense of absolute certainty. God, with His finger hovering over the smite button.

What might Barclay make of that?

He slid the scope into its mount on the barrel. He could dial in to compensate for wind, elevation, and bullet drop, but he rarely did for short-range shots. Besides, Scooter was a frenetic little beast, prone to sudden fits of motion. The holdover was a better option.

With the scope in place he checked the sight alignment. Then he loaded five .30 caliber cartridges into the clip. Some snipers made a point of loading only one. A tolerably stupid way to show off. You never knew when you might need another round.

Magazine loaded and locked. He peered through the scope for the second check of alignment. Exotic seaside overlaid by familiar cross hairs. Perfect alignment. Perfect rifle. His Springfield.

At 5:50 a.m. he lay prone with the rifle barrel resting on a sandbag. He pulled the bolt back, chambering the first round. Through the scope, he watched a heron swoop down the cliff to peck at a starfish marooned in a tide pool.

The sky lightened from dark purple to gray as Scooter's barefoot groupies clustered at the mouth of the cave. Men and women varying in age from a Balinese boy making a valiant attempt at facial hair, to a leathery old couple with multiple strings of beads looped around their necks.

It wasn't necessary to kill Scooter in front of people who cared about him. But the assassin chose to do it this way because he liked Scooter too, and he needed to prove to himself just how much that didn't matter. He was a professional, and Scooter, the mark.

At 6:08 a.m. the mark ambled out of the cave, holding hands with a woman in a white dress and tightly braided hair—the pula kahula who'd dropped in on Noel's wave yesterday. The mark scanned the crowd, unsmiling. Disappointed at Noel's no-show maybe. The pula kahula touched the mark's cheek, her eyes searching his. He squeezed her hand and left her side to greet the crowd where he passed out hugs and high-fives like canapés at a cocktail party. The pula kahula stood back in tranquil resignation.

INFRACTUS

Rumbling surf smothered the soundtrack, but through his scope the assassin watched the congregation. He'd had enough dealings with the entire Jackal spectrum to know that this particular beach party was no gathering of dissidents. The vibe was too gentle. Laughing, embracing, generous body language all around. This congregation was an actual congregation. No Bible, Torah, or Bhagavad Gita in sight, but that didn't mean the mark wasn't preaching.

"Holy shit," the assassin chuckled.

This was something he hadn't seen in a long, long time. He'd grown up severely Catholic, and at the Facility he studied many other religious texts out of spite. He could imagine the content of the sermon. Love one another. Say little and do much. No one who does good work comes to a bad end. You get snaked, you gotta snake 'em back. The Gospel according to Scooter.

A hint of gold in the gray light signaled the sunrise. The assassin glanced at his watch. He'd enjoyed the novelty long enough. Time to work.

He tucked the butt of the rifle against his shoulder and aimed at a point behind the mark's ear to ensure catastrophic brain injury. He'd minimize stock movement by holding his lungs empty. He'd fire between heartbeats. The Springfield had exactly three pounds of trigger pull and he took up each ounce slowly with the ball of his finger. The feeling rushed toward him like a glassy wave that shattered when something kicked the sole of his boot.

He dropped the rifle and scrambled to his feet, yanking a knife from his belt. In the glare of the rising sun, the assassin saw a dark silhouette unsheathing two identical blades. Not blades. Swords.

Katanas. The assassin squinted as the figure stepped forward—a woman, tall, in black fatigues, long red hair secured at the nape of her neck. Where the blighted hell had she come from? She glanced at the puny knife in his fist and his equilibrium rocked, as though the earth hiccupped beneath him. He dropped the knife, hearing it thud into the sand at his feet.

"Do I know you?" he asked.

Her blade whistled through the air and laid a thread of fire across his chest. She whirled in the opposite direction with the other blade. He lurched to the side. Too slow to avoid a second slash deeper than the first. He dropped to one knee at the edge of the stone shelf.

"Had we met before," she said in a low voice. "We would not be meeting now."

She swept her blades out wide. He extrapolated the inward arc. The katanas would cross, neatly decapitating him. He snatched up his rifle to block. With a shearing screech the swords crossed, cutting the barrel in two. The horrible sound rang in his ears like a Doppler. Even unarmed on the brink of a rough drop, retreat was barely conceivable. This lunatic fouled his comeback, and she destroyed his Springfield. For that alone, she was on borrowed time. But he was no match for her this way.

So, he ran.

Or he would have run.

Instead he teetered on the edge and fell.

Not his best exit.

He hit the sand neck first—so that was possible—in a knot of arms and legs interchangeable for all their immediate usefulness. His vision bleached and he struggled to suck air into his crumpled lungs, a challenge because he was still lying on top of his neck. At any rate it seemed like a swell idea to lie still.

A blurry head came into view above him, and someone yanked on arms that didn't feel like his arms. "Get up, man."

Riot advice. Summarily rejected by his jangled nervous system.

"Dude, I can't carry you. We got about ten seconds here."

The blur slid into focus. "Scooter?"

"Get up!"

Scooter tugged on the assassin's arms again. Heat surged into his joints as he unwound from his pretzel twist and inflated his lungs with salty air. He heaved himself to his feet and stumbled into a run. Not bad for twice-sliced and a fifteen-foot fall. He looked over his shoulder once. The rifle slayer dropped to the sand. She stuck the landing effortlessly, gracefully. Not on her neck.

Scooter led the sprint past bewildered groupies, into the cave, through the dark, and up the crumbled steps two at a time. Daylight exploded along with the plume of incense, coffee, and tea drifting from the warungs as they chugged to life.

They ran down the stone path and past the temple. Rivulets of blood streamed hot down the assassin's stomach as he tried to keep up with Scooter, who grabbed a hard right, darting between two bamboo stalls. The assassin skidded into the turn, nearly trampling a stray duck and about a million ducklings. Ducks were sacred to the Balinese, and they were everywhere. He didn't need any karmic complications. The narrow alley opened onto a dirt lot where he found Scooter standing beside a once upon a time blue mustang.

The assassin braced his arms on the hood of the car, gasping. "What the hell is going on?"

Scooter yanked the driver's door open. The hinge creaked, spitting flakes of rust into the air. "Get in, mate. I'll explain on the way to...someplace." He swung his head side to side, presumably scanning for the rifle slayer.

"D'you know her?"

Scooter slammed his fist on the mustang's pocked roof. "I know she's got swords, bro. Two of 'em. Get in the fucking car!"

The assassin threw himself into the passenger seat as the engine blasted to life. In seconds they were charging down the road. The assassin glanced behind them, the motion tearing at the cuts on his chest. The wounds sizzled. Did she treat her blades with a corrosive? And what were they made of that they could slice through the steel barrel of his rifle? His heart ached thinking about it. No sign of her following them, at least. He faced forward again. "How'd you know about the swords?"

Scooter jammed into third, "You're seriously sacking my chill, mate. Do us both a solid and shut your gob."

The engine mellowed to a low growl as they tore down the cratered asphalt. Farther inland, past the markets and earthquake-ravaged metropolis of Kuta, the geography gave way to agriculture. Terraced rice patties, groves of coconut palms, and neatly planted fields of sweet potatoes smeared past on both sides of the road.

After some time, Scooter turned his head and stared at the assassin, longer than he deemed prudent to keep one's attention off the road and its axle-shattering divots.

"What did you do?" Scooter asked.

"What?"

"She don't waste her time on jaywalkers and litterbugs. By rights you ought to be a pile of nuggets right now."

The assassin shifted in the lumpy seat that arguably held more sand than stuffing. "How'd you know I was there?"

"Hey!" Scooter said as they bounced over another crevasse. "I'm saving your caboose, dude, at considerable risk to my own. I'll ask the questions if you don't mind, Noel Bland. Worst fake name I've ever heard."

The assassin checked the cracked side view mirror. "She could be following us."

"She'll need to cadge a lift off someone. Unless a lot's changed, she don't know how to drive."

"Why are you helping me?"

Scooter strangled the disintegrating leather steering wheel. "Because it's what I do."

Near Denpasar, the smell of the ocean yielded to the stink of burning trash and algae fuel exhaust. Scooter shoulder-checked, weaving through traffic as Balinese rush hour commenced in a drowsy rampage.

Signal lights were a sometimes thing, as were designated lanes. Trucks—all competing against Scooter's car for the title of Miss Rusty Fabulous—jounced along, threatening to toss crates full of flapping chickens onto the road. Two men with three mattresses balanced on their heads zipped by on a motorcycle. The man on the back steadied the load, while the driver gunned the two-stroke engine, swerving tightly around the trucks, cars, and world-eating potholes. The assassin buckled his seat belt.

A mile past the city, traffic thinned until they had the road to themselves again.

"Where are we going?" the assassin asked over the hot wind whistling through the windows.

"Nuh-uh, tell me who you are first."

"You really don't know?"

"Should I?"

"You've made a nuisance of yourself where Panopticon is concerned. With your prayer meetings and stuff. I was about to put a hole through your head when that maniac showed up and tried to cut off mine."

Scooter's eyebrows shot halfway up his forehead. "You were gonna kill me?"

"Not sure why they didn't have you remapped."

"Meh, even if they tried, it wouldn't work."

"Everyone can be remapped."

Scooter tapped his fingers against the wheel. "What a world. Guy seems like a rad dude, you grab some chow, have a good jam, and wouldn't you know, he's a hitman. Are you even a vegetarian?"

"Why would I lie about that?"

"Why talk to me at all? Guess it's nice to be kissed first, but I think you got some issues, mate."

The assassin considered explaining. Though once they opened that can they'd have to eat it all and they didn't have that kind of time. He plucked at his wet T-shirt. Fresh blood trickled from the rents in his skin. He saw yellow spots dancing on the inside of his eyelids.

"Yo." Scooter nudged his arm. "You okay?"

"What's wrong with you?" the assassin snapped. "Anyone in your situation would be riot freaked, and you're asking if I'm okay?"

Scooter snorted. "Dude, you don't know barnacles about me. I've been around. Seen things that'll make your skin creep right off. You ain't one of 'em."

The assassin had a decision to make. He had another knife in his boot. Small, more tool than weapon, but it would finish the job he'd started. "Who's the redhead, Scooter?"

Scooter slouched in his seat, drawing one knee up and draping a hand over the wheel. "Yeah, I'm not feeling uber chatty just now. So, nerf me if you want. I know you're thinking about it. But she's gonna find you, and when she does she'll feed your cabbage water excuse for a soul to the drain."

"You could help me find her first. Enemy of my enemy and all."

A deep laugh rolled out of Scooter's little body.

"What's funny?"

"So many things, dude. I can't even . . ." Scooter chuckled again and blew a sun-streaked chunk of hair out of his eyes. "You got it all wrong, mate. She's not my enemy, she's my sister. Her name's Michael."

CHAPTER 22

By the time they reached Ubud, the assassin's wounds had clotted and his head felt less full of marshmallows. He found himself constantly tensed for impact as Scooter drove his Mustang through the market streets where everything from trucks to tricycles flailed along at a sedate pace and reckless trajectory. Pedestrians scurried single file down the sidewalks, past carts piled with melons and bananas, shops selling everything from animal feed to dental floss, and a garage that seemed to advertise plough and harness repair.

Scooter nudged his way through an intersection, yielding to a little girl leading a water buffalo on a tattered rope. Past the blooming gardens of the water palace, they crept into an alley and parked behind the bemo station. The ammoniac reek of chickens engulfed them like a hot blanket as Scooter parked under the overhanging thatched roof.

"What are we doing?" the assassin asked, following Scooter around to the front of the station.

Scooter cast him a grim smile. "I'm gonna crack a walnut with nothing but my epic personality. You're gonna hang back and keep your word-hole shut."

INFRACTUS

On the front veranda an old man on a bench carved into a piece of wood with a pocketknife. At his feet, a three-legged dog nosed through the fragrant shavings. Neither man nor dog appeared to be waiting for the bus.

The assassin retreated to the far corner of the veranda while Scooter called out a Balinese greeting, but in a lower, more reverent fashion than with Wayan the previous afternoon. The old timer's black eyes brightened with recognition and his hands stilled at their work. Scooter took a seat on the bench and conversed with the old man in clipped sentences.

The assassin understood only the odd word but certain mannerisms were universal. Tension in the shoulders, leaning in, backing off, pleading hands and crossed arms as the tone of the exchange progressed from friendly to mildly agitated on both sides. The assassin recognized negotiation in any language.

Traffic dwindled from a crowded dawdle, to nothing at all. Incense from the morning offerings lingered in the empty streets. Balinese Hindus no longer carried out their temple pujas or colorful cremation processions, but they kept their faith in their hearts—Panopticon's only blind spot. The assassin never understood the concept of faith. Belief, without question, without proof. Especially in times like these.

He still had that knife in his boot. Scooter was still the mark.

Am I still a professional?

Scooter's cajoling came to an abrupt halt. The old man's darkly etched face studied the assassin in silence, hands still, knife set into his unfinished carving. Then he folded the blade into its handle with an affirmative grunt.

INFRACTUS

Pressing his hands together in a prayer pose, Scooter murmured what the assassin supposed amounted to thanks. He scampered over, grabbed the assassin's elbow and dragged him around the corner, back to the alley.

"Crack your walnut?" The assassin tugged his arm out of Scooter's grip.

"Barely. Got us a hidey hole until we can shovel a plan together."

"I still don't understand why you're doing this."

Scooter scuffed his sandals in the dirt. "I've seen enough death."

Never had the assassin heard four words weighted so heavily. "Your friend didn't seem happy."

"Not really, no." Scooter pulled a dusty canvas tarp from the trunk of the mustang. "Lucky for us, the reason he ain't happy is the reason he went for it."

"And what's that?" The assassin grabbed one end of the tarp and helped cover the car.

"My man Putu says you're butakalas. A demon."

"He wouldn't be the first," the assassin said, thinking of Sister Claudia and her yellowed bible locked away in a box in Maine.

They hustled through a maze of dirt alleys and many more acrid chicken coops. At the edge of town, the assassin followed Scooter onto to a path leading into thick foliage that all but entombed a stone information wall. The monkey forest didn't see much traffic these days, and jungles didn't waste time reclaiming their land.

"Onward," Scooter said, and charged through the tree line.

Inside, the treetops meshed into a dark ceiling and breathing felt more like drinking warm water. Fronds, vines, and damp fleshy leaves that unpleasantly mimicked human touch pressed in on the assassin from both sides as he followed Scooter down the path. In some places the unchecked aerial root networks of banyan trees obscured the path entirely and they had to climb or crawl to get around.

The assassin's heart shifted in its cradle between his lungs, putting him off-balance. Somewhere between Uluwatu and Ubud, he'd begun to feel ground down and exposed. Not that it was sudden. More like he'd been losing thin layers of skin so gradually that he only noticed it now that he was completely flayed. Usually he had to hunt after his feelings, dragging them from their burrows like elusive prey, but lately those strong emotions stalked him. More dramatically since Grayson Hillaby. All those unpleasant rhetoricals, herding him unwillingly to one answer. He didn't want to do this anymore.

He was done.

Scooter vanished around a bend in the path. The assassin picked up his pace. Stone animals periodically peeked through the fluttering green around them. Komodo dragons, snakes, birds. Blinking eyes of flesh and blood macaques followed them.

Monkeys, or something else?

He wasn't exactly employee of the month. He'd failed Panopticon's test by withholding the location of Grayson's cell, and breached protocol by failing to leave a verifiable body with Liza. It didn't make sense for Scooter to help him. Unless Scooter wasn't helping him at all.

The assassin ducked off the path into the foliage, melting into the steamy darkness. The area wasn't huge, a few square miles. If he went straight on dead reckoning, he'd emerge out the other side soon enough. He cut through the thick green growth as silently as he could.

INFRACTUS

One thing he had to give Scooter credit for, he played like a pro. That fraternal conviviality, the "you look familiar" schtick. The assassin used those techniques on dozens of marks himself. His stomach lurched. From blood loss. Or a double dose of his own bad medicine.

What about Liza? Did Panopticon suspect? By asking Barclay to protect her, the assassin put him at risk. For all he knew, Laughing Corpse had already been razed to the ground.

As he trekked on he tried not to break stems or leave obvious footprints. Focused on concealing his tracks, he nearly collided with an eight-foot wall of orange stone. There were temples in the monkey forest. This must be one of them. He followed the wall until he came upon a statue of two monstrous children embracing one another, their fanged mouths open in an eternal scream

Butakalas. Demons.

He entered the courtyard through a split gate. Crossing the stone floor, he attached his surroundings to what he'd read in books. A drum tower stood in the center, and a few small pavilions dotted the remaining space. At the far end of the courtyard he saw the kori—a roofed gate leading to the most sacred portion of the temple. At the base of the kori steps, stone serpents slithered around a giant turtle. The foundation of the universe or something. The towering gate itself had three intricately carved gold doors, guarded from above by the monstrous leonine head of the bhoma.

This was Pura Dalem. Temple of the dead.

In spite of the heat, a chill raced through his blood. Silence settled over the courtyard, blotting out the rainforest chatter. Objects of solid stone seemed to shift in his periphery, as if what he saw was merely a veneer sliding over another reality. He chalked it up to acoustics and tricks of light, but there was something about this place.

The creepish pall evaporated when he caught a flash of red and black flickering through the green. The rifle slayer. The assassin drew the small knife from his boot and tucked himself into the corner next to the gate.

She had to be close, but he heard only the pillowy silence of the temple. His pulse decelerated as a black boot landed on the stones not a yard in front of him. A black-clad leg followed. She entered the courtyard, her footfalls soundless, her sheathed swords crossed over her back with the red rope of her hair hanging between them.

He sized her up for potential weaknesses. Roughly six feet, which gave him no height advantage. He might edge her out in strength, but that was a big "might" and it counted for almost nothing in the face of her brutal speed. Smart money was on sneaking out the gate while her back was turned. He lunged from his corner, grabbed her ponytail, and laid his knife across her throat.

"Looking for me?"

"Not anymore," she said in that low voice.

"Surprised?"

"I searched. I found. Not much surprise in that."

He tugged sharply on her hair. "I found you first. World of difference."

A weary exhalation rushed beneath the press of his knife, and she slipped out of his grasp. Just slipped. Even her hair simply poured from his fist like water. It wasn't preternatural, but the way she moved...another wave of vertigo hit him. "Who are you?"

"Someone who doesn't like to be touched." Her green eyes narrowed as she drew her swords. "Don't be afraid, human. I'll make it quick."

"I don't demand special treatment." He ducked her blades and tackled her around the middle. The impact drove her backward, though not off her feet. Damn it. But her arm struck a stone altar and her sword clattered to the ground. He snatched it up, gripping with both hands as its twin sliced toward him. The blades met in a brilliant clash.

Adrenaline gushed into his bloodstream as they parried, but the rifle slayer looked ready to yawn. She allowed him to escape on the cliff, and she let him sneak up on her just now. He was done being toyed with. He couldn't match her skill, but he could be an unpredictable idiot.

He transferred the sword to his left hand and swung in a wide horizontal cut. She easily dodged, but her ponytail whipped around a fraction of a second too late. Steel whispered through a lock of her hair. Time froze as they watched the red ribbon pool on black stones.

She snarled in a language he didn't recognize and smashed him in the face with her elbow.

He fell onto the stone turtle and rolled onto the kori steps. Blood erupted from his nose and mouth. Blind and reeling, he heard the grate of steel on steel, and the fiery sting of her blades sliced into his neck.

"Stop! Michael, don't. Please."

Scooter? Blighted fucking hell.

The blades cut incrementally deeper as the rifle slayer prompted the assassin to rise and herded him up the stairs toward the kori doors until gold-leafed deities cavorted against his back. He met her stony green gaze head on.

Scooter stood inside the split gate. "Yo, if you two are having a moment I can come back in fifteen."

"Are you trying to be funny?" the rifle slayer snapped over her shoulder.

"Yes?" Scooter smiled, and immediately sobered. "I mean no. Totally not trying to be...look, could we stow the sharpies and talk about this?"

The assassin winced at the withdrawal of steel from his flesh. His vision ghosted and blood puddled in the back of his throat. Scooter's sandals smacked against the stones. He darted around the rifle slayer and sandwiched the assassin's head between his hands. "You solid, mate?"

"Hoo are you peeble?" he gurgled, swatting at Scooter's arms. Anger felt both good and right. Certainly, it dulled the humiliation over his second ass kicking in as many hours.

"Let's you and me go inside a minute," Scooter said. "That cool with you, Mikey?"

The rifle slayer wiped her blood-streaked blades on her pant leg. Her face said it all. I suffer you to live. The assassin spat a mouthful of blood at her feet before Scooter grabbed him by the collar and hauled him through the middle door of the kori.

CHAPTER 23

Soothing gloom and the faint smells of incense and dried flowers welcomed them to the inner sanctum. The assassin found the nearest wall, slid down to the floor, and put his hand over his eyes. Each heartbeat felt like a hammer against his broken nose, and the lacerations on his neck burned like someone held an acetylene torch to them.

Scooter pried the assassin's hand away from his face. "Think you're so smart, ditching me like that?"

The assassin twisted away. "Bag off. I dode deed a durse."

"Shut up." Scooter rested his fingertips on either side of the assassin's smashed nose.

"Stob id." The assassin smacked him away again. "Stob agding like you're drying to save me."

Scooter shoved the assassin's shoulders hard against the wall. "I did save you. And I just did it again, dumbass. So that's two you owe me."

"You're sedding me up."

Scooter cocked his head. "I am?"

"They...sent you...ad her." The assassin pointed to the open kori door.

"They?"

INFRACTUS

"Are you wurging for the Eye?"

"Oculo Uno?"

He grabbed the front of Scooter's shirt. "Yes, or doh?"

"No," Scooter said, indignant. "Hell, no."

No trace of deception. Relief muted the infernal roar of his wounds, and he released Scooter, leaving a smear of blood on his shirt.

Scooter sat back on his heels. "Are you gonna calm your tits? Because I'm trying to help, but you need to let me."

The assassin said as much to Liza not a month ago. Scooter placed the pads of his fingers and thumbs on the assassin's face. Heat diffused through his skin, filled his sinuses, and branched out into every blood-filled capillary. Hot and hotter still. He tensed and clawed at the stone floor.

"Shh," Scooter whispered. "Nearly home."

Pain faded. The heat remained. One of Scooter's hands circled his neck while the other slipped through the sliced T-shirt to press flat against his chest. The assassin wasn't used to being touched, even casually. This was invasive, intimate. Anything but casual. Weirder still, it felt good. He knew, without a doubt, that Scooter intended no harm. The assassin relaxed and retreated from the back of his closed eyelids, falling deeper inside himself until he smelled rain, and salt.

Thunder rolled like a kettledrum through his solar plexus. The wind burned his cheeks as he stood in the gravel of English Bay, transfixed by waves racing inland and collapsing in a foamy explosion. A man sprinted down the beach. Shaggy gold hair. Yellow surfboard under one arm.

The assassin opened his eyes.

"Told you it would come to me," said Scooter, partially obscured by shadow.

The assassin took a trembling breath and waited for the chunks of reality to tumble back in to place.

"You want to know why I'm helping you. Well, there it is." Scooter slumped at the base of a carved throne. The seat of the gods. He looked hollow and sick, like someone who hadn't slept in days. "I'm helping you now because I shoulda helped you then. Had a feeling you were in trouble."

"What are you saying?"

"That I never forgot that kid on the beach."

Memories could be unreliable. That surfer would be in his fifties by now. The assassin rubbed his hands over his face and froze. His nose, though mildly sore, was back to its original configuration. He peeled back his shredded shirt. Under a smear of blood, the slashes on his chest had healed to a nascent pink. "Did you?"

"Make you pretty again? Only mostly. Better for both of us to let you handle the rest."

The assassin traced the tender film of new skin on his neck. "So, what? You're some kind of immortal magic mind reader?"

"Nope, nope, and nope." Scooter yawned and laced his hands over his stomach. "I don't age like human beans do, but I'm not immortal. I got the skills to channel the healing energy all around us, but it ain't even close to being magic. And mind reading is a dark art, yo. Violates His natural laws big time. He separated the think from the blab for good reason. All I did was prompt you to dredge the memory."

The assassin's next thought strummed unfiltered through his vocal cords. "His natural laws? Who's he?"

"God," Scooter said as though it should be obvious.

The assassin waited but the lie-detecting needle didn't so much as shiver. "Jesus Christ, you really believe that don't you?"

Scooter scowled. "Since I doubt you're close pals with my bro, Joshua, maybe you don't wanna be abusing his name like that."

The assassin brought his hands to the sides of his skull as though it might break open like an egg. "You're insane."

Scooter relaxed into an unfriendly smile. "I'm seraphim, and dissemble all you want because at this point I honestly don't give a flying shark what you believe."

The needle scratched wildly back and forth. Why did people so often preface their lies with the word "honestly"?

"Seraphim," the assassin said. "Angels?"

"Gold star for the stone-cold killer."

Occam's razor stated that all things being equal, the simplest explanation is the most likely. But there were no simple explanations here. It's a mysterious world, Mouse. You wanna keep an open mind, but not so far open your brains fall out. Blind faith is for suckers. Question everything. God is in the details.

He considered Zee's words while rubbing the itchy layer of dried blood off his face with a cleanish shred of T-shirt. Water would be nice. His mouth tasted like he'd been sucking on old world pennies.

"I have questions," said the assassin.

"Figured you might."

"If you're an angel, what are you doing here, passing for human, getting on Panopticon's nerves?"

"Not much for preheating the oven, are you?" Scooter rested his chin in his hands, his face pale and exhausted. "What I'm gonna tell you is a lot to chew on, so stop me if you need a beat to, like, process or whatever."

The assassin nodded.

"So, way before He said let there be light, God decided to grant human souls free agency. Plan was you'd evolve from amoebas to homo sapiens, at liberty to make your own choices, lifetime after lifetime, learning and growing, and when you'd learned and grown enough, your souls would ascend to the next kingdom of enlightenment."

"Good plan."

"It was, until you boneheads stopped dragging your knuckles."

"What happened?"

"Wrath, greed, pride, envy, sloth, lust, and gluttony."

"Seven deadly sins."

"A real cromag clusterfuck," Scooter said. "So, God calls a family meeting, asking for ideas. The Legion came up with the winning plan. Thirty-six seraphim at any given time, stationed here on Earth. We can't stop you dirt monkeys from jumping on the bed, but we can help pick you up when you fall and bump your noggins."

The assassin recalled Sister Claudia's interminable Bible reading sessions. "Legion? The demons Jesus cast into a bunch of swine?"

"Friggin' Azazel," Scooter muttered the same foreign oath his sister had earlier. "Bro, you gotta take those Bible stories with a pillar of salt.

Legion are not demons, a'right? There's different orders of seraphim. Legion are the pacifists, the healers."

"Is Jesus Legion too?"

"Naw, Josh is Luminary," Scooter said. "Order of enlightenment. Scholars, scribes, archivists of history. The Nerd Herd."

The assassin's head pounded. God, angels, demons. Accepting their existence called his entire reality into question. Worse still, it meant Sister Claudia had been right.

"What about the Devil?" he asked.

Scooter eyed the slice of courtyard visible through the open door of the kori. "What about him?"

"He exists?"

"Yeah, why?"

"Call it due diligence."

Scooter kicked his sandals off and wiggled his toes. "Lucifer got up in Dad's grill, went to war against his own family. Tore Heaven asunder and all that. Michael cast his traitor ass out, along with a third of the host, everyone who had his back. Now he's the Big Kahuna on Brimstone Beach."

"He as bad as everyone says?"

"How the hell would I know? I haven't seen my brother in five billion years."

Clearly a sensitive subject and the assassin sensed that now wasn't a good time to probe. Scooter's eyes were barely open. The power to heal came at a cost.

"One more question."

"Shoot."

"If you're an angel, where's your halo and harp?"

Scooter flipped his middle finger. "Harp this."

Within minutes Scooter fell asleep and the assassin started sorting the snarl of details racing around his brain. A nebulous God. Surfing Angels. Demon pranksters. Lucifer, the Great Ruiner of Everything. He couldn't positively determine the truth, only that Scooter wasn't lying. And he'd healed the assassin's injuries.

Blind Matt Murdock didn't have the luxury of relying on what he could see. He had to trust his instincts in a way few people could. That's what gave Daredevil his edge. Angels, God, Armageddon? When all possibilities are exhausted, what are you left with but the impossible?

The assassin picked himself up and peered out the door into the courtyard. He spotted Michael by the drum tower. She'd ditched her swords and jacket and appeared to be meditating, eyes closed, hands resting palms up on her knees bent into half-lotus. He slipped through the door and ventured to the top of the kori steps.

This was the first chance he'd had to observe her without the threat of imminent decapitation. Now he couldn't decide if she was plainly beautiful, or beautifully plain. There was nothing extra or unnecessary about her. She had the lean androgyny of an endurance athlete, and the fatigues she wore did nothing to diminish the genderless effect. Her one concession to femininity floated unbound to her waist. Shimmering strands of rust and blood cloaked her like a living thing. No wonder she'd flipped over a small bit being severed. He felt a pang of aesthetic regret himself.

"What's up?" Scooter asked standing in the doorway, bright eyed after his short nap, though still a bit gray in the face.

The assassin gestured to the rifle slayer. "Michael? The Archangel?"

"Thought she was a dude, right? Told you the Bible is fucked."

"Then why were you busted carrying one around?"

"You know about that?"

"I do now."

"Well it ain't just the big B. Got lots of books stashed here and there. The Torah, Quran, the Rigveda in Sanskrit. Even had a Portuguese Book of Mormon, but I lost that back in Cali."

"You've spent time in California?"

"Sick swell off Pillar Point."

The assassin touched the thin scars on his neck. "I don't want to believe you."

"Well I suggest you put on your big boy pants and get with the program. Because that there is the captain of Heaven's army, and my guess is she's praying for guidance on whether or not to waste your ass."

The assassin glanced up at the bhoma, its maw hanging open over the kori, and then at Michael, a frozen lotus blossom in the courtyard. "Praying to the Christian God in a Hindu temple?"

"Ever hear of the blind men and the elephant?" Scooter asked, skimming his hand over a stone Ganesha. "Each one touches a different part—trunk, tail, ears, tusks—and none of them realize it's a single animal."

"Meaning?"

"Most religions have some of the parts. None have the whole pachyderm. Judaism and Islam latched onto the mono-God notion. Christians got on board with my bro, Joshua. Wiccans are jazzed up on

Gaia and the balance of nature. My Hindu peeps got a handle on things too. All their gods are just different aspects of one giant god, demons aren't so much evil as they are the other side of the rupee, and Hindus also plugged into the idea of reincarnation and how all the shit you do now shapes future experiences. Karma, y'know?"

"About that," the assassin glanced at Michael. "I would have killed you, Scooter. Why am I still alive?"

Scooter shrugged. "Ask her."

"Ask me what?"

The assassin started at the sound of Michael's low voice. A moment ago, she'd been unarmed, sitting across the courtyard. Now she stood at the base of the kori once again wearing the harness that held her blades. "Have you a question, assassin?"

Only a million or so, though it would behoove him to choose his words respectfully. "You destroyed my favorite rifle, you bitch."

Scooter paled from gray to ashy white.

"That is not a question," Michael said, blowing a strand of blood red hair off her face.

"I'm not scared of you."

She arched an auburn eyebrow. "Shall I admire your courage, or marvel at your stupidity? I am Michael, and you, assassin, are of no importance at all."

The needle swung in a wide arc. "You're lying."

"You assume much."

"I assume nothing."

Michael ascended until they stood eye to eye. The assassin's gaze dropped to a purple bruise spreading over her arm. Considering how much of his blood he was wearing on the outside, it pleased him that he'd been able to hurt her, and he made no effort to hide it.

"Okaaaay." Scooter shouldered his way between the two of them. "I got a question. How'd you get here so fast, Mikey?"

She gathered her hair, once again securing it at her nape. "The young woman you abandoned on that beach offered transport. Concerned for your welfare, I believe."

Scooter shoved his hands in his pockets. "She's good people."

"To know your hiding places, she must be very good."

"Funny." Scooter jerked his thumb at the assassin. "What's the deal? Even this douche-canard doesn't warrant your personal attention."

Michael cleared her throat softly. "I came for you, Scooter. Of the Thirty-six Concealed Ones, you are the sole survivor."

The assassin said nothing, but inventoried every detail as Scooter's eyes went dead, like every mote of life had withdrawn and buried itself deeper than any human could manage. Michael's expression remained neutral but she reached out, gently taking Scooter's hands between hers. Around her wrists the assassin noticed a pair of silver cuffs. Close fitting with a dull finish. Too unpretty to be decorative, and too small to serve as armor. They struck him as proprietary somehow. A mark of ownership.

"A deep rot consumes this world," she said. "The murder of the Thirty-six is an untenable escalation."

"Thirty-five, doll, thanks to you." Scooter stood and scrubbed his hands over his face. "Why save me? Why not the others?"

Michael crossed her arms over her chest. "Legion, you have been living as a human too long. Seraphim are not so free to do as we like."

"Yo, I only meant—"

"Spare me your atrocious dialect. Our Father gave orders. I carried them out. Though I suspect I've only delayed the inevitable."

"What's inevitable?" asked the assassin.

"Not now, mate," Scooter said. "Grown-ups are talking."

Too stunned to do anything but comply, the assassin stepped back.

"Mikey, I get it," said Scooter. "But just because I care about these primates, doesn't mean I got any less love for the family. Doesn't mean I've forgotten who I am."

"You interfered."

"I did what I thought was right."

"Thinking can be dangerous. You ought not do so much of it."

"Then why's he still breathing?" Scooter pointed to the assassin. "You need him, don't you?"

"What would you need me for?" the assassin asked.

"Shut up," they commanded in unison.

"Go home, Scooter. Leave this business to those willing to get their hands bloody."

Scooter drew himself up to his full lack of height. "That was low."

"Truth often is, for those who regret their choices."

The assassin couldn't help slicing into the conversation again. "What does this have to do with—"

"Shut up!" they said, pivoting away from one another, Scooter wearing a bitter expression, and Michael expressing nothing at all.

The assassin eyed the split gate. Beyond the temple walls, the cry of peacocks and the rustle of leaves intermittently burst through the muffled silence of the courtyard. He had to get out of here. Whatever angel's game they were playing, he had no skin in it.

With heavy slaps of his sandals, Scooter plodded over to Michael and rested his cheek against her shoulder blade. "Missed you."

She turned around and the assassin sensed the tension ease.

"Our Father will not suffer the souls of man to be enslaved," she said. "I have come to destroy the abomination you call the Panopticon."

"With a sword?" the assassin blurted out.

Michael sized him up. "You tell me, and bear in mind your potential use is the only thing keeping your head attached."

"Knew it," Scooter said.

The assassin ignored him but strange words darted through his mind. She will come for you. You will understand. You will choose. Well he sure as hell did not understand anything about what was happening here. "If your God is so offended by the state of his ant farm, why doesn't He smite Panopticon himself?"

"Because every action's got its equal and opposite," Scooter said, as though speaking to a delayed child. "God has to play by his own rules, mate. Divine intervention means divine blowback. As in start gathering up two of every animal."

"And if you fail?" the assassin asked Michael.

She stared up at the cloudless sky visible through the canopy. "A less poetic version of Saint John's Revelation."

"A real shit show, yeah?" Scooter cracked his knuckles. "So, let's not and say we didn't. Where do we start?"

Green flame leapt in Michael's eyes. "We?"

Scooter quailed, opening his mouth and shutting it again. Her silence invited him to go ahead and bury himself, if only to save her the trouble.

"C'mon! The murderer gets to stay up with the big kids while I toddle off to bed?"

"Toddle lightly, Scooter."

"Captain, are you ordering me to return?"

Her hands clenched into fists at her sides. "I am asking."

Scooter got halfway to throwing his arms around her when she thrust him back so hard he smacked the stone wall. "Ow."

"What did I say about hugging, Scooter? What did I say?"

"To not to." Scooter gingerly rubbed the back of his head.

"This is why you are constantly in trouble. You don't listen. This isn't a game."

"Exactly why I need to stay. There's a lotta good people here." He glanced at the assassin. "Well, maybe not here. No offense, mate."

The assassin shrugged.

Scooter turned back to Michael. "I've had a feeling the last couple days. It can't be random, the three of us, together, now."

"You have no evidence to support that hypothesis."

Scooter touched his fist to the center of his chest. "I don't need any."

"And you would have us proceed *sole fide*."

By faith alone. The assassin wondered how long he could dissemble. Much as he hated to admit he had a dog in this hunt, he couldn't stop thinking of Liza. Even in a broken world, she and her baby deserved a chance to live. They mattered.

INFRACTUS

"You're committed to this?" the assassin asked Michael.

"I am the sword arm of the Lord."

He considered her evasive assurance. "I might have an idea."

CHAPTER 24

The assassin rested against the wall of the inner sanctum across from the Archangel Michael. She watched him. He watched her. They did not speak. They did not make eye contact. Scooter had left for provisions three extremely tense hours ago.

Cool stone pressed into the assassin's back, conducting what felt like a low level electric current. He'd lost a tolerable amount of blood, to say nothing of the mental shock treatment. Enough to put anyone off balance, but he couldn't shake the sense that there was something strange about this place.

"Gather round, yo." Scooter strolled through the kori door carrying a battered satchel. "I come bearing gifts. As per your request, mate." He produced a small notebook with a pen jammed through the coils and handed it the assassin. "Oh, and this too. Unless we run into a herd of zombies, you kinda stick out."

The assassin caught the white T-shirt and squeezed the spongy knit between his fingers. "Thanks," he said, and truly meant it.

"Don't think Santa forgot about you, Mikey." Scooter crouched and emptied the bag onto the floor. Foil pouches, a bag of dried jackfruit, and a large canteen tumbled out. "Hope you're hungry."

Michael held up one of the pouches. "This is food?"

"Only the finest rations for you." Scooter produced a knife from the bag. The knife the assassin had dropped on the cliff. With an elegant twirl of the blade, Scooter sliced open a packet, shoved in a plastic fork and handed it to Michael. "Mac 'n cheese."

Michael's nose wrinkled as she sniffed the contents. The assassin pointed to the knife. "That's mine."

Scooter flipped it in the air, caught it by the blade, and offered the handle to the assassin. "Want it back?"

"Serious?"

"Trust has to start somewhere, and I don't got much use for knives."

Michael stuffed a forkful of orange noodles in her mouth. Her throat convulsed and she spit the mush back into the pouch. The assassin opened his own pack. The noodles were cold, slimy and gritty at the same time, with no discernable flavor aside from salt, but it was fuel so he forced it down.

"You guys are too picky." Scooter opened his own pouch and took a bite, chewing once, twice. "Oh man. It's like an alien came in my mouth."

The assassin dropped his fork back in his pouch and shoved it away. Scooter reached for the canteen. The assassin sorted through the pouches and found some that contained black rice pudding. He tossed one at Michael. She devoured hers in a few ravenous bites and the assassin offered her the rest of his. She accepted without any thanks but nudged her share of the dried jackfruit at him.

Scooter scraped the last gluey morsels of macaroni and cheese from his pouch. "Once you get past the deadly revoltitude, the stuff's not so bad. How's the pudding, Mikey?"

"Don't call me 'Mikey.' Next time, I will hurt you."

"If I had a grain of sand for every time I heard that, I'd have my own beach by now. 'Course I'd be breaking that pesky vow of poverty, not accumulating worldly possessions and property yada yada."

The assassin drank water from the canteen, trying not to think of how many microbes he might be ingesting. "Poverty? Pacifism? Sounds monkish."

"It is." Scooter dug into one of the abandoned pouches of mac and cheese. "But with better outfits and one other notable exception."

"Sex?" the assassin said. "But I thought angels didn't have any~"

Scooter pointed his fork at the assassin. "You humans get some fucking weird ideas in your nogs. We're made in His image too, y'know? Same bits and the same jones to use 'em."

"The same? Hardly." Michael accepted the canteen from the assassin. "Humans are not known for their restraint."

Scooter gnawed on a piece of jackfruit. "They do like to party."

"And the Pula Kahula? Whose table was she dancing on last night?" the assassin asked, ducking the jackfruit flying at his face.

"She's a friend. That's all."

"Does she know that? The way it looked through my scope . . ."

"Scope? D'you even hear yourself? You got problems in your brain."

"What's the deal with this girl?"

"No deal, at least no deal that's got anything to do with her."

"Explain."

INFRACTUS

"Stop," Michael said, barely above a whisper, but with the commanding reverb of a gunshot in a gymnasium. It made the assassin's bones shiver.

He scraped his notebook off the floor and retreated to his corner of the inner sanctum. Scooter recovered from his pique and chattered non-stop while Michael half listened and barely tolerated. They didn't act like angels. They were regular people. Regular siblings. The assassin wondered what it might be like to have a family. Brothers and sisters. Parents. People you belonged to.

He opened his notebook and clicked the pen. Time to work. He'd start with what he knew. Social order through surveillance was the cornerstone of Panopticon's governing philosophy. Safety and security at the expense of privacy and liberty. Not that the world was any less dangerous. In order to keep people safe, Panopticon became the danger. Pure shell game. Misdirection. But it worked.

With that understanding, the only way to defeat the Eye, was to blind it. He daydreamed about this often, but always ran into the same problem. Bringing down Panopticon wasn't a one-person job. He'd need at least three or four trustworthy individuals with specialized skill sets. He would have better luck unicorn hunting. Until now. Maybe. He scribbled down the new details.

Archangels: muscle/warriors

Legion: healers/missionaries

Michael: commands all angels

God: commands Michael, doesn't get involved

Humans: slaves (God doesn't like it)

Liza: important, don't know why

INFRACTUS

Me: tech support/logistics

The croaking chorus of frogs commenced as dusk washed in through the kori door, bruising the little chamber with shadows. When it grew too dark to write, the assassin put down the notebook and listened to the two figures conversing on the other side of the room.

"Why this temple?" Michael said. "This island of all places?"

"Earthquake, doll." Scooter's smile flashed white in the gloaming. "About ten years back. I came over with a few docs who wanted to open a field hospital off the Eye's grid. Talked the Brahman into letting us set up in the temple."

"You take foolish risks."

"Nothing bad ever happened here before, Mikey."

"Scooter. These dimensional rubs are unpredictable in the way they transmute energy. When you introduce a mass of human suffering . . ." She paused, pressing her hands together. "Humans are born to die, Legion. I fear I will never understand your resistance to that."

Scooter's silence thickened with the shadows.

Interesting. The assassin had put the random dizzies and electrically charged vibe down to symptoms of physical and mental stress, but they were talking about this place as through it were the threadbare heel of a dimensional sock.

Two angels and a hitman camp out in a Hindu temple discussing string theory.

It was more than a bad joke. He didn't believe in fate or destiny but there was an interconnectedness at work, and the assassin knew he'd been caught up in something that would drag him along regardless of his belief in it.

Scooter stood up and stretched his arms over his head. "Welp, being marked for death takes it out of a guy. Our ride hits dirt at first light. I'm gonna catch some rack."

"I will take watch." Michael gathered her sheathed swords and paused at the door. "Sleep well, Legion."

"Good to see you again, doll."

Scooter curled up on the floor and Michael slipped outside, both without so much as a glance in the assassin's direction.

CHAPTER 25

I n spite of the stone mattress, Scooter fell asleep instantly. People like him always did. Presumably Michael was in the courtyard, maintaining her vigil. Fierce and feline. A flesh and blood version of the bhoma.

The assassin knew he wouldn't sleep. Jungles came alive at night and the darkness awakened with a cacophony of squeaking bats, insects, and, of course, the blighted frogs. All from outside though. Not so much as a mosquito buzzed within the walls of the temple. The assassin got up and ventured out.

Moonlight dripped through the canopy into the courtyard as the assassin crossed the stones. He stopped in front of the split gate. Illumination didn't rain into the forest the way it did the temple. Beyond the gate he saw only a rustling black void.

"Going somewhere?"

Her breath grazed the back of his neck and her steel pressed under his jaw. He couldn't breathe, let alone speak, without the edge slicing through his recently healed skin. She withdrew the blade. He rubbed his throat. "Couldn't sleep. Frogs."

"I understand," she said.

Adrenaline scalded his veins as he spun around. Michael's face glowed silver around the black depressions of her eyes, and the moonlight streaked her hair like threads of venom through blood.

"Something disturbs you, assassin?"

He swallowed hard. "You look different in the dark."

"It is no trick of light." A smile tugged at the edge of her charcoal lip. "I have many faces. In this place, I am the dark. Those who worship here would know me as Kali, the Destroyer."

"This place." He scuffed his boot on the black stones. "I can't trust anything."

"Throughout the universe there are pockets of space where the dimensional walls are thin. I should not have spilled your blood here." Her sword whispered back into its sheath. "At ease, assassin."

"Not a chance."

"Do not think to play the victim. You attempted to murder someone dear to me, you threatened my life, and you cut my hair."

"Yes, but when was the last time you had a day this interesting?"

"Is that a joke?"

"I'm not sure."

A frown marred her ghoulish face. "I would not harm you, assassin. You are now under my command, and as such, under my protection."

"I should tell you up front that I have issues with authority."

"Mine?"

"Everyone's."

"Trust is a burden. That you lack the strength to bear it hardly surprises," she said, conveying her low opinion of him with such elegance it was hard to feel insulted. "In light of your deficiency, I can only share with you a fundamental truth even gods cannot escape."

"I'm listening."

"Broken oaths are powerful weapons in the hands of one's enemies." As she spoke, the inhuman planes of her jaw and cheekbones gentled. "Come, we should not linger in the open."

The assassin followed her across the courtyard. "Don't you need to sleep?"

"Eventually," she non-answered. They settled on the ground against the wall, facing the split gate. She looked almost normal again as she slipped off her harness and placed her swords on the ground between them, marking a boundary. "You've yet to tell me your name, assassin."

He wasn't sure if she'd asked him a question or stated a fact. "I've tried a few. Nothing sticks."

"Perhaps for the best. Names have power."

Her words carried the ring of truth, even if he didn't wholly understand. For the hundredth time he wondered if he hadn't fallen into a tropical fever dream. "Who are the Thirty-six?"

She hesitated, tapping her fingers on the stone floor. "All seraphim are permitted the opportunity to cross the veil, leaving memory behind, to be born, live, and die as a human. At any given time, there are thirty-six such Concealed Ones on Earth, pursuing a life of fellowship and enlightenment in the hopes that their example will inspire others."

"Why do they have to be human?"

"Clever design." Michael said. "Earlier, you heard me say humans are meant to die, and it's quite true. Particularly for the Thirty-six, who often have their kindness and courage repaid with violence."

"Or crucifixion?"

"Indeed, some of the Thirty-Six have been better concealed than others," she said, twisting a silver cuff around her wrist. "The important thing is that when a human body dies, it releases the soul like a chrysalis opens for a butterfly. By contrast, an angel's body," she gestured to her own black clad torso, "is an interwoven part of the soul as opposed to a mere vessel. They aren't meant to exist separately. This means we do not age as humans do and we're quite a bit harder to kill, but when an angel's body does succumb to acute trauma or cumulative abuse, the soul must tear its way free. The resulting damage is catastrophic. These ragged wraiths wander in shadow, with no body, and no memory, existing in a perpetual state of nothingness. It can take millennia to heal the rents in their psyche to the point where they are once again able to manifest corporeal form."

Now that sounded like hell, more so than any cartoonish fire and brimstone imagining that Sister Claudia had used to try and scare him straight. Suddenly it dawned on him why Michael would allow all but one of the Thirty-six to die. "Scooter...he's not like the others."

"Ever the exception," she said in a tight voice. "His healing gift is divine in nature. He chooses to use it in the service of humankind and accepts the risk of wraithdom that comes with walking the earth in angelic flesh."

"He's been here a long time then."

"Only God can call an earthbound seraphim home."

"And you speak for Him," he said, recalling that layered seismic voice she'd used. "But now that you're here?"

"Only God can call me back. And He won't, not until the fate of your species has been decided."

"Do you care either way?"

Her face hardened into a mask of bone. "I am not the judge, assassin. I am merely the executioner. Surely you can relate."

"The Lord rebuke thee."

She bristled. "You quote human scripture as though it should amuse me."

"Does it?"

She tossed her braid over her shoulder, a haughty girlish gesture incongruous with the way her eyes flashed Kali-black in her silver face. Bad idea, nettling her like this. He ought to be careful, but right now it felt good to be careless. The assassin completely understood Scooter's choice not to play it safe in a human body.

"Can demons strut around on earth like angels can?"

Michael stared through the gate into the jungle. "By His decree, the fallen are denied corporeal form outside of their kingdom."

"Hell?"

She remained silent, wrists crossed over her knees, the silver cuffs dull in the bright moonlight. He decided to change the subject. "Your katanas are incredible."

"They are," she said, fingertips feathering over the blade. "If it matters to you, I regret the destruction of your rifle. I know what it is to treasure your weapon."

"Then you understand why I'll never forgive you." A pang of what he supposed must be grief seized him hard when he thought of his Springfield. "These cut right through it. What are they made of?"

"Nothing you'd find on earth. You can touch them if you like."

Reverently, he picked one up. An inscription of runic characters ran the length of the blade. "What does it say?"

She uttered a bitter laugh. "The Archangel Michael, who is like unto God . . ."

"And stands against the Dragon," he finished, a frisson of unease running through him. Twenty-five years ago, Sister Claudia dreamed of this sword. He set the blade down next to its twin. "Are they treated with anything?"

"Consecrated blades will burn the wicked." Their fingers touched briefly as he handed over the sword. "Excruciating, is it not?"

The assassin rubbed the fresh skin on his neck. "You've felt it?"

"I am naught but another sinner."

When she wasn't pulverizing him, The Archangel Michael was an interesting person. She spoke well, didn't fidget, or dither. She exuded formidable strength, yet nothing could be as old as time and not have a few scars. She was dangerous. She'd been burned by her own blades. She had his attention.

Together at last. Side by side.

He looks tired. He hasn't slept in days. Not that anyone could sleep in this place. There's some power here, but not like the lacuna. Most of what I imagine he's feeling is because of Her. She finally saw fit to hustle her tight ass down here, and now the game is on. The divine proximity of the one who is like unto God will erode all I've put in place. Memory blocks, time distortions, perception filters, agnosia, all of it will crumble. The reckoning approaches.

I shouldn't be here. Weak as I am in astral form, it's possible she'll detect my energy signature. She's been where I've been, after all, and it changed her. It changed everything. None of us would be in this situation today if not for her actions then. Much as it galls me to give that bitch any opportunity at all, his choice must be his own. For all that I've taken, I owe him that much.

CHAPTER 26

A t dawn, the assassin followed a bushy-tailed Scooter out of the monkey forest to a fallow field outside Ubud, where a battered Cessna Citation waited for them.

"That's our bird," Scooter said.

"Looks like it belongs in an aviation museum."

Scooter yawned. "Her chassis might be old world, but underneath she's retrofitted for transoceanic range at high alt. She'll get us to Cali, no prob."

"Says who?"

The Cessna's cabin door swung open and Wayan leaned out, waving. "Hello, my friends!"

The assassin smiled and returned the wave, speaking to Scooter through clenched teeth. "What the hell is he doing here?"

Scooter also grinned and waved. "Wayan's been piloting bules around the globe for years. Don't worry, I've been up with him lots. He even lets me drive sometimes. The beauty part is that the Eye ain't gonna question his flight plan."

"How much does he know?"

"Only that you're gonna fork over double fare on all nine seats."

"How generous of me."

INFRACTUS

The assassin glanced over his shoulder to see Michael hiking out of the trees. He wished they looked less like fugitives. She had her swords wrapped in her jacket, but between physical altercations and a night in the jungle, they had a grubby hunted aura about them.

"I don't believe we were followed," Michael said, joining them beside the plane. "Is this craft airworthy?"

The sun glinted off Wayan's wedding band as he beckoned to them. "All aboard, my friends!"

The assassin climbed in after Scooter and Michael. The interior of the plane was a stunning contrast to the peeling dimpled exterior. Four overstuffed seats upholstered in buttery brown leather ran down either side of the center aisle. Polished wood paneling glowed in the mellow light from recessed LED fixtures. The assassin hoped everything behind the closed cockpit door was as meticulously maintained as the passenger cabin. Not that he had an alternative. They had a shrinking window of time in which to make their escape before Panopticon put a burn notice on him.

Wayan closed the hatch and locked them in. The assassin noticed that while the man had a smile on his face, his hands were shaking.

"Welcome aboard Air Wayan. Have your seats, my friends, and fasten your belts. Wheels up in five minutes and flight time to California is thirteen hours."

Michael settled in the back while the assassin situated himself closest to the cockpit. He sank heavily into the leather and rubbed his gritty eyes. He'd been awake for over forty-eight hours and hoped to catch some sleep over the pacific. Scooter sprawled in the row behind him and in Balinese, conveyed their collective gratitude to Wayan. Still grinning, Wayan slipped into the cockpit, closing the door behind him.

"He seem nervous to you?" the assassin asked.

Scooter hugged the back of the assassin's seat poking his head around the side. "Well he ain't stupid. Probably knows he's doing something crazy illegal."

With a hiss the cabin pressurized and the jet stuttered into motion, rapidly accelerating. The assassin's stomach dipped when the wheels left the ground. For the next thirteen hours they were in a holding pattern, and a rather comfortable one at that. The smell of leather and the steady drone of the turbofan engines lulled him into a drowsy daze. He watched wisps of cloud streak past the windows as they gained altitude. He melted into the overstuffed chair and tumbled into sleep.

A distant chorus of voices chanted his name. His true name, over and over. He veered toward the sound, his feet trudging through something powdery, like snow or ash. He tried to open his eyes, but they were already open.

Layers of shadow undulated in the darkness, and with no visual reference points, his balance wavered. Every so often the shadows thinned, admitting an echo of light, though he couldn't identify the source. The chanting rose and fell in waves. He could almost understand, almost hear, but as always, he couldn't hold it in his memory. Whomever the voices belonged to, they lived in a place existing on the verge of sensory perception.

"Liminal," he murmured, his voice a strange lurch of sound within the bizarre acoustical space. The chanting stopped, and a single voice whispered in both his ears.

Wake up.

"Go away. I'm having a dream. An actual dream."

Dreams are what I've protected you from your whole life.

"By messing with my head, my memory?"

For good reasons that you will soon understand, but something's gone wrong.

"Not exactly a mastermind, are you?"

I'm not fucking around.

If you don't wake up now, you're all going to die.

The voice imbued the word "die" with a psychic shove, elbowing the assassin out of the liminal space where he gradually became aware of the purring engines and smooth leather under his cheek. He sensed someone pass by. Wide awake in an instant, he twisted around to find Wayan standing over Scooter, pointing a small revolver at his head.

The assassin pitched himself out of his chair into the aisle. "Wayan, put that down."

Sweat beaded on Wayan's upper lip and the gun quivered in his hand. "I am sorry. Truly sorry."

The assassin studied the revolver, a .22 caliber snub-nosed Ruger. Standard government issue sidearm. He had one himself, stored in his Acadia safe house.

"Dude, this isn't you," Scooter said, gently. "Let's talk, okay? Whatever it is we'll figure it out."

"My friend." Tears slid down Wayan's face and his finger tightened up on the trigger.

The assassin lunged. Wayan swung around and the report of gunfire shouted within the confines of the cabin. Heat unfurled from a focal point above the assassin's hip. Ears ringing, he saw Wayan gasp, and sway with six inches of steel protruding from the center of his chest. He dropped to his knees in the aisle.

"The Lord rebuke thee," Michael murmured, bracing one booted foot on Wayan's back to wrench her sword from his body.

Scooter scrambled out of his chair and gathered the dying man in his arms. Without a properly working pump to provide pressure, very little blood poured out of the wound in Wayan's chest. The assassin's heart was pumping just fine and he jammed his fist into his side to staunch the steady outflow.

"My friend," Wayan whispered, clutching Scooter's hands. "She say if I do this thing...she will give Nengah back to me...she say..."

"She?" the assassin asked, his gut plunging as the cockpit door opened.

Suit Two emerged in tailored tropical weight slacks and a sleeveless blouse that exposed the threadwork of scars coiling around the compact muscles of her arms, including the white ring she'd carved into her skin after the Ori Mane fiasco.

Shark-gray eyes landed on the assassin. "You had one job."

"Am I fired?"

Suit Two grinned with too many teeth and pointed her SIG at Michael. "Nice pocket knife, sweetheart. Drop it."

Michael let the bloody sword fall with a clank on the carpeted aisle. "How inadequate you must be to press a civilian into your service."

"Ooh, sassy redhead. Cliché much?" Suit Two's gaze then fell on Scooter as he cradled a quietly dying Wayan. She licked her bottom lip. The assassin knew she had a fresh corpse fetish. How far it went, he didn't want to know. "I was curious," she said. "Wondered if he'd kill someone he loved to save someone he loved more. People are interesting that way."

"What'd you do to Nengah?" Scooter demanded, his voice hoarse.

"The wife? Never met her. She's fine, I guess."

Blood saturated the assassin's pant leg. He wadded up a handful of his shirt and packed it harder against the bullet hole. Suit Two was a big problem, one he had to gain some traction on, and fast.

"Guess I'm a burnable asset after all," he said.

Suit Two tore her eyes from Wayan. "Not yet, you aren't."

"Then what the hell are you doing here?"

"I'm your handler, kid. I'm handling you. Your last couple assignments were sloppy. I came here to keep an eye, and you know, I'm actually surprised? Tipping points are usually predictable. With Radcliffe and Lusczak I saw it coming a mile away. Didn't see it with you."

"Where's Suit One?"

She covered her mouth with her gun hand, giggling. "I ditched him. He's probably sweating it out, wondering if I'm off my meds. He worries, you know?"

"And you take pleasure in that," Michael said. "Because your wounds are so deep and so old, you know not what it feels like to be whole."

The assassin was uncomfortably aware that Michael's observations applied at least as well to him, and that whether he liked it or not, he and Suit Two were fundamentally similar creatures.

"Something terrible must have happened to you," said Michael.

"Sweetheart, if you don't stop poking that pretty beak where it doesn't belong, I'm going to have to cut it off." She pointed her SIG like an accusing finger at the assassin. "Where'd you find this nosy cunt?"

A chill filled the cabin and the assassin fixed Michael with a hard stare, telling her to let him handle this. To do that, he needed to flip the power dynamic. "What's the play? Assuming you're not here to retire me."

"Glad you asked." Suit Two cheerfully aimed her gun at Scooter and Michael. "First, we take care of these. Then you and I pay a visit to Father Barclay's home for unwed mothers."

He dug his fingers into the soft leather cushion, his pinky finding the hole where the bullet that had gone through him lodged in the seat. "How did you know?"

"Kid, the only way y'all wouldn't leave a body was if there was no body to leave. Coming up with a short list of where you'd take her wasn't hard. Now you're going to finish what you started with that little tramp on the bridge, or I will."

"Not going to happen."

"So, stop me. Because I can't. It's my nature. I'm incorrigible that way."

Scooter shook his head at the assassin. Wayan was gone, the revolver hanging from his dead hand. Suit Two's pupils dilated and her eyes rolled back as her nostrils flared and her cheeks flushed. She was insane. Everyone knew it. Even she knew it. Cutting herself to ribbons, turning herself into a monster, something no one could love.

INFRACTUS

The assassin's hands smeared blood over leather as he slowly towed himself up the aisle toward Suit Two, closing the distance between them by another row, getting between her and Wayan's body.

"Barclay still talks about you," he said.

Suit Two's eyelids slid shut and opened again like a shark's nictitating membrane. "He does?"

"Told me he knew your parents, that he watched you grow up. He cares about you."

"Old man always did have a soft spot for head cases."

"He'd help you, if you let him."

"You think I don't know you're playing me?"

"I'm telling you the truth. And I think the intelligent adult inside you knows that."

"I'm not sure, kid." Suit Two's fingertips traced the filaments of scar tissue trailing down between the open buttons of her blouse. "It's been what? Three years since I had an intelligent adult inside me?"

Her attempt to bait him only proved he was getting to her. "I'm sorry I never cared enough to know you."

Her smirk vanished. "That wasn't our deal."

"I'm done, and you know it."

"Don't say that," she snarled, baring her teeth.

"Come with us. You've already escaped, this is your chance." He paused. "Don't go back to him."

"I said shut up!"

She ground her knuckles into her temple. This was his chance, the only one he'd get. He feinted for Wayan's gun. Suit Two reacted like a trained professional, aiming not at him, but at the Ruger. He knew she'd do this because she'd taught him the same technique. By aiming at a stationary object and anticipating the target's trajectory, you greatly improved your odds of a kill shot. Except he didn't follow through. Instead he awkwardly threw himself against her from the side and they fell into a row of seats.

He heard her gun thump to the carpet. With her back against his chest, she twisted until her full weight jammed the small of his back down onto an armrest. Her elbow jabbed into his wound. He saw white, but managed to get her in a headlock.

"Carmen," he said in her ear.

Her struggles ceased. "I always knew it would be you."

He tried to hoist them off the seat but he couldn't do it without letting her go. She'd kill Liza. She'd kill them all. She'd never stop. She couldn't. Sharks have to keep swimming or they die. She tensed on top of him, gathering strength.

"I'm sorry," he said.

A swift twist, and a dull crack. Her body slid onto the carpet in a boneless heap, head lolling. He saw shock in her dimming eyes. Then nothing. Problem solved.

"Assassin." Michael tugged him upright. "Assassin?"

With nothing left to distract him, the assassin clutched his side, overwhelmed by pain. "I'm not an expert on teamwork, but aren't there certain conventions? Like helping me when I'm unarmed and you have a sword?"

"I considered assisting."

"But?"

"You were handling it. Now come along."

INFRACTUS

The plane lurched as she slung his arm across her shoulders and dragged him around poor dead Wayan, to the back of the plane where Scooter waited with an open first-aid kit. He gave Michael a baleful look but said nothing. She retreated to the seat next to Wayan's body where she sat still as wax, staring out the window.

The assassin slipped off his shirt and Scooter silently sponged away the gore. He probed at the small entry wound, and palpated across the assassin's flank until he found another breach. "Good news, mate. Through and through. No need to go prospecting."

"Riot," the assassin said weakly.

Scooter chucked the bloody gauze in an airsickness bag. "So, we're headed for California to see Barclay?"

"You know him?"

"Who do you think hooked me up with docs and supplies for that off-grid hospital in Pura Dalem?"

"Small world."

Scooter stole another bereft glance at Wayan. He dug in his pocket, and pulled out a gold ring. "What d'you suppose I should say to Nengah when I give this back to her?"

The plane dipped. Scooter didn't want advice, but rather acknowledgment of the bleak truth. Wayan was dead. Anyone else they involved stood a good chance of ending up the same way.

Scooter shoved the ring back into his pocket. "You caught a bullet for me, bro. I owe you one."

"Convince Barclay to not shoot me on sight and we'll call it even."

"Deal."

Scooter laid his open palms on both sides of the assassin's bullet wound. Pain faded and intense warmth flooded the area. That weightless sense of well-being started to rush in when he grabbed Scooter's wrists and gently pushed him back.

"Enough."

"Dude, I've barely stopped the bleeding."

The assassin reached for the bandages. "I know what it does to you, and we need you need to fly the plane."

"What?"

"You said Wayan let you do it before."

"As in take the wheel for a few minutes, bro. I don't know how to work the controls."

"Don't let the instrumentation scare you. There's got to be a manual somewhere—"

"Are you high? It's a jet, not a Jeep."

The assassin grabbed Scooter by the front of his shirt, dragged him down the aisle into the cockpit and threw him sideways into the pilot's seat. "Scooter, I've had the kind of day where exit wounds are the good news. Now, if you haven't noticed, we're losing altitude, so stop making excuses, locate your balls, and fly this fucking plane."

Scooter straightened up and grasped the yoke with both hands, grumbling. "Would it kill ya to say please?"

The assassin swallowed a colorful reply and headed back into the cabin where Michael knelt next to Wayan. Suit Two's lifeless hand peeked out from between the seats, her fingertips protruding into the aisle

Michael wiped her bloody blade clean on the dead man's shirt. "Few are capable of doing what we do, assassin."

"What's that?"

"Whatever is necessary."

He found his own shirt and put it back on. The meaty reek of blood saturated the air of the cabin so heavily he could taste the iron.

"Uh, guys," Scooter called from the pilot's chair. "We got a humungo problem. I tried to lift us back up but the autopilot's locked me out. She must have programmed it, like a self-destruct."

The assassin read the GPS, shocked to see they were nearing the California coast. "How long was I sleeping?"

"Dunno, twelve hours maybe?"

"We thought you were dead," Michael added, almost cheerfully.

It never failed. Weirdness walked in and his sense of time walked out. He'd never slept half that long in a stretch before. To say nothing of what he was sure had to be a dream. His first.

Scooter tapped the map screen. "That's Halfmoon Bay. Looks like she'll make a water landing north of there. We got maybe ten minutes?"

The assassin scanned the controls. He knew nothing about navigation systems or their programming platforms. Radcliffe was right, he should have learned.

"Assassin?" Michael asked. "Are we certain the intent was self-destruction? Was your associate the sort of person to take her own life?"

She made a good point. Self-mutilation was one thing, but Suit Two was a creature of instinct, and what instinct was stronger than the will to survive? She knew he couldn't let her go, but she still fought to the end. Suit Two was not suicidal.

The assassin dashed out of the cockpit, hurdling over the bodies to the back of the plane. Ripping open the storage compartment, he discovered a coil of climbing rope, a nylon bag containing an inflatable raft and collapsible oars, and a parachute pack.

"You were right," he said to Michael. "This was her plan. Scuttle the plane. Make a clean getaway."

Scooter glanced back at Suit Two. "She's a buck twenty tops. Will her chute take all of us?"

"Do you have a better idea?"

No one offered alternatives. So, he laid out the plan.

The assassin donned the harness attached to the parachute pack, and used the rope to improvise a harness for Michael, tying it to his own with plenty of rope leftover. They waited. Two touch-averse people awkwardly pressed against one another. "Scooter, what's our altitude?"

"Nineteen thousand and falling."

"Kill the engines."

"Huh?"

"So we don't get sucked into a turbine when we open that door."

The plane shuddered into eerie silence. Scooter raced out of the cockpit and the assassin clumsily fed the rope through and around, getting Scooter tied on as quickly as possible. A lift in his stomach signaled the beginning of their dive. He put on the goggles so he'd be able to read the altimeter in his watch. "Time to go."

Scooter pulled back the locking lever and opened the hatch.

INFRACTUS

Nothing could have prepared the assassin for the experience of free fall. Rapid depressurization sucked them out of the plane. The wind howled and ripped at his clothes, his insides seem to fall faster than his outsides, and the skin of his face scraped back as they reached terminal velocity. He found it thrilling, but Michael and Scooter clung to him like kindergartners on their first day of school. Michael pressed her face into his chest against the wind and Scooter curled around him in a ball. The assassin wasn't sure what bothered him more, Michael's elbow jabbing his barely stabilized bullet wound, or Scooter's knee digging into his groin.

The altimeter reached three thousand feet. Pull height. Red cord. Blue cord. Hopefully he'd done it right. A surprisingly gentle upward tug pulled them out of free fall. He tilted his head back to see a white cloud of parachute bobbing over them.

Michael and Scooter relaxed their koala clutch as they drifted through the morning sky over the glittering sapphire carpet of the Pacific Ocean, edged by the yellow California coast. A muted boom rolled in the distance, like faraway thunder, though the sky was clear.

"That would be the plane," the assassin said.

"This is righteous!" Scooter said, twisting around for a panoramic view.

"Scooter," the assassin croaked. "Your knee."

Scooter dropped his leg. "No permanent damage, I hope?"

"Least of my worries," he said. "Okay, here's the plan. At twenty feet I'm going to release the parachute so we don't get caught up in it. We'll hit the water hard, but hold your breath and stay still. I'll cut the ropes, and you swim for the surface. Michael, you have the raft. Pull the cord as soon as you're free to. That's how we'll find each other."

The wind whipped Michael's hair loose from its ponytail. It curled around the assassin's neck and stroked his face like silky red feathers. Sister Claudia had a tomato garden with a lattice wall at the back crawling with sweet peas. On warm summer nights, he'd sneak outside and sit in the garden, reading comics by flashlight surrounded by that distinctive fusion of flowers and the green spice of tomato vines. Michael smelled exactly like it.

"How far are we?" she asked.

The assassin blew her hair off his face and consulted the GPS on his watch. "At splashdown, about twenty miles. Long way to swim, so hang on to that raft."

Seagulls swooped and circled beneath them as they reached five hundred feet. The assassin tried to ignore the cold crush of fear as the ocean drifted up to meet them. At thirty feet, he closed his hand around the canopy release handle. "Hang on."

Falling as a single object, they hit the water with all the grace of a turkey kicked off the high dive. The assassin breathed in salt water, tried to cough but only sucked in more. The ropes and straps tugged him in all different directions. Michael and Scooter squirmed on either side of him, but he saw only bubbly murk. He needed to cut them loose. He fumbled for the knife in his belt, but his fingers were numb. He was drowning.

CHAPTER 27

S omething slammed repeatedly into his back between his shoulder blades. He cracked open one eye, seeing only yellow. He coughed and spluttered, each heave of his chest sending a jagged beat of pain through his skull.

"Deep breaths, assassin."

His head rested on Michael's thigh and her hand jostled his shoulder, the same hand that pounded the water out of his chest. His lungs were raw after their latest salt water scouring, but he soon found himself breathing easily enough.

He wriggled over squeaking yellow rubber into a seated position. Their raft, inflated, was perhaps meant to hold one person and their gear, or maybe two people if they were friendly. Three was a definite crowd.

Scooter reclined beside the assassin, legs slung over the side. Michael coiled her hair into a red rope and wrung out the excess water. "You are well, assassin?"

"Disappointed?"

Scooter unfolded the oars. "Let's bring this teacup in."

It was a long day of rowing through calm water. By the time they were a mile out from the beach at Halfmoon Bay, the sun had dipped low in the sky behind them. The waves picked up. They made it to the trough of a ten-foot swell, still aboard their tiny raft, but the next wave capsized them.

The assassin lost count of how many times he got yanked under, held down, and pushed back up. Each time he broke the surface he breathed in equal amounts of water and air. Finally, he scraped shifting sand beneath his feet. Too exhausted to swim, he let the waves do the work of dragging him in and slapping him down on the beach.

A belt of pain squeezed around his bullet wound, making it difficult to take a full breath. How many times could he escape drowning when it seemed the universe was determined to dispose of him in exactly that manner? He lifted his head and saw a tall figure slopping out of the whitewash.

"Scooter?" Michael whispered.

They scanned the waves in the growing darkness. No sign of Scooter. The assassin's heart thudded and his throat tightened.

"There," she said, pointing down the beach.

"Yo, we made it," Scooter said staggering toward them. He pitched forward and Michael caught him before he could fall on his face.

The constriction in the assassin's throat dissolved and he found his voice. "What took you so long?"

"Spa day, dude." Scooter rubbed a raw patch on his cheek. "Sand facial, whirlpool bath, and a few too many Neptune cocktails."

Just then Michael doubled over, quietly vomiting into the sand.

"Aw, s'okay doll." Scooter held her hair back as she continued to retch up seawater. The assassin kept his distance, not sure what he should do. Had Scooter learned how to comfort people, or was it natural instinct? Holding the hair back was logical enough, but how did he know she would let him?

Michael glanced up and caught the assassin staring. She wiped her mouth with the back of her hand. "Are you sufficiently entertained?"

He didn't have the energy to argue. "Let's get out of here."

In spite of the fancy microchip gizmo security measures, it boiled down to completing a circuit. The assassin sifted through the wires under the steering column of the C-A that could have been his if not for the dog hair matted into the front passenger seat.

"Do we hafta do this?" Scooter whined.

The assassin ripped out the GPS beacon and tossed it onto the warm asphalt of the parking lot. "What's the big deal?"

"We're breaking one of the commandments."

"Legion, I grow weary of your moralizing," Michael said. "We are not stealing. We are commandeering resources unobtainable through conventional means."

"So, ...stealing, then?" Scooter plunked down on the pavement, stretching his legs out and leaning back against one of the C-A's tires. "At least try not to enjoy it so much."

"You're the most uptight surfer I've ever met," the assassin remarked from under the dash. "If I wanted to get greedy I'd boost that vintage Tesla over there, not this ugly chunk of plastic."

"Dude, how many cars have you stolen?"

"Really want me to answer that?" The assassin switched on the motor, the weak hum not nearly as gratifying as the rumble of a combustion engine. "The way you're counting off sins, I'm sure the owner of this heap has it coming. He probably coveted something, or worshipped a golden calf once."

"That's right, be a smartass."

"Enough," Michael said, but not in that dreadful God voice. "Every moment you two spend bickering is a moment I spend listening to you bicker, and my patience wears thin. Do not anger me."

The assassin opened the door to the back seat for her. "I'll drive."

The Napa Valley at night could be summed up in one word: dark. Something the people of fifty years ago had little experience with unless they were wilderness survivalists. In fact, light pollution had been a serious problem. Clearly those people had no concept of how terrible true darkness could be.

The assassin ignored the shredding pain in his side and focused on navigation. The stolen C-A's headlights struggled against the black and secondary roads in this area weren't well marked. The rolling hills and oak trees were presumably still out there, but who really knew? Perhaps when nightfall claimed the light it claimed the land as well. Maybe it was like that Bradbury story—maybe this was Mars. Christ, he missed books. He had quite a few stashed in his safe houses, and Barclay had several shelves full of books in his living room. The assassin had caught a glimpse of the old man's collection years ago and been curious ever since. What sort of books might be found in the private library of a priest turned terrorist?

He glanced in the rearview at Michael. They hadn't been on the road for ten minutes when she passed out. "She alive?"

Scooter had a peek. "Yup. Check the eyes. She's dreaming."

What might the Archangel Michael dream about? More and more questions. The assassin recalled the dream he had on the plane. At least he thought it was a dream. How would he know? Whatever it was, it had to mean something. If he cleared his mind he could sense the answer, like a candle at the end of a dark tunnel. But something blocked its light, something physical, like a wall.

"Hey," Scooter said. "Sorry about your friend. That couldn't have been easy."

"We weren't friends. She was my boss, and a bad habit. In that order."

"Wanna talk about it?"

The assassin stared ahead at the moving belt of highway. "I admired her authenticity. She was a wild animal and never pretended to be anything else. I guess I envied her freedom."

Scooter shifted into a cross-legged position. "Is that freedom? Or is it being a slave to the worst parts of yourself?"

Goddamnit, could Scooter just once not be right about everything? Being better was hard, and few people in his life had given him reason to think it was work worth doing. Sister Claudia, Jenny, Barclay. Even Zee had his moments. Like the time he found a case of little candy bars in the wreckage of a convenience store. They would've hauled a fortune on the black market, but Zee had something else in mind. *C'mon, Mouse. Let's take a hike.* They wasted an entire afternoon roaming the streets, giving candy bars to every dirty-faced brat they saw. Zee was never a slave to the worst parts of himself, he served them willingly, and the assassin supposed that kind of commitment, in its own way, was also worthy of respect.

INFRACTUS

The assassin applied the brake and the car crept down a red dirt lane, passing through a wrought iron gate. Always open, though not necessarily in welcome. He drove slowly. Slower than he needed to.

"Don't sweat it, bro," Scooter said. "I got this."

The assassin wasn't so sure. A lot depended on how Barclay liked being woken up in the middle of the night by someone who did wet work for his sworn enemy.

He stopped the car in front of the house and killed the motor. The headlights blinked out, plunging them into total darkness. He rolled down the window to let in fresh air smelling of dry earth and ripening grapes.

The porch lamp flicked on. A light in the night.

CHAPTER 28

The storm door swung open and Barclay followed the barrel of his Winchester onto the tidy veranda.

"Whoever you are, you'd best come out easy."

The assassin hoped he hadn't made a fatal error in returning to Laughing Corpse. "Game on, Scooter. Do what you do."

Scooter opened the door and called out, "Yo, don't shoot, Padre."

"Scotty?"

"Long time, mate."

Barclay lowered the rifle and his weathered face cracked into a smile. "Dare I ask how life's been treating you?"

"Like it caught me pile-driving its wife."

"Just so." Barclay swiped a broad-knuckled hand over his forehead. "Grandpa said nothing good ever happened after midnight."

"Grandpa sounds like a gas."

"What trouble've you brung to my door, then?"

Scooter scampered barefoot to the porch and gestured to the car with a thumbs-up. The assassin unbuckled his safety belt. "I'm going to get shot again."

"I accept that risk," Michael said, already climbing out of the back seat. "Considering each breath you draw is one more than you deserve."

A nap had done nothing to improve her temper. All things considered, one of Barclay's .30 calibers point blank would taste better than the murder of crow the assassin could expect to eat otherwise.

Getting out of the car was fun. Every damaged part of him had stiffened during the drive, and when he raised his empty hands it felt like a knife twisting in his side. The proverbial spear wound.

Barclay raised his rifle again. "What'n the furry hell are you doing here? Scotty, there's a thing or three you'll want to know about this man."

"Uh, rubbish on a board, takes an ass kicking so well you'd swear he likes it, and he totally tried to kill me." Scooter ticked the indictments off on his fingers. "Am I missing anything?"

Barclay kept his rifle trained on the assassin. "Starting to suspect you ain't a very good hitman."

The assassin swallowed a bristled knot of professional pride. "Father, a month ago you told me to stick to the path. This is what I found. And we need your help."

"Did I not make myself clear?" Barclay said.

The screen door opened behind the old man, and Liza Ayomori, pregnant as hell in a white nightgown, floated onto the porch and placed her hand on the barrel of the rifle. "Please, Barclay. He's not here to hurt us."

Scooter's head swiveled from the assassin to Liza and back to the assassin. "Holy shit, you're the guy? The Baby Butcher?" He scrutinized Liza. "Lookin' mondo peppy for a corpse, niblet."

Liza clutched Barclay's sleeve. "They need help."

Barclay's wary gaze landed on Michael. "Don't believe we've been introduced, young lady."

"You are correct," she said, wading into the pool of yellow light on the grass. "Introductions rarely benefit the execution of my duties, but your reputation as a man of faith precedes you, Mr. Barclay."

"That so?"

She held out her hand. "I am the Archangel Michael."

Pearl shuffled into the kitchen in her housecoat, yawning and combing her fingers through the cloud of her hair. "Colin? Is everything all right? Oh...hello." She surveyed the gathering of strangers and scrutinized the assassin. "Either you're wearing the shroud of Turin, or you've brought me another bleeder."

The assassin glanced at the rusty stains on his shirt. "It's all mine this time."

"Shall I fetch my suture kit? I'm quite a seamstress, ask our little Liza."

He didn't think Pearl meant it as a dig, but that didn't stop him from reliving the memory of his knife sliding through Liza's skin. Her blood splashing hot on his arm. Currently, little Liza was in the kitchen, pouring water into the coffee pot, standing on her tiptoes, the hem of her nightgown drifting above her delicate ankles. Pearl hadn't exaggerated. Only the thinnest of red scars marred Liza's throat. Like the bead off a fine tip pen.

Barclay cupped Pearl's elbow. "Didn't mean to wake you. Go on back to sleep if you like."

"While you entertain middle of the night guests with a gun over your shoulder?" Pearl's arched eyebrow invited a challenge.

Barclay conceded and tucked a wild lick of silver hair behind her ear. Not very priestly, but Barclay hadn't worn the collar in nearly twenty years. Pearl disappeared back down the hall. Barclay set his rifle on the fireplace mantle in the living room.

"You trust us that much?" the assassin asked.

"You're either telling the truth or I've gone senile. Rifle ain't much use, regardless. Take a load off, son. You look like hell."

He was only too happy to slouch into a chair at the big oak table. Half an hour later, Pearl and Liza served up enough breakfast to feed a marauding platoon.

"Whoa, doc." Scooter all but drooled on the plate of pancakes and sausages Pearl slid under his nose. "Shouldn't have gone to the trouble, but I'm glad you did."

"Real nice table, Pearl." Barclay poured coffee into her cup as she slid into the chair next to him.

Liza put a plate of pancakes in front of the assassin. "Barclay says you're vegetarian."

He stared at his food. Visual information. Shapes on a plate. "When I was fourteen, I survived a three-day riot by hiding in a pile of charred corpses."

Liza covered her mouth with her hand. "Ugh."

"Yeah." He drank some orange juice. It was cold and tart and about the only thing he could justify remaining upright for.

"Refill?" Liza hovered, pitcher at the ready. He shook his head. She seemed disappointed until Scooter snagged the offer and she filled his glass. "I thought angels were supposed to be all glowy with white robes and wings."

"Wings are a myth, niblet. As for the white robed glowworm stuff, you're thinking of Gabriel. Boy's gotta do it up in full regalia every time."

"Suitable for his duties as the Messenger," said Michael.

"And looking like a tool," Scooter added.

Michael ignored him. "The white robes of Heaven are rather impractical for those whose work is more...colorful."

"Oh," said Liza.

The assassin understood why Liza might be underwhelmed. With her matted hair, salt-crusted fatigues, and a spray of petechial hemorrhage around her red-rimmed eyes, the Archangel Michael was anything but angelic. Weathered, savage, in desperate need of a bath, and so viscerally appealing that it made the assassin's throat dry up.

She caught him staring. He drank down the rest of his juice. This wasn't something that happened every day. He seldom experienced physical attraction. His past lovers numbered in the single digits. A small assortment of men and women. Enough for him to conclude that even at its most pleasurable, sex was still tolerably revolting.

"Aren't you going to eat" Liza asked.

Being gut shot had a way of killing an appetite, but he didn't want to go into that. He chewed a few bites of what tasted like oily sawdust.

Scooter and Michael, however, tucked in with gusto. Michael especially. She shoveled it back like an Asian kid at a hot dog-eating contest. A spectator sport. He spectated, and tried not to be obvious.

After Scooter and Barclay finished clearing the dishes, the assassin flinched as Liza's arms wrapped around his neck from behind. He barely curbed the reflex to hurl her over his shoulder and body slam her to the floor. Did she not understand what kind of person she was dealing with? What did she want? Why was she being nice to him? What in the blighted blue hell was wrong with this girl?

"Think I'm done being awake," she yawned in his ear. "G'night."

"I'm going to catch a few more myself," Pearl said, patting Scooter's arm. "Give me a shake when you need me?"

"Yup."

Barclay's hand briefly swallowed Pearl's before she departed with a sleepy Liza. Juice and a few bites of food restored the assassin enough to get excited about the end of the world. Barclay fetched up a pencil and notepad for him, and he settled into strategy mode. Time to be bad.

Barclay refilled the coffee cups. "Anyone care to bring me up to speed?"

"Simply put, Michael is here to bring down Panopticon," said the assassin. "And we're going to help her."

"May I ask how?" Barclay's jaw tightened with skepticism. Reasonable, considering the Jackals had been trying to accomplish that very goal for the last fifteen years; the limited impact of their efforts further weakened with the incarceration of their fearless leader. After seven years rotting in the Colony, Ori Mane was probably dead.

"Here are the details so far," said the assassin. "We're going to destroy their surveillance network. They have hundreds of nodes, but there's got to be a central mainframe. The big brain. From there I'm thinking we use something low-tech. Explosives."

Barclay cracked his old knuckles. The sound of a knotty log popping in the fire. In Barclay parlance, this was a semi-serious outburst. "First of all, Captain Dynamite, we don't know where the surveillance mainframe is. And second, leveling one server farm won't do much but tick 'em off."

"That's the idea."

"Thought the idea was to cut the head off the snake, not inconvenience the tail."

Michael leaned into the discussion. "The assassin feels this is the best way to draw out whomever is hiding behind the Eye."

"Sounds like the best way to get bit."

"Father," the assassin said. "I know it's asking a lot. But we can't do this without you."

Barclay stared into his coffee as though reading the future in the dregs. "We'll need three things. The location of the mainframe, security clearance, and the access codes to get in."

The assassin considered this. "Panopticon wouldn't trust an important installation like this to the local Patrol. A high-ranking military officer would be in charge of the site, and clearance authorizations are embedded in their idents."

"The ident won't give us them access codes."

"No, but the officer will."

"Are you certain?" Michael asked. "Surely your military men are trained to hold up under aggressive interrogation."

The assassin pressed the sharp tip of the pencil into the pad of his finger. "You let me worry about that."

"Whoa." Scooter scraped his chair back. "No way. We're not torturing anyone."

"Scooter, this is what I do, and if you don't like it—"

"Simmer down," Barclay said, motioning for Scooter to rejoin them. "If there's a way to pull this off stealth-like without yanking any fingernails, I think we can all agree that would be ideal."

Scooter nodded vociferously. The assassin offered a noncommittal shrug.

"Peace, Legion." Michael placed her hand over Scooter's. "Your concerns are noted. Barclay, please continue."

"Thank you, m'lady." Barclay's fingers absently strayed to his shirt pocket where the assassin knew he kept his cigarettes and a box of matches. Everyone had their preferred way of sorting through problems. Barclay smoked through his, but this time it seemed to be enough just to know they were there. "Putting a pin in the 'where' and the 'who' for a moment, I see our biggest challenge being the 'how.' Military security protocol operates on a system of revolving access codes retrieved via authenticator tokens."

"Token?" Michael asked.

"A satellite linked fob," the assassin said. "When activated it downloads an access code."

"Valid only for sixty seconds," Barclay added. "That token is also linked to the officer's Guardian chip. If the officer ain't holding the token in his or her hand at the time of activation, it triggers an automatic lockdown. And if that happens, unless you got a nuke handy, you ain't gettin' in."

The assassin jotted down a list.

Token + Officer = Access Code

It occurred to him that they didn't actually require the officer, or his token. Those things were merely a data stream conduit. There had to be a way to divert that stream, and if anyone had experience diverting, it was Barclay.

"Could you write a virus?" asked the assassin.

Barclay brightened at the mention of his sketchy pastime. "Does a one-legged duck swim in circles?"

"Something that would intercept the access code once the token is activated?"

"Or replicate it." Barclay's blunt fingertips drummed on the table. "Upload the virus to the satellite. Officer activates the token. Code gets beamed down to him but also to an email account of my choosing. There's a problem though."

"Antivirus filters?"

"I can write something what has no current definition, but it'll get quarantined as soon as it's executed. Only be able to use it once."

"The quarantine will initiate a facility lockdown within minutes," said the assassin. "Timing is everything."

"We will coordinate for maximum efficiency," Michael said. "Let's move on."

The assassin found it interesting that Michael had no apparent issue with him taking point. She moderated when necessary, but mostly she listened, allowing ideas, even bad ones, to flow freely toward workable plans. Her ineffable authority combined with a light touch inspired confidence. She trusted them to do their jobs. It was a leadership style he could work with.

"We've established the 'how,' in theory," the assassin said. The pain in his side was manageable but his head ached and his vision had started to blur. "Next we need the 'where' and the 'who.'"

"Y'all can take a seat on that," Barclay said, powering up a small laptop that was scuffed, cracked, and patched with duct tape. "In my meanderings through the Eye's data storage cloud, I discovered a deeper layer of encrypted files. So, I started working on a cipher. What I found was a maintenance schedule. Care and feeding of government servers, including the surveillance mainframe. No locations or sensitive information at all. Thing is, even something as simple as a drive swap has to be authorized by the head cheese in an operation like this."

"Did you find a name?" Scooter asked.

Barclay shook his head. "As I 'spected it would be, the signatory data is password locked. If I knew the password, my cipher could decrypt it, otherwise the only way to narrow down who might have signing authority is to go through the side door. Track shipping manifests from the manufacturers of electronic components and cross-reference with military and government contracts. Knowing the Eye, there'll be dozens of intermediaries. It'll take weeks to get a short list."

"Nero," Michael said.

"Beg pardon?"

"Your mystery password? Try N-E-R-O."

Barclay brought up his cipher program and with several smooth runs over the keyboard with his gnarled fingers, he entered the letters and waited. The assassin couldn't see the screen but Barclay's eyebrows shot up.

"Hot damn," he exclaimed and then leaned back from the computer. "So's you know, it ain't a quick decryption. The cipher acts like a subroutine of the archiving software, so it'll take a couple days. Anything fast or targeted will get flagged, but it should give us a name. From there we can figure out where this place is. Can I ask how you knew?"

"I was sent to Earth with my orders, and a name. Nero," she said, absently twisting one of the silver cuffs around her wrist. "I thought it might be the assassin's name. But obviously not."

The assassin snapped the tip of his pencil on the notepad. "Don't you think you should have mentioned this earlier?"

"The information was of no use until now."

Not a lie. Not the truth, either. "What else are you holding back?"

"Dude," Scooter said. "Let's take a chill, yeah?"

Michael gave the assassin a dismissive once over. "I am under no obligation to disclose anything to you."

"I'll remember that next time you need me to pull your ass out of the fire."

"Let it go, assassin."

"We're supposed to be working together."

She regarded him with an incredulous tilt of her head. "Is this truly the hill you wish to die on?"

He slapped the notepad on the table. "You've got a lot hidden away, Michael, but I'm good at sniffing these things out, and every time you lie or otherwise prevaricate, it brings me one step closer to cracking you open like a secret-filled piñata."

She hauled him out of his chair and slammed him into the wall. His head bit the plaster and his knees sagged as dizziness swamped him. She held him up, her face so close he could see light exploding through the spaces between her auburn lashes.

"Listen well, human." Her voice dipped into a low tremor. "I am the sword arm of the Lord and slayer of the Dragon. I have laid waste to multitudes. Fall from my grace and know that I will end you. I am Michael."

His skeleton vibrated and glowing heat washed down his side. He didn't doubt that with the right word she could vaporize him into pink mist.

"Have you something to say, assassin?"

"Yeah, you smell nice."

A slight smile curved on her lips. "And you're bleeding."

He followed her eyes down to the right side of his shirt, once more drenched in crimson.

CHAPTER 29

Barclay perched on the edge of the coffee table in a fresh work shirt and jeans. Morning sun haloed his fuzzy gray head.

"How's it feel?"

The assassin poked the tender pink divots of scar tissue above his right hip, front and back. "Fine, surprisingly."

"You'll have Scotty and the good doctor to thank for that."

"So it seems." The assassin leaned back on the floral print sofa and listened to the mantle clock perforate the silence with its steady tick. Apparently, after losing consciousness in the kitchen, Scooter and Pearl fell on him like wolves, but instead of ripping him apart, they put him back together. They repaired his bullet wound, pumped fluids into the dried-up riverbed of his vascular system, and left him on the sofa to sleep it off.

"Would've gone a lot better if you weren't such a stubborn jackass," Barclay said.

"In a perfect world we'd be able to choose our allies."

"If the world were perfect we wouldn't have to." Barclay picked up a stack of folded clothes and dropped them in the assassin's lap. "Pearl took up a collection."

INFRACTUS

The assassin sorted through the pile, inhaling the smell of fabric softener. Disappointment came over him, as it had when he was a kid and Sister Claudia emptied a grocery sack of hand-me-downs on the kitchen table. He held up a T-shirt emblazoned with an enormous pink daisy. "I'm being punished."

"Better'n what you got on."

Anything would be better than the clothes he'd been sweating and bleeding into for the last three days. "How's Scooter?"

"Peaky, but I'm given to understand that's the way of it."

"If anything, he ought to see what he can do for Liza." He made a slicing motion across his throat.

"He did, but she declined."

"Why?"

"Y'ought discuss that with the young lady herself."

"Last woman I talked to threw me into a wall." He glanced over his shoulder into the kitchen.

"Just you'n me, son. What's weighing on you?"

The assassin forced himself to meet Barclay's eyes. "Suit Two...Carmen. She found out about Liza. She was gunning for you next."

Barclay bowed his head.

"I didn't want to, and I wouldn't have if I'd had any other choice."

Barclay genuflected. "Ain't no cure for a mad dog. God have mercy on 'er."

"Father, I know what this looks like."

"Just so," Barclay said. "You got problems with women, son?"

INFRACTUS

The assassin considered Liza, Michael, and Suit Two. He thought about Suit One, Scooter, and Barclay. He thought about God, or the idea of God, and fell on the obvious conclusion.

"Pretty sure I'm the problem."

"Perhaps the Lord led you here so's you can fix that."

The assassin kneaded the daisy shirt between his hands. "The Lord have any idea as to where I should start?"

"In the washdown, son. You smell like jail."

Barclay stood up and slapped the assassin on the back. As always, it felt like getting hit with a brick.

Clean at last and dressed in the daisy shirt and khaki pants that reminded him of the Facility, the assassin found Liza on the porch at the back of the house. He watched her, sitting in a chair with a bottle of pink nail polish, hunched over her belly trying to reach her toes. She flopped back with a breathless grunt.

He took the chair across from her and balanced her foot on his knee. "Hand it over."

She clutched the bottle tighter, withdrawing it and her foot before she relaxed, and surrendered. Her instincts were on point. Though she overrode them too easily. He held her ankle and varnished the rest of her toenails with neat strokes of the brush.

"Where'd you learn to do this," she said, switching feet.

"A friend." He brushed deep pink polish on her big toe. "She was a junkie, and when she got the shakes, she'd have me paint her nails."

"You had a friend?"

He smiled a little. "Smart girl."

"So smart I graduated early, aced the MCAT and effed it all up by getting pregnant."

"People make mistakes."

She wiggled the drying toes of her finished foot. "Is it true that in the old world these mistakes were easy to get rid of?"

"Easy enough." In fact, he'd often wondered why his birth mother would carry her pregnancy to term when she could've had him scraped out. "Would you have made that choice?"

She shrugged. "Just think it should have been my choice to make."

As he painted her nails, he put together the scattered details. That day on the bridge, he'd seen Jenny's face. Liza had the same lack of guile, the illogical optimism, and eighteen years ago, on the very day Jenny was murdered, Liza was born.

"D'you believe in reincarnation?" he asked.

She folded her hands on her stomach. "I did when I was little. My grandmother is a secret Buddhist, but when she told me I couldn't come back as a unicorn, mermaid, or dragon, I sort of lost my faith."

Her response only further cemented his theory. But it was time to set aside childish things. He screwed the cap back on the nail polish. "Liza, we need to talk about what happened."

Her hand went to the scar on her throat. "I don't want to."

"I know, and that's a problem. You aren't being honest with yourself."

"I tried to be angry," she protested. "But it gave me acid reflux. Even Dean told me to let it go, and he thinks you're a psychopath."

"Why won't you let Scooter help you?"

"Would that make you feel better?" Her voice cracked. "You ripped my life away. My parents, my friends, my entire future. Ayham and I... I don't think we were in love, but he's a good person, and now my daughter will never know her father. Because of you. You erased me. You mutilated me. This scar is mine. You don't get to take it back, and you don't get to tell me how to feel."

"Liza."

She grabbed his hand and pressed it against the side of her warm belly. He felt a thump against his palm.

"I still hate you," she said.

Each kick strengthened his resolve. Whatever he had to do, he would protect them. And God help anyone who got in his way.

CHAPTER 30

At Laughing Corpse the first crush of the season was an event. At dawn the assassin gathered with Michael, Scooter, and a large crowd of pickers outside the barn. The rag tag assembly consisted of fellow Jackals and their families, neighbors who had no idea this place was a terrorist front, and hill people who couldn't care less as long as they got their pay for a day's work.

Scooter yawned. "Finally, something that'll keep you two off each other's throats."

"The assassin is a slow learner," said Michael, oddly civilian in cheap sandals and a blue sundress. "I expect morale will improve once he accepts my authority."

The assassin told himself it was the rising sun heating the back of his neck. "I accept your authority, but if you're waiting for me to like it, go ahead and hold your breath."

"Your concession is imminent?"

"I like you better when you're unconscious."

Scooter moaned. "Guys, c'mon. It's too early."

A sharp whistle cut through the burble of conversation. The assassin saw Barclay standing in front of the barn doors.

INFRACTUS

"Like to thank y'all for hustling out here on short notice." Barclay's rasp carried to the back of the crowd. "Grandpa told me the first crush was more'n a day of work. He believed that gathering of friends and family was the secret ingredient and without it your entire vintage would sour. He never tested the theory, but he never had a bad batch neither. Think that's proof enough that as long as there's good people willing to work together, there's good chance things'll work out."

Subtle, the assassin thought as Barclay directed everyone to grab a pair of shears and a crate and deployed them into the vines.

By late afternoon, the wedge of hostility between the assassin and Michael had lost its humorous bevel. He wasn't surprised when Barclay summoned them back to operation headquarters outside the barn. There he guided them to a pair of lawn chairs with a large bucket and a heaping crateful of grapes between them.

"Sit," Barclay said. "I'd hoped a spot of hard labor in the vines would drain the fight out of you two, but it seems not. You're making folk nervous. So now you're gonna pick stems for a spell, and work it out. Understand?"

The assassin expected Michael to take umbrage, but instead an amused smile lit up her face. "I take orders from no father, save one, Barclay. However, in light of your generous hospitality, I will do as you ask."

"Much obliged, m'lady."

Barclay left and they obediently sat on the chairs and plucked stems, tossing the grapes in the bucket. Michael ignored the assassin completely, focusing on her task. He opened his mouth to propose a truce when a commotion broke the sullen silence.

Scooter rounded the corner of the barn with no fewer than a dozen whooping youngsters armed with water guns chasing him. A toddler headed up the rear of the mob, dragging a plastic pail and sloshing water onto the grass with every step. Scooter slowed down, allowing the kids to tackle him to the ground and drench him with their ordinance.

Michael laughed as the little one barged into the fray and poured the remaining drops in his bucket onto Scooter's head. Scooter fell back in corpse-like repose. The child squealed. Michael laughed again, a warm ripple of sound the assassin didn't know she could produce.

"You like kids," he asked.

"Very much. Though I do not often interact with them. Have you any children, assassin?"

He shook his head. "I'm not parent material."

"It is not what you are but what you do that matters."

"You don't believe that, at least not completely."

She studied him, her long fingers mindlessly working stem from fruit. "Have you always been able to sense deception?"

"Long as I can remember."

"I once knew someone with that gift," she said with a grunt of exasperation. "Maddening to say the least.

"Another Archangel?"

She gestured to the kids roughhousing on the grass. "With age comes a greater affinity for destruction than creation. The Panopticon is merely a symptom of greater human sickness. We may save this world, assassin. But only a new generation can change it."

The conversation just got juicy. If he squeezed her, more would come trickling out, but for once he didn't want to go there. Liza and Tara Hillaby were preparing to bring new life into a world on the edge of annihilation. The Archangel Michael believed in those children. Enough to stake her life on them. This was an important detail.

"Crush time!" Scooter raced across the grass toward them. "Women and children in the tubs. That means you, doll."

Astonished, the assassin watched as a five-three Scooter threw a six-foot Michael over his shoulder like a sack of tubers and scampered off in the direction of the huge wooden tubs full of grapes.

"What in hell are you doing?" she growled, landing a solid punch to Scooter's kidney. "Put me down, Legion, or I will castrate you with a fork."

"Aye, Captain," Scooter said, dumping her into a vat of grapes where she landed on her backside with a splat.

She rose slowly, evidently preparing to release an unholy blast of grown-up words, when a young girl hopped in the tub and stumbled into her.

"Oops, sorry," said the girl. "Gosh, your hair is so pretty. Is it real?"

Michael's face softened as she righted the child. "Quite real, though more burden than blessing as it plagues me with the sin of vanity."

"You talk weird," the girl said, shifting her weight foot to foot.

Liza and Pearl joined Michael and the girl in the tub. The assassin watched them stomp about like palsied gazelles, clutching each other's hands for balance. Renegade tendrils of red escaped Michael's clip and trailed over her bare shoulders. The grape juice on her skin glimmered over the long flexing muscles of her arms and legs.

Scooter clambered into the empty chair beside the assassin. "Close your mouth, bro. That's too much car for you."

"What?"

"Hey, I get it. Gnarlacious cutie who knows how to handle a sword—take that any way you want—thing is she ain't exactly available."

The assassin was going to ask what exactly that meant, when Liza called to them from the edge of the tub. "A little help, please?"

Scooter nudged him. "Go on, be a gentleman. I got 'em in. You can help 'em out."

The assassin approached the tub and Liza held her sticky arms out. He balked, unsure of where to touch her. He was dividing zones of her body into safe, not safe, possible weirdness etc. when she handled it for him, putting her hands on his shoulders for support while she clambered out.

"Thanks," she said and kissed his cheek.

He watched her waddle over to the water pump and rubbed the heel of his hand over his cheek.

"Having fun yet?" Pearl asked, flyaway hair floating around her flushed face. "He cares, you know. He thinks you can change."

"Barclay?"

She squeezed his forearm. "Don't disappoint him."

Pearl joined Liza at the pump, which left only Michael in the tub, wearing a soggy dress and a sardonic smile. "It appears we have them all fooled."

"Model citizens," he said, extending his hand.

After a moment's hesitation, Michael put her hand in his. The gravity of it was not lost on him as he looped his arm around her waist and boosted her out. And speaking of gravity.

"God, you're heavy," he grunted, setting her feet on the ground.

She laughed. "For an eternity I've longed for a man to compliment me thus."

"You're funny."

"I'm sticky." She withdrew her hand from his and plucked at her dress. Then she gasped as the spray from a nozzle hit her full force. "Scooter!"

"I'm helping," Scooter said, hosing her down. "You wanna be covered in flies?"

She turned so he could spray her back. "Don't forget my hair."

"Wouldn't dream of it, doll."

Work wound down in the red-gold light of sunset and two of the alpha males set up a charcoal grill. High priests at the sacrificial altar, preparing burnt offerings, thanking the gods for their plentiful harvest. Rather pagan, considering Barclay's Christian leanings. Then again, it was all a part of the same elephant.

While the grill-masters cranked out a mountain of meat parts, Barclay appeared at the assassin's side, handing out cups full of his private reserve. "Look at you and the lady, finally getting on like burning houses."

"Wouldn't go that far," the assassin said, holding Michael's cup while she wrung out her hair.

Scooter sipped and coughed. "Cowabunga."

"Problem, Scotty?" asked Barclay. "Mayhap you're used to the sort of libation what comes with an umbrella?"

Scooter gave Barclay a defiant glower over the rim of the cup. Michael accepted hers and emptied it in three noisy gulps.

"Slow down," the assassin said. "Unless you want to be praying to the porcelain god."

Scooter nuzzled her arm like a scruffy kitten. "Dude, when it comes to drink, Mikey's got the constitution of a tyrannosaurus."

Michael patted Scooter's head. "You exaggerate, Legion. Though not by much."

Scooter left with Barclay to help Pearl bring out the rest of the food, leaving the assassin and Michael to stack up empty crates. Near the picnic tables, the assassin observed Dean, the young medic, bring Liza a glass of lemonade. They laughed together and Dean's fingers remained touching Liza's even after she had them securely wrapped around her cup.

Michael followed his gaze. "Let them be, assassin. The girl is of age."

"Her life's been flipped upside down. She's lonely, and he's taking advantage."

"By engaging her in conversation?" Michael plucked his barely touched wine from his hand and topped off his cup and refilled hers from the jug.

The assassin forgot about Dean as he followed the cling of Michael's wet dress, adhering like shrink wrap along the curve of her spine and around her hips and stomach, revealing the indentation of her navel, the slope of her bottom ribs, and the contours of her small breasts. She handed him his cup and he drained half of it.

"My work is demanding," she said, splaying her bare toes in the grass. "It's been millennia since I've been on Earth long enough to appreciate moments of insignificance."

Even if it was only Barclay's plonk loosening her tongue, the assassin liked it. He liked it so much he forgot about her wet dress for up to a couple minutes at a time as they stacked the crates scattered about the lawn. By the time they finished he was buzzed, and while Michael remained sober they must have been on the same wavelength because they eyed the now deserted picnic tables and descended as vultures.

The assassin found cheese, bread, fruit, and some potato salad. Michael piled her plate high with scraps and handfuls of everything. They found a dry patch of grass to sit, and Michael tore through her food like a Neanderthal after a long winter. She chewed with her mouth open, scattered her lap with crumbs, dripped mustard on her dress, and smeared ketchup on her nose. Plate cleared, she went back for more and annihilated that too with undiminished enthusiasm.

"Marvelous," she said with her mouth full. "What is it?"

"Ice cream, and it's all over your face."

She managed to mop up most of it with her napkin, but she'd missed one spot. He reached out and dragged his thumb over the edge of her lip. He expected her to kick him in the ear. Instead, she sucked the tip of his thumb into her mouth.

The silky sweep of her tongue and the scrape of her teeth transmitted through his whole body. The ravening barbarian and the siren in a wet dress blended into a single creature too devastating to look upon. Like a gorgon, except only one part of him was turning to stone. He pulled his thumb out of her mouth and hugged his knees to his chest.

She wiped her hands with the damp towel she'd used to dry her hair. "I've always been a bit messy."

They passed the time together in silence as full dark claimed the valley. A bonfire crackled and they observed the people gathered around. Clusters of friends laughed and told stories, while parents cradled sleepy children, and Barclay made his way around to visit with everyone. The assassin was used to being the outsider, and it seemed Michael was no different.

He touched the cuff around her wrist. "What are these?"

She twisted the silver manacle, and he knew she was searching for precise words. "They were given to me after completing my human service, as one of the Thirty-six."

"You were human once?" Though she'd explained it as a common enough thing, it seemed beneath her somehow. "When?"

"From your perspective? Long ago."

"What happened?"

"What always happens. I lived. I died."

"An old woman, peacefully in your sleep?"

She shook her head. "A young man, violently, by my own hand."

He tried to picture Michael as a man. Broader frame, features less fine, but with the same austere genderless beauty. Why would this man take his own life? Sister Claudia said all suicides went straight to the spider garden hell. Michael clearly had not. The assassin wondered if the cuffs had something to do with that. Before he could ask, she got up, brushed off her skirt, and left.

That's right, Michael. Walk away.

You're good at that.

He sits alone by the trees, staring out across the valley. I'm too far away to see the look on his face. Just as well. It's not easy watching them bond. Probably a good thing I can't read their thoughts. Body language screams volumes though. He's totally into her, which would make me physically ill if I were corporeal. She doesn't deserve his love. Or his hate. God knows he's capable of both in terrifying measure.

He stretches out on the grass under the stars. I take comfort knowing I've got him right where I want him. His plans align nicely with my own. His memories will soon return. And when they do, She will get what's coming to her.

CHAPTER 31

That night the assassin had another dream. Rust and blood spun together in a red curtain. A warm weight bore down on him, and he found his mouth pressed against smooth skin salted with sweat and smelling faintly of flowers and tomato vines. He rolled over, and the silky curtain fell away. Strong fingers laced through his as he pinned them to the pillowed surface. He surged into that heat, eliciting a soft cry from the one beneath him.

Then everything changed. Red to ash. Flowers to smoke. The arms around him were bigger, the hands harder, and a delicate sigh rumbled into something deep and raw. An erotic charge bolted down his spine and he was close. So close.

The assassin woke to early morning sun and a fading echo of breath between his ears. He blinked and stared at the pale green numerals on his watch. Eight hours. He could get used to these long decadent stretches of sleep. The sex dream was disturbing, but surprisingly, not repulsive. What were the implications? Did all dreams have to mean something?

On the other twin bed, Scooter groaned and tugged his pillow over his head. The assassin detected no trace of a hangover, despite crashing into bed last night with a ferocious red wine headache.

INFRACTUS

Laughing Corpse typically rose at dawn but the assassin suspected there would be a general lie-in this morning. Upstairs in the empty kitchen, he started coffee for the caffeinators in residence. He poured a bowl of Cheerios for himself and took it into the living room where he opened the doors of a cabinet-style shelving unit. Alone at last, with Barclay's book collection.

The top shelf held paperback mysteries and spy capers from a quarter century ago, the last gasp of the printed page and fiction in particular. The Eye frowned on imagination. No surprise to see people getting duller by the day, cut off from the oxidizing psychic pollution of new ideas and free radical thought.

Below the mysteries he found old world hardcover classics: Dickens, Steinbeck, Wharton, the more depressing Russians, and the Brontes. The next shelf was memoirs, which he tended not to like because self-edited histories gave him migraines.

The other shelves were dedicated to grapes. Growing, harvesting, pressing, aging. Every volume appeared to be about a million years old. White striations marred the spines and the most frequently consulted pages had acquired a gentle wave from exposure to the elements.

The assassin heard shuffling in the kitchen. Moments later, a weary Barclay appeared in the living room. He raised his red mug to the assassin. "Mornin'."

"Overindulge last night, Father?"

Barclay took a healthy slug of coffee. "All things in moderation, son."

"Including moderation?"

"I reckon. How's your bunkie?"

"Avoiding direct sunlight. How's yours?"

Barclay frowned. "Got one hell of a cheek on you, son. Let's hope it proves useful. My cipher came up with a name yesterday evening."

"Why didn't you say something?"

"With all the Avengers sauced to varying degrees?"

The assassin couldn't muster any sincere opposition. He'd enjoyed those few insignificant hours with Michael, followed by a bizarre subconscious three-way. He swallowed the last Cheerio from his bowl.

"Father, what would you say if a person who'd never had a dream in his life, suddenly started having them, and it happened to coincide with the earthly arrival of an archangel?"

Barclay placed his mug on the end table. "You don't dream? Not even a bit?"

"Never, until three days ago. I've only had two dreams, and I've got no basis for comparison, but they were both...intense."

"Could be God is trying to tell you something?"

"Or perhaps not," Michael said, striding into the living room, androgynously attired in cargo pants and a black T-shirt, her hair dropping down her back in a tight braid. "Sometimes a dream is merely a dream."

"Possible," the assassin said.

"Wake the others," she commanded, with no trace of last night's familiarity. "We shall convene in ten minutes."

"Avengers assemble," he muttered, heading downstairs to drag a hungover angel out of bed.

Within the prescribed ten minutes they gathered at the kitchen table around Barclay and his battered computer.

"Sure you got to scare off so soon?" Barclay asked Pearl.

"Duty calls." She snagged a banana and poured coffee into a travel mug. "You've got the End of Days. I've got inflamed tonsils."

"I'll go with you," Liza said.

Pearl shook her head. "Sweetheart, until you get control of your upchucks, I can't have you sitting in on procedures. Another time, okay?"

"But I'm soooo bored. I'm used to being busy and now I can't swim, I can't go to school, I have no one to talk to, and I'm tired of knitting booties."

"In a few months, boredom will be a fondly remembered affliction."

Liza flumped back in her chair. "Stop treating me like a child. I'm five feet tall, not five years old."

Scooter ruffled her hair. "Get used to it, niblet. Happens to me all the time."

The assassin endured the entire time-wasting exchange using his pencil to make hash marks on the notepad in front of him. Finally, Pearl left and Liza stomped into the kitchen, slammed a frying pan onto the stove and began cracking eggs like they owed her money.

Barclay got right down to business, tapping a series of keys on his laptop. "We don't have an exact location for the mainframe yet, but the CO on the maintenance schedule is one Colonel Perkin Lindskog. Forty-five, married with two children, primary residence in Seal Harbor, Mount Desert Island."

"Maine?" the assassin asked.

Michael accepted a plate of scrambled eggs and toast from a sullen Liza. "Can we safely assume this mainframe would be nearby?"

"I'm familiar with that area," the assassin said. "There aren't any military bases or facilities on that island, let alone one big enough to house a server farm."

"We'll know more once we get our paws on Lindskog's ident," said Barclay

"Assassin, I believe this would be your area of expertise," Michael said, around a mouthful of buttered toast.

"May I?" the assassin asked, and Barclay slid his laptop across the table. A few keystrokes and the assassin loaded a program he'd cobbled together that started with Barclay's hack for a high-level survey of stored data in the mainframe. It plotted the subject's activities on a map based on GPS uploads, visual surveillance, and electronic hits from purchases and ident scans. A few weeks' worth of data would give a pretty good idea of how the subject spent their time.

"What've we here?" Barclay asked. "How specific are them search parameters?"

"Enough that you need a tolerably good idea of what you're searching for."

"This type of profiling don't sit too well with me."

"It's Old Testament justice, Father. An Eye for an eye."

"And we all go blind," Michael said, digging into Scooter's leftover breakfast after murdering her own.

"It can render a multilayered format too," the assassin pointed out. "With time lapse and smaller patterns within larger ones."

"Get much artifact?"

"Too much for my comfort."

"I might-could add a few refining subroutines."

"Wah wah wah." Scooter squeezed behind the assassin to refill his coffee at the counter. "I'm fresh out of geek repellant. This epic hangover is the only thing keeping me marginally cool."

"Should've known a munchkin like you couldn't handle my cellar's finest," Barclay said, typing his tweaks into the assassin's program. "There. Fire it up again. See what pops."

A neat graphic of Colonel Perkin Lindskog's day-to-day appeared on the map. The assassin picked up his pencil and began to grind away at the information, jotting notes and considering various scenarios. He stopped when he sensed Liza standing behind him.

"Did you run this program on me?" she asked.

"I did," he admitted.

"To figure out the best way to kill me?"

"Yes."

Her hand circled her throat where the scarlet thread lit up like a neon tube. Around her wrist, a silver charm bracelet sparkled in the sunlight. New, the assassin observed, since she hadn't been wearing it yesterday, and it had only one charm. A tiny blue fish. A fish he'd bet had Dean's fingerprints all over it.

Liza's chin trembled. "How can you still be this cold?"

"Because I haven't had a personality transplant."

"What's that supposed to mean?"

"I'm not a nice person, Liza. It's not in my nature. I'm very good at doing very bad things. The only difference between then and now is whose side I'm on."

His words pelted her like rocks, but she needed it. Jenny had seen only the good in people and thought dangerous creeps were just misunderstood. It got her killed. He'd failed Jenny. He would not fail Liza. The time for careful handling was over.

"I'm only telling you the truth," he said. "But if it offends you, say the word and I'll spin a pretty story where good triumphs over evil, and nothing is ever confusing."

Her cheeks burned in her pasty face. "Don't talk down to me."

"Then grow the fuck up."

"Dude, take it easy," Scooter said, wrapping a protective arm around Liza. "Don't listen to him, niblet. This is what happens when you're raised by thieves and psychopaths."

"I was raised by nuns. Thieves and psychopaths came later."

"The assassin makes a valid point," Michael said to Liza. "If you haven't the courage to face the reality of an unkind world, how can you hope to raise your daughter to be a strong woman?"

"Oh my god, you're both awful!" Liza kicked her chair away from the table and fled the kitchen. Michael appeared mystified.

"Ugh, you guys," Scooter rubbed his temples. "Think what kinda life she's had until now. She's not used to this and you expect her to just roll?"

Barclay lightly rapped his knuckles on the table like a judge's gavel. "You've all said your piece. Young lady's gone to lick her wounds. We've got work to do."

The assassin returned to his analysis. From the outset, Lindskog was a creature of deeply entrenched routine—which included his regular raising of mild-mannered hell.

INFRACTUS

Every Friday, Lindskog left home around nine p.m., probably after putting his kids to bed, and stopped at an ATM to withdraw five hundred creds from an account he did not share with Mrs. Lindskog. Then he drove into Bar Harbor to a public house called the Beluga. So Lindskog had a taste for horrible moonshine and expensive dates. Booze and traders. These military guys knew how to reinforce a stereotype.

"Okay," he said, shutting the computer. "Let's go to Maine."

CHAPTER 32

BAR HARBOR, MAINE,
PAN AMERICAN DIVISION

The assassin failed to smooth things over with Liza before they left. Not that he tried especially hard. On the drive to the airfield he realized, with some amusement, that sweet little Liza Ayomori was accustomed to being the smartest person in any given room. Now she was in over her head and did not take kindly to being called out. In parting, she'd offered only a terse "try not to get shot again."

"Chicks, man," Scooter said, curled up in his window seat as the tiny Learjet jounced through a patch of turbulence. "If you ask me—"

"I didn't."

"It'll blow over. Those baby-baking hormones, dude. Makes 'em nuts."

The assassin glanced across the aisle where Barclay sat reading one of his tattered paperback mysteries. The old man arranged the private flight, ground transportation, and accommodation through his byzantine network of contacts, and so far, there had been no surprises. Next to Barclay, Michael rested her head against the window, passed out. The assassin envied her ability to fall asleep anywhere instantly.

She wasn't speaking to him either, not since their strategy meeting at the kitchen table yesterday morning. He hadn't expected her to like the plan, but her silent treatment irked him. She consistently went out of her way to reinforce his status as an outsider. As if he'd forget.

"She knows I'm right," the assassin grumbled. "If she needs to act like a little bitch about it, let her."

"Liza?" Scooter asked.

"Uh...yeah."

"Want my advice?"

"Not particularly."

"Chillax. We need your head in the game, and the niblet's in good hands for now. She's got Doc Pearl and Dean."

"Right." The assassin slouched deeper into his seat. "Dean."

Unless Dean was prepared to make a big commitment, he had no business leading Liza on. She'd lost enough already. Though it was foolish, the assassin held out hope that he might be able to give some of it back to her.

Upon landing in another small airfield, they deplaned and found a C-A with the key fob in the center console.

"I'll drive," the assassin said.

They drove to Mount Desert Island and into the woods outside Acadia Park where they crept down a rutted lane that ended in front of a cottage. The assassin studied the place through the windshield. Curled shingles and peeling paint, but the windows were clean, which indicated an interior fit for human habitation. He stepped out of the car into the rustle of maple and elm trees beginning to lose their summer green.

Barclay reached up into the eaves trough and retrieved a brass key. The door opened with a creak, and they piled into the dim foyer. The assassin smelled damp wood and old fires.

Scooter slung his duffel bag onto an armchair. "Place has character."

Sketches of fish hung on the walls among at least a dozen deer and elk heads. Sturdy pine furniture showcased a genuine Maine black bear rug, and on the coffee table there perched a Boreal owl with an all too lively expression of caged fury on its face.

"Good enough for who it's for," Barclay said.

The assassin gave the owl a wide berth. "Are we sure this thing is dead?"

Michael said nothing as she stalked past the assassin and into the master bedroom, shutting the door behind her.

"Oookaaay," Scooter said.

Barclay set his computer bags on the dining table by the corner kitchen. "Other room's got a set of bunks. So, unless one of you wants to cozy up in a queen-size with a grumpy archangel."

"I'll take the couch," the assassin said.

After a few fragmented hours of sleep, the assassin woke to pre-dawn shadows and the unblinking stare of beady glass eyes from all directions, including that creepish owl glaring at him from its perch on the coffee table. He threw off the blanket and slipped out of the cottage. Ground fog slithered through the trees and cut his legs off at the ankles. He took off at a run down the lane.

INFRACTUS

His muscles heated into a fluid stride while earthy air chilled his lungs. When he crossed over into Acadia Park, he ran down the familiar carriage roads, knowing every rut, dip, and hump hiding under the carpet of fog and spongy larch needles. By the time he scrambled down the slope under the stone bridge, he felt alive again.

He heaved the granite slab open, hit the lights, and found everything as he left it. Cot, storage unit, batteries. He hadn't told the others about his safe house, only that he could source the necessary materials. From one of the cabinets he retrieved a backpack and loaded it with everything they'd need to melt the mainframe into a slag heap.

On the way out, he eyed the drawer containing the locked strongbox. Only six weeks ago he'd pawed through its contents. Six weeks ago, even his wildest imaginings wouldn't have come close to the reality of where life was about to take him.

Upon his return to their woodland critter necropolis, he saw a curl of smoke rising from the chimney. Someone was awake. He stood on the porch with his backpack full of explosives outside a house full of angels and wondered what in the blighted blue hell he was doing. God's work.

"Close the damn door!" Scooter barked, huddled in a blanket at the hearth.

"What's wrong with you?" the assassin asked.

"Near froze my vegetables off last night. Think it's gonna snow? Man, I hate snow."

"We're well aware of your preference for warm-weather crime." The assassin set his backpack on the table and unpacked coils of wire, slip-ties, and timers. "Where is everyone?"

"Barclay went for walk to suck down some coffin nails. And Mikey still hates you, so . . ." He cocked his head in the direction of the closed master bedroom door.

It didn't matter, the assassin reminded himself. So long as she did her job when the time came, it didn't matter.

Scooter eyed the items on the table. "Can I help?"

"Would bomb-making violate your oath of pacifism?"

"Gray area."

"You touch nothing unless I tell you to," the assassin said and blocked with both hands when Scooter threw off the blanket and vaulted over the sofa, arms open. "Do not hug me. I mean it."

"Okay, okay," Scooter backed off and perused the ingredients. "So. This is what bombs are made of?"

"You can say it. Blowing stuff up is riot cool."

"No, it's not."

"Lie."

"Fine, it's cool—long as no one gets hurt," Scooter said, crouching on an empty chair. "You always know when someone's bullshitting you?"

"Why?"

Scooter frowned. "Nothing. I used to know a guy...it's nothing."

The assassin unwound the copper wire and wondered about this person whom both Michael and Scooter had mentioned. Someone with the ability to see lies. Someone they seemed reluctant to talk about. He wondered about the sorts of secrets kept by angels.

Barclay and Scooter washed supper dishes while the assassin pulled up a chair next to Michael at the table. Her blunt fingernail traced a knot in the grain of the wood. Over and over, round and round. The assassin refilled her glass with iced tea. He'd given her as long as he could, but the hour was upon them.

"We could hold off," he said. "I'd be more comfortable with a few days to follow Lindskog around. Get to know him better."

"Just how much time do you think we have?" she asked, as though they weren't her first words in nearly two days. "You've been AWOL nearly a week, assassin. They are hunting you. One of their operatives caught up to us before we even left Bali."

"Only because Suit Two went rogue."

"The level of risk rises every day."

Sound logic, but something else had been eating at her since the morning after the crush. Something hiding behind her annoyance over tonight's plan. She hadn't lied, but the subtle scratch of deception lit the fuse of his temper. Not since he was a teenager had he been this quick to anger. He wanted to confront her. And before this was over, he would.

"So, it has to be now?"

"It does," she said. "Though I'm not sure why it's necessary for me to wear that."

"Lindskog isn't patronizing a trader bar for their blueberry rotgut, Michael."

She curled her hands around her glass. "You realize this is not how I usually go about my work."

"I do."

"Very well then." Michael chugged her iced tea, and wiped her mouth with the back of her hand. While charmed by her slovenly table manners, he hoped she could manage more civilized comportment for this evening.

"Do you need help with the makeup? Or hair?"

"Liza and Pearl provided intensive instruction on cosmetics, and rest assured I am bald as an egg from the neck down."

"I meant this." He pinched a lock of her hair between his fingers. "But for what it's worth, I admire your commitment."

Michael disappeared into the bedroom and the assassin gathered what he needed to don his disguise for the evening. In the shower, he scrubbed himself down to anonymity and prepared to slip into the skin of his favorite alias.

Carrall Hastings' motif was a curious fusion of poor impulse control and extreme self-loathing that started with tattoos. With stencils and ink, he fabricated a history of drunken mistakes and drug-fueled attempts at correction. An ex-lover's name became a bird, which later became a bat and a dragon and so on. The result of this obfuscation was a mess of blue, black, red, and green that resembled nothing in particular and yet covered the entirety of both arms.

Next, he dressed in the costume he'd retrieved from his safe house. Black jeans and a short-sleeved black button down, an ensemble tailored to make him appear even thinner than he was. He applied black eyeliner and black nail polish. Then he gelled his black hair, taking it from casual disarray to a swooping, spiking jungle, filled with hungry tigers. The bottle of cologne described the fragrance as woodsy, with a hint of mint. Typically, he'd take a bath in the stuff, but out of consideration for his partners in crime, he'd go with a lighter application.

INFRACTUS

Carrall Hastings. His first professional alias, and an outrageous shithead. Perfect for a certain kind of job. This was one of them. Carrall popped his collar and exited the bathroom in a cloud of perfume.

The chatter between Scooter and Barclay halted. His entrance shocked even the owl into slightly less withering silence. Time to warm up. Carrall sauntered over to the breakfast bar and rudely bumped into Scooter, nearly knocking him off his stool.

"That's some old-world goth." Scooter coughed. "And you smell like a Bulgarian stripper."

Carrall leaned in and pulled Scooter's shapeless hemp wallet from behind his ear like a quarter. "Misdirection, shorty."

Scooter grinned. "Sick trick, bro."

"That's nothing." Carrall shoved the wallet against Scooter's chest. "And I'm not your bro."

Scooter looked hurt before understanding dawned on him. "Ah. You're in character, yeah? So, who're we talking to?"

"Name's Carrall Hastings," he said, flopping into one of the armchairs.

Barclay rubbed his forehead. "Lord, here we go."

"You know this guy, Padre?" asked Scooter.

"Misfortunately, I do."

"Maybe not as well as you think. World's a stage, Father. We all pretend to be something. We all got secrets."

"Been an age," Barclay said. "Though when it comes to handing out opinions, seems you're generous as ever."

Carrall chipped at his black manicure. "Self-censorship's a disease. A goddamned plague."

"Perhaps," Michael said from the doorway of her bedroom. "Though the cure comes at the cost of sober second thought."

Barclay's tablet fell from his fingers, onto the bear rug. "I'll be damned."

Carrall silently seconded. Michael's ironed hair fell in a glossy red veil to her waist, so smooth he could barely detect the bit he'd shorn off during their skirmish in Bali. Liza and Pearl had coached her well. She'd applied her makeup in a thick but artful mask. And the dress...loose draping silk the color of pale champagne. And not much of it. The backless halter had a neckline that plunged halfway to her navel and a hem that floated midway down her long thighs. Revealing, but not cheap. On the contrary. It made her look very expensive.

"'Bout time, Red," Carrall grumbled.

She wrinkled her nose. "What are you supposed to be? An angst-ridden adolescent? You smell terrible."

"And you've got the social skills of a cadaver."

"You take these productions seriously." Her tone hinted at admiration. "Do I look appropriate?"

He dropped his gaze to her moderately high heels. "You'll do."

"What does that mean?"

He let his gelled head loll against the back of the chair. "Means you look like a five-hundred-cred fuck."

Barclay retrieved his tablet and slapped Carrall's arm with it. "Mind your vile tongue, boy."

"Like you weren't thinking it," Carrall said as Michael's posture stiffened.

"Don't take it personal, Mikey." Scooter hopped off his stool and stood between her and Carrall. "He's in character, and you've seriously got it going on in that dress, like really, really."

"Stop that," she said.

"I'm trying." Scooter clapped his hands over his eyes. "This is weirder for me than it is for you."

"You, Legion, are not on display like a barbecued duck."

Carrall watched the barbecued duck grimace and run her hands over pale silk. What would it feel like? Cool at first, but the warmth of her body would quickly melt through. Like ice cream. And then he was frantic to think of anything but that.

Michael wobbled to the couch. "How do people function in these shoes?"

Barclay caught her arm, steadying her before she could land in his lap. He handed Scooter a palm-sized card reader. "This doodad is real simple, Scotty. Insert the ident here, red light'll come on. Light turns green, you're done. Should take no more'n a minute."

"Cool," Scooter said. "Guess I got the easy job."

"Are you certain this will work?" Michael asked, crossing her arms and legs.

"Not if you do that." Carrall lunged forward to take hold of her wrists and pull her arms open. "Closed-off body language. Crossed legs is okay, but cross the top leg toward him, not away."

"Like this?" Studiously, she draped her hand on Barclay's shoulder and let the foot of her crossed leg brush against his shin. Barclay looked about as comfortable as a vampire in church.

"Better," Carrall said.

To Barclay's visible relief, Michael withdrew from his personal space bubble. "I'm a harlot," she said. "But what kind? Do I have a substance abuse problem and issues with my Father? Or am I a woman who freely chooses this life?"

Carrall expected little more than her grudging cooperation, but it seemed once Michael decided to do something, she was all in. "Whatever the reason, remember this is your livelihood. Don't fall all over Lindskog, but at the same time, every move you make is meant to tempt him down to lady town. Got it?"

Her eyes narrowed. "You speak with authority. Have you known many prostitutes?"

"In the biblical sense? Just one." He got up and plucked his jacket off a tree made of antlers. "We were kids. She was my friend."

He expected disapproval, but her painted face softened. He shrugged into his jacket. "Let's hit it."

CHAPTER 33

On the winding drive out of the woods down to Bar Harbor, buoyant energy surged within Carrall. Crime was his comfort zone. Or maybe this was what it felt like to be doing God's work. Michael's comment about Father issues had him thinking. A perfect, omniscient deity was a jagged pill. A flawed single dad on the other hand? That went down a bit easier. That, he could believe.

Carrall glanced in the rearview. Scooter fidgeted in the backseat.

"Stop worrying," Carrall said. "All you have to do is wait in the bathroom with Barclay's gizmo. I'll bring the ident to you, and I'll put it back. Simple as."

"Yeah," Scooter said. "Just crime, you know?"

"Yet you mock Gabriel for his adherence to regulation," said Michael.

"No, I mock Gabriel for his stodgy grampa 'tude and pretty-pretty hair."

"I admit he can be insufferable."

"Never understood why he didn't join the Luminary. Spend his eternity writing parables with Josh."

"Despite his piety and love of the archaic, Gabriel lacks the scholarly temperament required for Luminary work. And his penmanship is atrocious."

"What's this got to do with Lindskog?" Carrall asked.

"Are we doing the right thing?" Scooter asked. "This goes down and it's gonna blow back not just on him but his minions, his family."

Michael regarded Scooter with a severe expression. "You volunteered, Legion, knowing full well the sorts of unpleasant tasks I routinely perform at His behest."

Carrall had a vision of Michael kneeling on a marble floor, chained like a mastiff to the golden throne of her God. Let off her leash only when He had a dirty job that needed doing.

"Sorry, doll." Scooter slid his hands over the back of the seat to rest on Michael's bare shoulders. "Can I tell Gabe you said he was insufferable?"

"You may not."

Scooter slumped back in a pout.

Carrall wondered if the Archangel Michael ever thought of switching orders. Would she be content to study with the Luminary or take the Legion's vow of pacifism and heal the sick? What was her passion? What would Michael choose if those silver fetters fell from her wrists?

She regarded him with curiosity. "I want to ask you something. Though I realize it is not my right to know."

"Since when do you hedge your questions?"

"What happened to your friend?"

He couldn't imagine why she'd care. "She was murdered."

"And you dispatched her killer?"

"To put it mildly."

"Good," she said. "That is good."

They parked on the street across from the docks with plenty of time to settle in before Lindskog arrived. Carrall pointed to the weathered tavern. "There it is. We all set?"

Scooter bounced in the backseat. "Ready, Freddy."

"Michael?"

She gazed out the window, blinking lashes heavily larded with mascara. "What if this man does not find me attractive?"

"It's about distraction, not attraction. And don't worry. I'll be right there the whole time."

Her eyes flashed emerald in their smoky hollows. "I am unaccustomed to trading on my femininity, but this is not my first jaunt behind enemy lines."

Carrall was dying to know the story behind that cryptic statement, but there wasn't time. "We'll stagger our entry. I'll go in first, scope the place out, and wait for Lindskog. Scooter, I'll text you when it's your turn. Michael will make her grand entrance after that."

"Rock 'n' roll," Scooter said.

"See you on the inside."

❖❖❖

The interior of the Beluga hadn't changed in six weeks. Dim lighting, scarred wood, warped floorboards, cave-like booths, and vinyl-upholstered stools along a bar coated in flaking varnish. Carrall perched on a stool, reluctant to touch anything lest he get stuck to it. The decor hadn't changed, but the vibe couldn't be more different. His last visit had been on a Tuesday, and what he'd observed could be described as a sparsely attended funeral for the human spirit. Friday nights were a different kind of party.

Currently the room burbled with a blend of piped in smooth jazz and the melodic voices of women flitting about like exotic moths, chatting up the male patronage. There were other men as well, too good looking and well-dressed to be patrons. The traders came in all genders, shapes, colors, and ages. Friday night at the Beluga offered a buffet catering to every taste.

Colonel Perkin Lindskog came through the front door right on time. The man could be summed up in one word. Beige. Sandy hair, medium skin, and light brown eyes. Unremarkable height and build. Neither ugly nor handsome in tan slacks, white shirt, and expensive leather shoes. So far, Perkin Lindskog was everything Carrall's digital profile indicated he would be.

Lindskog claimed the booth closest to the front door. A dark, tucked-in void, private enough that Carrall wouldn't want to be on the Beluga's custodial crew. A young server with a tray under his arm made a beeline for Lindskog's table. The assassin recognized the server as the beautiful trader he'd met the last time. Lindskog and the server chatted back a forth in a familiar way. The server glanced over at the bar, said something else, patted Lindskog's shoulder and took his leave.

Carrall ordered a drink from the mute bartender but didn't touch it. The fermented blueberry fumes wafting up from the glass brought back all too fresh recollection of waking up on the beach beaten, bloody, and covered in vomit.

The server sashayed up to the bar, winking at Carrall. "Almost didn't recognize you. What brings you back to Bar hah-bah?"

"Besides your pretty face and that Yankee accent?" Carrall said, rolling his glass between his hands. "Fond memories, I guess."

The boy's face sobered. "Those fellas woulda killed me. I'd guess y'took a wicked beating. I'm sorry for it."

"Don't be."

"I owe you. An' that's why I said nothin' when a lady come round the next night asking 'bout a dark-haired gent from away."

Carrall dragged his finger along the rim of his glass. "Shark in an expensive suit?"

"That'd be her."

That explained how Suit One knew he wasn't in Venice. It reminded Carrall that Suit Two had an incredible gift. A spark of something special, and when she died, so did the spark.

"Kept my mouth shut, but truth to God I don't remember nothing after you fellas brung it outside. You in some kinda trouble?"

"Always," Carrall said. "Didn't realize you actually worked here."

The boy gave him a flirty smile. "Less competition for tips than trade on the weekends. I earn more schlepping drinks than I would shaking my arse, right Percy?"

The bartender grunted, ducking down to retrieve a bottle of actual vodka from under the bar.

Carrall stared into his own glass. "So, you do serve more than this bile."

INFRACTUS

"For special patrons, we do." The boy glanced over his shoulder at Lindskog and back at Carrall. "Dear heart, I don't know if you're here to trade, but if you are, there's a fifty cred buy-in."

Carrall had an uneasy feeling as he watched the boy collect his tray and deliver a vodka on ice to Lindskog, departing with another shoulder pat. Lindskog's gaze landed on Carrall and stayed there. Lindskog smiled, shyly, and raised his glass.

"Hey there, soldier," Carrall muttered to himself as he slid off the stool, walked toward Lindskog's booth, past it, and out the front door.

Carrall crossed the street and ducked back into the car.

"Is there a problem?" asked Michael.

"Remember how I wanted to spend a few days getting to know Lindskog and you said we didn't have time? Well, we brought the wrong meat to the market. Lindskog is queer."

Scooter's head popped between the front seats. "Even with the wife and kiddles?"

"Are you certain?" Michael asked.

"Trust me."

"Do we pack it in?" Scooter asked.

"Hell, no. Our strategy is solid, we just change it up a bit." Carrall outlined the new plan. In fact, the altered circumstances worked to their advantage. He had experience in this area. Michael chuckled.

"What?" the assassin said.

She laughed again. "This role reversal pleases me, on several levels."

"Whatever puts the starch in your knickers," he said, eyeing the silk riding up her thigh. "Not that I suspect you're wearing any."

Scooter looked skeptical. "Dude, you're not a people person. Sure you can sell this?"

Carrall checked his deranged hair and eye makeup in the mirror. "Watch me."

He really did need them to watch. Timing was everything. Michael and Scooter went in separately and staked out the bar before Carrall made his second entrance of the evening. He marched through the front door and tossed a fifty on the bar, which Percy swept out of sight without missing a beat. Then Carrall slid right into a startled Lindskog's booth.

"I was afraid you'd left," Lindskog said, moving down to make room for his presumptuous guest.

"Naw, making a call," Carrall said, picking up Lindskog's glass, tossing it back in one gulp and signaling the beautiful server for two more. "Had my secretary clear my schedule. But hey, if I got the wrong idea . . ." Carrall started to slide out of the booth.

"No." Lindskog laid his hand over Carrall's. "Please, stay."

Carrall settled back. "The direct approach. I like that in a fella."

Lindskog's fingers lightly closed around Carrall's wrist. "I guess when I see what I want I don't want to risk anyone else snatching it."

"Between you and me, I never had much use for snatch."

Lindskog chuckled. "Not much of a gentleman, are you?"

"If you wanted your knob swabbed by a gentleman, you wouldn't be here."

Lindskog's smile suggested he was mildly repelled and deeply intrigued. *Right where I want you*, Carrall thought, and as if on cue, the server arrived with two icy glasses of vodka.

"Thank you, Kris," Lindskog said, pressing a generous tip into the boy's hand.

"Call me cupid," the boy said and pranced off, tray tucked under his arm.

The conversation progressed the way most conversations do between strangers who feel obligated to observe certain pleasantries before penetrating one another. Sailing, travel, dog vs cat. Safe subjects. Lindskog told the truth, while Carrall's lies came easily as breathing.

At some point Carrall pondered what Scooter had said. If all went according to plan, Lindskog could very well get remapped, sentenced to a decade in a literal salt mine, or he might have a tragic accident. Panopticon's arbitrary system of crime and punishment meant you never knew what you were going to get. And what about those two little kids Lindskog had at home?

"Huh?" Carrall said, detecting an expectant pause.

Lindskog's eyebrows knitted. "I... I said I really... like you."

Carrall laughed. "Man, you're not used to people zoning out while you talk. You must really be somebody out there."

Lindskog shook his head. "No one special."

Interesting. Even with the lofty rank of Colonel, Lindskog knew it meant nothing. Lindskog knew he was a puppet. If nothing else, Carrall respected the man's self-awareness.

"Lemme ask you something," Carrall said, daring to nudge Lindskog's honesty a little further. "Your wife got any idea what you get up to on a Friday night?"

Lindskog hid his left hand under the table. "My wife understands."

Not quite a lie. Not quite the truth. Who was Carrall to judge? From what he gathered, marriage was complicated. He drained his vodka, letting it bite the back of his throat. "So what weird thing are you into?"

"Pardon me?"

"C'mon, a guy like you doesn't pay for vanilla."

"You don't know anything about me."

"I know your type," Carrall said. "Strapped into a wholesome existence. Everything neatly decided for you. But everyone's got demons, and you can do things to me you couldn't ever do to your wife and still watch her kiss your kids in the morning."

"Maybe." Lindskog's fingers, cold from the ice-filled glass, curled around the back of Carrall's neck. "Is that going to be a problem?"

Carrall reached under the table and slid his hand up Lindskog's leg. The moment their lips touched Carrall whispered, "First show me the money, you kinky bastard."

With a hungry shine in his beige eyes, Lindskog took out his wallet. The silver military ident flashed in one of the slots. Carrall nodded to Michael and Scooter at the bar. Get ready. Scooter got up and wandered down the hallway that led to the restrooms. Michael remained on her stool.

"Will this cover it?" Lindskog set his wallet on the table and counted out five one hundred cred notes.

"That kinda scratch'll cover any itch you've got," Carrall said.

The wallet was out. Time for some misdirection. This was where having different personas came in handy. Carrall Hastings had none of the assassin's incorrigible sexual hang-ups. Carrall pressed closer and slid his arms around Lindskog. The kiss wasn't bad. Not too wet. Not too dry. Polite vodka breath. Perhaps an excess of tongue, but overall Lindskog was a prince compared to some of the people Carrall had fucked for information or recreation. A few ounces of cheap vodka muted his alter ego's screaming revulsion. Carrall was doing his part. He hoped Scooter and Michael were ready to do theirs.

Lindskog's hands tunneled under Carrall's shirt. Without overselling it, Carrall responded with a quiet moan. He used his left hand to flip open the unattended wallet as his right hand dropped to Lindskog's belt, tearing leather from loop. Carrall slipped his hand into Lindskog's pants. At the same time, he blindly pulled the ident from the wallet. Lindskog groaned as Carrall worked him with a firm grip while placing the ident on the edge of the bench seat.

At a slight disturbance in the air beside him, Carrall peeked down at the bench. The card was gone. So was Michael. So far so good. She'd meet Scooter in the bathroom, skim the ident, then she'd find an excuse to drop by Carrall's booth and pass the ident back. In the meantime, he'd keep Lindskog in a holding pattern, so to speak.

"Let's get out of here," Lindskog whispered, grinding his rigid cock against Carrall's hand.

"Let's finish our drinks. Christ knows you paid enough for 'em."

"I'm paying a lot more for you." Lindskog pawed at the assassin's groin and frowned. "Everything all right?"

Carrall shrugged. "Did a few bumps earlier. Sometimes charms the snake right to sleep."

"I've got pills, the good ones. You want?"

Blighted fucking hell. He stifled a hysterical laugh. If Michael didn't return soon he'd have little choice but to stall Lindskog by downing a black-market Viagra. Over the years he'd consumed a smallish heap of drugs in the name of preserving his cover, everything from grass to glass, but this was an entirely different kind of upper.

Finally, she came to his rescue, emerging from of the hallway, all red hair, long legs, and pale silk. Carrall felt himself stir under Lindskog's heavy hand. Saint Michael defend us. Yeah, if he wasn't going to hell before . . .

"Gentlemen," she said as she approached their table. "Might I trouble you for the time?"

Carrall scowled at her. "D'you not see that we're in the middle of a private conversation?"

"I apologize," she said with a curt smile. "I did not mean to interrupt."

"Then get your tiny tits out of my face."

While a flustered Lindskog hurriedly fished his phone out of his pocket, Michael slipped his ident under the table into Carrall's hand.

"It's nearly midnight, miss," said Lindskog.

"Time to haul ass home, Cinderella." Carrall palmed one of the hundred cred notes off the table and shoved it down the front of her dress. "There, tip your footman before he turns into a hamster."

Why she didn't slap him was beyond his reckoning. She thanked Lindskog, spun on her heel and left through the front door. All Carrall had to do now was get the ident back in Lindskog's wallet, excuse himself to take a piss, slip out the side door, and they'd be in the wind, leaving Lindskog none the wiser. The blue-balled victim of a petty grifter. No way would he report it, not if he wanted to maintain a shred of gravitas.

Lindskog gripped Carrall's elbow as though ready to deliver strongly worded instruction on how to address a lady—when the music snapped off and the lights blinked out, flooding the room with that immense coastal darkness and the sound of waves crashing against the pilings below.

"The hell?" Carrall asked over the surprised gasps and scuffling in the darkened room.

"Shit," Lindskog whispered. "It's a raid."

The front door burst open. Women screamed as shadows in heavy boots stomped in. Acting quickly and relying on all the time he'd spent practicing things blind, Carrall groped for Lindskog's wallet and slid the ident back into its slot. Not a second later, rough hands yanked him out of the booth.

He fought his barely discernable assailants, landing several punches and elbow smashes. There wasn't a whole lot of sound, muffled blows, pained grunts. He didn't know where Lindskog was. If the Colonel got pinched, his clearance would be revoked, putting them back to square one. And what about Michael and Scooter? Had they cleared off before the bag team surrounded the Beluga?

The butt of a rifle struck his forehead, a knee crunched into his ribs, and a glancing kick to the jaw sent him reeling to the floor. Hot blood ran into his eyes as he crawled to his hands and knees. He heard thick-treaded boots shuffling back. A jolt of electricity seized him in a crushing grip. As soon as it began to abate, a second set of barbs caught him on the leg. A silent scream died in his knotted-up throat.

"One more bite." A voice stabbed through the darkness. "Trust me, you'll want to be certain this one is subdued before putting him in the van"

Crooked thoughts fell in a jackstraw pile, but he managed to slide one free. This wasn't a random raid. The baggers had come for him.

CHAPTER 34

A white room. A wrong room. No corners. Eggshell acrylic covered the floor, curving up into the wall and again into the ceiling, forming a seamless pod the size of a closet, or a football field. He couldn't say. When he tried to bring his hands to his thudding head, he found they were secured behind his back. Cold steel dug into his wrists. Handcuffs. Also, he was naked. Rarely a good combination.

The indefinable shape of the room screwed with his equilibrium. If he weren't anchored to a chair anchored to the floor, he might fall over. The space contained no focused source of light, but rather the floor, walls, and ceiling emitted a terrible glow that gobbled shadows like dirty kernels of popcorn. A room designed to reveal.

The only interruption in the blank expanse was a dull gray eye set into the floor. A drain.

The glowing wall abruptly opened in the shape of a black teardrop. A man stepped through the breach. Shiny hair, like a helmet. Sharp gray suit.

He scanned his own body. Ink swirls covered what he could see of his arms. Carrall Hastings. He'd been brought here. From the Beluga. Where he'd been working on Lindskog. Until the lights went out.

"Man, am I getting paid for this?" Carrall croaked.

INFRACTUS

"Mr. Hastings," Suit One said, standing with his legs braced wide, arms folded over his broad chest. "Half a dozen viper bites, a tranq dart, and awake already. I'm impressed."

Vipers. That explained the smeared short-term recall. Getting bit once with a stun gun was bad enough, and that wasn't the half of it. He noted a swollen right eye, burning ribs, and tender knuckles. Fighting? Yes. Before he woke up in this room where bizarre white light bleached the wrinkles and middle-aged sag out of Suit One's face until he resembled an overexposed photo of himself. A room designed to erase.

"Where am I?"

"You're starting to look like her." Suit One said, running his hot manicured hands over Carrall's multiple scars—bullets, blades, some old, some new—finally leaning in to examine the fresh pink whorl above his hip from when he'd been shot last week.

"If you're gonna get this close you may as well blow me," said Carrall.

The back of Suit One's hand cracked across Carrall's face, throwing him so hard his restrained arms tugged painfully at the shoulder joints. Suit One rubbed his knuckles on his white handkerchief. "Drop the act, this isn't a game."

The assassin rapped the handcuffs against the chair. "You're the one who bagged me up and brought me to your playroom."

Suit One clutched the handkerchief in his fist and exposed his weird tiny teeth in something approximating a smile, his face twitching with the effort. "Where is she?"

The assassin's critical thinking gears finally crunched into alignment. Suit One didn't know anything. This wasn't about Lindskog or the ident theft. They hadn't been busted. Michael and Scooter had what they needed to keep going. No one was coming for him on account of their agreement: you fall behind, you get left behind. Suit One was here on a deeply personal errand, which meant the assassin could contain this.

"The bartender, right? Your informant?"

"I suspected you would return to your old haunts. He said you were hustling. How the mighty have fallen."

The assassin tested his tongue against one of his front teeth and it wiggled. "So, your pit bull ran away and you think I've got her chained up somewhere?"

"Do you?"

"Haven't seen her."

A fist drove into his stomach and an uppercut to the chin snapped his head back. Suit One wrapped the hankie around his hand, face flushed and panting. "You're good. But you made a mistake."

"Only one?" he groaned.

"You didn't destroy the flight recorder."

"Huh?"

"I know you were both on that plane. Where. Is. She?" Suit One shouted, his lips gray around the edges.

"Y'know, I always wondered about you two."

Suit One grabbed the assassin's hair and wrenched his head back. "What did you do to her?"

The assassin laughed as blood ran down his throat. "What didn't I do to her? Let's just say I hope you weren't in the habit of eating lunch at your desk fifteen years ago."

"What you had was magical, I'm sure." Suit one let go of his hair and pulled a tablet and stylus from his jacket. "If you're not willing to supply me with any useful information, I'll have you sign and we'll get you prepped."

Now it made sense. A white room. Stark. Silent. No stimuli save that which was strategically supplied. A place where a thing was brought to be broken, scientifically. A remap suite.

Suit One dug his knuckles into the assassin's shoulders, exhaling a volley of arrowheaded syllables. "Mr. Hastings, do you consent to the terms of your rehabilitation as set out by the Department of Remedial Compliance?"

"Go fuck yourself, you smug asshole." The assassin glared up into Suit One's scuffed eyes, and behind the rage he saw grief. A septic wound, hot and inflamed.

Suit One lifted his knuckles. "Just tell me where she is. You don't understand. She needs me."

The assassin shook his head. "No cure for a mad dog. You might have loved her, but I did the one thing you couldn't. I put her down."

Suit One swung back, but dropped his hand abruptly when another black teardrop opened in the wall of the pod. Three men entered, kitted out in white jumpsuits, masks, and safety glasses. One man wheeled in a stainless-steel table perforated with tiny holes and equipped with canvas straps and buckles. Another man steered a cart with an electronic console on top and sterile-packed medical supplies beneath. They situated both the table and the cart in the center of the room over the drain.

Suit One smoothed his splintered hair down. "Apologies for the hour, Doctor. This citizen's violent behavior tonight resulted in injury to both tactical team members and his own person. Citizen now refuses consent."

The shortest of the white men shook his head. "I cannot ethically proceed without it."

"Persuade him to reconsider."

The doctor nodded to the other men in white. They converged on the assassin, unlocking the cuffs and lifting him to his feet. Pins and needles attacked his legs, but he allowed the techs to believe he was entirely helpless as they dragged him along. When they reached the drain, he picked up his feet and kicked. The table smashed into the pod wall. The techs fell backward.

"Idiots," Suit One growled and hammered two punches into the assassin's kidneys and a haymaker to the side of his face. His jaw broke with a crack that tore through his skull like shrapnel, and he hit the floor whereupon his ribs received another crunching boot full.

The techs scraped him up and slapped him on the table, securing the straps around his wrists and ankles. Forget fighting back, with his fractured ribs grating together, breathing was a tolerable enough challenge. A medicinal smell stung his nose. The white doctor stood over him with a syringe full of amber fluid.

"Camphor." Suit One's face elongated with the word. "Used in chemical convulsive therapy. Dosing is a fine line though. Underestimate by a couple milligrams, and it won't induce convulsions. Overestimate and you seize so hard you rip your joints apart. Mostly we eyeball it." He held out the tablet and stylus once more. "It's your choice."

The assassin fixed his gaze on the white nothing above. His heart rate slowed. He'd been through worse. He deserved worse. The IV needle slid through the skin of his inner elbow.

"Try to relax," the doctor said, and depressed the plunger.

An arctic chill crystalized in every capillary. In spite of his broken jaw his teeth snapped shut, barely missing his tongue. An enormous black flower bloomed in his head, cracking his skull. Roots tunneled into his stomach and weaved through his insides. He smelled strawberries.

Darkness...hush of rain on grass...wood smoke.

Light razored through his closed eyelids. His breath howled in his ears. Cold through his bones, freezing the marrow to slush. A steely blur descended from the ceiling. Ice water whooshed out in a torrent that filled his nose and mouth and sprayed into his lungs. He coughed and choked. His heels drummed on the gurney and his bladder released, a scalding contrast to the cold. He swung his head sharply to the side. Shallow breaths.

The downpour ceased. Hot gloves rolled him on his side as far the restraints would allow. He vomited onto the floor. The gloves rolled him back. Suit One brushed wet hair back and blotted his face with what he knew had to be that white handkerchief. Suit One tended him the way he might have tended Suit Two in the midst of a raving cutting crisis. "Shh, there now. It's over. Sign the consent."

The assassin spat a mouthful of bile in Suit One's face.

Round two.

A wolf pack, the alpha pair licking each other's wounds.

Round three.

Wild horses in a field at night. A foal stumbling alongside its dam.

Michael could handle the rest. The hero suit never fit him right and the cape got in the way. He was a very bad thing. Suit One placed the stylus in the assassin's numb hand. He scribbled something, didn't even know what, on the tablet.

Suit One peered at the signature. "Very funny."

"Sir?" the doctor asked.

Suit One patted the assassin's cheek before glancing up at the doctor. "Fry him. All the way back to hell."

Weak from the seizures, the assassin couldn't resist the white men as they pasted contacts to his temples and placed intravenous lines in both arms. They tucked a wire mesh blanket around his naked body and jammed a bite block into his mouth. They might have done that earlier. He tasted rust as the rubber scraped over his bitten tongue.

Only one thing mattered. They could carpet bomb his gray matter and beat him to a soggy flesh sponge. Anything they wanted. He'd done what he needed to do. Now he could let go.

"No change on the EEG."

"Level six."

Blood streamed from his nose and pooled in his ears. Electricity spidered under his skin. Bad choices. Haunt you for eternity. A dragon by any other name.

"Still no change."

"Level nine."

"It'll kill him."

"Nine."

Nine. His name once. After the blood and smoke. After everything. The Lord rebuke thee. Falling. Fallen.

"Wake up."

He heard the voice from some place far away. Wake up? He was already awake. Which way was up? His eyes wouldn't open. They were far away too. A whiff of something fresh and sweet, not strawberries. He scuttled about the void. A sudden tug jarred him to a halt. Then another, and another. A final yank and he came unmoored, hurtling through the dark and slamming back into the box of broken toys he supposed must be his body. Cold savaged him with serrated teeth. Only one of his eyes would open.

"Michael?" he tried to say but had no voice to say it.

She ripped off the restraints. "Scooter is holding the door. We must hurry."

"Michael?" he said in a clotted whisper.

She loomed over him, her hair volcanic red in the white light. "I'm here."

"You sure?"

"Don't look so surprised."

She hauled him up and a thick gurgle poured out of him as his injuries gnashed together. His feet slapped the floor. Rivulets of blood and water sluiced off his skin. When asked to support his weight, his legs laughed hysterically and folded like paper accordions. He pitched forward. She held him up. Part of him, anyway. The pulp. The rest drained away.

CHAPTER 35

Warm. Pleasantly unfamiliar, like he'd forgotten how to feel anything but cold. The ability to open both eyes also felt like a past life experience, but they opened and focused on a lamp made from a deer leg. Beyond that, black glass peeked through a gap in the plaid curtains.

The assassin lay on the couch under a heavy blanket. He drew it back to find himself dressed in a T-shirt and pajama pants. Not a trace of ink on his arms and the scent of soap lingered on his skin.

"It's almost five in the morning."

He craned his neck to see Michael sitting in the armchair in her rumpled dress, hair wild, jade eyes bleeding mascara.

"Scooter and Barclay gave you a good scrub. I thought—we thought—you would prefer to wake up clean."

"Thank you," he murmured, intensely grateful, yet appalled at the idea of being handled like a slab of meat with Michael standing by to empty his drool bucket. He swung his legs off the couch and sat up. A wallop of nausea promptly kicked him sideways again.

Michael handed him an empty trashcan. "I doubt you've anything left. Scooter's lap caught the last of it."

INFRACTUS

He slumped over the trashcan and dry heaved. His insides felt puffy, his bones hot, his skin tight. On a scale of zero to cholera, he'd give it a hard eight. Gradually, the nausea ebbed. Still, it wasn't nearly as bad as it ought to have been. Things like bludgeoned kidneys, a kicked-in ribcage, and a broken jaw tended to hurt quite a lot, yet he was in no acute pain and none of his teeth were loose anymore. Only one explanation for that.

"How is he?" the assassin asked.

"Sleeping it off. Unfortunately, his healing hand cannot rid you of the poisons in your blood. How do you feel?"

"Poisonous." He rubbed his hands together, grimacing at the sensation of tiny shocks.

Michael's toes tunneled into the bear rug. He noticed a blister on her heel. The shoes were gone, but the dress, the makeup...she hadn't left him, not even for the minute it would take to change her clothes or wash her face. She stayed.

He shoved the empty trashcan at her. "You're a goddamn lunatic."

"I am also the boss." She plunked the trashcan on the floor. "You'll recall I gave my word that I would protect you."

"How'd you even find the place?"

"We saw them put you in a black van. We followed. That was the easy part. Breaking in was less easy."

"You should have left me."

"I'm famished," she announced, rising from the chair and marching into the kitchen.

He watched her dig through the freezer. Ravenous, no doubt. The Archangel Michael had the resting metabolism of a rabbit and required frequent feedings even when not expending energy violating their agreement. Frozen foods clacked together as she rooted around. If she thought ignoring him would make him go away, she was in for disappointment.

"It was a stupid risk. For all you knew I'd already been bagged and tagged."

She emerged from the freezer with a plastic tub. "Mint chocolate chip. Is this better than the vanilla?"

"Depends what you like. Would you be serious?"

"No."

"No?"

"Tonight's run on absurdities made me realize something," she grunted, digging a spoon into the ice cream. "I am far too serious, far too much of the time. Now that I'm certain you won't expire in your sleep, I am taking a brief furlough."

He stood on watery legs and shuffled to the breakfast bar dividing the kitchen and dining area. "Can you at least tell me why?"

Slowly, she set the ice cream down and stared into the empty sink. "In reversed circumstances, would you have left me?"

His stomach charged up his throat, jamming halfway.

"That is why," she whispered. Then, with a tart smile to match her slutty dress and decaying makeup, she brandished the spoon at him. "Would you like some?"

What a question. Low rent looked good on the Archangel Michael. Too good. Earlier she'd been exquisite. Flawless. He couldn't fathom touching her for fear of leaving a fingerprint. Now she was a mess. What were a few more smudges?

INFRACTUS

Casually, he put his back to her. The edge of the counter bit into his sore kidneys. The owl glared from the coffee table. The assassin ignored it in favor of less judgmental objects—the deer leg lamps on either end of the sofa. Perhaps the same creature contributed to the handsome snarl of antlers over the dining table. Nothing wasted. Odds and ends fashioned into practical items that doubled as horrible conversation pieces. The owl wasn't much for talk though, being more of a hateful listener.

Michael came around to his side of the breakfast bar and climbed up on one of the high stools. She shaved a tiny bite out of her huge bowl of ice cream and popped the spoon in her mouth. A purr rumbled in her throat. Her tongue darted out, sweeping the remains from the spoon. Her eyes revolved toward him. "Do I have something on my face again?"

"No." He rubbed the back of his neck. "I like watching you eat."

"Watching me? Why?"

He flexed a hand that felt more like a foot, plucked the spoon from her fingers, and carved out a bite twice the size of her test sample. She opened her mouth, accepting it with the same low groan of pleasure as her toes curled around the rung of the stool.

"That's why," he said.

"How did I not know about ice cream?" She shoved a huge gloppy spoonful into her mouth, swiped a blob of chocolate off her chin with the heel of her hand, licked it off, and returned her spoon to the bowl to repeat the entire process.

"You're a barbarian," he said.

A milky laugh burbled out of her throat. "Do you know how long it has been since a man dared insult me to my face? And speaking of . . ." She reached down the front of her dress and pulled out a folded one hundred cred note. "I believe this belongs to you."

She pressed the polymer bill, pliant from her body heat, into his hand. He crumpled it and tossed it over his shoulder. "Do they count as insults if I actually like those things about you?"

She arched a brow over one raccoon eye. "You ought to focus on the things you dislike. I am not a good person."

Then why couldn't you leave me? He brushed his knuckles over the purple handprint circling her bicep like a tribal tattoo. "From the break in?"

"There were several guards." She swirled her finger in the melted ice cream at the bottom of her bowl. "It's only a bruise."

"Damn it, Michael. You're not invincible." It reduced his insides to paste. The idea of someone strapping her naked to a table, sticking needles in her arms, and electrocuting her.

"Assassin, you fret over my safety like a mewling infant, yet you relish danger. I have come to know this of you."

"I've never mewled in my life," he said through clenched teeth.

"What is it about extreme risk you find so seductive?"

No one had ever asked him such a question, so he'd never seriously reflected on the subject. "I suppose it's a cultivated taste. The streets were a rough place for a kid. Especially after A-Day."

"Adventus." She licked the melted ice cream off her fingertip. "And how did you survive when so many children did not?"

The assassin looked away, nearly praying for her to please, please, stop licking things. "I had someone. Taught me that if I could survive him, I could survive anything."

"How so?"

"I'd been living in Vancouver about a month when some punks mugged me. They were kids themselves, but it was five to one and I figured the few bucks I had on me weren't worth a concussion . . ." He paused, not sure why he was telling her this. "Anyway, Zee caught wind of it. He dragged me out of bed in the middle of the night, hauled me into a dead-end alley with the intention of showing me some moves. When it was over he dropped me back on my pallet, bleeding from every hole in my head, and he says to me, Next time someone tries to roll you, Mouse. You make 'em wish you were never born. Otherwise we do this again and again, until you learn."

"And?"

"I learned."

Michael reached for his hand. "Did you love him in spite of his cruelty, or because of it?"

"Don't." He withdrew from her touch, and from the memory of his complicated relationship with Zee.

"You do not wish to be touched," she said, her hand once again creeping across the counter. "But if I asked you to, would you touch me?"

This time he let her cool fingers mesh with his, and he swallowed hard. Backing off would be smart. But she was so close, smelling like crushed flowers, and looking like trash in all the ways he liked.

She brought her fingertips to his temple. "You've been hurt."

Her words caved his chest in, rubber band ribs snapping through hyaline lungs. His jaw rusted shut, turning his skull into a locked-down prison with gluey windows behind barbed lids blinking open-shut-open until his eyes bled white.

"Damage is a catalytic force." She fit his hand to the ligature circling her arm and brought his other hand to her scraped knee, dragging his wrist up her thigh until his fingertips edged under the pale silk of her dress. "Fractured pieces knit together. Making you strong. Making you hard. *Infractus ad fortem.*"

He slowly exhaled. "Michael...this isn't a great idea."

"Because you did not think of it?"

"Because you know I did."

Silk slipped under his hands as he slid them around her waist. She clutched his shirt and drew him tight against her body, her knees bracketing his hips. He fetched up a greedy handful of her hair and inhaled. Not enough. He wanted to taste her. Everywhere. Would she be okay with that? Should he ask? Or forget it all together? Apparently, he'd been throwing up a lot.

"Is this what you want?" she asked.

He pulled his face out of her hair. "Trick question?"

"You are unwell. I do not wish to take improper advantage."

True, his body felt like an alien costume with a stuck zipper, but he suspected she wasn't referring to physical injury. "Michael, I do want. I'm just not sure I can."

Mortified, he was thinking he should have taken one of Lindskog's weekenders, when her hands skimmed down his chest and stomach, and his damaged, drugged body actually managed to pull itself together and produce an erection. Go team.

He sucked in a breath and threw his weight against her, shoving her into the corner where the counter met the wall, holding her there with his body. Too hard. Too rough. Her legs tightened around him. She made a noise. Pain or surprise, he didn't know. It wasn't like he wanted to hurt her, but a part of him needed to hurt somebody. And he knew she would let him. She wanted him to.

"Why tonight?" He clamped his hands around her arms, hard enough to bruise mortal flesh. "Twenty years of Panopticon rule and suddenly it can't wait a few more days? I want the truth."

"I've grown weak," she said, twisting his shirt in her fists. "And weaker still with each passing day. I should not want this. I should not want you. I am Michael."

He loosened his grip. "You're more than that."

The cage he built couldn't hold her. She slid out of his arms and put the entire room between them as though he'd confessed to being a leper.

"Why did you say that?" she demanded. "Those exact words. Why?"

"Huh?"

"I do not know you," she said in a shrill whisper, her face salt white. "You do not know me." She paced the length of the couch, deer leg to deer leg, coming to a halt beside the owl. "If you speak of this, to anyone, I will spill your guts and see that you live to eat them. Understood?"

"Uh, okay?" he said, stunned at the sudden rejection, the eerie feeling of déjà vu, and the fact that everything she just said was a lie. At least in her mind. By the time he'd recovered his wits, she'd vanished in a swish of silk, the bedroom door clicking shut behind her.

Spite glittered in the owl's eyes. The assassin crumbled onto the couch. He'd done the right thing. Offered up his life for the greater good. And now he was alone with a wilting miracle of a hard-on for the Archangel Michael. Was there a lesson in this? He stuck his foot out and tipped the owl over on its face.

CHAPTER 36

The assassin stood on the veranda watching Michael on the other side, seated on a bench, obsessively polishing her katanas with a scrap of flannel. She hadn't spoken to him since emerging from the bedroom, her face bare of makeup and her hair tightly braided.

"Barclay said I'd find you out here," Scooter said, kneeing the screen door open and handing the assassin a mug of coffee. "How you feeling, mate? You were fucked up last night. I've seen healthier roadkill."

The assassin stared into his coffee, which he never drank but always accepted because he liked the heavy heat of it in his hands. "I should ask how you're feeling."

"Dandy, after some shut-eye." Scooter gestured toward Michael, bent to her task, rubbing the flannel in small circles along gleaming steel. "She been at that long?"

"Is two hours a long time to spend cleaning something that isn't dirty?"

Scooter grimaced and took a fortifying slug of coffee. "Morning, doll. Sleep well?"

"Quite," she said. "And the next time you call me 'doll,' I might reach down your throat and rip out your spine."

Scooter looked back at the assassin. "I sense a disturbance in the force. Did you guys have another fight?"

"I don't know," the assassin said to Michael. "Did we?"

She sheathed her blades and rose from the bench. "There is work to be done. We convene in five minutes."

She strode past them into the house. The screen door slammed shut behind her, forcing out a gust of pancake and sausage scented air. The assassin's stomach flopped. He set his untouched coffee on the railing and covered his mouth and nose with his hand.

Scooter spoke in a furious whisper. "D'you think I'm fucking retarded?"

"You're not supposed to say retarded," the assassin replied, staring off into the trees. "It's offensive."

"I dunno the specifics, but there are serious vibes between you two. Bro, I tried asking nicely, but now I'm telling you straight up. Keep your mitts off."

"Who is he?"

"Wha?"

"The guy. The one she's hung up on. The one who could see lies. The one who hurt her. Who is he?"

Scooter glanced over his shoulder at the screen door. "Leave it alone, mate. Some things can't be undone, and whatever happened last night—"

"Nothing happened, Scooter."

"Yeah, why don't I believe you?"

The assassin threw his hands up. "Could you just once not assume the worst from me? I did the heavy lifting last night, and for my trouble I got rolled by baggers, pumped full of toxic waste, and nearly lobotomized."

"I know," Scooter said. "I know, so let's take a beat and chill, okay?"

Scooter gently squeezed the assassin's arm. From that point of contact, a calming heat traveled up his shoulder and settled around a terrible well of rage in his chest. Usually that well was sealed tight, but throughout his life, certain things and certain people had a way of prying up the lid.

"Bro, you went through something harsh. You wanna talk about it?"

"No." The assassin yanked his arm away from Scooter's soothing touch. "And stop acting like we're friends. We both know I'm only here because I'm useful. I'm not your family."

"The hell you're not. We risked everything to bust your ass out of that place. I was just the wheelman, but Mikey? She charged through half a dozen armed guards to get to you."

"I never asked you to do that." The assassin slammed his fist down on the railing causing his coffee to jump into the wild bramble of the flowerbed. "I didn't want you to."

Scooter yanked his hands through his sleep-wild hair. "It's like talking to a rock."

"Then save your breath." The assassin stalked off the porch, onto the driveway, and down the lane.

"Hey, where you going? There's convening, like now."

"Can't."

Scooter called after him. "You make this shit way harder than it needs to be, mate. You're as bad as she is. What am I supposed to tell her?"

The assassin raised his fist in the air, flipped up his middle finger, and kept walking.

His stomach settled once he got away from the cooking smells, but fatigue quickly built in his legs as he hiked farther and farther into Acadia Park. He didn't go to his safe house. He wanted to be outside, where neither logic nor paranoia could close in on him.

He'd taken his anger out on the wrong person. His beef was with Michael, not Scooter. It wasn't even that she'd shut him down. But a simple "no" would have sufficed. She didn't have to imply that he'd manipulated her into doing whatever it was they'd done—which honestly was nothing. And Scooter piled on with the same assumption, which infuriated him, but there was more to it, a helpless ache inside the anger. Jesus Christ, his feelings were actually hurt. When the hell did that happen? Who was he becoming? Who had he been before any of this? His existential flail had many tentacles, all tracing back to one big question mark. Where did he come from? If he could determine that point of origin, then what? Like that would change anything?

Autumn wind scraped his cheeks as the elevation climbed and the trees thinned. Without intending it, he found himself on top of Cadillac Mountain. Underwhelming as far as mountains went. It was pretty and all, with mossy granite outcroppings crenellating the otherwise bald summit. To the west lay the forested expanse of the park and to the east, a misty myriad of islands dotted the harbor. In the distance he heard the ocean boom into a small cave-like inlet locally known as Thunder Hole.

The assassin wandered over to a clapboard building that served as a visitor's center. Acadia Park didn't get many tourists; nevertheless, the open sign was lit up.

"Morning," a young ranger in a windbreaker stood up behind the counter when the assassin ducked inside.

"Didn't expect to find anything up here."

"Park maintains a small staff. Us, mostly," the young ranger said, tipping his head toward the closed door behind the desk. "And we function as a maritime recording station: water temp, tides, waves, and what not. Panopticon worries about global warming; can you believe that? Everything old world is new again."

The assassin surveyed the information plaques on the walls, interspersed with dated souvenir displays. Racks of postcards and T-shirts emblazoned with black bears, fish, and birds. Bins full of polished rocks in all different colors like jelly beans. "First time in Maine, figured I couldn't leave without a hike up the tallest mountain on the north Atlantic seaboard. It's...small."

"More of a granite foothill," the ranger agreed. "Great views though, especially at sunrise."

The closed door opened and an older ranger emerged. When he spotted the assassin he quickly shut the heavy steel door behind him.

"It's this gentleman's first time up the peak," the young ranger said.

The older ranger zipped up his windbreaker. "You're a few hours late. Best time to see it is—"

"Sunrise," the assassin said. "Right. I should come back. Maybe bring the wife and kids."

"Family man?" the older ranger asked.

The young ranger's face split into an enormous grin. "My wife and I got one on the way."

"Congratulations." Where was this supposed fertility crisis? the assassin wondered.

"My missus and I weren't able. How many you have?" the older ranger asked.

"Triplets," the assassin said. "We're blessed—I mean, fortunate."

The young ranger tipped his cap. "Gotcha."

Something about the scene bothered the assassin. The absence of a New England twang in the rangers' voices. Such an obscure post staffed by flatlanders? Also, he identified the outlines of a shoulder rig beneath the windbreakers of both men. A rifle or a shotgun behind the counter, he could understand. Even a hip holster wouldn't be that out of place. Wildlife and all. But concealed carry for park rangers? Since when?

"Anyway, it's nice to get out of the wind for a few minutes." The assassin rubbed his ears. "When do the leaves start to turn?"

The rangers glanced at one another.

"That classified information?" the assassin asked.

"Sorry." The young ranger blushed. "We're not used to tourists. Or anyone, really."

"Get the odd local making the hike," the older ranger said. "Or kids wanting to party, but most of our visitors tend to be of the four-legged variety and the fattest gulls you ever seen."

"One time a bear wandered up," said the young ranger. "Shut us down for hours while we tried to chase it back to the mainland."

While the young ranger told the story of the bear, the assassin subtly checked out the door the older ranger had come through. Judging from the outside of the building, the space behind that door could be a small office. But the heavy steel door and sophisticated security panel on the wall were some serious protection for tide and wind speed records.

"Family's probably wondering where I'm at," the assassin said. "Nice to meet you fellas."

The rangers smiled and waved as he exited the visitor's center. He hustled down the mountain, ignoring the protests of his battered body. Something about the visitor's center reminded him of his own trollish hideaway under the bridge. The most secure of all his safe houses. Between misdirection and camouflage, it didn't need locks.

My prompts don't often get through to him. Maybe this one didn't either. Mohammed might have gone up the mountain all on his very own.

He hikes into the trees, focused, but weak. Last night...I didn't mean for it to happen, but I did nothing to stop it. I knew the remap wouldn't work, so why not let him suffer? Why not share in it? I curled up with him under that web of lightning until the moment I heard a panicked blur of thoughts from the guards outside.

I slipped away moments before she barged in. I spent so much time wondering how her arrival would affect him that I never considered what she might trigger in me. It's like a maelstrom opens up inside, sucking me down into that place where I'm still tied to that pillar, where the smoke fills my lungs, lending body to my unanswered prayers, and through the sizzle of my own meat, I hear the faint strains of a lyre. A great fire kindled long ago. No one knows I was the tinder.

I can't bear it, and I sure as hell can't control it. These days they call it post-traumatic stress. All I know is that when it comes to Michael, this universe is not big enough for the two of us. It's time to take the next step. I need Michael to see, and there is no shadow in the Light of God.

The assassin shambled through the cottage door on rubbery legs. The greasy smell of sausage hit him like a frying pan to the face, and he groped for the back of the couch to steady himself.

"Welcome back," Michael said, seated at the head of the table, regal as any queen, but something about the slant of her mouth held the tiniest bit of I dare you to fuck with me.

"Looks like you're about to leggo your Eggo, son," said Barclay from behind his computer.

The assassin dropped into the chair on the opposite end of the table from Michael.

"Considering all we risked to save your skin," she said, her eyes nailing him to the spot. "I would expect your presence at my briefing."

He glared at her. "Is there some greater purpose to twisting the facts, making it seem like I duped you into doing something you clearly wanted to do anyway?"

Her hands clutched the armrests of her chair so tightly her knuckles threatened to punch through the skin. "I'm sure I don't know what you mean."

"C'mon, Michael." He paused, letting her wriggle on the hook of her own lie. "Busting me out of the rehab clinic? That was your idea."

If a look could flay flesh from bone, he'd be an exposed skull. An iron-forged warrior with unchallenged authority, Michael could paint the walls with him any time she wanted. So, what was with the suicidal urge to dominate her? And not in a small way. He wanted to drag her out by her hair and hurl her down on the forest floor. He wanted her nails in his back and her gasping cry in his ear as he pushed into her body. He wanted her to want the same thing.

Not his usual style.

But strangely familiar, like they'd done this dance a thousand times before, only to forget and repeat the steps all over again. Maybe he was brain damaged. And was this how often normal people thought about sex? If so, how did they ever get anything done?

"Are you so disappointed to be alive?" Michael asked, interrupting his edgy daydream with a note of genuine concern. His anger dissipated.

"Thank you," he said. "I'm grateful, really. But we agreed."

"If you recall the transcript," Barclay said. "We agreed it would be foolish to go back for anyone what got pinched, not that we wouldn't do it should the predicament arise."

"You tricked me?"

Michael toyed with a loose thread on her sleeve. "It was easier than dealing with your tantrum if we refused."

The assassin slunk down in his chair. "I don't throw tantrums."

Barclay peered at him over the screen of his computer. "Y'do get a smidge irritable, son."

"And nasty," Scooter added. "If I hadn't told the niblet about your near dirt nap last night, she'd still be pissed at you."

The assassin covered his face with his hands. "You told Liza?"

"Mondo wiggage, bro. Full blownsies. We're talking the ugly cry. You should give her a call."

The assassin closed his eyes. The chemicals lingering in his bloodstream attacked his nervous system with random flashes of light, auditory distortion, and a gnashing headache.

"Sure you're up to this?" Barclay asked. "Mayhap you could use some sleep first?"

The assassin pressed his palms flat on the table, as though he could absorb some of its cool stability. "Tell me I didn't give Lindskog half a handjob for nothing."

"Half?" Scooter looked stricken. "That's cruel, yo."

"Seriously?"

"Bad for the plumbing is all," Scooter explained as he pulled one knee up and wrapped his other leg around it because the guy couldn't ever just sit in a chair. "But I gotta say, you crushed it last night. You're a sexy dude when you wanna be. Poor bastard didn't stand a chance."

Barclay cleared his throat. "On that note, I'm glad to say not a bit o' your, er...handiwork went to waste."

"What do we know?" said Michael.

"Lindskog's clearance is valid, and there's no record of a raid on the Beluga, nor any report of an incident at the rehab clinic. Extra-black bag operation, I'd guess."

"Suit One was after me," the assassin said. "As far as he knows, I was hustling for cash."

"Barclay, were you able to use Lindskog's identification to uncover the location of the mainframe?" Michael asked.

"Heck yes, and you're never gonna believe where."

"Cadillac Mountain?" the assassin said.

Barclay frowned. "How in hell'd you know that?"

"Just came from there." The assassin got up to retrieve the notebook and pen from his bag. "Rangers at the visitors' center aren't local, they're packing, and there's an awful sturdy door in the back of that shitty gift shop."

"According to the plans I accessed, that there door leads down into the hall of the mountain king," said Barclay.

"Are there more soldiers guarding the lower levels?" Michael asked.

"I don't think so," the assassin said. "The ranger was telling the truth when he said it was only him and his partner. And perimeter security is motion sensors and cameras. I doubt those guys know what they're guarding."

"Such minimal security for such an important installation?"

"Misdirection is the most effective security there is. Moats, razor wire, and soldiers would call attention to the site. The more people know about it, the greater the risk. Lindskog is one of the few military personnel with access to what's below. They don't need heavy security.

If there's an incident, the place goes into lockdown, and it's like Barclay said, you could drop a nuke on that mountain and still not get in."

"The guards need to be dealt with," said Michael.

Scooter lurched out of his pretzel twist, bare feet slapping onto the floor. "We can't kill them. Those guys aren't the Eye, they're just dudes doing their job. Can't we knock 'em out or something?"

"Like clunk their heads together?" the assassin sneered. "This isn't an old-world cartoon, Scooter."

"Beg pardon," Barclay raised his hand. "Moral implications aside, the ranger's Guardian profiles are tied into the security system. Their vitals flatline, the facility locks down."

Scooter relaxed slightly.

"There's a sweet spot," the assassin said. "Get past the rangers and raise a flag that will prompt Lindskog to activate his token, without triggering full breach protocol. Won't be easy. A wandering bear sent them into lockdown a few weeks back."

"I see." Michael leaned forward in her chair, a shrewd light in her eyes as she regarded the assassin. "Barclay tells me you are an expert marksman. Is this true?"

"Yes, but I don't think the pacifist loves that idea."

"Hear me out, Legion." Michael rested her hand on Scooter's and launched into her proposal. As a leader, she knew when to let the horses run, and how to deftly take up the reins.

While Barclay and Michael discussed the acquisition of specialized equipment, the assassin visually traced her hairline along her forehead and temple until it curved behind her unpierced ears and down to the nape of her neck. A soft flush colored her skin there as her blood stirred, no doubt in anticipation of their attack. She regretted what happened between them last night, but regretting half a mistake seemed a waste. The assassin wanted more of her mistakes, and he wanted them now.

Scooter kicked him under the table.

CHAPTER 37

A t one in the morning, the assassin, Scooter, and Michael were clad head to toe in black and huddled in some brush on the gentle slope below the summit of Cadillac Mountain. In the light of a nearly full moon, the assassin could see the shuttered windows of the visitor's center above them. He peered through the night vision scope of the gauged CO_2 air rifle Barclay acquired for him.

"Tricky shot," Scooter said. "Low ground. Think you'll make it?"

The assassin arched an eyebrow.

"Sorry."

"I still think this is a bad idea," the assassin said. "Tranquilizer darts are unpredictable."

"Pearl said there's enough beddy-bye juice in those suckers to drop a dude inside twenty seconds."

"A lot can happen in twenty seconds, Scooter."

"Legion," Michael said, nearly invisible in the shadow of a shrub. "We are doing our best, but you must accept the risk that someone may come to harm this night."

"Yeah, I know it." Scooter bounced around on his knees, his heavy parka making rustling noises.

"Sit still." The assassin shoved him off balance and he went spilling onto the rocky soil. "Jesus, what's wrong with you?"

"I'm freezing, and I'm kinda worried about the niblet."

So was the assassin. Barclay's part of the operation could be performed remotely so he'd returned to California yesterday afternoon. The destruction of the mainframe would shake Panopticon to their foundations and they would be relentless in their pursuit of the perpetrators. If things went sideways, the assassin didn't want the old man caught up in it. He almost sent Scooter back as well, but in order to get in and out within their narrow time frame, they needed his speedy little legs.

"Calm yourself, Legion," Michael said. "Pearl put Liza on bed rest only as a precaution."

Scooter remained grim. "That sound like Doc Pearl to you?"

The assassin didn't think so. Pearl considered pregnancy neither an illness, nor a weakness, nor even a delicate condition. She believed hard work, three squares, and a daily shot of whisky did more to ensure a long healthy life than any modern medical intervention. If she sent Liza to bed, something was wrong. Unfortunately, there was nothing they could do about it from the other side of the continent.

At the moment they were holding their position.

"Gagh," Scooter shivered, somehow managing to tuck his knees up into his parka.

"You exaggerate," Michael said.

"My cahones would disagree. This is a full retreat situation. I may never see them again."

"I don't hear the assassin complaining, though perhaps he lacks the anatomy."

"For the record," the assassin said. "that water is extremely cold."

Scooter chuckled. "Whatever you say, bro."

"On task, gentlemen," Michael said. "I believe it is time. Scooter?"

He flipped up the dark hood of his parka. "Ready to make like a bear and trip some motion sensors."

Scooter started crawling toward the tabletop summit of the mountain. Michael and the assassin followed, elbowing along on their bellies.

"I hope you're right about this," he whispered.

"You forget I command an army of my own. I have seen this type of scenario play out many times. After their recent false alarm, they will not initiate lockdown until they are certain the threat is legitimate."

Scooter crawled straight through the perimeter line Barclay had mapped out, and in the dark, bundled in his coat, he did uncannily resemble a little black bear. Sure enough, an exterior flood lamp came on under the eaves of the visitor's center and the door opened. A ranger emerged, service pistol drawn. The assassin peered through his scope. It was the young ranger from two days ago, and his gun was a very nice Beretta M9.

The ranger began conducting a visual sweep of the area. When he scouted around to the side of the building and out toward the perimeter, the assassin aimed. The guard was one hundred yards away. An easy target, except syringe darts didn't fly as fast or true as a bullet, and a torso shot was out because he might be wearing a vest. An arm or leg would do, but the ranger might have enough time to call out before the drug rendered him unconscious. According to Pearl, a neck shot ensured the fastest systemic delivery.

Through the scope, the assassin aimed at the pale sliver of the ranger's throat above the collar of his jacket. These pacifist measures were a pain in the ass. Just in case, he had his SIG and a couple knives in his pack. "Michael, if this doesn't work you know what I have to do, even if Scooter doesn't like it."

"Scooter has your back, assassin. Never doubt that."

Assurances didn't get more solid. The assassin held his lungs empty and squeezed the trigger with the ball of his finger. The dart fired with a soft pop. The ranger flinched, sank to his knees, and collapsed, still clutching his M9. A moment later the older ranger came out of the building. The assassin fired a dart into his neck and he went down even faster than the young ranger.

"Let's go," Michael said.

The assassin dragged the young ranger into the brush a little way down the slope of the mountain and Michael followed with the older ranger. Scooter met them at the door of the visitor's center.

"Do I make a great bear or what?"

"Well done, Legion," Michael said. "Are we ready?"

The assassin led the way inside. Behind the counter he found a card lock console with a keypad. The assassin's phone buzzed in his pocket. He dug it out and read the text from Barclay. A six-digit numerical code and the words "get a move on." He swiped the cloned ident and keyed in the code to release the mag lock.

The door opened, revealing a brightly lit staircase descending into the mountain. "We're in."

"Clock's ticking," the assassin said.

An arid draft blew steadily over them as they raced downward. The assassin couldn't imagine what kind of work went into hollowing out a granite mountain. The stairway switched back and forth, with cameras mounted at every landing. Barclay had said he would take the video surveillance system offline. Still, the assassin kept his head down as they passed under each lens.

The stairs terminated five stories down in a concrete walled vestibule with a steel door. The assassin keyed in the code again and opened the door to a blast of processed air.

"So far, so good," he said. "Right now, Lindskog's attempting to establish contact with the rangers. Barclay's taken down the comm system. He said it'll take Lindskog about five minutes to verify that it's not a technical issue on his end. After that he'll initiate lockdown. Five minutes. We need to be gone in three.

"On with it then," Michael said, herding them through the door onto a balcony overlooking an astonishing sight.

Row upon row of server racks lined ten thousand square feet of floor space under a dome of speckled granite. The very air seemed to vibrate at a high frequency that set the assassin's teeth on edge. This was Panopticon's Eye. These servers stored the dirty laundry of an entire civilization.

They zipped down the stairs into the center aisle of rack mounted servers where the found a large stainless-steel tank. The reservoir for the liquid cooling system that kept the mainframe from melting into a lake of slag. Similar to Barclay's set up at Laughing Corpse, the pipes running through the racks were filled with coolant. As a liquid in a closed system, it was stable, but in vapor form it was highly flammable. The assassin was counting on that added incendiary kick to incinerate every microchip in this place.

The assassin opened his pack and lifted out the largest explosive device armed with a detonator. The two smaller wrapped tubes stuffed with explosive he handed to Scooter, along with a knife to rip through the packing.

"Man, it's hot in here," Scooter shouted over the loud electronic hum, unzipping his parka and dropping it next to the assassin's back pack.

"Be careful with those," the assassin said. "Place them three rows over on either side of us. Unwrap them and shove them into the rack somewhere they'll be in contact with a cooling pipe. Get moving."

Scooter grabbed the knife, tucked the two packages under his arm and trotted off. Next the assassin held the large bomb while Michael taped it securely to the tank.

Scooter came running back, folded knife in hand. "All set."

"Good." The assassin set the timer on the bomb strapped to the tank for five minutes. "Let's get the hell out of here."

Halfway up the stairs, Scooter cried, "Wait! I left my parka by the tank.

"May it rest in peace," said the assassin. "Once you start the timer you don't go back."

"Why?"

"Because it's the rule."

"But it's freezing out there."

"Go fetch it then," Michael said. "Move, Legion, double time."

Scooter ran down the stairs into the rows of servers.

"You caved," the assassin said to her. "If we explode I'm blaming you."

They continued up the stairs and through the door, where Colonel Perkin Lindskog and his gun waited for them.

"Hands up," Lindskog said, eyeing the assassin in a way that couldn't quite hide the injury behind it. "What did I ever do to you?"

"It's not personal." Suit One said, descending the last few steps to point his own gun at the assassin. "Isn't that what you always tell them?"

Suit One appeared even more unhinged than he had two nights ago. His helmet hair was actually mussed and he hadn't shaved. His gray suit hung like saggy skin from his broad frame. When he lost Suit Two he'd lost his anchor. The assassin understood. And people thought him incapable of empathy.

"I see you've acquired a companion." Suit One shifted his focus to Michael. "I should warn you my dear, this one's attentions tend to be lethal."

Michael gave the assassin a sideways glance. She wasn't fast enough to stop a bullet. She trusted him to get them out of this.

"How'd you find me?" the assassin asked.

"After you escaped I traced your movements back. When they led to the Colonel here, I knew you had to be up to something. The same way I knew all those years ago that you were a mistake. You were trash then. You're trash now. And it's high time you were disposed of. Colonel, escort them upstairs."

"Move it," Lindskog said, herding them with his gun.

INFRACTUS

Each passing second brought them closer to being blown to kibble. The assassin wondered if he should say something about the bomb, and where was Scooter? Michael led the way up the stairs. Lindskog kept his gun on the assassin and Suit One had his gun on Lindskog.

"You should have shot me the other night," the assassin said.

"Perhaps," Suit One said. "But now I know who your people are, and I get to take one of them away from you."

The assassin swung around to find Suit One choking up on the trigger of his gun, aiming for the back of Michael's head. At the same time Scooter slipped out the server room door. A knife flashed in his hand and without hesitation he slung his arm around Suit One's neck, jerking him back. The cry of gunfire ricocheted through the stairwell.

Chips of concrete hailed down on their heads. Michael unsheathed a blade, holding it to Lindskog's throat, while the assassin snatched the M9 out of his hand.

Suit One coughed a coarse spray of blood and pitched forward, revealing a knife buried to the hilt in the back of his expensive suit. The assassin studied the placement. Upward angle, to the left of the spine, between the fifth and sixth ribs, tearing through the lung, the thoracic aorta, and finally the heart. Quick and clean. An expert kill.

Dead eyed, Scooter sagged against the wall.

"We have to go," the assassin said. "Now."

Michael and Scooter trudged up the stairs. The assassin beckoned to the Colonel. "There's a bomb in the server room that's set to go off in about a minute."

"I'm going to stay."

"This isn't the Titanic, Lindskog."

The career military man ran his hand over his decorated uniform, spattered with Suit One's blood. "I'm tired of being on the wrong side. Of everything."

"So, you're going to die the way you lived?" the assassin said. "As a coward and a government stooge?"

"What do you care?"

"I don't, but your kids might. Panopticon is going down, and this is your chance. Your one bite at the apple."

They ran up the stairs, out of the building, and scrambled down the side of the mountain to the place they'd left the tranquilized rangers. A muffled boom shook the ground beneath them, and the visitor's center erupted in a geyser of flame.

The assassin dusted himself off. "Collect your family, Lindskog. Dig those chips out of your hands and get yourselves off grid. Have your men here do the same. Somewhere remote would be safest. If things crash...you remember A-Day."

"Wait." Lindskog fished a card out of his pocket. "You run into trouble, call. If I can help, I will."

"Why?"

"I told you I'm tired of being on the wrong side, and eventually you're going to need someone on yours."

The assassin tucked the card into his pocket. "For your sake, I hope I never see you again."

They shook hands and the assassin headed down the mountain. He caught up with Michael in the woods, falling in beside her. Ahead he caught sporadic glimpses of Scooter shambling through the trees. "Is he okay?"

She shook her head. When they reached a small clearing, they found Scooter huddled on his knees. His back heaved like someone about to be sick, but instead of stomach contents an unearthly moan poured out of him, a slow crescendo building to an unbearable pitch that made the assassin's skin crawl.

Michael dropped to her knees, gathered Scooter into her arms, and rocked him the way a mother would her child. The assassin didn't understand. So what, if Scooter broke some stupid oath? It wasn't murder. He'd saved Michael's life. And he did it like a professional. The assassin was in no position to mitigate Scooter's grief. He had too many questions.

Michael abruptly stood.

"What is it?" the assassin asked.

"Quiet," she said, peering into the shadow and trees. "Whoever you are, show yourself."

In a whisper of foliage, the most beautiful woman the assassin had ever seen stepped into a shaft of moonlight. Long dark hair, dusky skin, large silver-green eyes, and her fatigues couldn't conceal the decadent curves of an old-world pin-up. A samurai sword hung from her narrow waist.

The woman bowed her head. "Captain."

"Uriel," Michael said. "I did not send for you."

So, this was the Archangel Uriel. The one Sister Claudia called the Light of God.

"I've come to assist you, Captain." The woman scrutinized the assassin and pursed her full lips. "This man is a murderer. He must be punished."

"Those were not my orders," Michael said.

"Circumstances have changed."

"Our Father has not informed me of any change."

"No?" Uriel's hand grasped the hilt of her sword. "And when was the last time you heard from Him?"

By now the assassin recognized when Michael was preparing for confrontation. She took two measured paces toward Uriel. "If you have something to explain, now is the time."

"Permission to speak freely, Captain?"

"Granted."

"You are compromised and derelict in your duty."

Michael glanced over her shoulder. "Scooter, assassin, you will proceed on foot without me."

"Not going to happen," the assassin said.

Uriel's radiant smile lit up the darkness. "Courage becomes you. Stay, repent, and die honorably."

"No one is dying," said Michael.

"You mean no one else?" Uriel's gaze landed on Scooter. "I knew this day would come. Tell me, Raphael. Is it like riding a bicycle?"

Scooter did not react beyond a slow blink, and Uriel's smirk wavered. The assassin observed a subsonic tremor of deception running through her every word and action. She had a secret, and she wasn't the only one. The assassin side-eyed Scooter.

Uriel unsheathed her sword. "Prepare to meet your maker, human."

Michael reached behind her back, drawing her katanas with a flourish. One pointed at Uriel, who halted in her tracks, and the other at Scooter and the assassin. In a voice that echoed off the trees and made the air shiver she said, "Go."

Scooter drags him off and he doesn't resist. I want to follow. Get away from Michael before she ignites another incendiary flashback. But I must see this through. I've got too many balls in the air. I failed to anticipate Suit One's tenacity and was an astral heartbeat away from using him as a meat puppet when little brother handled the problem. Like the old days. Still, that was too close. I can't have anyone dying. Yet.

"You haven't told them, have you," Uriel says. "About Nero. They still think they're after some cackling human villain."

Michael lowers her swords. "How do you know about Nero?"

"Not all under your command are as blindly trusting as Raphael...or as forgiving as Joshua."

Michael's flinch is barely perceptible. "Our Father wants this dealt with discreetly, lest it incite misguided rebellion on a larger scale."

"He wants you to clean up your mess. And you want to save face."

"Uriel, if you know something...if you know anything . . ."

Uriel's aggressive façade cracks. "This is so much more complicated than you know. Trust that I am only trying to set right what has gone terribly, unnaturally wrong."

"How is executing one human going to accomplish that? Talk to me, Uri. Whatever it is we shall face it together as we always have."

I honestly don't know what Uriel will say. I didn't force her to come here. I didn't even ask her to. I merely imparted three pieces of information. One, madness drove me to violate God's law. Two, I can't manifest my own body outside my realm. And three, she owes me, big time.

These are facts, and softhearted, guilt-ridden Uriel drew her conclusions. Now she will do what is in her nature. She wants to protect me, but she will not go behind Michael's back, and here we are. Poor dear. She likely won't survive.

"You have your secrets," says Uriel. "I have mine. Step aside."

"I cannot allow you to harm the assassin."

Uriel raises her sword in a ready stance. "Sister, I do not wish to fight you."

"Then don't."

Uriel slashes, a killing blow, which Michael blocks, trapping Uriel's blade between her own, and kicking her in the stomach. She staggers back and then charges with a direct thrust. Michael spins away, using her blade as an extension of her arm, inflicting a shallow cut along Uriel's flank.

Michael circles slowly. "I could have gutted you."

The real battle begins, and it's not fancy swordsmanship, observant of rules and etiquette. This is combat. Graceless and brutal. Uriel's boot digs into Michael's ribs. Her flinch gives Uriel all the opportunity she needs. It's finally happening. Were I corporeal, my blood would boil in the four-chambered cauldron of my heart. Uriel's sword cuts into Michael's shoulder and slices down to her inner elbow.

With her good arm, Michael punches her blade into Uriel's stomach. Even I've got to give Michael credit. That bitch invented mutually assured destruction.

"Enough." Michael steps back dragging her steel with her. Blood drips from her fingers onto the dead leaves blanketing the ground. "Uriel, I give you leave to return home. You will answer for this crime when my work here is complete."

Uriel sags against a tree trunk, hand pressed to her wound. "I sought to spare you pain, Michael. Soon, you will see."

"Uri—"

But Uriel is gone.

I'm disappointed in my sisters. Uri's steel rent Michael's flesh, and I'd rather hoped Michael would kill her for it. Now I'll have to find another way.

Michael falls to her knees and bows her head. So submissive.

I like it. But the flames creep closer with every second I linger in her presence. It's time to fly. I spread my astral wings and follow the Light of God.

CHAPTER 38

The assassin and Scooter made it back to the car they'd left in a ditch under the thick boughs of a pine tree. Within seconds their breath and body heat had completely fogged the windows.

Scooter braced a sneakered foot on the dash. The assassin let five minutes pass in blue-shadowed silence. Strangely he'd heard no sirens or helicopters. That didn't mean anything. Panopticon could handle the situation as loud or quiet as they wanted. His concern was their getaway plane, which left the airfield in forty-five minutes, whether they were on it or not.

Hopefully Michael wasn't too far behind, but in the meantime the assassin decided to steer Scooter out of his catatonia. "So... Raphael?"

"No one calls me that," muttered Scooter. "Not unless I've been naughty."

"Beautiful work back there. Slick. Fast."

"Said I didn't have much use for knives, not that I didn't know how to use 'em."

"You're good. Better than me."

Scooter dragged his gaze from the window. "Do me a solid and stop slobbering over my mad skills, okay? Ask your questions."

"I don't want to interrogate you," the assassin said, tasting the truth of the words as they formed in his mouth. "I want you to tell me who you are because you want to."

Scooter twisted around in his seat to face the assassin. "Gotta understand, mate, I've served as Legion a lot longer than I did as an Archangel."

"What happened?"

"I spent a billion bloody years soldiering in Heaven's army, defending Dad's universe against enemy incursions. Those were crazy days. Lucifer was on our side, Gabriel wasn't such a fop, and Uriel...anyway, it was intense."

"You didn't like it? The fighting?"

Scooter laughed. "Let's just say the only thing I hated about introducing your boss to the sharp end of the stick was that I didn't hate it at all."

The assassin shook his head. "But you made such a stink about not killing anyone and your vow of pacifism."

"Ever wonder why I had to take that vow in the first place?" said Scooter, an edge in his voice the assassin had never heard before.

"I had no idea."

"Everyone's got a secret identity, mate. Me, I'm a bloodthirsty badass. You, I dunno."

"I don't think that secret is ready to be told."

"Or maybe you ain't ready to hear it."

The assassin wanted to ask more questions but there was only one that mattered. "Scooter, are you still with us?"

"All in, dude. Uriel was right. It's like riding a goddamn bicycle."

The assassin unrolled the window and surveyed the trees. No sign of Michael. Something about Uriel didn't sit right. She hadn't lied, but she'd used evasive language. She didn't say "orders" had changed. She said "circumstances." A game of deception through perception, and Uriel had played it too carefully.

"What are you doing?" Scooter said as the assassin grabbed his pack from the back seat.

"I'm going back."

"Are you kidding—you're not kidding."

"Uriel didn't tell us the truth."

"She seemed fully sincere about killing you."

The assassin checked the weapons in his backpack. "Something's gone wrong. Michael should be here by now."

Scooter unbuckled his seatbelt. "I'm going with you."

"No, you're getting on that plane. Liza needs you."

"Twelve hours," Scooter said. "You don't check in, I'm coming back. Do not do anything stupid, mate. And by stupid, I mean going toe to toe with Uriel."

"Noted." The assassin stood in the ditch until the car's taillights disappeared. Then he ran back into the woods.

Twenty minutes later he arrived at the clearing. No felled trees or torn up earth as he half-expected from a scuffle between archangels. There was blood though, pooled on the leaves, black and shiny in the moonlight.

Two trails led in opposite directions, neither one toward the car. So, they'd fought and both were wounded. With nothing more to see, he crouched at the edge of the clearing, picked up a leaf tacky with blood and brought it to his nose. Beneath the wet iron odor, he detected a trace of slashed vines bleeding green. Michael.

After a mile of hiking through dense woods, he lost the trail. The crash of the ocean rode along on the cold wind. It was human nature to follow the sound of water. Michael wasn't human, but it was all he had to go on.

The rumble of the ocean articulated into regular beats, hollow and percussive. The tide was coming in. When he broke through the trees onto a paved road, he was a mere hundred feet from the upper observation platform of the Thunder Hole. Waves rolling out allowed air to enter a cavern normally under the surface, and when the next big wave rolled in it forced the air out in a boom that shook the ground. Water sprayed forty feet into the air and salty mist dusted his face.

When the mist cleared, he saw a figure lurching along the road toward the observation platform. He couldn't see a face but recognized the long-limbed silhouette.

"Michael!" Another boom thumped into his stomach and vaporized his voice. She stopped and listed over to the salt-crusted rail. "No, no, no... Michael, no!"

She poured like liquid over the rail, dropping into the churning water below. The assassin's feet were moving before he told them to, racing down to the lower observation deck. He scanned the surging inlet.

The next big wave would crush anything floating in that cavern. He refused to believe she could die that easily. Not when he was right here. All he needed was a glimpse. He closed his eyes and did something he'd never done before.

Please. I can do this...just show her to me.

His first prayer. Had he done it right? Was anyone listening? It didn't matter because on the other side of the inlet, clinging to the craggy wall like an albino crab, he spotted a hand. Thank you, he thought and dove over the railing.

Icy water swallowed him. He surfaced, spluttering and gagging on the salt. Black blades of water obscured his view of anything recognizable. He let himself ride up the trough of a small wave until he saw the glimmer of railing to his right. He swiveled his head left and spotted Michael still clinging to the rocks.

Wave after wave heaved him closer to the mouth of the cavern. He swam, not against but across the tide. His water-filled boots tried to drag him down but he made it to the rocks. Hand over hand he inched his way over. She shuddered when he came up behind her and buoyed her up so at least her face stayed out of the water. "It's okay. It's me."

Her cold mouth whispered something against his jaw as the water thundered into the cavern. A torrent of seawater crashed over them, and her head lolled heavily on his shoulder. So much for hoping she'd be able to swim herself back to safety. He considered the stretch of water separating them from the lower observation platform. Thirty feet. The waves were coming in bigger, ripping back harder. If he didn't time it right they'd be swept right into the cave.

He hooked his arm under the strap of her shoulder harness and used his legs to kick off the rocks as hard as he could. In the open water, he couldn't keep her face above the surface. It was all he could do to keep them both from sinking. Every wave herded them closer to the mangle zone. His muscles stiffened as cold water leached heat from his body. He kicked and pulled until his boot scraped over rock. The tightness in his throat eased, and he tugged Michael up the underwater slope.

He crawled up a foot, grabbed her harness, and dragged her up after him. Crawl and drag, crawl and drag, until his hand closed over the concrete lip of the platform. He left Michael on the rocks and climbed the rest of the way. When he hooked his hands under her armpits and hauled her onto the deck, she arched her back and let out a ragged scream. He overbalanced, using gravity to drag her the rest of the way up. Her boots skidded over the edge and she fell on top of him driving the air from his lungs in a salty gust.

"God, you're heavy," he gasped into the sopping pelt of her hair.

She rolled off of him, coughing. "What...the hell...are you doing...here?"

"Rescuing you. Now we're even."

"I would have been fine."

"Shut up and take your rescue like a big girl." He rolled to his hands and knees and crawled to where she huddled, shivering, against a large rock. "What's up with your arm?"

"It is not serious." She braced herself, preparing to stand.

"Don't lie to me." The assassin splayed his hand on her chest, pressing her back. "And don't argue. You're hurt."

With a reluctant grunt, she allowed him to remove her shoulder harness and her jacket. He tore her sleeve down, exposing a grisly slash running from her shoulder to the inside of her elbow. He cursed under his breath.

"This is bad," he said. It was worse than bad. Like someone had attempted to de-bone her arm. Miraculously, none of the bleeding was arterial, if it were she would have bled out by now. "Uriel did this?"

"I did worse to her. She ran away, thankfully. I would have hated to kill her."

"Not sure I'm with you on that." He tore her sleeve into strips and bound her arm tightly. Her lips pressed together but otherwise she showed no sign of the considerable pain it must have caused. "Can you stand?"

She glared at him, rising unsteadily, but under her own power. The Thunder Hole roared and icy mist rained down on them.

"We have to find shelter," said the assassin. "I've got a place in these woods, not much more than a hole in the ground, but it's safe and dry. Can you make it?"

She gazed up at the stars, swaying slightly. "Lead on, light bearer."

"What?"

"Hmm?"

"What did you call me?"

"What would I call you? You really ought to find your lost name."

She stumbled and he caught her uninjured elbow. "Stay with me, Michael."

"But you already left," she mumbled, leaning into him. "No second chances."

Despite her assertions, Michael was not fine at all. Delirious and muttering in strange languages as they ventured farther into the park down the carriage roads. He all but carried her while keeping vigilant for any sight or sound of Panopticon's soldiers in the woods. Two miles wasn't far, but cold and exhausted as they were, it might have been a hundred.

When they reached the stone bridge, he manhandled her down the slope. He left her slumped in the grass, still raving under her breath, while he found the latch in the abutment and wrenched open the granite slab.

Michael shoved her hair off her face. "What is this?"

"A place to keep things I don't want to lose."

"The dragon's lair."

"You're funny when you have hypothermia," he said, helping her to her feet and smuggling her into his safe house.

He heaved the door shut and hit the switch on the wall. Dim light flooded the tiny space. Michael held up the wall, eyes half-lidded, chin dropped onto her chest.

"How are you doing?" He cupped her face and her blown pupils sloshed over him.

"Stop fussing. I am not some frail human."

"Frail enough." He switched on the battery and cranked up the space heater. "Take off your clothes."

"Why?"

"Because they're wet and cold. Take them off and get under the blanket," he said, pointing to the cot.

He faced the wall to give her privacy. When he didn't hear her moving at all, he turned around to see her fumbling with the first button of her shirt.

"I... I cannot . . ." She grimaced, desperately attempting to maneuver the button through the hole with a growling sob of frustration.

"Okay, okay," he said softly, taking her stiff hands and lowering them to her sides. She leaned back, refusing to leave her feet. He understood. In a fight, once you lost your feet, you lost the high ground, and you lost it all.

He unfastened the buttons running the length of the torn shirt and peeled it off her body, taking care not to jar her arm. She wasn't wearing a bra but he hardly noticed as he hurried to unlace her boots, tug off her socks, and wrestle her wet pants down her legs, leaving her in nothing but a pair of black panties.

She fell forward, draping over him like a wet towel. He'd handled day-old corpses with more body heat. Her arm needed proper cleaning and stitches, but he hadn't replaced the med kit. Anyway, getting her core temperature up took priority.

The electric heater chugged out some welcome warmth as he lowered her to the cot. The heater wasn't powerful but every little bit helped. Every little bit.

He opened the bottom drawer of the storage unit and retrieved the extra blanket, folded on top of his lock box. He shook the blanket out and spread it over Michael. Then he stripped down to his underwear and slid under the covers beside her.

Skin on skin contact was crucial, so he lay on his side, pulling her limp—and goddamn freezing—body against him. He rolled so she was halfway beneath him with his arms and legs wrapped around her. Chest to chest. Belly to belly. Cocooned in blankets. He was glad she was out of it. He didn't need her staring at him while they pantomimed the get-naked-because-hypothermia cliché.

For a while she breathed erratically, slow and slower, fast and shallow. His eyelids grew heavy but he forced himself to stay awake. She began to shiver again, rising from unconsciousness into a fitful doze, wriggling against him, trying to burrow into the source of warmth. The movement aggravated her wounded arm and she moaned quietly. He held her, stroking her back and her hair until she relaxed into a deep sleep. Only when her breathing and pulse were strong and her skin was only cool as opposed to frigid, did he allow himself to drift off.

CHAPTER 39

The assassin gazed up at a domed ceiling of pale coral stone shot through with veins of black pearl, turquoise, and rust.

Glittering stalactites tapered to meet the towering stalagmites, forming a barrier of what looked like petrified connective tissue. The burble of water echoed off the stone, and he drew steamy sulfur-laced air into his lungs. It was nice to be warm.

You're here,

The voice chimed off the glittering walls of a cave somehow empty of space and time, with the rest of the world folded around it. A lacuna.

The assassin spun around, but saw no one. "Sister Claudia told me about this place. It is real, isn't it?"

Reality is perception. She should've told you that.

"Have I been here before?" asked the assassin, peering into the stalagmites.

You always ask the wrong questions.

The voice was distorted in such a way that assassin couldn't tell if it was male or female, old or young.

"What do you want from me?" the assassin asked. "I'm no one. I don't even have a name."

Of course you do. Why not ask Her? By now I'm sure She's brimming with fun facts to know and tell.

"Who?"

Have you fucked her yet?

"Michael?"

Figures. Takes an act of God to pry those knees apart. But if you manage it, you should know I'm not jealous. It's okay to love us both.

"Why won't you show yourself?"

You've not yet earned those details. Believe it or not, I want this to be satisfying for everyone, even Her.

The assassin's clothes stuck to his sweat damp skin as he sifted through every word. "You're lying to me."

What better way to point you to the truth?

"What good is truth if I don't remember it? My whole life you've been tunneling around in my mind, gouging out what you don't want me to know, leaving holes." The assassin couldn't explain the sick dread of trying to recall something, only to find the raw ends of severed neural connections where the memory should be. Of blinking once and finding hours had vanished between the closing and opening of his eyes. Now he understood why. "You're afraid of what I'll choose?"

A moment passed before the voice replied.

Aren't you?

CHAPTER 40

He didn't open his eyes immediately, preferring to take a blind inventory of his other senses first. He smelled earth and stone, the brine of seawater, and sweat. And blood. He was on his back with Michael's bandaged arm and her long leg draped over him. Her hair spilled across them like a blanket, and he felt the rhythmic slide of her ribs under his hand. She fit so comfortably in his arms he would have fallen back asleep if she weren't so warm. Too warm.

She shifted and her breasts crushed soft against his chest. Her leg slipped farther between his, provoking an immediate response. Physiology. That was all. It was the morning. He opened his eyes to find her staring at him.

"Am I dreaming?" she asked.

"You're awake. Do you know where you are?" he asked, attempting to assess her level of consciousness, "Do you know who I am?"

She continued to stare through eyes like bruises pressed into her ashen face. "You are too thin, so many scars, and your eyes are wrong...but you smell the same." She pressed her face into his chest, inhaling deeply.

"Michael, are you okay?"

She shook her head. "What have you done?"

Before he could ask her mouth crashed into his. Shock paralyzed him as her tongue swept between his teeth. Drinking someone else's spit was not hygienic, and neither of their mouths had seen a toothbrush recently. Not that his cock minded in the least, having gone from a routine systems check to full REDCON in the last five seconds.

Her heated body covered his and her hair fell around them. She tasted exactly as she smelled, of green leaves and sun. He drowned in it, feeling her spine snake under his hands, and her cool silver cuffs brush against his ears as she threaded her fingers into his hair. He gripped her hips, holding her hard against him, and she breathed into his mouth, a soft whimper he swallowed before she could take it back. That one was his forever.

"Michael," he managed to escape her mouth long enough to speak. "Are you sure about this?"

"No." She caught his lip with her teeth. "No... no... no."

Good answer. No slowing. No questioning. No talking. No thinking. He wanted to flip her on her back and fuck her senseless. He didn't want to consider that she might already be there. That in her injured delirium any consent she gave was dubious and while he was a lot of things, he wasn't a rapist. Of all the times for his goddamn deadbeat conscience to wake up and voice an opinion.

She sat back, blood-red hair tumbling over her shoulders. "What is it?"

The assassin lost his words as he gazed at her body, both harder and softer than he'd imagined. Subtle ridges of abdominal muscle framed the delicate indentation of her navel, and her breasts swelled gently beneath the sharp lines of her collarbones. He kicked his feet out of the blankets and propped himself up. "What's up with you? You don't even like me."

"Like you?" She tossed her hair like a bored teenager. "Like is a word bereft of passion. Banal and safe. I should think it nearly insulting were I to say I like you."

"You're not making a lot of sense right now."

She cocked her head. "I know who you are. It is you who seems not to."

He got up and pulled on his pants. She watched him, her chest rising and falling with each rapid breath. A lovely ravenous zombie, clutching her bandaged arm, her thumb stroking the silver cuff around her wrist.

"You know I was a man," she said.

He zipped his fly. "Right. Well, I don't have a problem with that, if you're wondering."

"Do you have a problem with zealots, or hypocrites?" She rose from the cot, her bare feet brushing across the stone floor. The black scrap of her underwear made her seem more naked than if she were fully nude. "Would it interest you to know that I was a wicked man with a hearty appetite for violence, drink, and harlots."

"Doesn't sound much like you—the booze and whores."

"I took many lovers, male and female both." She drew her fingertip down his chest like a surgeon's scalpel. "But there's something about a woman, is there not? The smell, the taste, the way her body gives way to yours. The power she has over you, even as you take her. You, a hard, strong man, brought to ruin as you sink deep and spend yourself inside her."

Was the Archangel Michael talking dirty to him? The assassin hardly breathed when she brought his hand between her breasts and held it over her thudding heart.

"Michael, please don't ask me to do something you'll hate me for later."

"Oh, but I have much better reasons to hate you." Her zombie eyes roamed his body and every beat of her heart under his palm invited him to take what he wanted.

He was only human.

Plunging his hands into her wild mane of hair, he kissed her as he shoved her down on the cot and nudged her legs apart with his. She flinched when he jarred her bad arm. He'd not meant to hurt her, yet that small bite of her pain kindled an undeniable appetite for more.

"Is this what you want?" he asked, though it wasn't a question. More of a judgment. An accusation.

"Yes," she hissed and tugged his face down to hers.

His hand found the back of her knee where her skin was hot and damp. He pulled her thigh up around his hip as his mouth traveled along her neck to her shoulder and down to her breasts. His weirdly active conscience grumbled that he was about to do a very bad thing, but his lizard brain was at the helm, and Captain Lizard contended that this scenario landed in conveniently gray waters.

His hand skated down her stomach into her panties where he found her smooth and hairless as a whore under his fingertips. He'd forgotten about her adventures in grooming, and the silky glide conjured an image of her in that scrap of a dress with blistered feet and muddy makeup. Her disastrous appearance exposed something honest and he'd wanted her then. Now she looked even worse and he wanted her more.

Stripped of her beauty and imperial bearing, her naked greed for his touch destroyed him. She moaned and rocked against his hand as he eased his fingers inside her. He tasted fresh salt on her mouth and opened his eyes to find hers tightly shut, but not enough to dam the tears.

His hand stilled. "Are you crying?"

Her eyes flipped open. She touched her cheeks and stared, bewildered at her wet fingertips.

"Michael?"

She didn't respond. He didn't know what to do. It was bad enough when Liza cried. He didn't think he could deal with this. But Michael didn't cry, she laughed.

"What's the matter with you?" he demanded.

She laughed harder. "We are terrible at this."

He stretched out beside her and flung an arm over his face. "You're the one who made it weird."

"You are the one who stopped. You might have brought me off first...like a gentleman." She dissolved into another fit of giggles.

He might've laughed with her, if not for the sickening squeeze in his groin. She wasn't wrong. They were killers at the top of their deadly game, and all thumbs in bed. Flailing around attempting to do sex at each other. If he hadn't stopped, by now he'd be...probably done. A disappointing performance, even hypothetically.

"Michael?"

"Hmm?"

"What are you hiding?"

"You tell me. You conducted a rather thorough search just now."

His aching balls found zero humor in her bawdy retort. "You've been acting nuts since you woke up. And if you think I'm letting this go, you really are out of your mind."

"I am in no mood for your interrogations."

She got up, found her pants and dragged them up her legs one-handed. He watched her slip into her shirt and pause, face tight as she held her bad arm to her chest. He went over and began fastening her buttons, starting at the bottom. The voice from his dream echoed faintly in his memory.

"Michael, what happened to you last night?"

Her trembling hands caught his. "Assassin. This is a complicated situation. I realize you have great difficulty trusting others, but I need you to trust me now. All will be revealed when the time is right. I give you my word...but please, I need you to—"

"I trust you," he said, surprised to find that he really did. "But I feel like you don't trust me."

Her gaze dropped to the floor. "I always have, at my peril."

CHAPTER 41

The assassin's feet slipped on dew slick grass as he shouldered the granite door closed. Then he stood back, thinking about the locked box in the drawer and knowing there was a good possibility he'd never come back here. Michael slouched against the side of the ravine, buried to her knees in thick fog. Conserving her energy, no doubt.

"You okay?" he asked.

"For now," she said, and allowed him to help her up the slope onto the bridge. The assassin scanned the trees and saw nothing, but that didn't mean Panopticon wasn't hiding in these woods. The assassin had a gun, but it wasn't much good against an army. They started down the carriage road, heading out of the park.

"Did Scooter make it back?" Michael asked.

"Shit." The assassin dug his phone out of his pack. As of ten in the morning, he had eight missed calls, and a text message:

CALL ME YOU FUCKER.

He glanced at Michael as he brought the phone to his ear. "I think he's in a mood."

Scooter's voice buzzed over their bad connection. "Way to leave it to the eleventh fucking hour, you drama queen dicksplat."

"Ninth hour, and you gave me twelve. So, who's being dramatic?"

"Kiss my furry ball bag, okay? I've been worrying my warts off here. What the shit happened to you guys?"

"Long story. How's Liza?"

"Pearl says the zips are separating from the zorps. Girl innards, mate. I dunno. I did what I could. Thing is, I couldn't do much."

"What do you mean?" The assassin allowed himself to lag behind Michael.

"I mean everything's got a price, bro, and bailing on my vow to do no harm put a serious kibosh on my fixits."

"Did you know this would happen?"

"No, and that's not even the worst part," Scooter's voice cracked. "Thing is, I've been praying, trying to find a way to make this right, y'know? But God ain't taking my calls. I reach out and it's like He's not even there. Dude. I'm in deep onions here, bugging out...all that bad I left in the past. I opened that door...kinda having a hard time closing it."

Scooter's shaky hush worried the assassin. A former Archangel with a seriously relapsed case of bloodlust and no reason to behave could only be a very bad thing.

"She's hurt," said the assassin before he could think better of it. "Michael and Uriel got into it and she's hurt."

"Bad?"

"Bad enough. I need you to hold it together until we get back."

"Then we got probs. Barclay says he can't risk sending a plane. The Eye's not doing much in the way of mobilizing from what Barclay can tell, but they're watching commercial and private aircraft like a hawk."

His hopes for a quick return deflated. "We'll drive. It'll take four days. Three if we cut across the Waste."

"That's your plan?"

"You have a better idea?"

"Yeah, get her to a damn doctor."

"She doesn't need a doctor, she needs a miracle."

"Dude, I just told you I can't. By waxing your boss, I think I really fucked myself."

"So, pray harder, Scooter. Find a way to get un-fucked, or we're going to lose her."

"Are you making shit up to keep me on the rails?"

The assassin glanced at Michael, plodding along ahead of him. "I really hope so."

A few crackly breaths. "Hurry."

The assassin shoved the phone in his pocket and hurried up the road. When he fell in stride next to her, he noticed the tension in her shoulders and the way she hunched over her bad arm, curled against her chest. He wouldn't make it worse by asking.

"How is he?" she asked.

"Not good. Seems God takes a dim view of vow-breakers."

"How much did he tell you?"

"A few details."

Drizzle fell from the chalky sky, and Michael's boots scraped through the vegetation. She surprised him by slipping her hand into his jacket pocket and folding her cold fingers around his.

"Tell me more," he asked, more interested in keeping Michael walking and talking than anything else. "How'd he get the nickname?"

"His tactic of scooting through the revenant army so swiftly that he'd have a dozen throats cut before they knew he was there. The 'scooter' became something of a nightmare legend among them."

Previously, the assassin would have said nothing about Scooter hinted at a history of violence. But last night he heard the bleeding edge of it in his voice.

Michael continued. "It was a long war, and he feasted on death until only blood brought him to life. I'd seen it happen before, with others."

"What did you do?"

"I wanted to pull him out, cloister him with the Luminary where a period of convalescence might heal the rents in his soul. But God counseled me against such action. Shortly thereafter, Scooter dropped his sword in the dust, and refused to pick it up again."

"Turned it into a plough?"

"You would reduce the birth of the Legion to an overworn quip? The new order of healers had to be born of an intimate knowledge of death and violence. Scooter's struggle made it possible."

"So, God gets what he wants, and Scooter pays for it."

Michael's hand tightened painfully around his. "Scooter made his choices freely, as we all do."

"All right," he winced. "But you've said it yourself, everything has a cost."

Her grip gentled. "Scooter and Uriel found themselves on diverging paths. Their differences proved irreconcilable."

"Scooter and Uriel?"

"Lovers for quite some time. Rumor has it they still enjoy one another's company on occasion." She leaned in as if anyone but a few scattered magpies might be within earshot. "It drives Gabriel into a covetous rage. Uriel is the great beauty of the seraphim, and he has courted her favor for eons to no avail."

Speaking of irreconcilable differences, the assassin suspected Sister Claudia would drop dead all over again if she were to witness the Archangel Michael gossiping about the sex lives of the Heavenly Host.

The drizzle got serious and Michael's hand slipped out of his pocket. Raindrops wet her cheeks and she stood absolutely still. "Heaven wept...for the morning star."

"Michael?"

"These woods ought to be crawling with soldiers. Where are they?"

"Doesn't mean they're not searching for us."

"Emptiness," she said, covering her ears. "It's all I hear. We need to get back to the others immediately."

"I'm working on it. When we get to town, I'll find us a car."

"A car?" she snapped. "Are you serious? Do I need to spell everything out for you?"

His hackles rose. "Spelling anything out would be a start."

She clutched her bad arm. "A journey by car will take three days at minimum. I will be dead in two."

"Got a better idea?"

"Not at all." She fell to her knees, pulling him down with her and wrapping his arms around her waist. "Keep your eyes closed. Clear your mind of intent, and above all, do not let go."

INFRACTUS

No time for questions. A buzz built in his ears and crawled under his skin. He slammed his eyes shut against the hellish cacophony shearing through his consciousness. Grating, metallic, and alive. Heat and cold. Wind and water. Absolute darkness and the white light of a supernova. An image of glittering stone flashed through his mind and wet sulfurous air swirled around him like the hot breath of a subterranean beast. All the while, Michael's arms held him like bands of iron. As if that panting creature needed only the finest sliver of space to separate them.

CHAPTER 42

NAPA, CALIFORNIA, PAN AMERICAN DIVISION

From the stand of oak trees behind the house, I listen to the mental murmur of those inside. The old man, rifling through secured networks trying to figure out why Panopticon, now blind, isn't circling the wagons or releasing the hounds. Meanwhile the doctor frets over the girl, and the girl silently bargains for her child's life with a God she only recently learned exists. All of them try not to speculate on the whereabouts of their two MIA team members.

The back door of the house opens and Scooter plods out. I can't read his mind, but I don't need to. He has forsaken vows written all over his little face. A demoralized sidekick suits my design quite nicely.

The young medic follows Scooter onto the porch. The girl fills his thoughts, day and night, and her child, while not of his blood, could be the child of his heart. He knows how close he is to losing them.

"We need to talk," Dean says.

"About what? There's nothing we can do. You said it a whole bunch, like a broken record." Scooter drops down onto the porch steps. I know his frustration is not with the boy but with himself. He tried to heal the girl, but the violence is fresh, and his power all too mutable.

"You know Liza almost lost the baby when he slit her throat," says Dean.

"And if it weren't for him she'd be a pile of ashes in an urn. He cares about her, Deano. In his own way."

"Why are you defending him? Why does everyone love this guy so much? He's a killer for Christ's sake. Why didn't you leave him to be remapped? He fucking deserves it."

"Now really ain't the time, mate."

"People who are sick in the head like that don't change. They just get better at tricking you into giving them what they want."

Scooter scrapes his fingers over his scalp "Dude, I get that you got a crush and want someone to blame. But right now, I need to chill and repacify, so make like a wave and break, yeah?"

"Whatever." Dean retreats and pulls the screen door open. "Just saying he's probably banging your sister right now."

"Hey, grommet" Scooter calls out over his shoulder. "We need him on this. But when it's over if you wanna stuff him in a sleeping bag and kick him into a lake, I won't stop you."

Dean's face fractures into a grin and he disappears inside the house, leaving Scooter angry, confused, and afraid. As well he should be. Dean is right. You can't trust anyone in this world, not the ones you love, not God, not even yourself. Scooter intends to recommit to his vows, but I can tell he's reliving it. The weight of the blade and the fleshy resistance of a human heart. Vindicating and terrible. Shame that I can only save the souls of mankind. My brothers and sisters deserve better.

Even Michael.

I know her pain. I was there when she opened the gates and let it spill out. Kneeling in the desert between shifting dunes, her tears scorched the sand like acid and her screams gave birth to mountain ranges as they shuddered through the shifting plates of the Earth's crust.

The violence of her release carried to a faraway land where two brothers toiled in their father's field. The sky darkened with thick clouds, and wind shrieked through the wild oats, creating a boiling ocean of grain. Cain and Abel stopped their work and began to argue.

Every time it starts small. A slighted ego, a step in the wrong direction, the strike of an archangel's fist on the earth. A single spark ignites a blaze that creates its own weather. Michael started this fire, and I was far from the first to be burned.

Motion in the trees. Scooter hesitates before strolling barefoot across the grass, clearly hoping for a fight. Inside the tree line he stops and listens.

"Scooter." Uriel lurches from behind one of the gnarly oaks. And the game is on. This is what I'm here for.

"Uri?" He's shocked by her grave countenance. Sweaty hair sticks to her face, her bronze skin gone ashen with blood loss, and her fist jams into her side. She falls into his arms and he lowers her to the mossy earth.

"She told me to go home...but I can't...not yet."

"How'd you get here?"

"I need your help."

He traces the path of a tear down her clammy cheek. "Uri, you are putting me between the millstones."

"I ask only for a chance to fix this. Scooter, I'm begging you."

She clutches him and his resistance crumbles. He lifts her shirt to expose the puncture just under her ribs. A small wound. Deceptive.

"How bad is it?" she asks

"Ain't bad at all," he lies. "Relax. I've got this."

He places his hands on her wound. His brow tightens as he attempts to invoke the healing energy. He frowns deeper and opens his eyes.

"Uriel?" He pats her waxy cheek, checks for a pulse. She's not breathing. "Uri...c'mon baby, wake up."

And this is where the situation goes to shit in a way I never could have predicted. I expect him to scream or cry or whatever it is one does when one's soul mate eats it. Instead, he lays her beautiful corpse back on the ground and stacks his hands over her heart. In the nothingness of my being I feel suction, and there's a sound, like tearing burlap. A blast rips through me. Not just energy. Life. Scooter siphons it up and funnels it down. By the time Uriel wakes, he's unconscious on the grass beside her, and every one of the oak trees is dead.

Naughty, naughty, Raphael. But I do understand. Love makes criminals of us all.

"Scooter!" Uriel cracks her open palm across his face.

"Ow," he mumbles.

Sobbing, she hauls him into her arms. "Why did you do that? You could have been killed, you stupid, stupid . . ."

He lifts his head from her bosom. "I'm not the only one digging into some sketchy use of power."

She's on her feet in an instant, brushing leaves and grass from her bloody fatigues. "I have to go."

"Uriel, don't."

"Tell Michael...Tell her I love her."

He heaves himself up, catching her wrist as she walks away. "What about me?"

She turns her head, her lips brushing his. "You and I have said it all."

She kisses him once, twice, and down the rabbit hole they go. There's something beautiful about them, on the ground, surrounded by the fresh corpses of old trees. Making love at the epicenter of death.

Sweet Uriel, you were gone but now you're back. I suppose I'll to have to kill you myself.

CHAPTER 43

A skittering sensation over his skin. Like spiders. When the assassin forced his eyes open he found himself at the edge of a road, under an enormous sky vaulting over desert hardpan.

His skin crawled and his nose still burned with the stench of sulfur. He dug out his phone and the GPS indicated that he was over two thousand miles from Maine, in what used to be Nevada. The Waste.

How in the blue hell did he end up in the Waste? And where the hell was Michael? The air shimmered over a low rise a few yards away. Gun in hand, he crawled up the slope. When he reached the top, he found Michael in the fetal position at the bottom of a crater perhaps four feet deep and so recently blasted the dust and heat hadn't yet dissipated.

He scrambled down the side, singeing his hands on burnt earth. Michael's eyes were open, but her pupils bled through the irises and into the sclera through dozens of capillaries black as tar. He'd witnessed something like this in Bali, but that time the darkness was on the outside, clinging to her like an amorous shadow. Now it was inside her.

He nudged her shoulder. "Hey, you okay?"

In a flash she had him on his back, her knee in his chest, hands squeezing his throat. Her stygian eyes simmered in their sockets as she bared her teeth at him.

"You broke your promise," she said in a rough voice, scraping a blackened fingernail over his cheek. "Lying serpent. I could show you pain. Such exquisite suffering."

"Sounds great," he croaked. "Michael . . ."

She blinked. The squeeze on his windpipe eased. She lifted her knee off his sternum. He was relieved to see the black veins receding, though her fingertips remained smudged with soot.

"I apologize," she said. "I have never brought a human through a dimensional tear with me. I did not anticipate the side effects."

"You've done this before?"

"Once or twice, though God strictly forbids it. The Tear requires an invocation of dark energies that are unpredictable and corrupting."

"So, you risked God's wrath and a case of the black-eyed monsters to drop us in the Waste?"

"What?" She peered over the rim of the crater. "Were you thinking of this place?"

"Not exactly, but I had a flash of a cave or something...for a second." It surprised him. The memory. He expected another ragged blank spot, and while he didn't understand how they got here, he definitely remembered the trip. The cave, the light, the noise.

"For the love of Christ." she growled, picking up a stone and hurling it out of the crater. "Clear your mind of intent. One simple instruction and you bungled it. If you'd done as I asked we would be at Barclay's vineyard by now, you knuckle-dragging primate."

A knot tightened between his shoulder blades. "If that's an insult, you should know I've been called worse by better people."

"Of that I have no doubt."

She stomped off and managed to climb up and out of the crater one armed. He followed and joined her at the side of the road. She breathed fast and hard through blue lips and her body baked with fever he could feel standing next to her. Even her resilient angel's body could only endure so much, and he sensed her approaching that upper limit.

He stared down the road bisecting the seemingly endless desert. "How did a vague thought of a place I've never been derail your vision of Laughing Corpse?"

"Your human body. Your connection to the Earth is stronger than mine, therefore your will to power is greater. That cave must be nearby."

"Can't you try again?"

She laid her hot hands on either side of his neck. "If the journey did not kill you, I certainly would." She squinted over his shoulder. "Am I hallucinating or is that a car?"

He followed her gaze and in the hazy distance he spotted a car zooming down the highway. No point running. The barren landscape offered no place to hide. As the car drew closer, blue and red lights flashed on the roof and a siren howled through the dusty bowl of post A-Day Nevada.

"What the hell is a patrol doing in the Waste?" The assassin pulled his gun from his jacket pocket and discreetly tossed it into the crater. They'd probably seen Michael's swords, but blades weren't illegal.

"Let me do the talking," he said.

INFRACTUS

The orange and white cruiser coasted to a halt on the shoulder. A middle-aged patroller climbed out of the passenger seat in a deliberate way, suggesting a multitude of protesting joints. Sallow skin drooped from his jaw. He hitched up his uniform pants and smoothed the orange sash over his blue jacket. A patrol-issue viper jutted from his hip holster.

The driver emerged next. About the assassin's age and height but with an additional fifty pounds of muscle on his solid frame. The snap on his viper holster was open. The assassin recalled electricity flying like drain cleaner through his veins. The broken cop limped toward them. His nameplate said Patrolman Rainey.

"You folks wanna explain what you're doing out here?" Rainey asked.

"My wife and I," the assassin said. "We're from Montana. Her sister was in a wreck yesterday. Flights to San Francisco were booked up, and we don't know how much time she has."

"So, you figured you'd take your chances cutting through the Waste?"

"Our car broke down this morning and we've been on foot ever since. She's got these swords, family heirlooms, didn't wanna leave 'em in the car, but they aren't sharp enough to cut through butter." The assassin looped his arm around Michael's waist. "We saw you coming. We thought...well, we didn't expect to see a patrol."

Rainey sniffed. "We take a jaunt through the borderlands a few times a week. Maintain a presence. Kites are a pest we don't want crossing state lines."

The assassin regarded Rainey warily. "The Eye says kites don't exist."

"Call 'em what you want, they'll kill you just as dead." The tall one joined his partner on the passenger side of the cruiser. His tag said Patrolman Keelut. "We ought to cite you two for illegal trespass. Throw you in the remap lottery or maybe toss you over the Colony walls. We're not much more than an hour's drive from Area 51. You'd make a nice supper for Ori Mane and his dogs." Keelut's tone suggested he was only mostly joking, and he'd obviously never seen the colony.

"Please officers," Michael said in sweet voice. "I only want to see my...my sister...once more. You must have families yourselves. Surely you understand?"

She lowered her chin demurely and even batted her damn eyelashes. Too much. But her hamming probably wasn't an issue, considering the way Keelut checked her out in a way he likely thought was subtle.

Rainey pinched the tip of his purple nose. "'Fraid we're not going to be much help to you folks."

Keelut drew his viper out of its holster. "Even if we wanted to, our friends might object."

A rumble in the distance had the assassin squinting down the road in the other direction where it curved around a desert mesa. A truck ripped around the bend, stirring up a sizable wake of dust. Kites. Michael abruptly shoved him to the ground. In doing so her arm caught the barbs of a viper strike meant for him. It was Rainey's weapon, not Keelut's that delivered the jolt. She dropped to the gravel, seizing up, unable to make a sound. The assassin knew that pain. There was a reason he hated patrollers. Rainey's chances of surviving this shrank to zero, and Keelut's weren't much better.

"Hands up. This one ain't no stun gun," Keelut said, pointing a very nice Glock 7 at them.

The assassin complied as a rust pocked pick-up truck skidded around the cruiser and stopped in the middle of the road. Eight kites spilled out of the bed like a barrel of dirty monkeys armed with hunting knives, machetes, bats, and pipes.

"Idiots," Rainey drew his own pistol. "You're supposed to wait until we call for you on the walkies."

"Boys got restless," the lead kite said, scratching a beard that was probably full of lice and crouching beside a prone Michael. "Howdy there, Missy."

She bit down on a scream when he twisted her wounded arm, dragging the sword harness off her back. Her face went green, but her eyes met the assassin's, telling him to hold. He locked every muscle in his body against doing the opposite.

Keelut searched through the assassin's pockets, coming up empty since his backpack and gun were hidden in the crater. "We'll take the swords. Some collector will pay good cred for those, even dull."

"What the fuck, Rainey?" asked the lead kite, placing the blades on the hood of the cruiser. "These two got nothing."

"Deal's the same as it's always been," Rainey said. "We get first pick, you take the rest, and you stay inside your own territory. Take it or leave it."

"Dibs on the girl," said Keelut.

The kite rubbed a lock of Michael's hair between his dirty fingers. "Naw, you called the swords. We get the trim. I got a whole crew back at the nest and they'd love to party with these two."

"Ten minutes," Keelut argued. "I won't rough her up much. Your guys won't know the difference."

Rainey glanced at his watch. "Can't rape them all, Keelut. She looks sickly anyhow. You wanna catch something? Take the blades and let's get the hell out of here. My dogs are barking."

"Sorted then," the kite said with a rotting smile. "Whaddya say, Missy? You and your man wanna come home and meet the family? Spend some quality time?"

"Michael," she said.

"Huh?"

"My name is Michael. Not Missy."

Keelut chuckled. "Dumb slut thinks she'll need a name where she's going."

The assassin's mind galloped. The odds were atrocious, but the time for playing along had passed. Keelut's bloodlust made him dangerous. It also made him the weak link. The assassin laughed quietly.

Keelut nudged his temple with the gun. "The idea of getting passed around tickle your funny bone?"

"No, that sounds terrible." The assassin said. "But don't you find it strange that we're not begging for our lives?"

Clearly unused to having thoughts, Keelut's guard dropped as he processed the information. Time to act. The assassin lunged for Keelut's gun as Michael leapt through the air and landed with her knees on the lead kite's shoulders, her toes braced against his chest. The kite staggered, but the counterweight of her body kept him from falling. His dirty face peered up from between her thighs.

"Quality time," she said. "This what you had in mind?"

The question was rendered rhetorical by a dull snap. The kite crumpled to the ground, his neck broken. Michael swiped her swords from the hood of the cruiser. The marauders raised their weapons, but her blades were already unsheathed and she descended on them like a Valkyrie.

The assassin had Keelut's gun. But Keelut was already dead, his body cleaved in two on the diagonal. The top half fell to the asphalt, trailing loops of reeking intestines before the lower half pitched over as well. Rainey recovered his wits and raised his pistol. The assassin neatly fired one of Keelut's bullets through Rainey's brain stem, but that was the extent of his participation. For her grand finale, Michael spun around and drove both swords through the chest of the man behind her, and the man behind him. With a solid thunk, her katanas were embedded in the grill of the truck. The dying men hung off the blades, a grisly, twitching hood ornament.

The assassin pocketed Keelut's gun and navigated around the bodies until he reached her. "You are the perfect woman."

"Hardly, though I understand why you might think otherwise," she said, wrenching her swords out of the truck with a sharp tug. The corpses slid off her blades like raw kabobs. She used one of the dead men's shirts to clean her swords before sheathing them. Blood trickled down the inside of her wrist and dripped onto the hot pavement. A frown wrinkled her forehead. She swayed on her feet.

The assassin helped her to the cruiser and lowered her into the passenger seat. "I'll be right back."

A search of the cruiser produced a couple bottles of water and a thoroughly picked over first-aid kit. The kitemobile yielded a bottle of moonshine and a jacket that smelled like someone had been buried in it. As he crossed the bloody asphalt, he noticed a few crows had arrived. They hopped about, scoping out the choicest bits before other scavengers could lay claim to the salvage.

Michael reclined in the seat, one bent leg outside the car, her boot resting on the gravel. "Find anything?"

He held up the bottle.

"You expect me to drink that poison?"

"I expect you might want to."

"Not necessary."

She eased out of her jacket, exposing her arm. Fresh blood softened everything so the improvised bandage didn't stick. That was the extent of the good news. He doused a wad of gauze with bottled water, and sponged away the mess, uncovering a deep trench of purple-red flesh that radiated heat like steam from a perturbed volcano. She bore the pain impressively, calmly staring through the windshield into a sky burned white by the desert sun.

"Sure you don't want a drink? Or a belt to bite down on?" He twisted the cap off the moonshine and an astringent aroma of wood alcohol wafted out. "This is going to hurt like hell."

She leaned back and closed her eyes. "Do it."

Grasping her forearm, he slowly tipped the bottle. The first drops sizzled over exposed muscle and raw nerves. Her eyes flew open. She kicked the glove box so hard it exploded in a hail of plastic shards. Clawing the front of his shirt with her good arm, she hauled him up so they were nose to nose. She snatched the bottle and drained a third of it in three noisy gulps before handing it back.

"Ready?" he asked.

Hands clenched into fists and breathing rapidly, she nodded. He gripped her arm and poured.

By the time he'd finished with the alcohol and irrigated once more with water, she sprawled limp on the seat. A flush burned on her cheeks and beads of sweat coasted down her neck to rest in the hollows of her throat and clavicles.

"It's infected," he said.

Her mouth melted into a smile. "I feel quite well."

"I'll bet."

"I think I'm drunk."

"Then you definitely are."

"That was excruciating. Did you enjoy it?"

He screwed the cap back on the moonshine. "Enjoy?"

"You have a streak of cruelty in you. Do not think I haven't noticed."

Her uncomfortably astute gaze drilled into him as he wrapped gauze around her arm, taking care to make it snug but not so tight as to aggravate the angry wound. A fine balance and not an easy one to strike given his complicated relationship with pain. He pulled the bandage taut. She winced and regarded him with suspicion. "Did you do that on purpose?"

"Michael, if I ever hurt you on purpose you'll know it." He dropped the tape into the kit and snapped the lid shut. "I've got a question. When you were burnt and scary, you called me a lying serpent. Why?"

Her warm vulnerability froze over. "I do not recall."

"Now you're lying." He grasped her jaw forcing her to look at him. "I could make you tell me."

She twisted her head until her lips brushed his palm. "I know."

Sex, violence, and forbidden fruit. Talk about subtext. The assassin busied himself putting the first aid kit in the trunk and rummaging through the pockets of Keelut's bottom half until he found the key fob.

Stepping over bits of kite on his way back to the cruiser, the assassin tried to puzzle out the duality of his feelings for Michael. Clearly, he was willing to die for her, and nearly had more than once, yet a bitterness seethed in the darkest crevice of his heart. Zee's voice buzzed in his memory like a tenacious mosquito.

Know what hate is, Mouse? It's love, unzipped and turned ugly side out. The two aren't sold separately, and they got no secrets between them. Go ahead, and hate me all you want because we both know it's only half the story.

He ducked into the driver's seat, and she placed her hand lightly on his arm. "Something vexes you?"

He shrank from her touch. "Could say that."

The key fob activated the computer console and since the dead patrollers were still logged into their server, the assassin snooped through every bulletin for the last twenty-four hours.

"You were right," he said.

"Hmm?"

"No APB. They're not searching for us. There's no mention of the explosion at all." He switched on the radio and tuned it to the stream. "Let's see what they're talking about out there."

. . . Disease and Contagion Control units dispatched yesterday to the city of Darwin, Australian Continental Division in response to an outbreak of hemorrhagic fever. Video footage is currently unavailable, though DCC has determined the virus responsible for the epidemic appears to be an airborne strain. As the death toll in Darwin spirals into the thousands, with many more quarantined, unverified reports indicate the outbreak may have already spread off continent as far as Indonesia. In an effort to contain this epidemic, Panopticon Aviation Authority has grounded all intercontinental travel until further notice.

Michael switched off the radio. "The destruction of the mainframe and now this blood fever. It cannot be a coincidence."

In this case, the assassin's instincts aligned with Michael's. Certainly, Panopticon was capable of weaponizing a virus, but it was a drastic move that smacked of endgame. It seemed Michael wasn't the only one resorting to extreme measures.

"Let's get out of here," he said, steering the car onto the highway.

CHAPTER 44

S afely on the California side of Lake Tahoe, the assassin watched with relief as the mint condition GMC—with only a thatch of blond hair visible over the steering wheel—cruised to a halt at the side of the road. The door opened and Scooter dropped out like a joyriding twelve-year-old.

"Fuzzmobile?" Scooter kicked the front tire of the cruiser. "I ain't even gonna ask."

"Barclay let you drive his good truck?" the assassin said.

Michael emerged unsteadily from the passenger side of the cruiser. Scooter's face darkened. "Permission to speak freely, Cap?"

"I did not realize you had any other setting," she muttered.

Scooter crossed his arms over his chest. "The Tear? Are you nuts?"

"Dire straits, Legion. And I need not defend my actions to any man, least of all you."

Her sharp words carried with them the last of her energy. Her eyes rolled back and her knees buckled. The assassin managed to catch her before she face-planted in the gravel. His back protested when he hoisted her up, all dangling arms and legs, and staggered toward the truck. "It's like carrying a giraffe."

Scooter opened the door to the back seat. "Don't forget the elephant sized balls. Those add a good twenty pounds each."

"Let it go, Scooter," said the assassin, gracelessly cramming Michael into the back of the truck. "Can you do anything for her?"

"Not yet, but Doc Pearl's the next best thing."

"How's Liza?"

Scooter shrugged.

"She still hate me?"

"Ain't exactly singing your praises—but when Dean started in on how you're a psycho and a creep, she directed him to verb the reflexive pronoun, if you catch my grammatical drift."

Scooter leapt into the driver's seat, where the assassin expected him to tie blocks to his feet to reach the pedals. The assassin settled for the passenger side and breathed in the mellow tang of leather and tobacco. His shoulders unraveled as he sank into the soft seat. They'd made it back to California. They were alive. Liza had told Dean where to go and what to do when he got there. Everything was good. For now.

A few minutes down the road, the assassin gave Scooter a once-over. "You're a wreck. Have you slept at all?" he asked. Scooter let his uncharacteristic silence speak for itself. "You can't let this eat you up, Scooter. Guilt is a useless emotion."

"And I'd eject it like a bad warp core if I were made of robot parts like you." The little angel braced both hands on the wheel and pressed himself back into the leather upholstery. "I saw Uriel this morning."

Michael stirred in the back. "Uriel came to you? Is she all right?"

"No, she was fully not all right." Scooter's shoulders hunched. "Until I sorta brought her back."

Michael poked her head between the gap in the front seats. "Pull over. Now."

The assassin held onto the door handle and kept his mouth shut as Scooter cranked on the wheel and fishtailed to a stop.

"Am I getting a spanking?" Scooter asked.

"Don't tempt me, you foolish piece of tripe."

"I fucked up. You think I don't know?"

"Fucked up?" Michael shouted. "You raised the fucking dead, Scooter. Your souls could have been obliterated."

"Yeah, but they weren't."

"And you suppose that is the end of it? Have you forgotten Lazarus? Joshua flexed his might to raise a dull-witted peasant and John the Baptist's head wound up on a platter. Resurrection finds its level. Always. A life for a life."

"I totally killed a bunch of Barclay's trees. Think that counts?"

"Is that a joke?"

"Depends on the padre's sense of humor, I guess."

Michael's face calcified. "You put Uriel at risk of something immeasurably worse than death. That this amuses you only proves what I've long known to be true. She deserves better than you, Raphael."

The assassin leapt into the argument. "Hey, you broke the rules too, by doing that tear thing."

"To put it in a context you would understand, assassin, it's the difference in damage between a pellet gun and an automatic rifle."

"Why would I need a gun analogy to understand?"

"I didn't plan it," Scooter said, his voice full of wet gravel. "But when I tapped into that black mojo and realized what I could do...I couldn't let her go."

Michael's stony expression softened. "She would have returned to us."

"After two thousand years as a wraith. She wouldn't be the same. No one ever is."

"The price of eternal life." Michael rested her hand on his shoulder. "Scooter, with great power comes even greater temptation to alter the universe to your liking. You must resist."

"Here's a question," the assassin said. "Why would God give you the ability to do all this stuff and then say you're not allowed to do it?"

Scooter grunted. "Beats my brains out."

The assassin twisted around to Michael. "Care to weigh in? Make it about guns if you can, otherwise I get confused."

"I would ask Him," she said. "But it seems He has nothing to say to me."

"Whoa, you too?" Scooter asked.

Michael fell back against her seat. "Uriel alluded to it as well."

"Mikey, this ain't right."

"Does it matter?" the assassin said. "We already put out Panopticon's Eye, and Barclay says he's working on a way to jam the Stream. We'll cut them off, run them down, scorch the earth. We don't need God to save us because we're going to save ourselves." The assassin paused to gauge Michael's response only to find she'd slipped back into a feverish doze. "Fine waste of a pep talk."

"What's in this for you?" Scooter asked. "Aside from saving your own leather, which you don't seem to value much in the first place."

The assassin wasn't in any mood for deep dive psychoanalysis.

The right thing is like a blowjob, Mouse. Ain't no one doing it out of the kindness of their heart, so unless you need to know, don't ruin it by asking why.

"I'm on your side, Scooter. Isn't that enough?"

"Maybe at first, but not anymore."

The assassin yawned and stretched his stiff legs out under the dash. "Redemption."

"Huh?"

"That's what you want me to say, isn't it? That I've had my come to Jesus moment and I'm a changed man?"

"Except we both know that's a raft of whale shit."

"I've done terrible things. Maybe I regret a few of them. But I'll never feel as guilty as you want me to."

"Then why are you doing this?"

"Same reason I've always done anything." The assassin stole another glance at Michael. "Because I need to know."

To his surprise, Scooter laughed and then sighed. "Thanks, mate. And by the way, if we live through this, Dean might try to kill you. Take it easy on the kid."

"I'll consider it." The assassin rubbed his scruffy jaw. "But speaking of knowing things, how do you think your ex-girlfriend plays into this?"

"That's the part I don't get," Scooter said. "If Uri was willing to invoke the Tear to get to me, she coulda used it any time to drop in and waste you all ninja-like."

"Instead, she forced a confrontation with Michael."

"Got herself corpsified."

"Why would she risk it?"

Scooter drummed his fingers on the wheel. "Someone made a mess. Uri's trying to clean it up."

"She attacked us immediately after we destroyed the mainframe. That's no coincidence. Whomever she's covering for must be connected to the Eye." The assassin mentally sorted through the details scouting for a common thread. "We've assumed it's humans behind Panopticon, but what if it's not?"

"Naw, mate. God wouldn't allow interference on this level."

The assassin chewed it over. "But demons can possess people, right?"

Scooter shook his head. "Only a certain kind of weak-minded human. Even then it's like riding a bucking bronco. Takes crazy energy to stay in the saddle. That's why the possessed don't do much but fling shit and spaz in tongues. Forget precision work. To possess enough people to tug Panopticon's strings would require the invocation of dark megatonnage on an epic scale. The only demon with even close to that kind of juice is Lucifer, and it's not his style."

"Don't be so sure," the assassin pressed. "Didn't Lucifer go to war against God over his belief that humans couldn't be trusted with the freedom to make their own choices? Sounds a lot like Panopticon, don't you think?"

Scooter's brow furrowed. "Even if he could pull it off, and that's a big if." Scooter glanced over his shoulder at a deeply asleep Michael and whispered, "There's no fucking way Uri would raise her sword against the dragon slayer to protect the dragon."

"We need to consider other possibilities."

"You're the one always saying the simplest explanation is the most likely. You've got no proof that there's anything but human beans behind the Eye."

No proof, but thousands of details. The assassin felt them fall like drops of paint onto a blank canvas. A-Day set the stage for a new world order. Zee said it would take resources. Fat Bella said Panopticon was a massive private security outfit and army for hire. The perfect plug-in government. Panopticon tried to remake the world in their image. It didn't work. There were agitators, Jackals, and thirty-six earthbound angels that inspired the people around them to be better. Panopticon somehow knew to target these Concealed Ones. They sent the assassin himself after Grayson Hillaby, a man so full of goodness it practically wept from his angel-green eyes.

Drip. Along came Scooter.

Drip. Then Michael.

Drip. Then the dreams.

Drip. The morning after her clash with Uriel, Michael woke up full of secrets.

Drip, drip, drip.

He stepped back to assess the big picture. Incomplete. But the negative space around an object could be defining enough.

"Where is Uriel?" the assassin asked.

"Uh...she left."

"You let her go?"

"Like to see you make Uri stay put when she don't want to."

"Let's switch."

"What?"

"I'm driving. You can barely see over the wheel."

They changed places, and the small bit of control it gave him improved the assassin's outlook dramatically. Down the road he noticed scrubby weeds creeping from the ditch, covering the shoulder of the highway and edging into the lanes. A blotch of yellow slime exploded across the windshield with a wet slap, followed by another and another.

"Holy bug guts, batman," Scooter said.

When the wipers smeared away enough to see through the glass, the assassin realized the vegetation covering the road was actually a thick carpet of grasshoppers. "Scooter? Did you hear about the outbreak in Australia?"

"Yup. And it looks like we got locusts. Juicy ones."

"Still think this is entirely the work of humankind?"

In answer Scooter clambered over his seat, his bare feet scraping the roof as the truck splatted through a swarm of grasshoppers.

"What are you doing?"

"Weirdly, I feel better," Scooter said, tumbling around in the back until he was right side up again. "And if you're right, we're gonna need our number one ass kicker."

The assassin flicked the wipers on high and hoped whatever Scooter could do would be enough.

CHAPTER 45

Hot air, sweet with the smell of grapes, poured through the open windows of the truck as they drove through the gate and down the dirt lane. Mankind might be hanging over the abyss, but at Laughing Corpse it was Wednesday, and the presses were running.

"I'm starved," Michael said when they parked in front of the house with its familiar white paint, tidy veranda, and hanging flower baskets. "And I would gladly kill for hot water and a bit of soap."

"Yup, she's feeling better," Scooter mumbled.

"How do you feel?" the assassin asked.

Scooter yawned and kicked off his sandals. "Like something the dog's been keeping under the porch, but it's all good, bro."

It was good. Michael's face remained pale, but she otherwise radiated good health.

"Barclay approaches," she said.

The assassin watched the old man crest the hill and hike across the grass in swift strides. The assassin got out of the truck. The heat of the day wasn't as oppressive here in the hills surrounded by vines. Barclay sighed as if he hadn't taken a breath in days. "Lord, y'all had us up in a worry."

"We're not so easy to kill," the assassin said.

"Pearl didn't sleep a wink. Up all hours baking bread and such. I don't interfere when she gets to kneading at midnight."

Michael's stomach growled. "Bread?"

"More'n even you could eat, m'lady," Barclay said and clapped the assassin on the back. He lurched forward as though struck with a shovel. The old man surveyed his truck and its curing shell of grasshopper guts. "What in tarnation did you drive her through?"

"Egyptian plague."

"Just so." Barclay reached into the front pocket of his shirt for a cigarette. "Where's Scotty?"

Michael jutted her chin toward the open door of the truck where two brown feet hung off the back seat. The assassin peeked into the cab to find Scooter on his back, out cold.

"Let him rest." Michael laid her hand on his shin. "He's been through enough. I was rather harsh."

"One way of putting it," said the assassin.

Michael rubbed her forehead and sighed. "Uriel put him in an impossible position."

"What would Jesus do?"

"Is that a joke?"

"Funny, right?"

"It is, when you consider Scooter violated natural law to save the love of his existence, and Joshua did it to impress a harlot whose backside he fancied."

"Did it work?"

"Joshua is a puppy. He wouldn't know what to do with a woman even if he were to fall face first into the paradise of seventy-two virgins."

"Careful what you wish for."

At the sound of a clearing throat, the assassin and Michael found Barclay standing at the edge of the driveway behind them, unlit cigarette clamped between his teeth. "Don't suppose this business has what all to do with a petrified grove of oak trees out back?"

"Allow me to explain." Michael launched into a succinct briefing, bringing Barclay up to speed.

"Raphael, huh?" Barclay said.

"Do you think less of him?"

Barclay scraped his thumbnail over a match head and lit his cigarette. "Ain't yet met a good man what don't got some ugly in his past. Only it seems to me our situation is a might hairier than it was two days ago."

"The hairiest," the assassin said. "But the plan doesn't change, Father."

"Feels like flying blind," Barclay said, exhaling a vigorous stream of smoke. He looked over the assassin's head and uttered a raspy curse. With callused fingers he pinched off the end of his cigarette and tossed it into the rough at the edge of the drive. The assassin saw Pearl hurrying down the lawn toward them.

"Scatter, it's the pulmonary police!" Pearl waved her hands in mock hysteria. "For Christ's sake, Colin. It's the end of the world. Smoke 'em if you got 'em."

Barclay brushed his fingers over her cheek. "Sorry, dear."

Pearl leaned into his touch a moment and then examined the assassin. "Curious. Will you ever arrive not covered in blood, in dire need of calories, and bearing tidings of great doom?"

The assassin shrugged. "It's my thing."

Barclay left to shut down the machinery for the day. Michael called the shower and accompanied Pearl back to the house. The assassin stood alone by the truck. Aside from Scooter's intermittent snores, the air had gone silent, no birds chirping or insects buzzing. The assassin felt a breeze on his skin and through his hair, blowing in black clouds from the west. Thunder rumbled in the distance like the beat of approaching horses. A harbinger of very bad things.

The storm door creaked and Liza plodded out onto the porch. She didn't smile or wave. She merely tracked the assassin's approach across the grass until he stood below her with the porch rail between them.

"You were dead," she said flatly. "I dreamed it. I saw you. In the water."

He plunged down the images her words dredged up. "Should you be out of bed?"

"Dean says it won't hurt. What he means is that it doesn't matter."

"Liza." He dug his hands into his pockets as if they held the right words and all he had to do was scoop them out. "I'm sorry. About what I said."

She rested her hands on the shelf of her belly. "I don't want your apology. I want an explanation."

INFRACTUS

He rocked back on his heels. She was only a kid. He didn't have to explain anything. "When I talk to people, most of the time I'm working under an alias."

"You know what to say, because you know what you're after."

"But when I'm just me, and it's not part of a grift, I get it wrong a lot of the time. I didn't mean to make you angry."

Liza scowled. "You're not really sorry. You're just sorry I got upset."

"Is that different?"

"Are you for real?"

"I've never told anyone what I just told you."

"You want a cookie? Jeez, typical guy. Share a feeling and expect to get away with murder. Literally in your case."

"I think you're overreact—"

She pattered barefoot down the steps to stand in front of him on the grass. "Before you finish that sentence you ought to consider that I am hormonal, gassy, and extremely dangerous. Now, since you clearly don't get it, would you like me to explain?"

He nodded. "Ballistic metaphors are helpful."

"You were right, I need to grow up." She blinked and tears spilled down her face. "But I'm not weak because even when I want to shoot you in your dense brick of a head, I'm still strong enough to love you, because you need it."

She fell into him and he held her as well as he could with her belly in the way. No one had ever said those words to him before. He wasn't loveable. Certainly not worthy of the pseudo-dad status she'd conferred upon him. While he couldn't definitively classify his feelings toward her as love, they were certainly paternal.

INFRACTUS

Though on one point she was mistaken. He'd never dismissed her as weak. She'd been terrorized, brutalized, and ripped away from everyone who meant anything to her, yet she still cared. She still hoped. That was a rare breed of strength. Like Jenny, but she was more than that now. She was Liza, and she obviously had more to teach him about being human.

"That was good," he said. "Bringing the gun in."

She sniffed and released him with a shove. "Welcome home, dummy."

CHAPTER 46

The assassin listened to rain patter on the roof, sluice along the meticulously maintained gutters, glug through the down spouts, and finally pour into barrels at the corners of the house. After a hot shower, a shave, and some clean clothes, the assassin felt almost civilized again.

Michael's freshly washed hair cascaded down her back as she chose the farthest kitchen table seat from the assassin. Her way of telling him she'd noticed how he'd distanced himself since their return. But he needed space. He felt crowded and battered. Not by her, but by a clash of opposing forces within himself.

Scooter and Pearl brought salad, fresh baked bread, and a huge dish of pasta tossed with chicken, mushrooms, and tomatoes. The assassin tried to recall the last time he ate and came up with a blank.

"Veg," Pearl said, placing a separate plate of meatless pasta in front of him. Next to the plate she put down a tall glass of something thick and pink. "Whey protein. Much as I appreciate a fine set of cheekbones, you're not leaving this table until you finish that."

The assassin sniffed at the vaguely strawberry scented concoction. "Didn't have to go to the trouble."

Pearl settled next to Barclay. "Drink it, or I'll tie you to the chair and funnel feed you like *foie gras*."

The assassin picked up the glass. "Looks terrific."

"Awesome bread, Pearl." Scooter wiped up the last traces of vinaigrette on his plate with a slice of bread. "And this salad is epic."

"Liza made that," Pearl said.

"Well, niblet, you know the way to a man's heart."

Liza pressed her napkin to her mouth. "So do you, apparently."

The assassin barked out a laugh. Scooter grimaced. "Who told you?"

"Dean."

"Of course," the assassin muttered into his protein drink.

"'Fraid I took the liberty," Barclay said. "Felt I should explain why Scotty came home neutered."

"Whoa," Scooter protested. "Can we not call it that?"

Liza narrowed her eyes at the assassin. "Why don't you like Dean?"

"Yeah, mate." Scooter dog piled on the change of subject. "Deano's a stand-up guy and you're not the dad of her." He looped his arm around Liza. "Did Dean use the word 'neutered'?"

The assassin set his glass on the table. "I don't want you to get hurt. You're not in the best place to be making those kinds of decisions."

Liza gave him a flat glare. "Why? It's not like he can get me pregnant."

"An unwise choice of supporting argument."

"What's that supposed to mean?"

"It's called opening the door, Liza. You're a debate champion. Figure it out."

INFRACTUS

"God, you're doing it again. Just leave him alone. Don't you dare hurt him."

"I won't," he said, taking another sip of his drink. "Unless he gives me a reason."

She clutched the silver charm bracelet around her wrist. Beside the fish there now hung a tiny jade elephant.

Scooter slouched in his chair. "I guess neutered is the right word. But I'm better now. I fixed everyone."

Liza tapped Michael's shoulder. "Would you please order this high-handed murderer to leave Dean alone?"

Michael glanced up from her efforts to consume her body mass in carbohydrates. "Would it do any good?"

"Has it ever?" he asked.

She maintained eye contact as her white teeth sank into a piece of bread, tearing at it like a lion. The assassin wondered. Would it be outrageous to lunge across the table through salad, pasta, and a half-full glass of whey protein, tackle her to the floor and have her right there in front of whoever cared to stick around and watch?

Scooter kicked him under the table.

The meal progressed along established lines of conversation during which delightfully little in the way of communication occurred. The assassin ate his vegetables and finished his thousand-calorie protein shake. At last Michael set her fork down and licked her fingers. "An excellent meal, Pearl. I cannot recall its equal."

Pearl brought her hands together in a prayer pose. "Atheists make the best cooks because we know we're on our own."

Barclay sighed. "Breaks bread with angels and still she doesn't believe."

"Don't rush me, old man."

The assassin collected plates and cutlery while Pearl filled the big sink and handed him a fresh towel with an air of ceremony. "What a good washer doesn't get, a good dryer will."

The work went smoothly, accompanied by slosh of lemony bubbles and the squeak of rubber gloves. The cotton towel grew damp with every dish it traveled across and soon she handed him the last plate. He passed it through the rinse sink, dragged the towel over both sides, and stacked it with the others.

Pearl studied his movements. "Foster kid, huh?"

"How'd you know?"

"We're expert dishwashers. Dead giveaway."

The assassin hung the towel over the oven door handle. "Chores kept us out of trouble, in theory. How'd you end up in the system?"

"Single mom. Missouri. Meth." She pulled the plug and the water gurgled into the drain. "You?"

"Born and turfed on the same night in Whitehorse. Raised by a nun who insisted I was a demon."

"Hmm, I should have known."

"That I'm Catholic?"

"Canadian." She tossed her yellow gloves on the counter where they landed with a splat, and she picked up a glass pie plate containing something brown and crisp that smelled of baked sugar and butter. "Would you grab the ice cream? I think it's behind the..."

INFRACTUS

Pearl's voice trailed off and a crash filled the silence as Barclay's water glass slipped from his hand and shattered on the floor.

CHAPTER 47

The assassin squinted at the man-shaped nimbus of light. Liza screamed and crawled halfway into Scooter's lap. Barclay remained frozen, his fingers positioned as though they still held the glass now in shards on the linoleum.

"Fear not, for I am a Messenger of the Lord," said the incandescent crasher. "You sent for me, my Captain?"

Michael rose from the table, shielding her eyes while Scooter grumbled. "Damn, G. You've made your glittery entre. Could ya dial it down a few lumens?"

The painful glare dimmed to a shimmer of white robes, flaxen hair, and radiant beauty twisted into a sneer. "You're a disgrace, Raphael. No respect for decorum, for your superiors, or even your own vows."

"You're not my superior."

"And now you've led Uriel astray."

"You need to get over it, mate."

"One day she will get over you, Raphael. And when that happens, I'll be there. Think about that."

Scooter chuckled. "Anything's possible, but as of this morning she was definitely still under me, if you get what I mean, so why don't you go on and think about that."

"Enough." Michael whispered, and the kitchen fell silent but for the tapping of rain. "Perhaps the two of you could resume your eternal pissing contest on your own time."

Scooter dropped his chin, chastened but not nearly contrite.

The beautiful glowworm delivered a sweeping bow. "My humblest apologies, Captain. I am at your service."

"Rise," Michael said with an annoyed quirk of her mouth. "Everyone, this is—"

"The Archangel Gabriel," Barclay said.

Pearl held out the dessert dish with shaky hands. "Would you like some pear tart?"

Gabriel beamed at the awestruck reaction to his presence. "You are kind, but I must decline as I am astral at present."

Pearl put the tart on the table and sat down, sliding her arms around Barclay, protective and seeking protection all at once. The assassin immediately and deeply disliked the brilliant newcomer, barging in and petrifying his people.

"Gabriel," Michael said. "Have you spoken to Uriel recently?"

"Not in weeks," Gabriel ran a harried hand through his perfect hair. "Michael, I admit I am shocked by these developments. What's more, I've been praying for days and not once have I established contact with our Father."

"I know."

Gabriel's glow dimmed further. Scooter pulled up his chair and straddled it backwards. "Mikey, what's going on?"

"I do not know," Michael said, and the assassin felt her eyes on him even as her partial lie tickled his gray matter. "But he does."

INFRACTUS

He pressed his fingertips to the window above the sink and felt the cold strike of raindrops through the glass. Her grazing half-truths were adding up. She was hiding something big, and he wasn't surprised. The dreams, the voice, the negative space outlining his own shape all pointed to the obvious conclusion that he was somehow linked to the Panopticon. A big problem.

"Our answers are locked inside the assassin's memory," Michael clutched his arm and drew him into the middle of the kitchen. "Gabriel, you must lift the veil."

"Captain, you cannot be serious."

The assassin tugged his arm from Michael's grasp. He didn't want to be touched, and he really didn't want anyone rummaging through his head. One remap was enough, even if it didn't work especially well. "What do you mean, lift the veil?"

"The veil," Gabriel said. "Is a protective barrier shielding the memories of this life from the collective memory of a soul's entire existence. God conferred upon me the power to remove that barrier, but without His divine assent, the sheer volume of information would damage your human neurology. At best you'd go mad. At worst it gets unpleasantly tactile. Michael, are you certain this is wise?"

"There are risks." She twisted her silver wrist cuff. "But we cannot wait for Him when we have the means to act now."

The assassin felt like he was on an operating table, being argued over by two surgeons with conflicting opinions. He turned to Michael. "You were going to do this without talking to me?"

"I am talking to you now."

"No, you're talking about me, to Lord Fancyskirt, whom you neglected to mention would be joining us. He almost scared a baby out of Liza."

She cocked her head at a familiar haughty angle. "It is called a need to know basis, assassin."

He almost laughed. "You are so full of shit."

"Insolent meat," Gabriel thundered. "How dare you speak to the Archangel Michael in such a manner? How dare you speak to her at all? You are not fit to black her boots, human."

"Not her boots I'm interested in, Astral Boy."

Michael slammed her palm down on the kitchen table. "Do any of you have any idea what kind of pressure I am under? God has left the building, as they say, and who does that leave to keep this cosmic machine running?"

Scooter raised his hand. "Pick me. I totally know this."

"Rhetorical, you idiot. But correct. And since I have neither the power, nor the omniscience, nor the infinite patience of a God, here is what I propose. The next man that whinges at me over something not being fair, or right, or safe, or insists that I consult him on my every decision, will find his tongue knotted about his testicles. All in favor please indicate with your continuing silence."

The assassin raised his hands in surrender. Scooter made a zipping motion across his mouth. Gabriel bowed.

Again, Michael tugged at the silver cuffs. The assassin's well-trained brain filed it as a nervous tell. Old habits die hard, and cataloguing a person's weaknesses came to him more naturally than the mammalian dive reflex.

"Gabriel, in the absence of divine assent, I will not order you to lift the veil on the assassin, but I am asking. Will you do it?"

Gabriel's expression betrayed a glimmer of hurt. "My sister, there is nothing I would refuse you. Have I given you reason to think otherwise?"

Michael regarded Gabriel with the respect due a fellow soldier. "Never have I doubted you, brother."

Liza, Barclay, and Pearl perched rigid in their chairs while Scooter relaxed, munching on a toothpick. With Gabriel placated, Michael addressed the group as a whole.

"Uriel attacked me last night. To protect an individual, perhaps. But in a broader sense I believe she was trying to protect us all." She pulled back her sleeve, revealing a thin scar running along the inside of her arm. "Her blade showed me what is true, and it cannot be disputed, for there is no shadow in the Light of God."

"And this undisputable truth is?" the assassin asked.

"You are not human. Not entirely."

The words punched into his brain and he found he had none to throw back.

"Mikey, are you sure?" asked Scooter. "He ain't one of us. His eyes are wrong...half wrong anyway."

Gabriel peered at the assassin as if an ingredient label were pasted to his forehead. "If not one of the seraphim, what is he?"

"Lift the veil and find out," said Michael.

"Can I talk to you a minute," the assassin asked and they retreated to the back corner of the kitchen where they could whisper in less than complete privacy. "What do you mean I'm not human?"

She anxiously twisted her cuffs. "Do you love me?"

"What?"

"It is a simple question."

"Michael, stop." She'd galled her wrists to a raw pink, and he trapped her hands between his. "Stop hurting yourself."

"Why can't you say it?"

"Why can't you?"

She pressed her forehead to his. Her hair brushed over his knuckles and under the artificial perfume of shampoo he smelled green vines climbing toward the sun. He was a very bad thing, but when he was with her, even at his worst, he was better. They both were. But that wouldn't stop them from turning on each other. She knew how he felt, but he wasn't about to confess it like a crime, not in front of people, and not with a huge secret standing between them. So, he stepped back. He let her go.

"Do it," he said to Gabriel.

Gabriel held out his luminous hands. "May God protect you, whatever you are."

The assassin complied and felt a halo of warmth circle his head. The gentle heat morphed into light, growing brighter until it burned. In his head he felt a pull, a loosening, and as the veil lifted from his mind, it also lifted from the eyes of those who would know him for who he truly was.

"This isn't real," Scooter said in the distance. "It can't be real. Mikey . . ."

Images appeared in the light, faint at first, then more defined. The assassin fell out of the kitchen, out of his own body, out of time, into an alien landscape of flames and smoke where blades clashed in a song of blood. Soot filled his nose and mouth as he dragged his sword through the muck. Something slammed into his shoulder and the world spun like a gyroscope. He could no longer see the horizon, only black stars piercing a crimson sky. His shoulder hurt.

He heard someone—Uriel—running across the battlefield of the past, screaming a name.

His name.

"Lucifer!"

LINER NOTES

A year after the great fire of London, John Milton published *Paradise Lost*. You can read his epic poem chronicling the Fall of Man, but at ten volumes of blank verse in archaic English...it's a bit of a slog. I'll save you some time. Milton's tale of Adam and Eve's eviction from the Garden of Eden isn't actually about Adam. Satan quickly steals the spotlight. And why shouldn't he? He was the first to fall.

Like Milton, I had a childhood steeped in religion, and though I left the Mormon church as a teenager, the scripture I'd studied since I was a small child remained in my head. I'm not sure how many atheists entertain the idea of writing biblically derivative apocalyptic science fiction, but I was definitely feeling it. I started crafting a narrative that both adhered to and subverted the existing mythology, and choosing a protagonist was a no-brainer. Whether vengeful or tragic, Satan is the guy we relate to. The original fuckup, fallen from grace, stripped of everything but free will. Who doesn't love an anti-hero? I knew that even if I tried to give the story to someone else, the Devil would take it right back.

So, that's how *Infractus* started, and eight years later...well, the story isn't quite finished. More adventures await. Hopefully not too far down the road.

Sarah L. Johnson - Calgary, Alberta - October , 2017

MENTIONS

Milton wrote that "the mind is its own place, and in itself can make a Heaven of Hell, a Hell of Heaven." A book is its own place too, but it can't make itself into anything without an army of Fallen to help guide it out of Chaos. A debt of gratitude is owed to my mentor Lee Kvern and the Writer's Guild of Alberta, beta readers Robin van Eck and Meghan Way, Gaurav Sethi (Van to my Ada), my writing group, and the Alexandra Writers' Centre Society. I also need to acknowledge Rob Bose, and the Coffin Hop Press crew, who rescued *Infractus* from the lake of fire and gave me the Coffin Hop shirt off their back. Thank you all.

And finally, a massive shout out to my family, particularly Spousal Unit, a man who knows when it's time to pour a double gin & tonic and coax me into the hot tub. I love you.

S.J.

ABOUT THE
AUTHOR

Sarah L. Johnson lives in Calgary with her noisy family and two bewildered cats. She runs ultra-marathons, does daily battle with curly hair, and writes fiction that pokes its nose into a variety of genres: literary, sci-fi, fantasy, noir, horror, and once a romantic comedy that was so very terrible it shall be blasted from the obelisks of recorded history. Her work has appeared in a number of journals and anthologies including *Room Magazine*; *Shock Totem*; the Bram Stoker nominated *Dark Visions 1* (Grey Matter Press); *It's a Weird Winter Wonderland* (Coffin Hop Press), and *Year's Best Hardcore Horror Volume 2* (Comet Press). Her short story collection *Suicide Stitch* was released in 2016 by EMP Publishing.

Find Sarah on twitter **@leadlinedalias**

or at **www.sarahljohnson.com**

COFFIN HOP PRESS

New Crime. New Weird. New Pulp.

Visit us online at
www.coffinhop.com